THE TRIBUNAL

THE TRIBUNAL

A novel by Peter B. Robinson

iUniverse, Inc.
New York Lincoln Shanghai

The Tribunal

iUniverse, Inc.

For information address:
iUniverse, Inc.
2021 Pine Lake Road, Suite 100
Lincoln, NE 68512
www.iuniverse.com

ISBN: 0-595-30754-X

Printed in the United States of America

To my wife, Jeanne—"the wind beneath my sails"

and my daughter, Jennifer—the turbo-jet!

Acknowledgements

Many people helped make this, my first book, possible.

Jeanne and Jennifer Robinson had to live with me while I wrote it, and suffer through my endless readings and revisions.

Bruce Henderson, a fabulous author, helped turn my amateur writing style into something more acceptable. My friend and agent, Shana Keating, a great lawyer in her own right, offered me many useful suggestions and unfailing optimism.

At the International Criminal Tribunal for the former Yugoslavia, Christian Chartier, Chief of Public Information Services, was most gracious with his time and arranged a tour of some parts of the Tribunal that even defence lawyers don't get to see. Jan Maarten Terwiel, the Director of Education of the Scheveningen prison complex, where the Tribunal keeps its inmates, gave me a wonderful tour and showed me his own, impressive book.

Judge Ewald Behrschmidt of the Court of Nuremburg, Germany, graciously gave me a bird's-eye perspective of the Nuremberg trials and let me sit in the very chairs occupied by those who defended at Nuremberg almost 50 years ago.

My good friend and colleague Tomislav Visnjic of Belgrade taught me what it was like to be a defence lawyer at the Tribunal, and gave me the opportunity to try it out myself.

To all of these people, I will be forever grateful.

The Security Council, expressing once again its grave alarm at continuing reports of widespread and flagrant violations of international humanitarian law occurring within the territory of the former Yugoslavia, and especially in the Republic of Bosnia and Herzegovina, including reports of mass killings, massive, organized and systematic detention and rape of women, and the continuance of the practice of "ethnic cleansing", including for the acquisition and the holding of territory,...decides hereby to establish an international tribunal for the sole purpose of prosecuting persons responsible for serious violations of international humanitarian law committed in the territory of the former Yugoslavia.

—United Nations Resolution 827 (1993)

Since its inception, the Tribunal has become a fully operational legal institution rendering judgements and setting important precedents of international criminal and humanitarian law. Many legal issues now adjudicated by the Tribunal have never actually been adjudicated or have lain dormant since the Nuremberg and Tokyo trials.

The Rules of Procedure and Evidence guarantee that Tribunal proceedings adhere to internationally recognised principles of a fair trial.

—International Criminal Tribunal for the former Yugoslavia document (2001)

P R E L U D E

─────────────── ▼ ───────────────

"All rise! <u>Veuillez vous lever!</u>" the black-robed usher bellowed in English and French, the two official languages of the International Criminal Tribunal for the former Yugoslavia.

Trial lawyer Kevin Anderson leapt to his feet. The adrenaline from the impending verdict flowed hard and fast inside his well-conditioned body. He had tried more than two hundred cases and lost only a handful. Waiting for a verdict was always a heart thumper. With what he had at stake here, this one was a heart stopper.

The three judges filed solemnly into the courtroom. They wore black robes with bright red satin covering the chest and shoulders and striping the cuffs. Crusty old William Davidson of Great Britain led the procession, carrying an old leather book in which he had made notes during the trial.

Kevin studied Judge Davidson's face for some indication of the decision, but the judge's eyes were impassive behind his thick glasses, his mouth fixed in its usual scowl.

Next came the President of the Trial Chamber, Juana Orozco of Chile, with jet-black hair pulled tight behind her head. She looked down; the normally pleasant smile absent from her face. Finally, Francisco Linares of the Philippines marched in, wearing the same blank expression that he had maintained throughout the month-long trial.

"Good morning, ladies and gentlemen," Judge Orozco began when everyone had been seated. She looked out at the visitors' gallery, separated from the courtroom by a wall of bulletproof glass. Normally empty, the gallery was standing room only.

Journalists and court watchers had flocked to The Hague to see the result of the War Crimes Tribunal's most notorious case yet; the prosecution of the infamous Serbian warlord known as "Draga", leader of the Black Dragons. Draga was accused of leading his paramilitary group on genocidal attacks in Bosnia at the behest of Yugoslavian President Slobodan Milosevic.

"Will the accused please rise?" Judge Orozco ordered.

A tall, clean-shaven athletic-looking man wearing a dark blue double-breasted suit rose to his feet. In America, he would have been mistaken for one of the lawyers. However, at the Tribunal here in Holland, all the lawyers wore robes.

Kevin's gaze met the deep brown eyes of the woman he loved, seated next to him at the counsel table. He took her hand and squeezed. With his other hand, he reached inside the pocket of his robe and rubbed the lucky stone that their eleven-year-old daughter, Ellen, had given him. Ellen had sat in the audience for many of his verdicts, and now, her life depended on this one.

A wave of panic engulfed Kevin. He looked up at the judges. The proceedings were moving in slow motion. He took a deep breath, trying to calm himself.

"The Trial Chamber has reached a verdict in this case," Judge Orozco intoned. "It is a majority verdict, as required by our rules, but it is not unanimous. The verdict on all of the counts of the indictment is the same."

Kevin struggled to process this information. A 2-1 verdict. But for acquittal or conviction?

Judge Orozco continued. "Separate majority and dissenting opinions will be filed in due course. Only the result will be announced this morning."

Kevin looked around the courtroom, desperate for a clue. If any of the court personnel knew what the outcome was, they didn't show it. The clerks, guards, and interpreters all had their eyes fixed on Judge Orozco, her black and red robes framed by the sky blue background of the United Nations flag.

Kevin gave up his attempt at cognitive analysis.

Instead, he closed his eyes, rubbed the stone, and prayed.

EIGHT MONTHS EARLIER...

CHAPTER 1

▼

"I can't believe we're moving to Holland tomorrow, Daddy."

Kevin Anderson beamed at his eleven-year-old daughter, Ellen, as they huddled together over a two-scoop vanilla sundae with chocolate sauce and whipped cream.

She was beautiful, with her long brown hair gathered into a ponytail by a purple scrunchy; fun-loving, liquid-brown eyes, and a batch of girlish freckles on her nose.

"It's going to be an adventure," he said, smiling.

Her expressive face had morphed from a smile into a frown. "I'm really going to miss my friends. And my new school is so big. How will I ever find my way around?"

"You have plenty of experience finding your way around," he said, nodding toward the Game Boy that sat on their white marble table at the soda fountain. "You get around Super Mario Land real well."

Ellen's face broke into a wide grin. "Can I play while we finish our ice cream?"

Kevin caught that infectious smile. If she had asked him for the moon at that moment, he would have somehow found a way to get a lasso around it.

"Sure. We've got time."

"Yeah, if we go home now, we'll just have to help Mommy pack."

They exchanged conspiratorial smiles.

He hadn't cared much for babies until he held Ellen in his arms seconds after she was born. Never before had he experienced the unconditional love that he felt for his daughter from that moment forward. There were mornings now he dropped her at school, and watched as she walked away, leaning against her heavy backpack, ponytail flapping. He'd sit there and look at her, thinking how lucky he was to have her as a daughter. Sometimes she would look back like, "Dad, go!" And of course, he did. But he couldn't wait to see her again. He was a highly-regarded federal prosecutor, but his favorite job was being Ellen's dad.

Ellen picked up the Game Boy and flicked it on. Its annoying, all-too-familiar tune filled the air.

Kevin watched his daughter squinting at the little screen, oblivious to the world around her. He went back to the ice cream, now without competition.

Less than an hour ago, he and FBI Special Agent Bud Marcello had been seated side-by-side at the prosecution table in San Francisco's Federal Court-house. As Ellen had watched from the public benches, a jury had convicted a prominent Santa Rosa City Councilman of bribery. It was Kevin's last federal trial for the next year, and the final case of Bud's long and illustrious law-enforce-ment career.

Tomorrow, Bud Marcello was retiring from the FBI after 30 years, while Kevin was heading to Holland where he had landed a one-year assignment to prosecute war criminals in The Hague at the United Nations' sponsored International Criminal Tribunal for the former Yugoslavia.

After twenty years as a federal prosecutor, Kevin was looking to do something different for a year, and at the same time, he wanted Ellen to experience living and touring abroad before she got to the age where she wouldn't be seen with her parents.

When he returned to California, Kevin planned on landing with a prestigious law firm where he could try civil cases in federal court and make enough money to fund Ellen's college education. Ellen was a straight "A" student. The day before, she had completed the fifth grade. To Kevin, she was Ivy League material already; Harvard, Yale, Princeton—none were too good for his little girl.

A trip to the Ghirardelli Chocolate Factory, with its large clock tower over-looking San Francisco Bay, was Kevin and Ellen's tradition whenever he finished a trial. As he heard Ellen exclaim in frustration while pressing the buttons on her Game Boy, Kevin got up and filled two cups of water from the dispenser.

Ellen finally paused her game and looked up. "I was thirsty. Thanks, Dad."

"Ready to head home?"

"We have to look at the machines on the way out."

Ellen took a swig of water, got up from her chair, put the Game Boy in its case, and headed for the rear of the soda fountain. Kevin followed, snatching a napkin from the holder as they left. He caught up with Ellen and handed her the napkin without a word. She knew the routine. Grimacing, she wiped her mouth and handed the dirty napkin back to Kevin as they reached the exhibit showing how Ghirardelli chocolate was made. Ellen studied the placards, which she read every time they came here. She examined the machinery used in making chocolate candy.

"I wonder what the chocolate will be like in Holland," she said.

"The Dutch make some of the best chocolate in the world. They're famous for it. I hear they even sprinkle chocolate on their toast."

Ellen's face lit up. "Now that's a habit I could get into. But I'm really going to miss my friends."

"You'll have all kinds of new friends."

"I've lived in the same house since I was born. I've gone to the same school since kindergarten. There's only a hundred kids there, and I know them all. There's more than a thousand kids at The American School of The Hague. And it's in a foreign country where I don't know the language."

"Scared?"

Ellen nodded.

"So am I," he admitted. "A little, anyway."

He put his arm around her shoulder as they watched the sea of milk chocolate wash back and forth in the large vat.

"Hey, have I ever steered you wrong?" he asked confidently.

"You made me take those drama lessons and play in that dumb softball league."

Kevin grinned sheepishly. "Besides those two."

Ellen rolled her eyes, then reached for his hand and cupped it in her own. Kevin loved it when she let him hold her hand. He knew it wouldn't last much longer.

They strolled out of the ice cream place and into the parking garage. When they got to their minivan, Ellen grabbed the Game Boy and resumed the challenge.

Kevin didn't object. He had slain his dragon in the courtroom today, and now Ellen was trying to slay hers.

As was their tradition, Kevin maneuvered the van over to the part of Lombard Street known as "The Crookedest Street in the World." Ellen paused her game as the Andersons' van joined the procession of cars carefully snaking their way down the switchbacks of the famous crooked street. She waved happily to the tourists who stood at the bottom of the street, snapping pictures.

Kevin and Ellen had been down this street dozens of times, but they still shared in the thrill.

"I wonder what it would be like to live on this street," Kevin said.

"Oh, I don't think I'd like it, Daddy. Too many tourists and too much traffic. And it's so steep; you couldn't possibly ride a bike here."

"Good point."

"I like our house in Santa Rosa. It's on a nice, flat dead end street where I can ride my bike, and has lots of trees, and our creek. There's too much concrete in San Francisco."

Kevin agreed. San Francisco was exciting to visit, but he loved living in Santa Rosa, with its safe, family-oriented atmosphere, beautiful rolling hills, and an abundance of parks and nature trails. Their house backed up to Annadel State Park, where he ran along meandering footpaths whenever he could. It was one of his great pleasures.

"Did you find out about our house in Holland?" Ellen asked.

"Yeah, I got an e-mail this morning. We got the one I was hoping for."

"What's it like?"

"A lot different than what we're used to. Three stories tall, but really skinny. They call them row houses because a bunch of houses are together all in a row."

"Will I have my own room?"

"Better than that—you'll have your own floor. The downstairs has the kitchen, living room and dining room. The second story has the master bedroom, an office, guest bedroom, and the bathroom. The third level has two bedrooms. You can have one for yourself and one for your friends."

"Cool!"

"There's a canal in front that runs down the middle of the street."

"Can I swim in it?"

"I don't think so. But I hear that sometimes it freezes over in the winter and people ice skate on it."

"Great! I hope Mommy packs my skates."

Ellen looked worriedly at Kevin. "Will we do the Breakfast Club in Holland?"

Once a week, he drove Ellen and two of her friends, Jordie and Britt, to school. They set out early in their minivan, picked up her friends, and then stopped for a donut, muffin, or croissant to eat on the way. Kevin had been doing this since kindergarten. The three girls called themselves "The Breakfast Club." Kevin was their driver and an honorary member, mostly because he always paid for the goodies.

"I'd love to, but I think you'll be biking to school. Everyone does it in Holland. And our house is only about ten blocks from school."

"Wow! Will I get to pick out my own bike?"

"Sure."

"I'm going to get a purple one with a bell." Purple had become Ellen's favorite color recently, after one of her friends had observed that pink was for little girls.

Kevin drove the van north, past the Marina Green and the stately Palace of Fine Arts, and on to the Golden Gate Bridge.

Ellen had turned back to her game.

"Let's tell Mommy the verdict," Kevin said as they passed the first huge orange span of the bridge.

"Call her," Ellen replied, not looking up from her game.

Kevin reached for the cell phone, but realized that he would soon lose the connection as they drove into the tunnel on the other side of the bridge. To his right, he saw a huge container ship getting ready to glide under the Golden Gate out into the Pacific Ocean. Behind it in the bay sat Alcatraz Island, with its faded yellow prison buildings, steel water tower, and flashing beacon. Hundreds of white sails dotted the bay on this sunny June afternoon.

Ellen took a deep breath as they passed the rainbow arch that formed the entrance to the Waldo Tunnel a mile north of the bridge. She had been holding her breath and making a wish in tunnels since she was two years old. Fortunately, this was a short one. Ellen expelled her breath when their van emerged from the tunnel. She would never divulge her wish. She just said that it was the same one as always. Kevin thought he knew it—she had been wanting a puppy for some time.

Kevin dialed home.

Ellen, distracted from her game by the tunnel, snatched the phone.

"Daddy won his trial! And we had ice cream!"

They joined the commute north on Highway 101 through Marin County as Ellen recounted her day to her mother. Kevin reveled in the enthusiasm that Ellen expressed about their day together. When she finally surrendered the phone and returned to her Game Boy, there wasn't much left for Kevin to report.

"Hi, honey," Kevin said.

"Congratulations."

"Thanks. It's nice to go out with a win."

Kevin and Diane had been married for twenty-one years. They had met in law school. Although she'd graduated near the top of their class, she hadn't liked practicing law, and eventually had gone to work as a writer for a legal publishing company. When Ellen was born and with Kevin earning a federal prosecutor's salary, Diane had cut down to part-time writing from home. Recently, she had stopped taking legal writing assignments from her regular clients, and Kevin wasn't quite sure why. He knew that she had been depressed since the death of her last parent, her mother, in the past year. An only child, Diane seemed to have lost some of her passion for life since then.

"How's the packing going?" he asked.

"Well, Ellen's room is mostly packed up. I just need to get the stuff I'm throwing out into the trash so she won't try to reclaim it."

Kevin smiled. Ellen, a pack rat at heart, insisted on saving every piece of paper, Kid's Meal toy, and art project that came into her possession. It was only through Kevin and Diane's periodic secret sweeps that Ellen's room was not totally engulfed.

"I haven't even begun to think about packing the things we're taking with us. Moving is so much work. I wish we could just stay put."

They had just done ten years' worth of staying put, Kevin thought. He didn't say anything; he'd learned to listen to Diane complain, and offer words of understanding.

"I'm sorry I haven't helped much with the move."

Diane sighed. "I'll see you in a little while. Don't let Ellen have more sweets."

"Of course not," he said in mock indignation.

Kevin knew Diane didn't want to go to Holland. A homebody, she was comfortable in Santa Rosa and among their circle of close friends. Kevin hoped the change of scene would be good for Diane, who had finally come around to the idea because she didn't want to stand in the way of an experience for Ellen that few children got. If Ellen had not been in the equation and it had simply been a matter of Kevin wanting the experience, he suspected he would have been moving to Holland alone.

He wondered what the relocation would mean to them, and what would happen in their marriage. As they had gotten older, the differences between them grew and bothered Kevin more. He was forty-five years old, and he wasn't yet ready to live on cruise control. With an innate zest for living, he still wanted to have adventures and make new memories, while Diane seemed weighed down and even haunted by old ones.

Kevin had never cheated on Diane, and he was not one to admit failure by divorce. And, of course, there was Ellen to consider now. He was in for the long haul. But he worried that he and Diane were disconnecting, and was scared to death that their marriage had begun to resemble that of the couple in *American Beauty*.

An hour later, Kevin pulled the van into the driveway. Ellen raced into their sprawling ranch house, leaving Kevin to carry in her Game Boy, backpack, as well as his own things. By the time he headed up the stairs, Ellen was passing him on her way down.

"I'm going next door to play with Lauren," she said breezily.

"Thanks for a great day, Ellen."

"Me, too. Love you," she called back to him from halfway down the stairs.

Kevin's face broke into a wide smile. He made it to the top of the stairs and put down his load. There were boxes everywhere.

Diane, wearing sweats, appeared in the hall. "I'm pooped," she announced.

Kevin suddenly felt tired. The adrenaline of the trial and the sugar from the sundae had worn off. It was good to be home, even one that looked like a warehouse. Tomorrow, the movers would be taking everything away to storage—the things going to Holland with them would come along in five suitcases and two trunks. The day after, the family who had rented the house for a year would be moving their belongings in.

"Are we still going out to dinner?" Diane asked.

"I guess so," Kevin replied. "I'm beat, but I want to take Bud out to celebrate the verdict and his retirement."

"Whatever." Shrugging indifferently, she said, "All the cooking utensils are packed up anyhow. And Ellen wants to spend the night next door."

Kevin didn't bother changing out of his suit. Diane put on a light blue summer dress. At forty-four, she still hardly ever wore makeup. Her smooth, moist skin and beautiful smile lit up her face, although the smile had not been coming out much lately. Diane wore her brown hair short now, and it was streaked with gray, which she made no effort to conceal. The most striking thing about her was that she didn't act like she was beautiful; she carried herself with a reserved simplicity and looked good without trying.

Kevin and Diane drove to downtown Santa Rosa and strolled into his favorite restaurant: Mac's Deli. Mac's was a Santa Rosa institution; a hole-in-the-wall delicatessen that served huge sandwiches to the town's movers and shakers. Diane didn't care for Mac's—she preferred fancier restaurants when they went out, and also, she didn't like having to share Kevin with "the entire room" whenever they ate there.

Bud Marcello and his wife, Sherry, were already seated in a booth. The burly FBI Agent had grey, curly hair that looked a bit more unkempt than usual. He seemed to also be making less of an effort to conceal his bulging waistline now that he would no longer be subject to the Bureau's grooming rules.

Marcello rose and kissed Diane on the cheek.

"Come on," he said to Kevin with a chuckle, "let's take our victory lap."

Kevin winced. As Santa Rosa's first and only federal prosecutor, he was a bit of a legal-community celebrity. But he shied away from gloating whenever he sent someone on their way to federal prison. Tonight, Kevin decided to humor the gregarious agent. After all, Bud needed to start drumming up business after tomorrow.

"Got your new business cards printed up yet?" Kevin teased.

"Right here," Bud said, slapping his breast pocket.

Kevin had worked with Bud Marcello for the last eight years. Bud was a tenacious investigator with a keen sense of fair play, and Kevin had come to trust him completely. He was also the most irreverent FBI agent Kevin had ever met. If Bud needed some information, he would bypass the Bureau's cumbersome procedures and just go get it, leaving FBI supervisors and bean counters tearing out their hair.

Kevin and Bud walked around Mac's, talking to various lawyers and politicians sitting in the booths. News of the local councilman's conviction had spread, and the pair was roundly congratulated. Political animals always went with a winner.

After Kevin and Bud had rejoined their wives, other locals frequently stopped by, talking about the trial, Kevin's move to Holland, and Bud's plans as he liberally passed out his new cards.

Kevin saw Diane silently steam as their meal was repeatedly interrupted.

"Are you looking forward to living in Holland, Diane?" It was Gaye LeBaron, the legendary columnist for the Santa Rosa <u>Press Democrat</u>. LeBaron was sharp and very perceptive, but Diane was savvy enough not to spill her guts to the local scribe.

"I'm too busy packing to think about it," Diane said, managing a weak smile.

Shortly after dinner, Kevin and Diane took their leave.

"Stay away from the dark side," Kevin kidded Bud, who was fully prepared to take on work from criminal defense attorneys in his new private investigation business.

There was no conversation in the car as the Andersons drove home. Kevin had enjoyed savoring his victory with his friend. Diane was so wrapped up in her anxiety over the move that she hadn't even asked him for details about the verdict, as she usually did. As he drove, Kevin shook it off. It was time to disengage from the councilman's trial anyway, and to look forward to his new challenge of prosecuting Bosnian war criminals. He found himself hoping once again that the move would prove to be good for Diane and their marriage.

When they got home, Kevin went to say goodnight to Ellen. He strode into her room where she had rigged a pulley system between her bedroom and Lauren's next door. Kevin printed out the words "Good night, Love, Dad" on a piece of paper, opened Ellen's window, and attached the paper to the rope with a clothespin. Then he pulled the rope through the pulley and watched as the note glided its way across to Lauren's.

When they heard the sound of the rope scraping the pulleys, Ellen and Lauren appeared in Lauren's bedroom window and retrieved the note. Ellen read it, grinned, and blew him a goodnight kiss.

He got up and went to check his e-mail for the last time.

WELCOME, said the familiar AOL greeting. YOU'VE GOT MAIL.

He scanned the list of incoming mail. One entry caught his eye: a message from his contact at the Tribunal in The Hague. He double clicked on it and read:

We are sorry to inform you that a budget freeze has been imposed upon the Office of the Prosecutor. At this time, we must withdraw our offer of a position for you. We will keep your application on file if the funding becomes available.

Rupert Schmidt, Director of Personnel

Kevin felt the air go out of him.

CHAPTER 2

▼

"Rupert Schmidt, please."

Kevin stood inside the guardhouse at the entrance to the International Criminal Tribunal for the former Yugoslavia in The Hague. He had repeatedly tried from home in California to reach Schmidt by e-mail, fax and phone—to no avail. The Tribunal official was obviously going to great lengths to avoid him. "Who may I say is here to see Mr. Schmidt?" asked a young guard wearing the sky-blue United Nations uniform.

Peering into the guard's booth through the glass, Kevin saw control panels, closed circuit television monitors, and an automatic rifle hanging conspicuously from a rack.

"I'm Kevin Anderson from the United States. Mr. Schmidt hired me to work as a prosecutor."

The clean-cut guard's face broke into a friendly smile. "Welcome to the Tribunal, sir." He picked up a phone and punched in some buttons.

Kevin hoped his name wasn't on a list of people who had been <u>unhired</u>. He looked around the small guardhouse, spying a metal detector, X-ray machine, and some lockers. Another blue-uniformed guard stood near the metal detector.

After a minute, the guard put down the phone and motioned Kevin closer to the glass. "I'm sorry, sir, but Mr. Schmidt is not in at the moment. He's expected back soon. Why don't I give you a visitor's pass and you can sit in on the court this morning? When Mr. Schmidt arrives, I'll tell him where you are."

"That sounds good."

Kevin was relieved that he was finally getting closer to the elusive Mr. Schmidt, to whom he planned to make a personal appeal. He was also anxious to see the inside of a courtroom at the Tribunal.

Kevin collected the pink visitor's ticket that the guard passed through the slot in the glass, and then walked through the metal detector. He headed out the door of the small guardhouse, toward a large triangle-shaped building some thirty feet away. The three-story building had large brown pillars and was surrounded by a high steel fence. It looked to cover half a city block.

He entered the Tribunal building and found himself in a small lobby. To his right and left were glass doors marked "Employees Only." Straight ahead was a white marble staircase with another metal detector and security guard.

Kevin approached the guard and showed his ticket. When the metal detector beeped, he was ordered to stand with his feet spread apart and hands outstretched. The guard ran a wand over Kevin's body. The sensitive machine had picked up the metal in Kevin's rubber jogging watch.

Kevin was then directed to the top of the stairs, where yet another guard greeted him. Next to her was a fresh-faced man in his early thirties carrying a reporter's notebook.

"Follow me," the guard said. "We're going to Courtroom 2."

She led Kevin and the other man down a maze of corridors. Finally, she stopped, pulled up an industrial-size set of keys hanging from her belt, and opened a large metal door on the left. Kevin followed the other man into a tiny glass booth, with four chairs, perched in a corner of a surprisingly small courtroom with a low ceiling. The door closed behind him and he heard the key turn in the lock.

On each seat was an electronic translator—the size of a small cellular phone—connected to a headset. Following the lead of the other man, who seemed like he had done this before, Kevin picked up a headset and put it on. He sat down, and then looked out into the courtroom. Kevin felt very conspicuous sitting in the glass cage.

"This must be what monkeys in a zoo feel like," he said softly.

The man smiled kindly.

On the other side of the glass, Kevin saw his first war criminal. The accused man sat to Kevin's left. He was an older, gray-haired man wearing a worn suit. He was flanked by two large U.N. guards. In front of him were his lawyers, two tall men wearing black robes. Kevin leaned forward to get a look to his far right and saw the prosecutors, a man and a woman. In the center of the courtroom were the court clerks and ushers, also dressed in black robes.

Kevin rose quickly when he heard the usher announce the arrival of the judges. Three judges strode into the courtroom, wearing snazzy black robes with red satin. As he listened and watched, Kevin was fascinated by the various nationalities that appeared to be working in the glass courtroom. Of the three judges, one was an African woman, another a Caucasian man with an Australian accent, and the third an Asian man. The clerk spoke in French, the prosecutor in English, and the defense lawyers in BCS—the acronym for the Bosnian-Croatian-Serbian language.

Kevin guessed that the African woman sitting in the middle was the President of the trial chamber. She turned toward the defense attorney. "You may begin, Mr. Krasnic."

A distinguished, silver-haired man stood up and began speaking in BCS. The witness, who Kevin could not see from the visitors' gallery, answered in that language as well.

Listening to the English translation on his headset, Kevin soon gleaned that this case was a prosecution of a Bosnian Serb general whose troops had participated in the invasion of the Bosnian city of Srebrenica. Near the end of the war in Bosnia, the Bosnian Serb Army had entered the U.N. protected area of Srebrenica and rounded up the Muslim men, killing some 7,000 of them.

The witness had been called by the defense, so Kevin assumed that the prosecution had finished presenting its evidence. The defense lawyer asked the witness a series of questions apparently based upon a detailed statement that the witness had already given.

The witness was a Muslim. During the war, he had been a city official in Zepa, another U.N. safe area. He testified that the General had been involved in negotiations at Zepa when the Srebrenica massacre occurred, and had treated the Muslims in Zepa fairly.

Kevin scanned the tiny visitors' gallery. He was locked in the room with the other man, who was taking notes. He wondered what would happen if either of them needed to use the bathroom. Kevin was sorry he'd had a second cup of coffee after breakfast.

When the defense lawyer finished questioning the witness, the presiding judge turned to the prosecutor. "You may begin your cross-examination, Mr. Stone."

A ramrod-straight man with short black hair stood up and approached the podium.

"May it please the Court," Stone began, with a clipped British accent that suggested aristocracy. He turned toward the witness, peering over small, rectangular wire-rimmed glasses perched on the end of his sharp nose. He appeared to study the man in the witness stand as if judging a type of fowl or perhaps selecting a cut of roast beef.

"How many times have you rehearsed this rather tawdry performance with the defense lawyers?" the Englishman finally asked.

Kevin was shocked at the confrontational nature of the question. He waited for an objection from the defense, but none was made.

"What do you mean?" the witness sputtered.

"You are here to answer questions, sir. Not to ask them."

Kevin looked at the defense lawyers, expecting an objection for badgering the witness.

The lawyers, however, made no effort to intervene.

The prosecutor marched on. "The defense lawyers prepared your statement for you, did they not?"

"No."

"You mean to tell us that you sat down entirely on your own and typed out this fifteen page statement covering all of the events that are relevant to this trial?" The prosecutor took off his glasses and leaned forward, challenging the witness.

"Yes, sir, I did."

The prosecutor threw the glasses down. "I don't believe that for a moment."

Kevin eyes widened in surprise. A lawyer couldn't express his personal opinion that a witness was lying! He knew if he ever tried that in federal court, there would be a thunderous objection from the defense, followed by a stern rebuke from the judge.

In Courtroom 2, neither the defense lawyers nor the judges said a word.

The prosecutor continued: "What do you think of what the Serbs did to your people in Srebrenica?"

"Well, um, I don't know. I didn't personally see anything happen."

"Sir, you were a collaborator with the Serbs, weren't you? A traitor to your people." The glasses were back on the prosecutor's nose but he seemed never to be looking through them as much as he was using them as a prop.

Kevin shifted in his seat. This prosecutor was pissing him off, and he was about ready to stand up and object himself.

The other man in the visitors' booth was calmly taking notes.

The witness now sounded as if the prosecutor was getting under his skin. "I was <u>not</u> a traitor, sir," he said emphatically. "That is a very unfair thing to say."

The prosecutor continued undeterred. "Several people we've interviewed say you were particularly cruel to your own people."

Kevin shifted in his chair. "I can't believe this guy," he said under his breath. It was improper to ask a witness to comment on what someone had said out of court, let alone face anonymous accusations. Still, there was no objection from the defense.

When the judge mercifully called for the regular morning recess, Kevin and the other man waited in the visitors' booth until the accused was taken out of the courtroom. Then, the door was unlocked, and a guard told Kevin and the other man that they needed to go back to the lobby to wait out the recess.

Kevin sat on a bench, hoping that he might be summoned to Rupert Schmidt's office. The lobby was empty except for Kevin and his fellow observer from Courtroom 2. Kevin decided to talk to the man, who was standing by the coffee machine.

"I'm Kevin Anderson," he said extending his hand.

The man shook Kevin's hand. "I'm Nihudian."

"I'm a lawyer from the United States. This is sure a lot different than the courts in America."

"Yes, I imagine so," Nihudian replied haltingly.

Kevin suspected Nihudian's reserve was due in large part to a language barrier. He decided to forge ahead anyway. "Are you a reporter?"

Nihudian shook his head. "No. I am from Bosnia. I am a teacher there. This summer I work for the Bosnian embassy. Every day, I come here to watch this case."

"What do you think of the case, so far?"

Nihudian was silent for a long time. He was a handsome, dark-eyed man with a fresh, boyish look. He could have passed for a law clerk or young lawyer. "I think the prosecution is going to win," he said finally. "They have a very strong case."

Kevin decided not to comment on how unfair he thought the prosecutor had been. After all, Mr. Stone was a future colleague. "What did you do during the war, if you don't mind my asking?"

"I was a policeman and a soldier. But now I am back to teaching high school."

Just then, a guard approached Kevin. "Come with me," he directed.

"I have never spoken English for so long," Nihudian said, "Thank you for the opportunity."

"Your English is excellent. I'm sorry that I don't know your language. Maybe I'll see you around here again."

The guard led Kevin through the side doors leading to the Tribunal offices. After walking down a bare corridor, he pointed to an office and said, "Right in there, sir."

Kevin entered the office. There were three people inside, each working behind a desk. The man behind the desk farthest from the door rose and said in English with a heavy German accent, "Mr. Anderson, I am Rupert Schmidt. What can I do for you?"

As he looked at the short, wiry, balding man in front of him, Kevin immediately sensed that Rupert Schmidt was going to be dismissive. So, he walked the length of the room to the man's desk and extended his hand. "Nice to meet you, Mr. Schmidt."

Rupert Schmidt's return handshake was limp.

Without waiting to be asked, Kevin sat down on one of the chairs in front of the desk. When he saw Kevin making himself comfortable, Schmidt reluctantly sat down.

"Mr. Schmidt, you hired me as a prosecutor. I'm ready to go to work."

"But your position was not funded, Mr. Anderson. Weren't you notified?"

"Yes, I was notified—the night before I left. By then, it was too late. I had already quit my job, rented out my house, leased a place in Holland for a year and enrolled my daughter in school here."

Rupert Schmidt appeared unmoved. "I'm sorry, but what can I do? We don't have the money to pay you. The United Nations froze our budget." He paused and added somewhat peevishly, "Perhaps if your country paid the back dues that it owes to the United Nations, we would have the money for more prosecutors."

Kevin wasn't going to take the bait.

"Mr. Schmidt," he said, leaning over the man's desk, "I have nothing to do with that. I was promised a job here as a prosecutor. The Tribunal should honor its commitment to me."

"I'm afraid there is nothing I can do at the moment," Schmidt said, avoiding eye contact. "However, I can take your phone number and if something develops, we will call you straight away. Meanwhile, you can check with my office again in a week."

Kevin didn't know what to say. There was no point arguing with this by-the-numbers bureaucrat. He would use the week to get his family settled.

"Mrs. Kelly will see you out," Schmidt said briskly as he rose from his desk, signaling that the meeting was over. "You can give her your phone number here in The Netherlands."

Kevin saw someone get up from one of the other desks in the room. "Right this way, sir," said a gray-haired, plump woman, who Kevin took to be Mrs. Kelly.

Kevin followed the woman out into the corridor. She had a notebook in her hand, and she took down his phone number.

"You brought your family here as well?" Mrs. Kelly suddenly asked him in an accent that sounded Irish.

"Yes, I have."

"It's a shame about your job offer and the funding."

"Yes, it is. I was really looking forward to working here."

"Well, perhaps something will come up."

"I sure hope so," Kevin said with a forced smile. He opened the door and turned to say goodbye to Mrs. Kelly.

"You know," she said, handing Kevin some papers, "maybe you can work as defense counsel. Their funds have not been frozen because, of course, those arrested must be given a lawyer. If you're interested, fill out this application."

"Thank you," Kevin said, taking the application.

Lowering her voice, she said, "I'm sorry about what happened. Please don't judge us all by him. Get your application back to me and I'll see that it gets to the right place."

Mrs. Kelly had a gleam in her eye as she turned back toward her office.

The warmth of the sun felt good on Kevin's face when he left the building. The Tribunal was a cold place with its own set of strange customs and rules. Nevertheless, Kevin was excited about the glass-enclosed courtroom with the judges in red satin. He wanted to be working in that courtroom on the other side of the glass. He had no doubt he'd be more professional than the prosecutor he had seen at work in there today.

He took a tram from the Tribunal to the Central Station, and then switched to a bus to the suburb of Wassenaar. The public transportation system in Holland was excellent. As he rode on the bus, Kevin noticed that every street had a bicycle lane. People of all ages were riding bicycles.

When he got back to the row house in Wassenaar, it was noon. Diane and Ellen were still asleep, no doubt jet lagged; it was still only 3 a.m. California time. Unable to adjust to the 9-hour time difference, they'd been in and out of bed all night.

Kevin put the defense application in a drawer. He did not want to defend war criminals. He had been on the side of the good guys his whole career. He didn't move here to defend some mass murderer.

Kevin prowled around their new home, looking for something to eat. It was lunchtime and he was hungry, but they hadn't yet gone grocery shopping. He went into his bedroom where Diane and Ellen were asleep. He moved the curtains, allowing some light to stream in.

Ellen's eyes opened. "Where am I?" she yawned.

"In the city of Wassenaar, province of South Holland, country of The Netherlands, continent of Europe," Kevin replied. "Does that answer your question?"

Diane stirred at the sound of voices. "What time is it?" she groaned.

"Twenty past twelve in the afternoon," Kevin answered. "You two need to get up or you won't be able to sleep tonight. And I'm hungry."

Ellen stretched her arms high in the air. Kevin couldn't resist. He struck quickly, tickling under her arms, and then on her sides. She squealed, then squirmed out of Kevin's grasp and ran up the stairs to the third floor.

"Missed me, missed me, now you got to kiss me," she taunted.

Kevin started up the stairs.

"You guys!" Diane called. "Someone's going to get hurt on those stairs."

Looking at the stairs, Kevin realized Diane had a point. The stairs in the row house were extremely narrow and steep. It was the Dutch way of saving space. They were geniuses at that sort of thing.

"You can't come up to the 'Ellen level' without permission," Ellen yelled down.

"Well, get dressed while you're up there," Kevin yelled back. "We need to go grocery shopping or I'm going to start eating the candy you brought with you."

"Don't you dare, Daddy!"

One hour and two threats later, the Andersons drove the few blocks to the "Albert Heijn" store, the local supermarket. When they got there, Kevin wrestled with the shopping carts stacked up outside, trying to get a cart. He backed off when he saw a line of people waiting behind him. The person behind him calmly approached the cart, put a coin in a slot near the handle, and easily separated the cart from the others.

Diane and Ellen, standing nearby, howled with laughter. Diane mercifully fished a Dutch guilder from her purse and Kevin managed to score them a shopping cart.

By now, Kevin was famished. He piled all kinds of groceries in the cart as they made their way down the aisles.

"Let's try some of this," he said, adding canned herring to the cart.

Diane and Ellen stuck with familiar American brands, and lots of vegetables.

When they had filled their cart, Kevin maneuvered it toward the checkout counter in the front of the store. He was disappointed to find that the line was long, but they patiently waited their turn. Just as Kevin was about to begin unloading the cart, a kindly old woman said to him in English, "You haven't weighed your vegetables."

Kevin looked at the woman. Was she some kind of a nut?

"Americans make that mistake all the time," she said. "There are scales over by the vegetable section."

Kevin was suspicious until the woman picked up one of her own vegetable bags and showed him a pre-printed price sticker.

"Thank you very much," he said.

He moved their cart out of the line and headed back to the vegetable section, wondering if anyone would notice if he took a bite out of an apple.

Diane and Ellen followed him, cracking up.

"They're your vegetables," Kevin said in mock sternness to Diane and Ellen. "You guys weigh them."

Diane and Ellen pulled the vegetables out of the cart and weighed each of them.

Then they headed back to the checkout area. The line was even longer.

"We'll wait outside," Ellen announced, grabbing her mother's hand. "I'm bored."

When Kevin finally reached the cashier, he dutifully unloaded the cart full of items. He relaxed when he saw that the cashier was ringing them up. He wondered where the bagger was as his groceries stacked up behind the cashier.

"Who bags the groceries?" he asked as he paid the cashier.

"You do," the cashier replied curtly.

"No problem," Kevin said. "I didn't know. We just moved here." He scanned the counter again. "Where're the bags?"

"You have to bring your own."

"What?" Kevin exclaimed a bit too loud. "Really?"

"Yes," the cashier replied. "That is how we do it here in The Netherlands." The man's English was excellent.

Kevin looked with despair at his huge mound of groceries. He searched frantically for Diane and Ellen. In desperation, he said to the cashier, "What should I do? I don't have any bags."

"You can buy some over there," the man replied, pointing to an odd looking machine against the wall.

By now, Kevin would have gladly paid a small fortune for grocery bags. He ran over to the machine while the other customers waited in the ever-growing line at the checkout counter. Kevin felt his face getting red as he fumbled with the coins for the bag machine. He raced back over to the counter with five bags, praying that they were enough. Kevin threw his groceries in the bags as fast as he could and loaded them into the cart. He wiped the sweat from his forehead and staggered out of the supermarket.

"Daddy, what took you so long?" Ellen asked impatiently.

They went home and had their first meal in Holland.

Afterward, the three of them headed out for a leisurely stroll.

"When do you start work?" Diane asked nonchalantly.

Kevin hadn't yet told her he was unemployed, and he dreaded doing so.

CHAPTER 3

▼

After hearing nothing from the Tribunal for a week, Kevin called Mrs. Kelly to ask if she had any news.

"I'm afraid not, dear. That's really too bad, coming with your family and finding out you have no job," Mrs. Kelly commiserated. "At least the weather is good. Enjoy it while you can. It gets rather gray here."

"We may only be here for the summer. I can't afford to stay without any income."

"How's your family enjoying Holland?"

"You're very kind to ask. We love living in Wassenaar. It's got everything: woods, parks, sand dunes, even a windmill."

"They call Wassenaar the Green Oasis of Holland for a reason. Of course, it's nothing compared to Ireland. You have a daughter?"

"Yes. She's eleven."

"How's she getting along?"

"She started summer camp at the American School this week. She's already made friends and is riding all over town with them on her new bike."

"It's very safe here. That's one of the things I like about it. With all the violence at home, you know. And what does the missus do?"

"She's volunteering at the American School, helping get the library ready for the school year. The truth is my family is happy and busy. I'm the one at loose ends."

"Oh dear, Kevin. I do hope something breaks soon."

The next week, Kevin visited the Tribunal in person. He brought Mrs. Kelly a bottle of California wine from Sonoma County. She was delighted with the gift, but sorry that she still had no good news.

When Kevin returned to the lobby, he saw a familiar face.

"Nihudian," he called. "How are you doing?" He strode over to the bench where Nihudian was sitting and offered his hand.

Nihudian shook it warmly. "Quite well, thank you. I just finished another morning in the monkey cage."

Kevin smiled. "Do you have time to grab something to eat?"

"Sure. Have you been to the beach?"

"No, I haven't."

"Come on. I'll introduce you to the favorite food of the Dutch. My treat."

The two men walked outside and through the guardhouse. Kevin told Nihudian about his expected employment as a prosecutor at the Tribunal, and the difficulties that had cropped up. At the corner, they hopped on a tram.

"The Yugoslavian Embassy's over there," said Nihudian, pointing to the south.

"What is the relationship between Bosnia and Yugoslavia anyway?" Kevin asked.

"Bosnia was one of the six republics that made up the Yugoslavian federation. Like one of the fifty states in the United States. Yugoslavia included Serbia, Croatia, Bosnia, Slovenia, Macedonia, and Montenegro.

"When did it break up?"

"In late 1991, Slovenia declared its independence, followed by Croatia, and then in early 1992, Bosnia. That's when the war in Bosnia started. Bosnian Serbs wanted to remain part of Yugoslavia, united with Serbia, while the Muslims and Croats living in Bosnia wanted to be independent."

Nihudian stood up as the tram came to a stop in front of a huge old hotel with a dome shaped like the U.S. Capitol. "That's the Kurhaus Hotel," he said as they got off the tram. "It's where the rich and famous stay in The Hague."

Kevin wondered if Nihudian was taking him for some fancy meal, and hoped that the Bosnian was not planning to spend his hard-earned money on lunch with Kevin. But instead of going inside the Kurhaus, Nihudian and Kevin followed a path around to the back of the hotel. It led to a wide strand of boardwalk and beach with a long covered pier, food and souvenir stands, and waterfront restaurants. Kevin saw the high surf of the North Sea bringing wave after wave onto the beach.

"This is Scheveningen, The Hague's big resort area," Nihudian said. "It's packed on the weekends." He pointed to an old metal food stand behind the Kurhaus Hotel. "That's the place."

"Two large orders of French fries with mayonnaise," Nihudian told the man behind the counter.

"This is it," he said handing Kevin a plastic container overflowing with French fries. "The Dutch delight."

Kevin loved French fries, but wasn't sure about the mayonnaise. They walked over to a bench where they could watch the waves and people on the beach. Many of the women were topless.

To his surprise, Kevin loved the fries and mayonnaise combination. He took a deep breath of salt air. "It doesn't get any better than this," Kevin said, picking out another French fry and dipping it in mayonnaise.

Nihudian laughed. "It's a long way from Bosnia, that's for sure."

"What was Bosnia like before the war?"

"That seems like ages ago. Marshal Josip Broz Tito ruled Yugoslavia from the end of World War II until he died in 1980. Tito managed to keep the three major ethnic groups, the Serbs, Croats, and Muslims, united under a very tightly controlled central government during that time. In Bosnia, it was not uncommon to find a street with a Serb, Croat, and Muslim living next to each other. Everybody got along fine."

"What went wrong?"

"After Tito died, politicians like Slobodan Milosevic, the President of Serbia, started fueling the fires of ethnic hatred, encouraging Serbs to seek revenge for injustices they had suffered in the past at the hands of the other ethnic groups. Ruthless Serbian gangsters formed paramilitary groups. They bombarded the people with paranoia that the Muslims were going to slaughter the Serbs. Pretty soon the people started believing it."

"Who was the war in Bosnia between?"

"Good question. It started out with the Serbs against the Muslims and Croats. Then the Muslims and Croats starting fighting each other. They got back together and fought the Serbs again until the peace agreement was signed in Dayton, Ohio, in 1995."

"What group do you belong to?" Kevin asked hesitantly.

"I'm a Muslim."

"Were war crimes committed?"

"Oh, definitely. There was brutality on all sides. The Serbs carried out ethnic cleansing, where they would come into a village, take the Muslim men to concentration camps, and force the Muslim women and children to leave. Only Serbs were left, and entire Muslim populations were eliminated. In the camps, the Serbs shot, beat, and tortured Muslim civilians. It was awful."

"It sounds like World War II all over again."

"Don't get me started on that. After World War II, the world leaders said the holocaust would never happen again. Well, it did happen again, in my country, and the world didn't do anything to stop it."

Kevin saw the powerful emotions that the war still stirred in Nihudian.

"Enough of the history lesson," Nihudian said. "Let's get back to the Tribunal so I don't get fired."

Kevin threw their empty containers into a garbage can and walked back to the tram stop with Nihudian.

"Tell me about some of your famous cases," Nihudian said along the way.

"My cases aren't that famous. But as long as it's my turn, I'll tell you a few of my war stories." As they rode together on the tram, then walked back to the Tribunal, Kevin regaled Nihudian with the highlights of his prosecution career: a Neo-Nazi group committing murders and armored car robberies to start an all-white state; corrupt public officials taking bribes; bankers looting savings and loans; and police officers shaking down and beating up drug dealers.

When they arrived at the Tribunal, Nihudian said, "Courtroom 2 is going to be dull compared to that. Are you coming to watch today?"

"For a while, I guess."

Soon, Kevin and his new friend were led back toward the visitors' booth in Courtroom 2. As they approached the last corridor, Kevin spied the obnoxious prosecutor, Mr. Stone, standing near another guard in the hall about ten feet away.

"That's him," Stone said to the guard when Kevin and Nihudian approached.

The guard stepped in front of Nihudian, and handed him a piece of paper. "You have been subpoenaed as a witness for the prosecution," the guard said to Nihudian. "You must come with me."

Nihudian recoiled, and looked at the paper he was now holding. Before Kevin could say anything, the guard led him, alone, into the visitors' booth. The guard banged the metal door shut, and locked Kevin inside.

<u>What was that all about?</u> Kevin wondered. There was no one to ask, though, as he was alone in the monkey cage. He thought about banging on the door, but decided to try to find out what happened at the recess. Kevin donned his headset and listened half-heartedly to Mr. Krasnic, the defense lawyer, take another witness through his testimony.

An hour later, the door to the visitors' gallery swung open. The female guard who had escorted Kevin to the courtroom appeared. "Come with me, sir."

Kevin looked at her, thinking there was some mistake. "Me?"

"Just follow me, sir."

Kevin followed the guard as she marched silently down the corridor. She led Kevin into a windowless room. Kevin saw the room was bare except for a table and three chairs. Sitting in one of the chairs was Nihudian.

"What's going on?" Kevin asked the guard.

"This man is a witness," she said curtly. "He says he wants you to be his lawyer."

Kevin looked at Nihudian. Nihudian was pale, a worried expression on his face.

"I'm sorry," he said to Kevin, "You're the only lawyer I know."

"Mr. Stone will be with you at the next recess," the guard announced, shutting the door behind Kevin and locking it.

Kevin sat in a plastic chair across the table from Nihudian. "What's this all about? Are you under arrest or something?"

"They want me to testify about some conversations I overheard. I was in the Muslim army in 1995 when the Serbs began attacking Srebrenica. I was part of a team that intercepted radio communications of the Bosnian Serb Army. Each member of the team worked in shifts, and wrote down the conversations in notebooks. Apparently, the prosecution has gotten access to the notebooks, and they want me to testify."

"How did they find you?"

"The guard said that they sent a list of witnesses they needed to the Embassy, and the embassy told them they could find me in Courtroom 2."

"Well, it seems straightforward enough. The prosecution just needs you to authenticate your handwriting in the notebooks so they could use them in court. Do you have any problem with testifying?"

"I have a wife and two little girls in Bosnia. I don't want anything to happen to them. And if I am a witness, I might lose my job at the Bosnian embassy. They hired me as a neutral person to observe the cases and report what's going on."

Kevin nodded. "Those are legitimate concerns. Perhaps you can tell this to the prosecutor. Maybe they can find some way not to use you or keep your identity secret."

"That is why I wanted a lawyer. Can you help me?"

Kevin thought for a minute. He certainly didn't want to get on the opposite side of the prosecutor's office. On the other hand, Nihudian was a witness for the prosecution. They would be on the same side. "I guess I can help you. It seems simple enough."

Nihudian smiled and his face relaxed. "Thank you so much, Kevin."

Soon, the door flew open. The prosecutor entered, his black robes flowing behind him. "I'm Bradford Stone," he said, extending his hand to Nihudian. Then he looked at Kevin.

"I'm Kevin Anderson. Nihudian has asked me to represent him. I'm a federal prosecutor from the United States. I've actually been hired by your office to work as a prosecutor, but the funds are frozen so I haven't started working yet."

"I see." Stone's voice did not reflect any camaraderie. "This man is a simple fact witness. He doesn't need counsel."

"Well, he has some concerns about the safety of his family and his employment. I thought I might be able to help him resolve these things."

"There's no need," Stone said emphatically in his clipped British accent. "We can take care of all that." He turned to Nihudian. "If you'll just come this way now."

Nihudian looked at Kevin.

Kevin wasn't sure what to do.

Nihudian stood up, and so did Kevin.

"You need to wait here," Stone said to Kevin. "I'll call a guard to escort you out."

Kevin was surprised. "I'm the man's lawyer."

"No, you're not."

Kevin was silent. He didn't want to offend the prosecutor, but he had promised to help Nihudian. He didn't know what to say.

Stone turned around and continued toward the door.

Kevin walked on behind him. "What do you mean I'm not his lawyer?"

Stone turned back to face Kevin. "Are you on the list of assigned counsel?" he asked arrogantly.

"No."

"Then you're not authorized to be his lawyer, are you? The man is a witness. He doesn't need a lawyer."

Kevin looked at Nihudian. Should he just back off? He didn't want to hurt Nihudian's standing, nor his own. Nihudian looked scared.

"I want this man to help me," Nihudian said in a weak voice.

"He's not authorized to help you. He's not on the list of assigned counsel."

Stone reached the door and opened it for Nihudian.

"Nihudian," Kevin asked, "Do you have a Euro?"

Nihudian and Stone stopped. Nihudian reached into his pocket and produced a Euro coin. Kevin took it from him, and said to Stone, "The man has just retained private counsel. He won't be needing assigned counsel from the list."

Stone's face was crimson; he was clearly agitated. "Both of you—wait right here." He slammed the door behind him.

Kevin looked at Nihudian.

"The prosecutors here are a bunch of bullies," Kevin said, shaking his head.

"You are so powerful, Kevin. Just like Johnnie Cochran."

Kevin groaned. Apparently the O.J. Simpson trial had made its way to Bosnia.

"I am so grateful to have you on my side," Nihudian said.

"Well, you just got my services for one Euro. Let's hope you didn't overpay."

A few minutes later, Bradford Stone returned.

"Right this way," he said brusquely, opening the door for Nihudian and Kevin.

They followed him upstairs to an interview room.

"This is Allen Jacobson. He's one of our investigators." Stone spoke to Nihudian, ignoring Kevin.

Nihudian and Kevin shook Jacobson's hand and sat down.

Jacobson produced a notebook and passed it across the table. "Do you recognize your handwriting in this?" he asked Nihudian in accented English.

"Before we get to that," Kevin interjected, "my client has some concerns about his safety and employment that we would like to clear up."

"You'll have to take that up with Mr. Stone,"

Kevin turned and saw that Bradford Stone had left the room.

The investigator opened a page of the notebook.

"Is that your writing?" Jacobson asked Nihudian.

Kevin couldn't believe these people. "I'm sorry," he interrupted, "but I'll need to speak with Mr. Stone before my client answers any questions." Borrowing a famous line from Brendan Sullivan, the lawyer for Colonel Oliver North in the Iran-Contra hearings, Kevin added, "I am not a potted plant."

Jacobson shook his head slowly.

Kevin was perplexed. Either he was doing something wrong or these prosecutors had no respect for people's rights.

Jacobson frowned, got up from his chair, and left the room without saying a word.

"I hope I'm not getting you in trouble, Nihudian."

Nihudian rubbed his forehead. "I hope I'm not getting you in trouble, Kevin." He looked at the notebook on the table. "Do you want me to see if this is my writing?"

"No. Interview rooms are often bugged with hidden microphones. I don't think we should talk about anything here."

Kevin and Nihudian sat in silence.

After a few minutes, the door opened and Jacobson walked in with another man. "This is Charles Oswald. He's the Chief Deputy Prosecutor."

Oswald offered his hand to Kevin. He was an older man, mid-fifties perhaps, with white hair, a jowly face, and glasses. He spoke with an accent that Kevin thought was from Australia or New Zealand. "Mr. Anderson, what seems to be the problem?"

Kevin explained Nihudian's concerns about his family and his job at the Bosnian embassy. He tried to be as friendly as possible. After all, Oswald might be his future boss.

When Kevin had finished, Oswald replied, "We deal with these things all the time. There is no problem. It is most unusual for a witness to have counsel, however."

"I'm really just trying to help him out," Kevin said in a conciliatory tone. "Perhaps you can explain how you will address his concerns and we can get on with the interview."

"Yes, well, I'll have Mr. Stone come back here and do that. Good day."

With that, Oswald turned and left the room.

Bradford Stone appeared a few minutes later. "I understand I'm to give you a lecture in witness procedures," he said sarcastically to Kevin. He sat down and explained that Nihudian's identity would not be revealed to anyone other than the defense lawyers and that he would be referred to in court by letter and not name. There would be no need to tell the Bosnian Embassy that Nihudian was testifying.

Kevin was anxious to smooth over any feathers that were ruffled, and Nihudian appeared to be satisfied with the prosecutor's assurances.

Jacobson again opened the notebook. "Can we go ahead now, counselor?" he asked Kevin, a hint of bitterness in his voice.

"Sure."

Nihudian identified his writing in the notebook and explained how the notebooks were prepared simultaneously while he was listening to the Bosnian Serb Army radio communications.

Jacobson and Stone seemed satisfied, and ended the interview in half an hour.

"You cannot go back into Courtroom 2 until after you've testified," Stone instructed Nihudian. "You'll be testifying a week from tomorrow. In the meantime, the defense attorneys might contact you for an interview. There's no need to talk to them."

Kevin bristled. Where he came from it was unethical for a prosecutor to discourage a witness from talking to the defense.

"We'll make that decision if and when he's asked," Kevin asserted.

Stone shot him a cold look. "Be in the lobby promptly at 8:30 in the morning next Wednesday," he said to Nihudian.

Kevin hoped that now that Nihudian had proven to be a useful witness, his own standing with the prosecutor would improve. He wanted to end their meeting on a good note. "I'll just watch Nihudian's testimony from the visitors' gallery," he told Stone as they were leaving.

Stone stopped and turned to Kevin.

"Yes, do that," he said, his voice dripping with scorn. "You won't be seeing the inside of the courtroom anytime soon. Your career here as a prosecutor is over before it even started. Pity."

With that said, Bradford Stone stormed away.

CHAPTER 4

▼

That night, Diane hurried to get ready to go out with some of her new friends from the library, so Kevin said nothing to her about his disastrous day at the Tribunal.

After Diane left, Ellen insisted that they play Harry Potter. For more than an hour, Kevin pretended to be an eleven-year-old English boy, accent and all, while Ellen played the role of Harry's friend, Hermione. After many miscues on Kevin's part, which Ellen patiently corrected, they once again defeated the forces of the Dark Lord just in time for bed.

"Daddy!" Ellen cried excitedly as he tucked her in. "The new Harry Potter book comes out tomorrow. You've got to get it for me! It's over seven hundred pages!"

Ellen was a voracious reader and the Harry Potter series was her absolute favorite.

"I guess we won't be hearing from you once you get your hands on that."

"Let's have father-daughter talk," Ellen said, snuggling under her covers.

"Okay. What about?"

"Let's talk about how our days went." Ellen bounced up in the bed. "I'll go first. At camp, we made cranes and bats by folding paper. It was cool. It's called origami. And we played a game called wood crick. It's kind of like cricket. Then Mommy picked me up and took me to get some school clothes. I like Nordstrom better."

"Now, what did you do today?" she asked, fluffing up her pillow.

"I didn't exactly have the greatest day," Kevin said, wearily plopping on the edge of the bed. He told Ellen about his efforts to help his new friend, Nihudian, and his encounter with prosecutor Bradford Stone.

"What are you going to do?" she asked, as if hearing an exciting bedtime tale.

"I don't know."

"Dad, that guy Stone is nothing more than a big bully."

"Ellen, you're absolutely right."

"You tell me not to let bullies boss me around."

"I do."

"Then just forget about the creep."

Kevin smiled at the utter simplicity of the sound advice he'd just gotten. "That's exactly what I'm going to do." He rose from her bed. "Now go to sleep, my angel."

Ellen was yawning, but continued stretching out her bedtime. "The song. You have to sing me the song."

Kevin started singing their new favorite bedtime song called "Butterfly Kisses," and soon heard Ellen's rhythmic breathing.

The next day, Kevin rode the second-hand bike he'd bought from a neighbor to the American Book Center in The Hague. There, he picked up the latest adventures of Harry Potter. Then, he met Nihudian. He wanted to go over the testimony Nihudian would be giving in court. If he was going to be his lawyer, he was going to do it right.

"Come on," Nihudian said when they met near the bookstore. "I'm going to take you for another Dutch delight."

He led Kevin through the Binnenhof, an old, walled enclosure of stone buildings that housed the Dutch Parliament. They walked under an old brick arch. Nihudian pointed to part of the building shaped like a cylinder with a turret-like roof. "That's where the Prime Minister of the Netherlands has his office." Behind the building was a huge fountain of water in the large pond that bordered the Binnenhof.

"Look at this," Nihudian said, pointing like a tour guide to the church-like building in the center. "That's Knights' Hall, the oldest building in The Hague. It dates back to the Medieval Era of the 13th century, when it was built by the Count of Holland as a hunting lodge. Once a year, Queen Beatrix rides her golden carriage here from her palace and opens the session of the Dutch Parliament."

"That is ancient," Kevin agreed. "In California, a building from the 1800s is considered old."

They walked through the arch on the opposite side.

"Now, for lunch," Nihudian said. He led Kevin to another food stand just outside the Binnenhof, near a green statue of a Dutch monarch on a horse. A white seagull was perched on top of the statue's head.

Nihudian took care of the ordering. "Two orders of kibbeling with fish sauce."

The man behind the counter handed them two plastic containers full of fried fish pieces. Nihudian and Kevin carried their lunch over to some white plastic chairs overlooking the Binnenhof pond.

Kevin dipped a piece of kibbeling in the sauce, and immediately proclaimed it delicious. "You sure know your Dutch food, Nihudian."

As they sat and watched the fountain spewing water high into the pond, Kevin quizzed Nihudian about his role in intercepting the conversations and about the notebooks. Nihudian's testimony seemed to Kevin to be routine.

"I decided I am going to tell my boss at the Bosnian Embassy about having to testify," Nihudian said after they had finished their lunch and were strolling past small shops lining the street toward the tram stop in the center of The Hague.

"Do you think you'll lose your job?"

"I might. The people who work in the diplomatic area are very sensitive. But I could get in more trouble if they find out from someone else. Besides, the Tribunal will be in recess for the month of August, so I have less than a month of work left anyway. Someone new will take my place in September, and I'll go back to teaching."

Kevin was disappointed that his friend would soon be leaving. He was also surprised about the court recess. "You mean that the whole building closes down?"

"Yes. Everyone goes on holiday."

That was news to Kevin. If he didn't get hired by the end of this month, he would be out of work for August as well. A quarter of his planned year here would have been frittered away—leaving only nine months left. The prosecutor's office might not even want someone for such a short stint. His prospects appeared to be dimming further.

When Nihudian's tram arrived, the Bosnian shook Kevin's hand before boarding.

"Thanks, Kevin. I feel so much better with you on my side."

Kevin hoped his client would feel the same way after testifying.

That afternoon, Kevin delivered the Harry Potter book to a very thankful reader.

"Oh, Daddy!" Ellen exclaimed, throwing her arms around Kevin's neck. She ran into the living room, sat down on the couch, and began reading.

For the next week, Kevin would hardly hear a peep from her.

*   *   *   *

The day before Nihudian was to testify, Kevin called Mrs. Kelly.

He had told Diane that he was waiting for some paperwork to be completed before starting at the Tribunal. But now, three weeks had passed.

"Still no good news," Mrs. Kelly said sadly. "But I hear you have a new client."

"Oh, I'm just helping out a prosecution witness," Kevin said, embarrassed that word had gotten to her. "But I'm afraid I may have offended Mr. Stone."

"He's a bother. It was a mistake to have hired that pompous young man in the first place."

"He told me I'd never work as a prosecutor there. Do you think that's true?"

"I don't know. He does seem to have the ear of the Chief Deputy, Mr. Oswald, I'm sorry to say. I'd send in that defense counsel application. There's no word on the funding freeze, and who knows what mischief Bradford Stone might cause."

Kevin thanked Mrs. Kelly and hung up the phone. When Diane and Ellen came home from the American School, Kevin was glum.

"We need to talk," he said over dinner that night. "It seems there's a funding freeze on in the prosecutor's office and they can't hire me after all. And this prosecutor, Bradford Stone, seems to have it out for me. We might have to go back home at the end of the summer."

"I just got used to being in Holland, Dad," Ellen whined. "I'm not ready to go back home. I want to go to the American School for sixth grade with my new friends."

Kevin looked at Diane for her reaction. She seemed to be thinking.

"Is there any other work you could do for the court, like being an assistant to a judge?" she asked finally.

"No. The only other thing I can do is put my name on the court's list of defense lawyers. I don't want to do that. I'm a prosecutor."

"You're defending Nihudian," Ellen piped up. "He's not a bad guy, right?"

"He's just a witness," he said. "That's not the same. I've always been on the side of the good guys."

"That bully Stone isn't one of the good guys," Ellen retorted.

"The prosecutors here do seem like they have too much power," Kevin said. "The Tribunal probably needs good defense lawyers to keep them honest. But I just don't think it's for me."

Diane took a sip of wine. "You wouldn't be defending Milosevic or any of those war criminals who did all that ethnic cleansing, would you?" As if recoiling from her own words or thoughts, she looked up with a start. "Those people were no better than the Nazis."

Her normally warm brown eyes had turned hard and piercing.

"I want to stay here, Daddy," Ellen said. "Please, please. You always tell me to try new things. I am, and I like it."

"Well, I suppose I can put in the application anyway and keep our options open," Kevin said, more to not disappoint his daughter than anything. "I hear it's difficult to get assigned a case though, so don't count on it. The defendants all want Yugoslavian lawyers who speak their language. They probably won't trust an American, especially one who's spent his career as a prosecutor."

"Just go for it, Dad. They'll want you once they find out how good you are."

Diane frowned, but kept her thoughts to herself.

The next morning, Kevin tucked the defense application into his jacket before leaving the house.

"I've put a magic spell on you, Daddy," Ellen said. "You're invincible today. Or did the spell say invisible? Oh well."

"Invisible might be good," he laughed.

Kevin gave her a big hug as she squirmed to get away.

"Good luck," Diane said, giving Kevin a quick kiss as they stood in the doorway.

She had surprised him by taking to Holland so well. He thought she'd jump at the chance to return home to California. She did seem to be enjoying herself, having found work she enjoyed and some new local friends. Kevin realized that if they were forced to return home early, he would have two disappointed females on his hands.

At the Tribunal, Kevin left his completed application with Mrs. Kelly. He nervously waited for Nihudian in the lobby. What if Nihudian didn't show up? Bradford Stone would surely think Kevin was behind it. Nihudian would be a fugitive, and Kevin would be charged with aiding and abetting. His imagination was in overdrive.

To Kevin's relief, Nihudian appeared right on schedule.

"I told the people at the Embassy about my situation," Nihudian said. "They were very understanding, but they thought it was best that I should not continue my work here. So, I am going home tonight."

"I'm sorry you lost your job over this."

"It's for the best. My daughters were so happy when I called and told them I will be home tonight. I have missed them."

"How old are they?" Kevin asked.

"Eleven years and seven years."

"My little girl is eleven. Daughters are pretty great."

Nihudian got a dreamy look in his eyes. "The best, my friend. God's gift."

A few minutes before 9:30, Bradford Stone appeared in the lobby and summoned Nihudian, without greeting Kevin. While Nihudian went with Stone, Kevin was escorted to the Courtroom 2 visitors' gallery. Kevin felt nervous for Nihudian.

Once the session started, Bradford Stone slowly and thoroughly led Nihudian through the events chronologically, beginning with Nihudian's training. He ended with Nihudian reading entries from the parts of the notebooks that the prosecution thought important to its case.

Stone's direct examination took about one hour. The judges seemed satisfied with Nihudian's direct answers. Kevin held his breath as Vladimir Krasnic, the defense lawyer, rose from his chair to begin his cross-examination.

Krasnic launched into a highly technical discussion about the capability of the interception equipment. He questioned whether the model Nihudian was using was as effective as other models. He asked about the radio frequency used when intercepting the conversations. Nihudian's answers were simple.

"I don't know how the equipment worked," he replied more than once. "I just turned it on and wrote down what I heard."

After about forty-five minutes of technical questions, Krasnic told the judges. "I have just a few more questions, Your Honors."

Kevin allowed himself to relax a bit. Maybe Nihudian would get through this without any hitches. Or was the lawyer saving his best cross-examination for last?

"Did you yourself commit any war crimes?"

"No."

"Did you murder any civilians?"

"No."

"Did you rape any women?"

"No."

"Did you treat any prisoners inhumanely?"

"No."

"Yet it is true, is it not, that before you would speak to the prosecution in this case, you insisted on having a lawyer?"

"Yes."

"Now, you are not a wealthy man, are you?"

"No."

"Yet you retained a lawyer from the United States to represent you did you not?"

"Yes, I did."

"Did the Bosnian government pay for your lawyer?"

"No."

"You paid him with your own funds?"

"Yes."

"Can you tell this Court how much you paid this lawyer?"

Kevin looked at Bradford Stone in anticipation. That question was irrelevant. There should be an objection. But Stone sat there silently.

"One Euro."

"One Euro, that's all?"

"Yes."

The President of the trial chamber, the woman from Kenya, interrupted. "Witness," she asked, "what kind of lawyer would work for one Euro?"

Before Nihudian could answer, Bradford Stone was on his feet. But it was not to make an objection. "You can see for yourself," Stone announced. "The lawyer is sitting right there. His name is Kevin Anderson, or something." He pointed to Kevin, sitting in the small booth on the other side of the glass.

All eyes turned to Kevin. Kevin fought to keep himself from turning beet red, a battle that he lost. He also tried to look confident, but felt unbelievably embarrassed.

"I guess you get what you pay for," Stone volunteered, offering Kevin a snide smile. There was laughter in the courtroom.

The judges shook their heads. "Perhaps we are paying our assigned counsel too much," the Australian judge observed dryly.

More laughter.

Kevin was devastated. He had been made to look a fool. He had represented Nihudian to protect his rights. None of that had come out. Instead, he was the object of ridicule.

"Why did he ask how much I paid you?" Nihudian asked when they met in the lobby.

"I don't know what that was supposed to prove."

"I'm sorry, Kevin, if they embarrassed you. If they gave me the chance, I would have told them what a great lawyer you are. And a great friend."

"It's alright, Nihudian," Kevin replied. "You were a truthful and credible witness. It's been an honor to be your lawyer."

Kevin and Nihudian walked out of the Tribunal together.

"You have my address and e-mail," Kevin said. "Be sure and keep in touch."

Nihudian took Kevin's hand and shook it firmly. "I will someday repay you, Kevin Anderson." He turned and headed down the street.

Kevin walked over to his bicycle. His first case at the Tribunal was over. It had been a success for the client, and a disaster for himself.

Not feeling much like returning to the Tribunal that day, he got on his bicycle and rode home to Wassenaar. Things sure weren't turning out the way they were supposed to.

Over the next two weeks, Kevin called Mrs. Kelly twice, but nothing had changed. It was almost the end of July. The Tribunal would be closed in August. It looked like Ellen would not be attending the American School after all.

On the Wednesday of the last week of July, Kevin was alone in the house, taking his turn reading the latest Harry Potter book, when the phone rang.

"Mr. Anderson, I'm with the defense unit at the Tribunal. We have a case for you if you're available."

Kevin's heart started beating faster.

"Great," he said, not sure whether it was great or not.

"The accused was arrested last night by the United Nations forces. And he speaks English. Do you want the assignment as his temporary counsel? As you know, it will be up to the accused whether to select you as his permanent counsel."

Kevin's mind was racing. His instincts told him that if he asked to think it over, the assignment would go to someone else. With the prosecutor's job looking virtually hopeless, Kevin had the sense that it was now or never for him at the Tribunal. It wouldn't hurt just to be someone's temporary lawyer.

"Yes, I'll accept the assignment."

"Good. You can go out to the detention center and meet your new client tomorrow. His court appearance will be the day after tomorrow at 2:00."

"Thank you for selecting me."

"You can thank your friend—the Irish one."

Kevin smiled at the thought of Mrs. Kelly. "I'll do that. Goodbye, now."

"Wait! Don't you want to know your client's name?"

"That would help." Kevin was a rookie at this defense business.

"Dragoljub Zaric."

That name meant nothing to Kevin.

"He is better known as Draga," said the court official.

Now Kevin remembered reading something about "Draga" in the local English-language newspaper a few weeks earlier. He was a flamboyant Serbian fugitive they'd been trying to find for some time. Kevin wondered what he might be getting himself into.

"Can you tell me anything else about him?"

"Well, he commanded a paramilitary group called—the Black Dragons."

"And the charge?" Kevin asked, holding his breath.

"Genocide."

CHAPTER 5

▼

Kevin's body tingled with excitement, but he dreaded telling Diane.

He knew he had made a kind of promise to his wife, but at the same time he was sick and tired of being on the sidelines. In his heart, he knew that he would never get a job with the prosecutor's office—even if the funds became available any time soon. He had made too many stout adversaries in that department.

When he heard the gate open and saw Diane and Ellen walking their bicycles into the back yard, Kevin opened the door and greeted them.

Once they were all inside, he could wait no longer.

"I've got some news. I've been assigned as temporary defense counsel at the Tribunal."

"Does that mean we can stay, Daddy?" Ellen asked excitedly.

"I don't know yet," he said cautiously. "The defendant will have to decide to keep me, and I'll—well, there's some other considerations."

"Well, I guess congratulations are in order," Diane smiled wanly.

"Goody, goody," Ellen squealed. "We can stay!"

That night, alone in the living room, Kevin switched on CNN. The story he was looking for came third after the top of the hour.

"United Nations troops arrested the infamous Serbian warlord Draga last night at the Romanian border with Serbia," the announcer reported. "The arrest of Dragoljub Zaric was made after a rival Serbian gang reportedly kidnapped him and delivered him to U.N. officials. Zaric has now been transported to The Hague where, along with Slobodan Milosevic, he becomes one of the most significant persons arrested for the War Crimes Tribunal."

A picture of a brash, confident man in his mid-thirties, tall, and well groomed, flashed on the screen. He was wearing a black beret and black Ninja-like uniform. Other footage showed him at his wedding, when he was married to a popular Serbian movie star, and at a Belgrade stadium cheering on the local soccer team.

Kevin found a yellow legal pad and began jotting down notes.

"The Black Dragons, a paramilitary group headed by Draga, is believed responsible for thousands of deaths during the war in Bosnia. Draga has been one of Europe's most wanted fugitives. In addition to his alleged war crimes, Draga is wanted by authorities in Belgium, Sweden, and Germany for a string of robberies in the 1980s. He previously escaped from a German prison. Security is expected to be tight when he makes his first appearance before the U.N. War Crimes Tribunal."

Kevin turned off the TV as the announcer went on to the next story.

He was surprised to see that he had been silently joined by Diane and Ellen.

"Is that your client, Daddy?" asked Ellen, wide-eyed.

"Well, for the time being," he said, sneaking a quick look at Diane.

"He's handsome," Ellen said. "He can't be all bad—a movie star married him. Will you be on TV, too, Daddy?"

"Ellen, you have that report to work on," Diane said sternly. "Run upstairs now."

When they were alone, Diane sat on the couch. She put her head in her hands.

"When you went to Seattle and prosecuted that Neo-Nazi group, I was so proud of you. I was hoping I'd feel the same way about your work here. But now—"

"Look, honey," he stammered, "this wasn't what I had in mind."

Kevin saw that her face was filled with pain and fury.

"Not what you had in mind? Kevin, are you crazy? Milosevic is Bosnia's Hitler and this guy Draga is Himmler for God's sake! And you're his defense lawyer?"

"I—uh, well, I really didn't know who he was when I agreed."

"You know now! What are you going to do about it?"

"I have a responsibility here, Diane. I'll have to meet with him. It's just temporary."

"You're on the wrong side!" she hissed.

Diane rushed from the room.

*   *   *   *

The next day, Kevin rode his bicycle to the Tribunal's detention center, located at a Dutch prison near the dunes at Scheveningen. It was not far from where he and Nihudian had eaten fries with mayonnaise.

At its entrance was a huge brick gate with a coat of arms on the top. The prison complex, built in the 19th century, had been used by the Nazis to imprison members of the Dutch resistance when Germany occupied Holland during World War II.

After showing his ID and passing through a metal detector, Kevin was directed to a brick building called "Unit 4," and eventually to a windowless interview room.

A few minutes later, the door opened and Kevin found himself face to face with the infamous Draga. He seemed even bigger than he had on television. His muscular arms were huge.

"I'm Kevin Anderson." Kevin extended his right hand. "The Tribunal has assigned me to be your lawyer—at least for the time being."

Draga looked at Kevin's hand, but did not take it. He remained standing.

"An American?"

"Yes."

"I don't need a lawyer."

Kevin looked up at Draga standing over him, trying not to show any fear.

"What do you mean you don't need a lawyer?"

Draga spat out his words: "This War Crimes court is a joke. There is no justice here. They paid a bunch of hooligans to kidnap me from my home. They dragged me here in chains. I am a prisoner of war. This is nothing but an imperial American show trial to justify its genocide against the people of Serbia."

"Your English is very good," Kevin said, trying to diffuse Draga's anger. "But you still haven't told me why you don't need a lawyer."

Draga glared at him. "I am not going to participate in this illegitimate court. Let them do with me what they wish."

Kevin looked at Draga. His first case as a defense lawyer was starting badly. Did he really want this angry man for a client? "Look, it's your decision. I can tell you that the Tribunal will probably assign you a lawyer whether you think you need one or not."

"What can you do for me?" Draga demanded. "Get me out on bail?"

"I suspect not."

"Help me escape?

"Definitely not."

"Then you are wasting my time."

"You don't seem to understand, Mr. Zaric. The Court is going to give you a lawyer whether you want one or not. And no lawyer is going to get you out on bail or help you escape."

"Can I represent myself?"

Kevin thought about that. He wanted to be honest with Draga. "I suppose so."

Draga was silent again.

"But even when a person is allowed to represent himself," Kevin continued, "the Court usually appoints a lawyer as standby counsel. So you're going to have a lawyer in your life one way or the other."

"I don't need a lawyer."

They were back to square one.

In some sense, Kevin was relieved. It seemed to be working out for the best. Obviously, he wouldn't be on this case that long. It would be a professional escape, and a personal one as well.

Kevin shrugged. "Tell it to the Court tomorrow. Meanwhile, until I'm off the case, I'm required to appear in court with you."

Draga said nothing.

"I brought a copy of the charges against you," Kevin continued, placing a thick group of papers on the table.

Draga made no effort to pick them up or look at them.

"Basically, you're charged with about every crime that occurred during the war. The Tribunal has what they call 'superior responsibility.' Under their rules, commanders are responsible for the war crimes of their men if the commander knew or had reason to know of the crimes and failed to prevent them or punish the persons who had committed them. It's very broad."

Draga showed no reaction.

"Tomorrow, you'll be asked to enter a plea."

Draga turned and walked toward the door from which he had entered, signaling an end to the interview.

"I guess I'll see you in court tomorrow," Kevin said weakly.

Draga turned and stared at Kevin. "I told you. I don't need a lawyer." Then, he opened the door and left the room.

Kevin walked out of the prison and got back on his bicycle. As he rode on the bike path along the sand dunes towards Wassenaar, he realized how much he preferred being a prosecutor. As prosecutor, he'd always called his own shots. This defense work felt too much like being someone's stooge.

The next day, Kevin was shown to Courtroom 1 at the Tribunal where Draga would be arraigned. The courtroom was much bigger than Courtroom 2, and had a large visitors' gallery—separated from the courtroom by bulletproof glass—that held about 150 people. Kevin looked out and saw that every seat was taken.

The prosecution team was at its table on one side of the courtroom: Charles Oswald and Bradford Stone.

Kevin frowned at the sight of his nemesis, Stone.

When he moved toward the defense table, Kevin was surprised to see defense counsel Vladimir Krasnic, who had made such a point to embarrass him during the cross examination of Nihudian, seated in one of the chairs.

"Ah, it's the one-Euro lawyer," Krasnic said.

Kevin tried to smile.

"Well," Krasnic said, straightening the front of his robes, "I don't believe your services will be required in this case, even at your discounted rates."

"What do you mean?"

"Mr. Zaric will be requesting that I be his assigned counsel."

Kevin could not believe what he felt. He knew that Draga had the right to choose his assigned counsel from anyone on the Tribunal's list. And a big part of him wanted off the case, today, now. And yet—he was <u>disappointed</u>. Was it the excitement of finally standing in the Tribunal's courtroom wearing a black robe, only to be shown the door? Did he wish for an opportunity to lance Stone where it would hurt the most: in his puffy British ego?

When Kevin heard a door open behind him, he turned and saw Draga enter, surrounded by light blue uniformed guards. As soon as Draga appeared, the smooth, silver-haired Krasnic was on his feet, making his way to talk with him. The two men greeted each other warmly.

Kevin sat down. He could see it would be over quickly.

Diane would be pleased, and Ellen would be disappointed.

"All rise! Veuillez vous lever!" the usher bellowed, as an elderly judge entered the room. It was William Davidson of Great Britain. He was reputed to be the most cantankerous of the Tribunal's judges.

"Call the case," he ordered.

The clerk announced, "Prosecutor against Dragoljub Zaric, case number IT-96-30. Counsel, announce your appearances please."

Kevin rose with the other lawyers.

"Charles Oswald and Bradford Stone for the Office of the Prosecutor," Oswald said in a firm voice.

"Vladimir Krasnic for Dragoljub Zaric, Your Honor."

It was Kevin's turn. "Good morning, Your Honor," he said, edging over to the podium where Krasnic was standing. "I am Kevin Anderson. I was asked by the Registrar to be temporary counsel for the accused." He then sat down.

Judge Davidson said nothing for a moment. Then he addressed Vladimir Krasnic. "Mr. Krasnic, has the accused retained you to be his counsel?"

"No, Your Honor. He is requesting that I be his assigned counsel."

"Very well." Turning to Draga, Judge Davidson asked, "Mr. Zaric, do you request that the court assign Mr. Krasnic to represent you?"

Draga was looking down. He did not look up or say anything.

"Mr. Zaric, can you hear me?" the judge asked, tapping on his microphone.

Draga stood up slowly and looked directly at Judge Davidson. He spoke in a loud, defiant tone. "This court has no jurisdiction over me. You have kidnapped me from my sovereign country. I am a political prisoner. I refuse to participate in your show trial."

Draga sat down.

Judge Davidson's face reddened. "Mr. Zaric, do you request that Mr. Krasnic represent you or not?"

Draga again was silent. He looked at the judge defiantly, crossed his arms, and said nothing.

"Mr. Zaric, I ask you for the third and final time. Is it your request that Mr. Krasnic represent you?"

After a second or two of silence, Vladimir Krasnic rose. "May I have a moment with my client?"

"Yes. I believe that would be advisable." Judge Davidson's tone signaled a warning.

Krasnic walked over and whispered to Draga. The two men spoke out of earshot, then Krasnic returned to the podium. "Your Honor, I believe that Mr. Zaric feels that by requesting counsel, he is somehow consenting to the legitimacy of these proceedings. He does not wish to do that. Perhaps the Court will accept my representation, as an officer of the Court, that Mr. Zaric desires the Court to assign me as his counsel."

Judge Davidson shook his head. "No, Mr. Krasnic. This man isn't going to get any special treatment. The temporary counsel assigned by the Registrar will represent Mr. Zaric until he makes a request for a specific lawyer."

Judge Davidson looked at Kevin. "What did you say your name was, counsel?"

"Kevin Anderson, Your Honor."

"Mr. Anderson, are you ready to proceed with the arraignment?"

"Yes, Your Honor." The words came out weakly. Kevin's heart was racing at this turn of events.

"Will the accused please rise?"

Kevin turned and looked at Draga. He was still seated, staring coldly at the judge.

"Will the accused please rise," Judge Davidson repeated more forcefully.

Draga made no effort to move.

"I order the guards to bring Mr. Zaric to his feet."

The two guards flanking Draga attempted to pick him up out of the chair. They struggled to do so as Draga went limp. Soon, two more guards rushed over. The four of them lifted Draga out of his chair and propped him up in a standing position.

Kevin caught Draga's eye as the struggle ended. Draga glared at him.

"Mr. Zaric, have you received a copy of the indictment?"

No response.

The judge looked at Kevin. "Counsel, have you provided a copy of the indictment to the accused?"

"Yes, Your Honor."

The judge looked back at Draga. "What is your true name, sir?"

Kevin was on his feet. "Your Honor, I respectfully direct my client not to answer that question."

"I beg your pardon," Judge Davidson said, surprised.

"The burden is on the prosecution to establish that the person in this courtroom is the same person accused in the indictment. I request an identity hearing be held for that purpose."

Kevin had seen good defense lawyers do this in federal court.

Judge Davidson looked annoyed. "Counsel, I understand that you are new here. It is standard procedure in this Court for the accused to state his true name for the record at the initial appearance."

Looking at Draga, Judge Davidson continued, "What is your true name, sir?"

Kevin hesitated for an instant, and then was on his feet. He was determined to protect his client's rights. "With all due respect, Your Honor, my client should not be compelled to give evidence against himself. It is the prosecution's burden to prove that he is the person accused in the indictment. I request that the Court require them to do so at a hearing."

Judge Davidson was exasperated. "Sit down, counsel." He turned to the prosecution table. "What is the prosecutor's position on this?"

Bradford Stone rose and smiled at the judge. "Clearly Mr. Anderson is inexperienced with our procedures. Why, Mr. Krasnic has already told the court that the person here is Mr. Zaric."

"Perhaps the prosecutor wishes to call Mr. Krasnic as a witness," Kevin retorted, "at a hearing which is required for that purpose."

Kevin saw Krasnic glare at him.

Judge Davidson ignored Kevin. He looked at Draga. "Mr. Zaric, if you do not now declare your true name, I shall hold you in contempt."

Draga said nothing.

Kevin rose again. "Your Honor, my client cannot be held in contempt. He is simply following the advice of counsel in this matter."

"Then I will hold you in contempt," the judge growled.

"Your Honor," Kevin pleaded, "will you at least ask the prosecution what law they rely on for the proposition that an accused may be compelled to state his true name when the issue of identity is contested?"

Judge Davidson turned to the prosecution. "What does the case law hold on this point, Mr. Stone?"

Bradford Stone looked surprised. "Well, Your Honor," he sputtered, "I don't recall a case on this point. But we have always proceeded this way. I don't know that it has been challenged before."

"All the more reason to proceed cautiously, Your Honor," Kevin chimed in.

The judge glared at Kevin. "Court will be in recess. I will see counsel in my chambers." The judge rose from his chair, throwing his glasses on the bench.

"Your Honor," Kevin called out.

The judge stopped. He glowered at Kevin.

"I regret to say that I cannot go into chambers with the Court. My client does not trust me as it is. I request that all proceedings in this case take place in his presence in open court."

Judge Davidson turned and stormed off the bench.

Kevin sat down as the guards led Draga from the room.

Vladimir Krasnic chuckled. "You're going to need your own lawyer if you keep this up," he said as he walked away.

Kevin looked out in the gallery. People were filing out, some shaking their heads.

Judge Davidson returned to the bench thirty minutes later. "Mr. Anderson, you will be given ten days to file a memorandum in support of your position. The prosecution shall respond ten days thereafter. The Court will then rule on the matter. This arraignment is continued until 4 September at 1400 hours."

Stone was on his feet. "Your Honor, surely the Court is not seriously considering counsel's position."

"I am bending over backwards to give counsel more time to research and consider his position. He is new and unfamiliar with our procedures. I don't want him to do something he will later regret."

The judge looked at Kevin sternly.

Kevin was on his feet. "I appreciate the Court's consideration, Your Honor, but I request that an identity hearing be held forthwith."

"Request denied."

"Then I request that my client be released from custody, Your Honor. He is entitled to such a hearing without delay. September is over a month away."

"Sit down, Mr. Anderson, or you'll be joining him in custody," the judge barked. "Court is adjourned."

Everyone stood up as Judge Davidson strode from the bench.

When Kevin turned around, Krasnic was already at Draga's side, whispering to him. When the guards led Draga away, Krasnic turned to Kevin.

"Don't waste your time on the research, counselor. I'll be preparing a written request for counsel that Mr. Zaric will sign tonight."

Kevin was tired. "That's fine. I think I'm finished for today."

"With that performance you have finished your work here—forever."

CHAPTER 6

▼

After court, Kevin hid out in the defense counsel room, hoping to avoid the news media that had gathered. As he waited, he wondered how things had gone so badly. At home, Diane was beside herself and Ellen was on edge about staying for school. Here at the Tribunal, he had managed to offend the judge, alienate the prosecutors, and annoy a fellow defense counsel. Plus, his client hated him. All this from doing what he thought he was supposed to do: serve as a responsible advocate for his client until being replaced.

As a prosecutor, he had felt invincible; almost as if he could do no wrong.

As a defense lawyer, he had so far done nothing right.

Just after 5 p.m., he ventured down to the lobby. He had almost made it to the front door when a tall man with dark hair and a hawk-like face approached him.

"I am Toma Lanko of the Bosnia News Service," he said in an Eastern European accent. "Mr. Anderson, we have all seen pictures of Draga in his Black Dragon uniform and at his wedding. The man in court is clearly the same man. What is the point of your actions in court today?"

It was a fair question.

"Like any defendant, my client has the right to make the prosecution prove every point. Every issue must be challenged right from the beginning without any presumption of guilt. The only way that international courts will ever be accepted as a means for doing justice is for the accused to be given a vigorous defense and a fair trial."

Kevin firmly believed what he had said, and he would have defended those principals even as a prosecutor. They were Criminal Law 101 at law school.

"But Draga seems to want no defense at all," said the newsman.

"Well, as his lawyer, I'm obligated to give him the best representation that I know how. If he doesn't like it, he is certainly free to replace me with someone else."

Kevin had not wanted to be trapped; they had kept moving, and were now outside the courthouse. It was cold and gray outside, and Kevin pulled up the collar on his coat.

"Why would you want to defend a cold-blooded killer like Draga?"

"The prosecution has to prove that. The law says he's presumed innocent."

Kevin began to wonder about the reporter's objectivity.

"My role in the system is to defend the individual against the power of the state," Kevin went on. "When the police bring a murder suspect who they have just wounded into the emergency room at the hospital, the surgeon doesn't pass judgment on the man. He just rolls up his sleeves and works as hard as he can to save the man's life. That's what I'm going to do."

Kevin excused himself.

At least the Tribunal would be closed for the next month, he thought as he mounted his bicycle. After two days as Draga's lawyer, Kevin felt like he needed a vacation already.

When he reached home, he found Ellen in the kitchen having a snack.

"Hi, Daddy. Do you still have a job?"

Kevin smiled. "For the time being, although I'm not sure that's good or bad."

"Are we staying?" Ellen asked, "My school starts in two weeks."

He sighed. "For now."

Diane came down from upstairs. She tried to offer a smile. Kevin couldn't help but notice that she didn't ask him how his day in court went, as she almost always did.

"Ellen and I were talking about maybe going into Amsterdam this weekend for some sightseeing," Diane said.

"Sounds good," he said. Maybe that would cheer him up.

"Can we go to Anne Frank's house?" Ellen asked excitedly. Her fifth-grade class back home had studied the Holocaust, and Ellen had done a book report on *The Diary of Anne Frank*. Kevin had told her at the time that they would be able to visit Anne Frank's house in Holland. The kid didn't forget a thing.

"That would be very good for all of us to see," Diane said pointedly.

Yeah, Kevin thought, that ought to cheer me right up.

The next day, the Andersons took the train to Amsterdam. When they got off at their destination, they found themselves among a mob of people heading to and from the trains at the huge Central Station. The Andersons struggled to reach the street, where they found throngs of people walking, bicycling, and getting on and off trams.

"This place is too crowded," Ellen complained. "I thought Holland would be a peaceful place with people walking around tulip gardens in wooden shoes."

Kevin led his family down the first side street that he saw. He, too, wanted to escape the mass of humanity. He spotted a sign in English that said "Coffee Shop."

"Let's go in here and sit down for a minute," he suggested.

When they entered, Kevin saw that the coffee shop looked more like a tavern. There was an old wooden bar in the center and a few tables near the front. He led Diane and Ellen to one of the tables.

"It's nice to get away from all those people," Kevin said. "It's more crowded than New York City." He pulled out a map to locate the direction of Anne Frank's house.

Diane and Ellen were scanning their surroundings. Diane picked up a menu from the table. Ellen wrinkled her nose. "What's that weird smell?"

Kevin immediately smelled the odor of marijuana. He looked around and saw a teenager smoking a joint at the bar. A few tables away, he saw a couple smoking hashish from a water pipe.

"I think that's the smell of marijuana," Diane said.

She showed Kevin the menu, which listed many varieties of cannabis for sale. "I don't think this is the kind of coffee shop they have in America," she said.

"Ugh, I hate drugs!" Ellen exclaimed. "Let's get out of here."

Kevin got up and headed for the door, followed closely by Ellen and Diane. He waved to the bartender, who smiled like this sort of thing happened all the time. When they were outside, Diane pointed out the marijuana leaf symbol on the front door.

"Oops," Kevin said. "More culture shock. I'm glad you hate drugs, Ellen. So do I." He was grateful for the anti-drug campaigns that had reached Ellen's school.

"How did you know it was marijuana, Mommy?" Ellen asked.

Kevin chuckled to himself. <u>Nothing</u> slipped by this kid.

"Let's see if we can find Anne's house," Diane said, deftly changing the subject.

They headed back toward the main street. Kevin tried looking at his map as they walked through the crowds, but as a city built on canals in the 16th century,

Amsterdam was hardly laid out in a grid pattern. He soon found himself hope-
lessly lost.

"I think it must be this way," he said, relying on his sense of direction, which
had never been good.

"Can't we ask someone for directions?" Diane asked.

"I think we're getting close," Kevin said.

"What's that girl doing?" Ellen asked as they turned a corner and walked
down a street bordering a small canal. Ellen pointed to a window of the building
on the corner.

Kevin saw a large-breasted woman standing in the window, wearing only a red
lace bra, red panties, and black-netted stockings. She was smiling at the passers by
and sucking her finger in her mouth.

"Look, there's another one!" Ellen exclaimed.

A woman in black underwear stood coyly in the window of the next building.

"Wonderful," Diane said. "You've taken us to the Red Light District." She
grabbed Ellen's hand and turned back around the corner.

Before Kevin could say anything, Diane was asking a policeman for directions.

"What's the Red Light District, Dad?" Ellen asked.

"I'll explain it to you later, Ellen."

They finally found Anne Frank's house—in the opposite direction. The narrow five-story house facing a canal called the Prinsengracht, had been joined with
the house next door and converted into a museum. They paid the entrance fee,
and then walked from room to room, looking at photographs from the Holocaust
and reading passages from young Anne's diary that were displayed throughout
the museum.

"Come over here, Daddy," Ellen called when they had gone upstairs. "Look at
this!"

It was the wooden bookcase that had been built to hide the entrance to the
secret annex where Anne Frank and seven others had hid from the Nazis for more
than two years. Ellen pulled open the bookcase like a door, and led the way up
narrow stairs.

Anne's bedroom was tiny and contained small pictures and postcards that she
had used to liven up the bare walls. The museum placards told how Anne and her
family had to be quiet as mice, lest the workers in the warehouse below hear their
footsteps.

"I could never have done it," Ellen declared, "unless I had my Game Boy and
Harry Potter books."

When he came to the end of the museum, Kevin watched a video interview of Anne's father talking about how he had found out that his daughter had died in a Nazi concentration camp just one month before the camps were liberated. He later recovered her diaries and was finally able to get them published.'

Tears welled up in Kevin's eyes as he thought of how much Ellen meant to him, and how horrible it must have been for Anne Frank's father to have his daughter taken from him and imprisoned. And then to find out that she was dead! <u>How did the poor man even want to go on living after that</u>? Kevin wondered. He doubted he would.

As they left the house, Kevin put his arms around Diane and Ellen and squeezed.

His hassles at the Tribunal seemed trivial. His family was everything.

That night, Kevin and Diane stayed up long after Ellen went to bed. They sat on pillows on the floor in front of a roaring fire in the old, stone fireplace.

"That night when the story was on CNN," Diane said, tears welling in her eyes, "what I saw were concentration camps. So many people died. The Nazis killing millions, and then the Serbs wiping out villages in the name of 'ethnic cleansing.' I thought of my grandmother and grandfather being marched into the gas chambers…"

Kevin's mother-in-law, Ruth, had learned only a few years earlier during a visit to Israel, when she located a distant cousin, the details of her missing parents' fate. To hear of their murders from an eyewitness had proven too much to bear for Ruth. Although by then an old woman, she had relived the horrible pain as if she were a young girl finding out her beloved parents had just been taken from her. Ruth went to her grave not long after, and a day didn't go by those last months of her life that she didn't cry for her parents. The death certificate identified advanced arteriosclerosis as the primary cause of Ruth's death, but everyone who knew her understood that she died of a broken heart.

As Diane opened up, Kevin listened and felt her pain.

He thought about Draga and the Bosnian Serbs. Diane was right—if the accusations against him were true, then what he and his men did to the Muslims was not much different than what the Nazis did to the Jews, and there were probably girls Ellen's age, like Anne Frank, who had suffered and died. If Draga and the Black Dragons had done those things, Kevin knew he was on the wrong side of this one.

He held Diane in his arms, but made no promises to her.

After helping her to bed, Kevin threw another log on the fire, and sat and stared at the flames.

He had wanted so much to be a prosecutor at the Tribunal. Part of him knew that Diane would have been proud of him for playing that kind of role in what amounted to a present-day Nuremberg Trials—and he had known he needed that from her. But events had swept him in the other direction. He found himself in the new and uncomfortable position of defense counsel, and the main thing he was holding onto now was the first tenet of criminal law: the presumption of the accused's innocence until proven guilty.

As he stared at the flames, he recognized there was something else working on him.

As a prosecutor, he knew how to put a case together. He knew how to play fair and achieve results. From what he'd seen in the Tribunal courtrooms, the prosecutors, led by that pompous ass, Bradford Stone, played by a different set of rules. They personified, in Kevin's mind, the worst sort of abuse of government power. And he now wondered gravely—how many people had been railroaded by these same prosecutors?

It was just as well that Draga wanted another lawyer; of that, Kevin was certain.

But until that time came, he would do his level best to keep the prosecution honest.

*   *   *   *

It was raining lightly on Monday morning, but Kevin decided to ride his bike to the prison anyway. The rain turned heavy and Kevin was soaked when he arrived. A sympathetic guard gave him a towel. Kevin dried himself off as best he could before entering the interview room for his second meeting with Draga.

The guard shut the door behind him. Draga was already standing in the room.

"Good afternoon," Kevin said pleasantly. "How are you today?"

No answer.

"I wanted to come by and find out if you were going to be signing Mr. Krasnic's papers or if you wanted me to continue as your lawyer?"

No answer.

Kevin paused. "Well, until the Court relieves me, I'm your lawyer. So I'm going to do the job as best as I know how. I'd like your help."

No answer. Draga was staring at Kevin with his arms folded. He had an expression of annoyance on his face.

"Is there anything at all you'd like to talk about?" Kevin asked.

No answer.

"Okay," Kevin said with a shrug. "Well, let me tell you a little about this court and what you can expect."

He sat down, while Draga remained standing.

"The International Criminal Tribunal for the former Yugoslavia was created in 1993 by a resolution of the United Nations Security Council. It has jurisdiction to try people for war crimes committed in the former Yugoslavia. You will be tried by three judges, although Judge Davidson, as the pretrial judge, will be handling most of the court appearances before the trial. Before your trial, you are entitled to copies of the evidence that the prosecutor will use against you, as well as any evidence that points to your innocence. That's called discovery. You also have the right to raise any legal challenges or discovery issues by filing pretrial motions."

Draga remained standing, his eyes fixed on some imaginary point of interest on the ceiling.

"Let me tell you what I'm going to be doing on your behalf. If you have any objections, or suggestions, be sure and let me know. First, I will obtain the discovery from the prosecution, and bring a copy for you to read as well. Do you have any problem with that?"

No answer.

"Next, I am going to prepare some pretrial motions to be filed with the court. As you know, I'm trying to make them hold an identity hearing in your case. I also want to challenge the circumstances of your kidnapping and arrest. I need your help on that one. Can you tell me what happened that day?"

No answer.

Kevin tried to appear unfazed. "What I thought I might do," he said, "is go to your Embassy and make a formal request on your behalf that they investigate and arrest the persons responsible for your kidnapping, I don't imagine your government wants to condone this kind of thing. Do you have any problem with my doing that?"

No answer.

"Good," said Kevin, trying to get a rise out of Draga. "I'll let the Embassy know I have your full approval."

No answer.

"I also want to file what is known as a 'graymail' motion. It's a request for information on you in the files of the major intelligence agencies in the world like the CIA."

Draga looked over at Kevin, showing interest for the first time.

"It's a routine motion in a case involving international events. The strategy is to try and put the prosecutor in a position where they have to choose between revealing sensitive intelligence information and dismissing the case. Once in a great while, the intelligence agencies won't reveal the information and the case gets dismissed. But most of the time the intelligence agencies deny having any records relevant to the case, and the motion is rejected."

"Do you have any reason to believe that intelligence agencies have information on you?" Kevin asked.

No answer. Draga turned away and resumed his study of the ceiling.

"Well, I'll give it a try, anyway. Then, after all the pretrial motions are decided, your trial will begin. I'm not sure when that will happen. I would guess that your trial would start sometime next spring. They don't have the death penalty here at the Tribunal. That's one piece of good news. But, if you're found guilty, I think you can expect a life sentence."

Draga turned and walked out of the room. He had not said a word to Kevin.

Undaunted, Kevin bicycled over to the Yugoslavian Embassy. As he passed the huge stately buildings of the Embassy district of The Hague, he thought more about Draga's arrest. If he could prove that the U.N. forces had planned and encouraged Draga's kidnapping and arrest, he could file a motion to get the case thrown out. And what if he succeeded? Was he doing too much here? he wondered. He dismissed the worrisome thought, knowing that the motion would surely be denied. Besides, it was the kind of thing that defense attorneys did. Too, he liked the idea of tweaking the insufferable prosecutors.

The building housing the Embassy of Serbia and Montenegro was an old three-story brownstone in need of repairs, and surrounded with ragged landscaping. Like some poor cousin, it stood alongside the stately embassies of Germany, Colombia, Finland, and the Ukraine. The economic sanctions imposed against the government of Slobodan Milosevic appeared to have taken their toll.

Kevin tried the front door, but it was locked. He found an intercom near the door and pushed the button. A female voice said something in Dutch.

Kevin spoke into the intercom. "My name is Kevin Anderson. I'm a lawyer for a citizen of your country who is in jail here in The Hague. He needs your help. Can I speak to someone about his situation?"

There was a long pause. Then, there was a click from the lock on the door.

Kevin opened the door and entered.

A short man with a gray mustache and goatee greeted Kevin in the hall. He was wearing a white shirt, unbuttoned at the collar, and a bright yellow sport coat. A large pot belly pushed his pants down below his waist. "I am Zoran Vacinovic, Special Assistant to the Ambassador. How can I help you?"

Kevin offered his hand. "I'm Kevin Anderson. I was appointed to represent Dragoljub Zaric at the War Crimes Tribunal. As you probably know, he was kidnapped within the borders of your country and handed over to U.N. forces. On his behalf, I wish to file a formal request for your government to investigate his kidnapping and to prosecute those responsible."

Vacinovic paused. He did not look like much of a diplomat to Kevin.

"Is that so?"

"Yes."

"What makes you think my government will cooperate with an American lawyer?"

"Well, our interests in this are the same. If I can prove that U.N. officials conspired to kidnap my client, then perhaps I can prove that the arrest was illegal and win his freedom. Then, maybe it will not happen again in the future to one of your citizens. That would be a good thing for your country, would it not?"

Vacinovic stroked his goatee. "That would be a good thing."

"Then will you forward his request to the proper authorities?"

Vacinovic eyed Kevin warily. "Mr. Anderson, a lot of people are not happy that an American lawyer was assigned to represent Mr. Zaric. I'm not sure how long you'll remain in that capacity."

"Well, anything you can do to uncover the circumstances of Mr. Zaric's arrest will be very helpful to whoever ends up representing him."

Vacinovic walked to the door and opened it. "I'll see what we can do. Good day, Mr. Anderson."

It felt like a diplomatic brush-off, and Kevin left disappointed. Draga would be better off with a Serbian lawyer. At least his lawyer would have received a warmer reception at the Embassy.

For the rest of that week, Kevin worked at the Peace Palace, a magnificent building with a large clock tower jutting into the gray skies of The Hague. It housed the World Court, formally known as the International Court of Justice, which decided civil disputes between countries, and contained a law library containing the largest collection of international law books in the world.

As he walked through the building, Kevin felt like he was in a true temple of justice. A marble statue of Lady Justice greeted visitors on the main staircase. Elaborate murals by French artists depicted the wisdom of settling disputes with judges, rather than by war. Stained glass donated by Great Britain depicted the world as it had been torn by wars, and as it looked when people lived in harmony and settled their disputes civilly.

Kevin was inspired by the bust of Mahatma Gandhi he came across in one of the corridors of the Peace Palace. The sculptor had captured the peacefulness and simplicity of Gandhi's persona. Gandhi had persevered in the face of much greater adversaries than Bradford Stone and Vladimir Krasnic, and had survived much greater indignities than being laughed at in court, or rebuked by a judge.

So could he.

*   *   *   *

Ellen started school the next week. Some of her friends from camp were in her sixth grade classes, and the school had assigned each new student a returning student as a Student Ambassador. Ellen had scored well on two placement tests that the school gave her, and was assigned to the advanced Math and Spelling classes. "I even have a seventh grade spelling book," she told Diane and Kevin proudly that night.

On Thursday, Kevin waited for the postman. The prosecutor's response to his motion for an identity hearing was due. When the postman came in the afternoon, there were two envelopes for Kevin, one big and one small.

The small one was from Vladimir Krasnic. Kevin read Krasnic's motion on Draga's behalf asking that Krasnic be assigned as his counsel, but curiously, there was no signed request by Draga. Kevin doubted that Judge Davidson would allow Draga to change counsel unless he personally signed the request. Had Draga changed his mind?

The big envelope was from the Office of the Prosecutor. Kevin flipped through the pages and saw that there were two stapled packets. One was a response to his motion.

When he came to the second packet, Kevin gasped. It was entitled:

"Motion to Disqualify Attorney Kevin Anderson for Conflict of Interest."

CHAPTER 7

▼

In the prosecution's motion, Bradford Stone claimed Kevin should be disqualified because he had a pending application to be a prosecutor. He contended that Kevin's desire to work as a prosecutor would prevent him from providing a vigorous defense to an accused. Several cases from the United States and other jurisdictions, as well as law review articles, were cited in support of the principle that a lawyer has a conflict of interest when he has applied to work for the other side.

Stone also attached Kevin's application and cover letter, in which he had expressed his desire to prosecute war criminals at the Tribunal. Stone even found an article about Kevin in the Santa Rosa newspaper, quoting him as saying that he looked forward to helping "bring to justice those responsible for the ethnic cleansing in Bosnia."

Kevin held his head in his hands. It was so true that he had wanted to be a prosecutor—heck, he'd even been <u>hired</u> as one only to have it taken away. Nonetheless, that did not prevent him from defending Draga, or any client, to the best of his ability.

So far, he <u>had</u> provided a vigorous defense, and in so doing he'd alienated everyone in the system—including his own client. Kevin no longer had any illusions of working as a prosecutor at the Tribunal. He had to admit, though, that there was an appearance of a conflict of interest when a defense lawyer had his own personal agenda to curry favor with the prosecutor. He had certainly felt that conflict when representing Nihudian.

Kevin looked over the response to his motion for an identity hearing. It was very powerful. Stone attached news media articles with photographs of Draga in his Black Dragon uniform. It was clearly the same man sitting in the Tribunal courtroom. Stone labeled Kevin's motion as "frivolous."

When Ellen arrived home, Kevin gave no hint of his latest problems at the Tribunal.

"Dad, some of my friends are going down to the Langstraat this afternoon on their bikes. Can I go with them?"

The Langstraat was the pedestrian mall in the center of Wassenaar where lots of little shops were located. Kevin had noticed many kids Ellen's age, or younger, bicycling to the Langstraat without their parents. While he liked the idea of giving Ellen the independence that Dutch parents gave their children, Kevin was concerned. After all, she was only eleven, and a stranger in a foreign land.

"Let's wait and ask Mommy on that one. She should be home any minute."

When Diane arrived, Ellen ran outside and popped the question.

Diane came in the house and said to Kevin, "I don't know about her going so far on a bike without an adult."

"But, Mom, it's less than a mile away," Ellen pleaded. "It's not much further than school. And four girls are going with me."

Diane looked at Kevin. "What do you think?"

"I guess it would be okay. Everyone else seems to let their kids do it."

"See, it's okay with Daddy. Please, Mom, please."

Ellen knew how to play one parent off the other.

"I guess so," Diane finally said.

"All right!" As Ellen ran up to hug and kiss her mother, she winked at her father.

In fifteen minutes, Ellen's friends rode up on their bicycles and Ellen was off on her shiny new purple bike with a sing-song bell attached to the handlebars. Diane had given her some spending money, and a phone card to use if she needed to call home.

After Ellen left, Diane and Kevin talked about the wisdom of their decision.

"That's one of the nice things about living in Holland," Kevin said. "It's seems a lot safer here."

A few minutes later the phone rang. Diane and Kevin both jumped, thinking it might be Ellen.

Kevin got to the phone first. "Hello."

"Is this Kevin Anderson?" asked a man with a heavy accent.

"Yes."

"This is Toma Lanko from the Bosnia News Service. Do you have a minute?"

Kevin signaled to Diane that it was not Ellen. "Sure."

"Do you have any comment on the prosecutor's motion to disqualify you?"

Kevin was taken by surprise. He had just gotten the motion himself a few hours earlier. "I'm sorry, but I don't think it's appropriate for me to be arguing motions outside of court. I'll have plenty to say about it at the hearing.'"

He found himself speaking with more bravado than he felt.

"I've spoken with Draga on the telephone this afternoon," the reporter went on. "Here is what he said: 'They sent a prosecutor to defend me? This is just more proof that this court is a farce. It is obvious I will receive no justice here.' Do you have any comment on that, Mr. Anderson?"

Kevin was stung by the words of his client. "I'm sorry, but I can't get into a public debate with my client. I'm sure you can understand."

"I understand, but without your response, my story is not going to make you look very good."

"You have a job to do. I appreciate you giving me the chance to comment. But I just can't go there."

"As you wish. Have a nice day."

So far, it had been anything but a nice day.

The next morning, Kevin switched on his computer and located the web site for the Bosnia News Service. He saw the headline: **Draga's Lawyer Exposed as Prosecutor**. The story reported that the Tribunal had assigned Draga a former prosecutor who had never defended anyone in his life. It quoted Kevin's letter and the Santa Rosa newspaper article in which he had said he wanted to help bring war criminals to justice. The article also contained Draga's quote. A spokesman for the prosecutor's office agreed that Kevin's appointment had been inappropriate but said that there was no deliberate attempt to saddle Draga with a lawyer who would not look after his interests.

"After all," the prosecution spokesman was quoted as saying, "we were the one who brought this conflict of interest to the court's attention." The article concluded by noting that Kevin had refused to comment.

Kevin knew that he had to confront this problem right away and not wait a month until court resumed. He typed a letter to the prosecutor, formally withdrawing his job application. He no longer wanted to work for those people. The practical side of him knew that there was no chance they would hire him now anyway. Kevin rode his bike to the Tribunal and dropped off the letter.

Then, he rode over to the prison, where he was led into an interview room. When Draga arrived, Kevin walked up to him and looked him straight in the eye. "I have no conflict of interest. I will fight for you as hard as I know how."

Draga looked away.

"Before I came here," Kevin continued, "I did want to prosecute. I thought they were the good guys. But since I've been here I've seen how they abuse their power. If I get the opportunity, I'm going to jump up and down on the defense side of the scales and do my best to see that it balances out."

Draga said nothing. Both men were still standing less than a foot from each other, with Draga towering over Kevin.

"If you don't want me to be your lawyer," Kevin said, "you can just tell the Court on September 4th and the judge will be happy to assign you someone else."

Draga walked over to the door, opened it, and left. He had again said nothing. The meeting had lasted all of thirty seconds.

$*$ $*$ $*$ $*$

On Monday, September 4th, Kevin donned his robe and entered Courtroom 1 shortly before court was scheduled to start. Vladimir Krasnic took his seat at the defense table with Kevin, but selected the chair farthest away.

Judge Davidson strode to the bench like a man with a purpose.

"We have several matters to take up at this hearing," he said in an authoritative voice after the case was called. He looked down at the leather book where he made his notes. "I see we have a motion filed by Mr. Anderson, one by Mr. Krasnic, and one by the prosecution. We will also complete Mr. Zaric's arraignment today."

"We will first take up Mr. Anderson's Motion for an Identity Hearing. Mr. Anderson, do you have one shred of evidence to offer that the man seated in this courtroom is not the same Dragoljub Zaric as accused in the indictment?"

Kevin rose quickly. "No, Your Honor."

"That's what I thought. Your motion is frivolous, counsel, and a waste of the Court's time. It is denied."

"Your Honor," said Kevin, who remained standing. "Four years ago, an innocent man named Goran Lasic spent over three months in custody because this Court had no procedure in place to hold an identity hearing. Perhaps you will find, after a hearing, that the accused in this case is the man charged in this indictment. But unless you rule that an accused is entitled to such a hearing, you are permitting a system to exist which is fundamentally unjust."

"Your motion is denied, counsel," Judge Davidson said loudly. "Now sit down!"

Kevin obeyed. The hearing had not started off well. Kevin wondered why Judge Davidson had not begun with the disqualification issue.

"We shall now arraign Mr. Zaric," the judge ordered. "The Court, having found beyond a reasonable doubt that the accused is the same Dragoljub Zaric as charged in the indictment, now calls upon the accused to plead." Turning to Draga, Judge Davidson asked, "What is your plea, Mr. Zaric, guilty or not guilty?"

Draga said nothing.

"Mr. Anderson," the judge said, not missing a beat, "as counsel of record for the accused, do you request that a not guilty plea be entered on his behalf?"

"Yes, Your Honor. Without waiving any rights or defenses, including that of the jurisdiction of this court, I ask that not guilty pleas be entered as to each count of the indictment."

"Not guilty pleas will be entered."

Kevin suddenly realized what Judge Davidson was up to. He's a smart old coot. The judge had wanted Draga to have an attorney to enter his plea for him. The judge had deftly avoided any possible roadblocks to that end result. If he had disqualified Kevin at the outset, the arraignment might have had to be postponed again.

Judge Davidson looked down at the leather book in front of him. He appeared to be working off a script, and was moving smoothly through his agenda.

"Now that the accused has been duly and properly arraigned, we shall turn to the prosecution's motion to disqualify Mr. Anderson." The judge turned to the prosecution table. "Does the prosecution have anything to add?"

"No, Your Honor," a confident Bradford Stone responded.

"Mr. Anderson, this is a very serious allegation. It brings dishonor to you and to this court. What do you have to say for yourself?"

Kevin rose to his feet. "There is no conflict of interest, Your Honor. I have unequivocally withdrawn my application to work for the prosecution. I have no personal stake in this case, and no interest contrary to that of the accused."

Judge Davidson's face reddened to a bright pink. "Mr. Anderson, you have used extraordinarily bad judgment, and shown a lack of respect for this Court. We can't waste our time with inexperienced lawyers making frivolous motions and violating the canons of ethics. The Motion to Disqualify is granted."

Kevin felt about two inches tall. He was unsure whether he should get up and leave. Since no one told him to go, he remained in his seat, trying to maintain a poker face. He wanted to disappear.

Judge Davidson turned to Vladimir Krasnic. "That brings us to your motion, Mr. Krasnic."

"Yes, Your Honor." Krasnic displayed the confidence of a man whose competition had just been eliminated.

"I would like to grant your motion. I know you to be a very competent counsel and one who understands and obeys the rules of this Court."

Krasnic smiled, and bowed slightly to the judge.

"But I need to have some indication from Mr. Zaric that he wishes to choose you as his assigned counsel. I will state on the record that by doing so, he will not be waiving any challenges he has to the jurisdiction of this Court, or any other matter. But our rules require that the accused choose an assigned counsel from our list. Otherwise, the Tribunal staff makes the assignment."

"May I have a moment with Mr. Zaric?"

"Of course."

Kevin watched as Krasnic walked over to Draga and spoke to him. Kevin couldn't bear to look at anyone else in the courtroom. He didn't dare see who was out in the visitors' gallery.

"I'm sorry, Your Honor," Krasnic said when he returned to the podium, "I cannot convince Mr. Zaric to address the Court."

"Very well, Mr. Krasnic. I will direct the staff to assign new counsel for Mr. Zaric."

Krasnic looked disappointed. Then he brightened. "Excuse me, Your Honor, might I make a suggestion that I believe will accommodate all interests?"

"Yes, what is it?"

"Perhaps Mr. Zaric could be provided with the list of the assigned counsel. The court could take a short recess while Mr. Zaric circles the name on the list that he chooses as his counsel. That way he would not have to address the Court, yet he can make his preference known."

"That is a very unusual procedure," Judge Davidson grumbled.

"It complies with the Court's rules. Perhaps it will allow Mr. Zaric to save some face, Your Honor." Krasnic gave an indulgent smile to the judge.

"Very well. Mr. Zaric, the court will furnish you with a list of all of the lawyers eligible to be assigned a case in this court. You shall indicate your preference by circling one name. If you do not do so, your assigned counsel will be chosen for you."

"Thank you, Your Honor," Krasnic responded gratefully.

"Court is in recess for fifteen minutes."

Kevin rose as Judge Davidson left the courtroom. Kevin looked over at Draga, who was being fawned over by Krasnic. Draga never looked in Kevin's direction. Kevin was a nobody in the courtroom, and he knew it. He wanted out as quickly as possible, and yet he hated the thought of going home and telling Ellen he was unemployed again and to say goodbye to all her new friends because they would be heading back to California immediately.

As Draga left the room carrying the list of lawyers and a pencil, Krasnic walked over to the prosecutor's table. Kevin heard him arranging for the discovery materials to be delivered to his office. Kevin wished that court would be over, so that he could just leave. He was totally humiliated.

After precisely fifteen minutes, Judge Davidson returned to the bench. He looked over at Draga's chair. It was empty. "Where is the accused?"

"One moment, Judge," replied the guard stationed inside the door. The guard spoke into his hand-held radio. In a moment, the door opened and Draga was led to his seat.

"The usher will retrieve the papers from the accused," Judge Davidson said.

The black-robed usher approached Draga and took the papers from him. He delivered them back to the judge.

Judge Davidson flipped through the papers. "I see that you have circled a name, Mr. Zaric." He held the paper up closer to his eyes and donned his glasses. "Kevin Anderson?"

Kevin was shocked at the mention of his name.

Krasnic's head went back as if hit in the jaw.

In disbelief, Judge Davidson looked at the paper again.

Kevin looked over at Draga; Draga broke out into a big grin.

"You two deserve each other," Judge Davidson muttered. "Mr. Anderson, you are reinstated as counsel of record for Mr. Zaric. Court is adjourned."

CHAPTER 8

▼

"I'm glad you're still Draga's lawyer, Daddy," Ellen said after Kevin told her and Diane what had happened in court.

"Why?" he asked his daughter.

"Because those bullies pick on everyone."

"Any other reason?" he smiled.

"Oh Daddy, <u>you</u> <u>know</u>. I'm not ready to go back home."

"So why did you let Draga choose you as his lawyer?" Diane asked.

"It wasn't my choice. It was his. I just hope he'll talk to me now."

"Let's have a party for Daddy," Ellen exclaimed. "I'll make a cake!"

"You have homework to do, young lady," Diane said too sternly.

"Party pooper!" Ellen walked into the dining room and sat back down at the table where her homework was spread out. Kevin had tried to make her do her homework at her desk on the third floor, but Ellen hated being banished to her room. She wanted to be where the action was, so she could monitor and contribute to every conversation. After a few attempts, Kevin had given up. Now a threat to send her to the third floor to finish her homework was enough to get Ellen back on task.

At about 8 p.m., the doorbell rang. Ellen raced to the door and opened it. Soon she was back in the dining room. "It's for you, Dad."

Kevin went to the front door. He was surprised to see Zoran Vacinovic, from the Serbian Embassy, and another man standing in the doorway.

"Mr. Vacinovic, come in."

Vacinovic and the other man entered. "I was in the area so I decided to drop by rather than call tomorrow. I have someone I want you to meet. I hope you don't mind."

"I don't mind."

"This is Mihajlo Golic. He is your client's brother-in-law."

Kevin shook the man's hand. Golic was huge—at least 6-foot-4—and had a handshake like a vise. Kevin led the men into his living room. He introduced them to Diane and Ellen, and then took them upstairs to his office.

"Your daughter is beautiful," Golic remarked.

"Thank you. She's a great kid."

Vacinovic got down to business. "Mr. Golic is a former Belgrade police detective. He wants to help his brother-in-law. I thought perhaps you could use him as an investigator now that it looks like you're going to be representing Mr. Zaric."

Kevin looked over at Golic. His appearance was very professional. He was dressed in a shirt and tie with a gray tweed sports coat. He looked to be in his early forties, with an Arnold Schwarzenegger physique.

"It's kind of you to offer your assistance," Kevin said to Golic. "Have you done any private investigation before?"

"Yes."

"He has worked on several sensitive assignments from our government since leaving the police department," Vacinovic interjected. "He has also worked on security matters for some of the largest companies in Serbia."

Kevin was surprised and delighted to be getting this kind of substantive help. "I'm going to need an investigator in Serbia," he said. "I can submit a request to the Tribunal so Mr. Golic can be paid for his work."

"That will not be necessary," Vacinovic replied. "My government will pay Mr. Golic. We consider your client a loyal and patriotic citizen. It is our duty to help him."

Kevin pulled out a legal pad from his top drawer.

"Mr. Golic," he said, "the first thing I would like you to do is to find out everything you can about your brother-in-law's arrest. I want to know if the United Nations hired someone to kidnap him or paid a bounty for his arrest. Can you do that?"

"That is no problem," the big man said softly. "I will begin working on that when I return to Belgrade in three days time."

"Excellent."

"Can you send him the reports you get from the prosecutor so that he is informed about the case?" Vacinovic asked.

"Yes, that's a good idea. There'll probably be other witnesses to interview as well. I'll make a set of reports for you as soon as I get them from the prosecutor."

Kevin was pleased. He had a professional investigator, and at no cost.

As Vacinovic and Golic were getting ready to leave, Vacinovic said, "Oh yes, there is one more thing. Mr. Golic would like to see his brother-in-law while he is here, and to give him the regards of his family. Can you arrange a visit for him?"

"I think so. Let me call the prison right now."

Kevin called and asked about their visiting policy for family members. He learned that inmates could have visits with family members on weekends. But Golic would be leaving before the weekend. Kevin asked about defense investigators, and learned that an investigator could have a visit at any time so long as he had a letter of authorization from the defense counsel. Kevin reported what he had learned to Vacinovic and Golic.

"Could you prepare a letter so that he can visit his brother-in-law as soon as possible?"

"Sure." Kevin turned on his laptop computer, typed a short letter, printed it out, and then signed it. "Here you go," he said, handing the letter to Golic.

Kevin walked the two men to the front door and said goodbye. He watched as they got into a Black Mercedes, with Golic driving.

"Who was that pair?" Diane asked suspiciously as Kevin returned to the living room to find that Ellen had gone to bed.

"That's the guy from the Serbian Embassy and my new investigator, who happens to be my client's brother-in-law."

"That huge guy is an investigator? He looks like a bouncer. What are they doing coming to our house at night?"

"They said they were in the area."

"Why do they want to help all of a sudden?"

"I don't know why things changed with the Embassy. But it can't hurt. If the brother-in-law doesn't work out, I'll just get another investigator."

"I don't feel good about any of this," Diane said warily as she turned to go into their bedroom. "Not who you're defending and not who wants to help."

"I know how you feel, Diane, and I understand. But honey, we came a long way for me to have the experience of trying cases at the Tribunal. I'm finally doing it, even if it's on the other side of the courtroom. I'm in my element. I can handle it."

The next day, Kevin received three boxes jammed with papers. The first box contained a cover letter from Bradford Stone. "Enclosed are pages 1-5843 of the disclosure materials," he wrote. "You are reminded of the protective measures adopted by the Court. You may only distribute copies to your client and persons working for you. You are also required to maintain a log of all copies that are distributed. At the end of the case, all copies and originals must be returned to the Office of the Prosecutor."

Kevin lugged the boxes over to his desk. He pulled out a stack of papers from the front of the top box where the cover letter had been. There was no index, and the papers, although in numerical order, were a collection of diverse pages from different witnesses in no apparent order. The first page was the beginning of an interview with one witness, the second page was a page from the middle of another witness' interview, and so on.

The old prosecution shuffle. Before numbering the disclosure, someone had shuffled all of the papers together like a deck of cards. The material was all mixed up. The prosecution had an obligation to provide disclosure, but was not required to organize it for the defense. Kevin had run across this sort of pettiness before. It would take him time to organize the materials, but time was one thing Kevin had.

He started separating the materials by the town or village where the events that were being talked about occurred. When he had gone through the first box, he had thirty-seven different piles. It had taken him almost four hours. After sorting the next two boxes, he would then have to go through each pile and try to gather the pages from each witness' statement and put them together.

By the time Kevin began riding his bicycle over to the jail, it was about 4 p.m. Kevin was hungry, but he was anxious to meet with Draga now that Draga had chosen him as his counsel. Kevin hoped that Draga would at last begin speaking to him.

When Kevin passed a pizza place, he got an idea. He remembered reading a news account of an interview with Draga from a few years ago. Draga had remarked that the only thing he liked about America was its pizza. Kevin stopped at the pizza place and ordered five pizzas to go. Thirty minutes later, he strapped them to his bike carrier and resumed his trip to the jail.

When he arrived at the jail, Kevin gave the pizzas to the guard. "I brought some dinner for the crew, and one for me and my client, if you will allow it."

"You bet. Thanks!"

Kevin was led into the interview room. A few minutes later, Draga was led into the room. The guard placed the box of pizza on the table. "I heard you like pizza," Kevin said to Draga. "I thought we could have dinner together."

Draga looked at Kevin and said nothing. He opened the pizza box and helped himself to a slice. Then he sat down.

Kevin did the same. "Look, I understand that you don't want to participate in your defense. Why don't we just talk about something else? Not as a Serb to an American, but as one human being to another."

Draga said nothing.

Kevin started to launch into a monologue about the Tribunal's procedures.

Draga interrupted him. "The pizza is good," he said.

Kevin smiled. "I like it too. What kind of toppings do you like?"

"Pepperoni."

"Me, too. Next time it will be pepperoni."

Kevin was starved, and had already downed two pieces.

"Don't eat so fast," Draga told him, "It's not good for you and it's not polite."

Draga looked like he was savoring every bite.

And so it began. Kevin and Draga talked about food, movies, and cars. Kevin said nothing about the case. After they had polished off the pizza, Draga said, "Thank you. This is the best meal I have had in months."

"What do you do all day?"

"Play cards. Watch television. Work out on the exercise equipment. Write letters to my family."

"Do you get along with the other prisoners?"

"Yeah. I knew some of them from before. They're all afraid of me. I like it that way." Draga smiled. Then he turned it around. "What do you do at night after work?"

"Help my daughter with her homework. Then we play or read together before her bedtime. By that time, I'm usually ready for bed myself. It's not too exciting."

"You are with your family. That's the main thing."

"Yeah. You must really miss your family."

"I do. I was gone a lot, but when you're locked up like this, you really wish you'd done things differently. I would give anything to help my children with their homework."

Kevin remembered having almost the same conversation with Nihudian. Two people on opposite sides of a war, and both wanting the same thing.

"Help me with your case. Help me understand the facts. Maybe one day you can return to your family."

Draga laughed derisively. "They'll never let you win my case. Not in a million years. Just get me a speedy trial. I don't want to sit here for a year."

"Why did you choose me?" Kevin asked as the subject moved closer to the case.

"I liked the way you wouldn't take any crap off that old judge. Krasnic made me sick the way he sucked up to him. And I knew Krasnic would just delay my case so he could bill more hours and make more money. I don't want any delays."

"What good is a speedy trial if you get a life sentence?"

Draga didn't reply.

"Allow me to ask you something that many defense attorneys would never dream of asking their client."

Draga raised his eyebrows in interest.

"Did you do what they have charged you with?"

Draga took a deep breath. "I am a soldier," he said. "Not a butcher."

"Well, that's as good a place to start as any. I received three boxes of witness statements and reports from the prosecution today. When I get them organized, I'll make a set for you and bring it here. There are over five thousand pages."

"Don't bother. There's plenty of fiction to read here in the library."

Kevin smiled. "Are you going to help me with your defense?"

"No."

Kevin didn't want to push it. "One more thing. I met your brother-in-law, Mr. Golic, last night. He's offered to do some investigation for us. He's also going to come and visit you."

"He was here this morning. Thank you for arranging that."

"He's a big guy like you. How are you two related?"

Draga hesitated for a moment. "He's the husband of one of my sisters," he finally replied. Then he changed the subject. "What's on the menu for next week?"

"Any requests?"

"Oh, I don't know. Why don't we do some nice American steaks and mashed potatoes? I'm a meat and potatoes kind of guy."

"Well, I'll see what I can do. I don't know of any take-out steak houses in The Hague. But I'll look into it."

"Now, what's new with the Oakland Raiders?" Draga asked.

Kevin laughed. It figured that Draga's favorite team was the bad boys of American football. They talked sports for a while, then it was time to go.

"Don't forget the A-1 sauce," Draga said as Kevin departed.

Kevin spent the next week and a half organizing, and then reading, the prosecution's disclosure. The reports were awful. According to over a hundred witnesses, members of the Black Dragons had murdered, tortured, beaten and raped Muslim men, women, and children in Bosnia. One witness reported seeing Draga personally murder a Muslim civilian. Draga had also made numerous public statements in which he threatened to kill Muslims who did not leave Bosnia. The prosecution's case appeared overwhelming.

When he finished reading the reports, Kevin had a copy service make two copies. The day they were ready, he drove to the Tribunal so he could deliver one copy to the detention center for Draga, and then to the Embassy and left a copy for Vacinovic to send to Mihajlo Golic.

Kevin decided to remove the statements of the protected witnesses from Golic's copies. Golic would have no need for those reports. The Muslim victims were not going to talk to a Serb from Belgrade. Kevin would need to find a Muslim investigator to interview the victims.

Kevin wrote a cover letter to Golic asking him to interview as many members of the Black Dragons as he could find. He also instructed Golic not to copy or disseminate the contents of the reports to anyone else. Then he wrote out a log, showing that he was distributing one copy of the materials to his client and one to his investigator

After stopping at the prison, Kevin headed over to the Serbian Embassy. It was just before lunchtime and he hoped Vacinovic would be there. He was. "I have the box of materials and a letter for Mr. Golic in my car," Kevin said. "Perhaps we can have lunch together, and then I can leave them with you?"

Vacinovic agreed. They left the Embassy and drove in Kevin's car to the Plein, a square adjacent to the Dutch Parliament buildings where there were many excellent restaurants. Kevin got lost trying to find a parking lot, but after circling around a few times, he found a space on the street to park his car. The two men walked to a restaurant that Vacinovic recommended featuring Balkan food.

During lunch, Vacinovic gave Kevin a long history of how the Serbs had been persecuted through the years by the Turks and Muslims, as well as the Croats, who had been on the side of Hitler in World War II.

"But the Court won't allow that as a justification for anything that Draga is charged with," Kevin interjected. "What else can I use as a defense for Draga?"

Kevin wondered if Vacinovic would say "his innocence," but he did not. In fact, he didn't try to answer Kevin's question. "It is important to show that the Serbs were victims," Vacinovic continued. "We were simply defending ourselves. Draga's trial will put the Serbs in the world spotlight. We must use it to show the truth, once and for all."

Kevin politely nodded as he listened to Vacinovic's point of view.

He drove Vacinovic back to the Embassy, although not before getting lost again. He was used to his bicycle and unfamiliar with the auto routes around The

Hague. When they arrived at the Embassy, Kevin gave Vacinovic the box of materials for Golic and drove home.

He told Diane and Ellen about his day, and the important question he had asked Draga, and his client's response.

Diane looked as if she wanted to roll her eyes, but she didn't.

"Maybe people just dressed up to look like the Dragons," Ellen offered. "You know, like how kids wear American camouflage stuff because it's cool."

"I'll have to look into that. I don't have much more to go on right now. In fact, this case is pretty hopeless. Thousands of Bosnian Muslims were killed and beaten by men in Black Dragon uniforms and the only defense the guy from the Embassy can offer is that the other side started it 600 years ago. Draga says he didn't do it, but he won't cooperate in mounting a defense. I don't think F. Lee Bailey could win this one."

"Oh, Daddy, you're so much better than him."

Ellen came over and climbed into his lap. It was her turn to tell him about her day.

That night, Kevin decided to read something to get his mind off of the case for a while. He picked up a novel and stretched out on the couch. When Diane came down from putting Ellen to bed, the phone rang. It was just before 9 p.m.

"Mr. Anderson, this is Zoran Vacinovic."

"Yes, Mr. Vacinovic," Kevin replied.

"A group of investigators from the Tribunal were just here." Vacinovic sounded agitated. "They searched the Embassy looking for the materials that you gave me today."

"What?" Kevin was stunned.

"They claimed that you and I had conspired to violate some protective orders of the Court."

Kevin was speechless.

"This is an outrageous breach of diplomatic procedures. We have never heard of an Embassy being searched. My country will be protesting this in the strongest possible way."

Kevin felt shaky. Had he broken some Tribunal rule? He was just giving the materials to Vacinovic to send to the investigator. He had even taken out the reports from the protected witnesses.

Just then, Kevin heard a loud banging at the front door.

Someone shouted: "Police, open up!"

CHAPTER 9

▼

Kevin dropped the phone and raced to the front door. He opened it only a crack, and immediately a half-dozen armed men and women in blue United Nations police uniforms burst past Kevin, fanning out in the house.

"What's going on here?" Kevin demanded.

A tall man in a dark suit and Colombo rain jacket came in behind the police. "I'm John Wells, Chief Investigator for the Office of the Prosecutor at the Tribunal," he said in clipped English. "We have a court order to search these premises."

Wells directed Kevin to sit on the couch next to Diane. The color had drained from her face; she looked as if she expected her family to be dragged into the streets.

"Please," she said, "our daughter is asleep on the third floor—"

A few seconds later, a sleepy Ellen, in her pajamas and carrying her bathrobe, staggered down to the living room escorted by a police officer. She ran for her parents, her eyes like those of a frightened fawn caught in the headlights of an oncoming vehicle.

"What's happening, Dad? Who are these people?"

"They're police from my work. Everything's going to be okay."

A uniformed officer picked up the phone that Kevin hadn't hung up. "Is anyone there?" the officer asked. "Who is this, sir?" After a pause, the officer said, "Mr. Anderson is unavailable. I suggest you call him in the morning."

The officer hung up the phone and turned to Wells. "He was on the phone with Vacinovic from the Serbian Embassy."

Wells looked disapprovingly at Kevin.

"May I see the court order?" Kevin asked.

Wells handed some papers to Kevin. "Read it and weep," he said sarcastically. Kevin began to read the documents, with Diane and Ellen looking over his shoulder. The top page was indeed an order, signed by Judge Davidson, authorizing the search of Kevin's home, his office at the Tribunal, the Serbian Embassy, and a box held by Dutch postal authorities. He flipped the page and began reading the attached affidavit of Chief Investigator John Wells:

As counsel for Dragoljub Zaric, Kevin Anderson was provided with reports and witness statements, which were governed by a protective order issued by the court. The order provided that because of danger to the witnesses, copies of materials concerning protected witnesses were not to be distributed to third parties other than the accused and persons working directly for the defense.

This morning, I observed Anderson loading boxes into a car at the Tribunal. Thinking that Anderson might be distributing materials covered by the protective order, I followed Anderson and observed him travel to the Tribunal detention center. Inquiry with the jail indicated that Anderson had delivered three boxes of discovery materials for his client.

Thereafter, I followed Anderson to the Embassy of Serbia and Montenegro, where he exited in the company of Zoran Vacinovic. Vacinovic is a former officer in the Yugoslavian secret police and a long-time confidant of former President Slobodan Milosevic. Vacinovic is believed to have been assigned to The Hague to monitor the activities of the War Crimes Tribunal.

I observed Anderson and Vacinovic get into Anderson's car and drive off. Anderson thereafter engaged in counter surveillance driving, circling the same block and making quick turns. This is a common method of determining if one is being followed.

Anderson and Vacinovic were thereafter observed meeting at a restaurant in the central area of The Hague owned by a reputed member of the Serbian underworld. After the meeting, Anderson again engaged in counter surveillance driving, so as to lose anyone who might be following. I was unable to follow Anderson, but other investigators observed the pair arrive at the Serbian Embassy.

Once back at the Embassy, Investigator Allen Jacobson observed Anderson take a heavy box from the trunk of his car and hand it to Vacinovic. The box was identical in appearance to one that had been provided to Anderson by the company that had copied the discovery. It was also identical to the boxes that Anderson delivered to the jail earlier in the day. Investigator Jacobson observed Vacinovic carrying the box into the Embassy.

About an hour later, Vacinovic was observed carrying the same box to the Post Office. I requested the Post Office hold the box so that it could be searched once a court order was obtained. The box is addressed to one Mihajlo Golic in Belgrade, Serbia.

A review of the financial authorization forms filed by Anderson with the Tribunal revealed that no investigator had been retained by Anderson. Therefore, it appears that Anderson has violated the terms of the protective order, and that a search of the box seized at the Post Office, the Embassy of Serbia and Montenegro, and Anderson's office and home is necessary to locate additional protected material and to find additional evidence of the conspiracy to violate the Court's protective order by Anderson, Vacinovic, and others.

The affidavit was approved and submitted to the Court by Bradford Stone.

Kevin's felt a wave of relief. They had gotten their facts wrong. He had not delivered any materials subject to the protective order to Vacinovic. Golic was Kevin's investigator, and the prison had a letter to prove it. He had enclosed a letter in the box directing Golic not to copy the materials. Kevin had even kept a log of the copies he had distributed, as required by the Tribunal. And as for his "counter surveillance driving," he had driven the way he had that day because he was lost, not to avoid being followed.

Then, a surge of anger welled up inside Kevin. These heavy-handed prosecutors had no right to invade his home and scare his family.

"Could you come over here, Mr. Anderson?" Wells was sitting at the dining room table with materials from Kevin's briefcase spread out before him.

"This is a very serious matter, Mr. Anderson. I need to ask you some questions."

"This _is_ a very serious matter," Kevin said. "You have stormed into my home at night like the Gestapo, scared my family to death, and rummaged through privileged attorney-client papers. And you're dead wrong. I followed the protective order to the letter. I've got nothing more to say to you."

Wells shook his head. "If that's the way you want it, counselor. We'll be seeing you in court."

"No, I'll be seeing _you_ in court."

Wells and his troops left a few minutes later, taking all the documents with them.

"Don't worry," Kevin told Diane and Ellen, "I haven't done anything wrong." He explained to them what was in the affidavit and what he had actually done.

"What are you going to do, Daddy?"

"Well, I think I'll file some kind of emergency motion tomorrow morning and see if I can get the judge to order the return of all the papers they took. After that—I don't know—maybe we'll sue them for home invasion."

He couldn't believe how much like a defense lawyer he was sounding.

Diane was still shaken. "This isn't like America, Kevin. These people at the Tribunal have more power than you. Be <u>careful</u>."

"I will, honey. And you're right; they have way too much power."

Diane and Kevin let Ellen sleep with them in their bed that night. After Ellen had fallen asleep, Kevin got up and went back downstairs. He spent the next few hours drafting his emergency motion on his computer. He recounted segregating the discovery, and explained his so-called "counter surveillance" driving. He demanded return of all of the items seized, as well as Draga's release from confinement as a sanction.

At some point, Diane appeared, and offered to make them tea.

With steaming cups in hand, they sat at the kitchen table, speaking in hushed tones in the quiet and darkened house.

"I'm sorry that I brought this home to you and Ellen," Kevin said sadly.

"You know, all along I've thought that you were on the wrong side," Diane said. "But after what happened tonight—my God, these people are scary. If they can make you look guilty in their reports and investigation, what can they do to other people?"

"This whole thing was a mistake. We should have stayed home."

"There was a time I would have liked to hear that. But now, you've got to do your job. If you believe your client is innocent—"

"I can't know that for sure, Diane. Nothing is black and white around here."

"Okay, but do what you have to do. I'm here with you—and for you."

Kevin was remembering why he had fallen in love with Diane.

He reached out to touch her cheek. She intercepted his hand and kissed it.

*   *   *   *

At breakfast, Ellen asked, "Daddy, are the policemen going to come back?"

"I don't think so. And today, I'm going to make them sorry for what they did."

"I can come with you to court today," Ellen said excitedly. "I can be a witness."

"No," Diane said quickly and emphatically.

"Maybe you can come another day," Kevin said. "I'd like that."

"Okay. I wanna see you kick butt at Draga's trial," Ellen replied enthusiastically.

Kevin laughed, and so did Diane. He was glad to see that the nocturnal visit from the police had not taken any of the spunk out of their daughter.

Kevin showered and dressed. There would be no time for his usual jog this morning. As he sat down for breakfast, he flipped on CNN. A picture of Draga appeared.

"Tensions are running high today in Serbia and Montenegro," the announcer said, "after the search last evening of their Embassy in The Hague by investigators from the U.N. War Crimes Tribunal."

Kevin motioned for Diane and Ellen to look.

"Court officials claim that Kevin Anderson, an American lawyer for the infamous Serbian warlord Draga, passed confidential information to an Embassy official about Muslim witnesses whose identity has been kept secret for fear they would be killed."

A picture of Kevin was beamed on the television.

Kevin groaned.

"This morning, leaders of the Serbia and Montenegro government announced that they had expelled the Ambassador from The Netherlands in protest."

The announcer went on to the next news story.

"Wow, Daddy, you're on CNN!" Ellen exclaimed. "I hope my friends at home saw that."

"That's not exactly the kind of publicity I want," Kevin said, wondering what his former colleagues at the U.S. Attorney's office would be thinking.

When Kevin rode his bike near the Tribunal building, he could see news cameras set up outside the guardhouse. "Do you expect to be arrested, Mr. Anderson?" shouted a reporter as Kevin approached the Tribunal guardhouse.

"Not at all. I haven't done anything wrong."

The news cameras were rolling as Kevin stopped in front of the guardhouse.

Six or seven reporters gathered around Kevin.

"Was your house searched last night?" one of them asked.

"Yes, it was. The prosecutor's office seized privileged communications between my client and me, as well as documents outlining our strategy for defending the case. I'm filing a motion this morning for the immediate return of those items."

"Did you pass confidential materials to an official of the Serbian secret police?"

"No, I did not."

Kevin noticed Judge Davidson striding briskly up the walk toward the guardhouse.

"I'll be happy to provide you copies of what I file with the Court this morning," Kevin said. "They contain all the true facts."

He hustled up to the Registrar's office to file his motions, and then went to his office. Later that morning, Kevin received a copy of an official protest lodged at the Tribunal by the government of Serbia and Montenegro.

Then, the phone at his desk rang. It was Nihudian.

"Kevin, I saw you on the news. Are you okay?"

"So far. You saw that I have a new client?"

"I did. That guy is really lucky to have gotten you. You are so powerful, Kevin."

Hearing from Nihudian made Kevin smile.

"Thanks, but I'm not feeling real powerful right now. How have you been?"

"I am fine. I am teaching history at a high school in Sarajevo and enjoying the time with my family."

"That's great. Say, would you happen to know a good private investigator in Sarajevo? I need someone to interview the Muslim witnesses in Draga's case."

"I don't think you could find an investigator in Sarajevo willing to help Draga. Let me think about that. I'll ask my students. Maybe we can come up with someone for you."

"Thanks, Nihudian. It sure is nice to hear a friendly voice."

When he checked his e-mail, Kevin found a score of messages from concerned family, friends, and colleagues in the United States. Bud Marcello's e-mail brought a smile to his face. It read simply: "And you told me to stay away from the dark side?"

He answered them all. "No problem," was the gist of what he told everyone. "It's just a small misunderstanding that will easily be straightened out."

On his way out of the Tribunal he checked his mailbox. There was an envelope from the Registrar. Kevin opened it, hoping it was a notice of hearing on his motion. Instead, he saw the heading: "Order to Show Cause why Attorney Kevin Anderson should not be held in Contempt of Court."

Kevin was ordered to appear in court on Monday morning for a Rule 77 hearing on whether he should be held in contempt of court for violating the protective order. The order, signed by Judge Davidson, noted ominously that Rule 77 provided for "punishment of up to twelve months in jail and a fine of 20,000 Euros" for anyone found in contempt of the Tribunal.

Kevin felt weak in the knees as he walked outside to his bicycle.

Would Judge Davidson dare to put him in jail?

CHAPTER 10

▼

Two hours later, Kevin was in jail, visiting Draga. Kevin had picked up Chinese food, and the two men sat in the interview room, eating out of cartons with chopsticks.

"I'll reserve a cell for you next to mine," Draga said after Kevin brought him up to date on his legal difficulties.

"That's a comforting thought."

Kevin passed the chow mien to Draga. "Trade you for the fried rice."

Draga dug at the rice one more time before handing the carton to Kevin.

"Want me to defend you at the hearing?" Draga asked.

"Oh yeah, you've really impressed Judge Davidson with your courtroom decorum. You're the perfect choice."

The two men laughed.

Talking to Draga made Kevin feel better, even if the man was absolutely no help.

"I called my contact at the Embassy," Kevin reported, "and asked him to get your brother-in-law here for Monday's hearing. I'm probably going to need him to testify that I had hired him as my investigator."

Draga nodded, passing the chow mien back to Kevin, and digging into the pork.

"He's supposed to be bringing me some reports of the investigation he's done on your kidnapping. The version in the prosecution's discovery just doesn't make sense. If you were just unexpectedly handed over to the U.N. at the Romanian border, how did Allen Jacobson, the chief investigator for your case, get on the scene to try to interview you within two hours after you were found?"

"I didn't say a word to that jerk."

"There's more to the story than we're being told," Kevin said.

"I have some business to discuss with you," Draga said.

Kevin perked up. Had Draga changed his mind about assisting in his defense? Draga pulled out a torn piece of newspaper. "Here's the odds for this weekend's NFL football games. Let's see if you can pick the teams better than I can."

Kevin looked sideways at Draga. "You want me to help you bet on football?"

"No, I want us both to bet on the games against each other. We can do it all season. Then, at the end, the winner pays off."

"I'm about to go to jail for contempt and you're facing life in prison and you want us to bet on football games?"

"I can pick the winners in your own country better than you."

Kevin eyed his client. "No, you can't. I follow football all year."

Draga handed Kevin the paper. His picks were already circled.

Kevin studied the point spreads while Draga dug the remains out of the cartons.

"How much are we betting?" Kevin asked.

"How about a hundred dollars a game?" Draga replied.

"Are you crazy?"

"How about a hundred Euros, then?"

"Where would you get that kind of money? Wait, I don't want to know."

Draga smiled. "Okay, let's just play for sport. Ten Euros a game."

"That's more like it. I'll win enough off you this season to take my family out for a nice dinner."

Draga laughed. "The Chinese was great. Thanks for lunch."

"Let's hope we're not cell mates by Monday. Who would bring in the take-out?"

"See you in court, counselor."

Sunday was Diane's birthday, and Kevin, determined not to spoil her special weekend, decided not to mention the contempt order.

On Saturday, he and Ellen took the bus to The Hague and then shopped for presents. Ellen picked out matching orange sweatshirts for Diane and herself with Queen Beatrix's family's coat of arms on them. Ellen always managed to receive presents on other people's birthdays. At the Royal pottery factory in Delft, an old city just south of The Hague, Kevin bought Diane a blue and white serving plate with a scene from one of their favorite Rembrandt's, "The Night Watch."

On Sunday afternoon, Kevin and Ellen took Diane to the Madurodam, an outdoor museum in The Hague where the scenes of cities and towns all over Holland were elaborately displayed in miniature.

"We know you like to stay close to home, Mommy," Ellen explained thoughtfully. "This way you can visit all of Holland without leaving The Hague."

They walked along the canals of Amsterdam, past the famous spire of the Dom church of Utrecht, and the busy port of Rotterdam. Ellen's favorite spot was the Mars candy factory. There, if you deposited ten cents, a miniature truck would take a piece of candy from a conveyor belt and deliver it to you.

Every child visiting the Madurodam was given a passport, which contained a challenging game of locating various buildings throughout the museum. Diane and Kevin tried to keep up with Ellen as she raced around answering the questions in her passport. As they were leaving, Ellen turned in her passport at the front desk. She had gotten all the questions right, and was awarded a stamp in the passport.

Just as Ellen ran over to show Kevin and Diane the stamp, she bumped into a man walking into the Madurodam.

"Don't I know you?" the man asked.

Ellen thought she recognized him. "You're helping my dad, aren't you?"

"Yes."

The man followed Ellen over to where Kevin and Diane were waiting.

"Mr. Anderson, I have just run into your lovely daughter. Or should I say, she has just run in to me," said Zoran Vacinovic of the Serbian Embassy.

"Hello, Mr. Vacinovic. I hope Ellen wasn't too rough with you."

Vacinovic smiled. "Not at all. I was coming to show Mr. Golic some of Holland."

Kevin saw his huge investigator coming up behind Vacinovic. They shook hands.

"Thank you for coming back to Holland, Mr. Golic," Kevin said.

Golic turned to Ellen. "And how are you, young lady?"

"Great!" beamed Ellen. "I got all the questions right in my passport. Want to see?" Without waiting for an answer, she whipped out the passport and showed it to Golic.

"I just received some reports from Mr. Golic," Vacinovic told Kevin. "I will bring them to court tomorrow. I think you will find them very interesting. And I've arranged for an attorney from Belgrade to be in court tomorrow as well."

Kevin nodded. He turned to Golic. "I'm sorry to take you away from your family."

"It is no problem."

"How are you related to Draga anyway?"

Golic hesitated. "How do you say it in English?" he asked. Then he answered, "I am the brother of his wife."

"The movie star?" Ellen piped in.

"Yes," Golic said with a smile.

"Cool!"

"I don't want to keep you and your lovely family on such a day," Vacinovic said. "We'll see you tomorrow." He and Golic waved goodbye and melted into the crowd.

"What's happening tomorrow?" Diane asked.

"I'll tell you later."

Diane frowned. "That guy shows up at the strangest places. First he came to our house at night, now he's at Madurodam—a children's place—with his big friend and no kids. I don't trust him."

"Do you think he's following us?" Kevin asked, open to the possibility.

"I don't know."

"I know one thing. Mr. Golic is not my client's brother-in-law."

"How do you know that?" Ellen asked.

"Do you remember how he said he was the brother of Draga's wife?"

"Yeah."

"Well, when I asked Draga how they were related, he said that Golic was married to one of his sisters."

"I don't get it."

"Well, there's two ways you can be a brother-in-law. You can be married to somebody's sister, right?"

"Yeah," Ellen said, following Kevin so far.

"Or you can be the brother of somebody's wife."

"I get it. Golic and Draga gave you two different stories?"

"Right."

"You're smart, Daddy."

"Coming from you, that's a real compliment."

Kevin put his arm around Ellen as they walked back to their car.

On Monday morning, Kevin was seated at his usual place at the defense counsel table when Judge Davidson swept into the courtroom.

"Prosecutor versus Dragoljub Zaric," the Deputy Registrar called. "Case number IT-96-30. State your appearances please."

"Bradford Stone for the Prosecution."

"Kevin Anderson for the accused,"

"And I am a lawyer from Belgrade, Your Honor," the man seated next to Kevin announced. "I am an attorney for the government of Serbia and Montenegro. My government would like to join in the Motion for Return of Property filed on behalf of the accused."

Judge Davidson looked at the lawyer sternly. "This is a hearing on Mr. Anderson's contempt."

"I thought perhaps the Court might address the legality of the searches of our Embassy and Mr. Anderson's home as well, since the issues appear to be intertwined with the alleged contempt."

Kevin appreciated the Belgrade lawyer's use of the word "alleged."

"We'll see about that," Judge Davidson muttered. Turning to Kevin, he said, "Mr. Anderson, this is the time set for you to show cause why you should not be held in contempt for violation of this Court's protective order."

"Thank you, Your Honor. I'm ready to call my first witness."

"We don't need to hear witnesses. Let me hear what you have to say for yourself."

"You Honor, I would like to call a witness who will establish my innocence. It will be much more convincing than anything I have to tell you."

"Well, make it quick," Judge Davidson grumbled.

"I call John Wells."

Wells' head bolted up from the back row of tables on the prosecution side of the courtroom. Bradford Stone, too, was startled, and was soon on his feet.

"Your Honor," Stone whined. "He has no right to call our chief investigator as his witness. It's just an excuse for mischief."

Judge Davidson turned to Kevin. "This better be relevant to the contempt, counsel, or I'm going to cut your examination right off. Mr. Wells, come forward and take the solemn declaration."

Wells walked to the witness chair and promised to tell the truth. When he was seated, his look of surprise had been replaced by the look of a snake coiled and ready.

"Mr. Wells," Kevin asked pleasantly, "as part of your investigation in this matter, did you recover the box of materials from the Post Office that I was seen giving to Zoran Vacinovic at the Embassy of Serbia and Montenegro?"

"Yes, I did."

Kevin wanted to get right to the point and not give Wells an opportunity to take any gratuitous swipes at him. "It's true, is it not, that not a single piece of paper in that box related to a protected witness or was covered by the protective order?"

Wells hesitated, trying to find a way to answer the question and damage Kevin. Finally, he replied, "That appears to be the case."

"I have nothing further," Kevin announced, sitting down after asking only two questions.

Judge Davidson struggled to assimilate what he had just heard. He slowly turned to Bradford Stone. "Cross-examination, Mr. Stone?"

Bradford Stone stood erect, his chin pointed in the air. "Mr. Wells," he asked, "who did Mr. Anderson give the materials to?"

"Zoran Vacinovic," Wells replied, then added, "a high ranking member of the secret police."

"What ethnic group makes up the secret police?"

"They are all Serbs."

"And who are the people most likely to retaliate against Muslim witnesses before this Tribunal?"

"The Serbs, especially those in the secret police."

"Now, when you searched Mr. Anderson's home, was he on the phone with someone?"

"Yes, Zoran Vacinovic."

"And what was Mr. Anderson's demeanor when you searched his home?"

"He was extremely hostile," Wells responded.

"In your experience, is that the normal reaction of someone who has done nothing wrong?" Stone asked haughtily.

"People who have nothing to hide don't act like that."

"No further questions, Your Honor," Stone said, sitting down triumphantly.

"Any redirect examination?" the judge asked Kevin.

Kevin was sorely tempted to take Wells on, but his instincts told him to leave it alone. Surely he would not be found in contempt simply because he was outraged at the search of his home. "No, thank you, Your Honor."

"Mr. Stone," Judge Davidson inquired, "do you wish to call any witnesses?"

"No, Your Honor. Mr. Anderson has called our witness for us. It is plain that Mr. Anderson violated the spirit, if not the letter, of the protective order. Conspiring with a member of the Serbian secret police is a serious matter, regardless of whether the materials were literally covered by the order or not. We don't know what kind of information Mr. Anderson passed on to the man orally during their two hour lunch, on the telephone, or at other meetings."

"Mr. Anderson," Judge Davidson said when Stone had finished, "Do you have anything further to say before I rule?"

"I think Mr. Stone said it best, Your Honor."

Judge Davidson shot him a quizzical look.

"He said 'we don't know.' They didn't know what was in the box when they invaded my home and a foreign embassy. Now we do know. And it is clear that no violation of the protective order took place. What is clear, however, is that the searches were illegal, and I would ask the court to order the material returned immediately."

"What is your position on the search issue, Mr. Stone?"

"Your Honor, there is no reason for the court to have to concern itself with the legality of the search. We do not intend to use any of the seized evidence at Mr. Zaric's trial. Therefore, even if the search was illegal, which it most assuredly was not, there is no evidence for the court to exclude, and no prejudice to the accused from the searches."

Kevin was on his feet. "Your Honor, that doesn't solve the problem one bit. They seized attorney-client materials from my home dealing with our defense strategy. Just having knowledge of the contents of those materials taints their whole case and prejudices the accused, whether they directly use the evidence or not."

"Wait until I ask for your position before stating it," Judge Davidson rebuked Kevin. "Now, Mr. Stone, what about the so-called privileged materials?"

"That is also no problem. Our office has erected a Chinese wall for all of the items seized during these searches. Neither Mr. Jacobson, the investigator on Mr. Zaric's case, nor I have seen these materials and they will be shielded from us and anyone else who works on this case. Therefore, there will be no use made of any privileged materials against the accused."

"Very well," Judge Davidson replied.

Kevin wanted to offer a rebuttal, but the Judge didn't call on him, so he remained silent.

The lawyer from Belgrade, however, rose from his chair. "Our government's interests have not been addressed. We would like you to rule the search illegal so that the world knows the truth."

"The Court will be in recess," Judge Davidson ordered. "The world will know the truth when we reconvene in thirty minutes."

CHAPTER 11

▼

Precisely thirty minutes later, Judge Davidson took his seat at the bench. His face, an impassive mask, was impossible to read.

Looking down at his leather book, he began:

"The Court issues the following three orders. First, the motions of the accused and the government of Serbia and Montenegro challenging the searches are denied. The Court finds that the searches of the Embassy and Mr. Anderson's office and residence were completely lawful and supported by the information known at that time. However, since the prosecution does not plan to use evidence from those searches at the trial, the items seized, and all copies of those items, shall be returned to Mr. Anderson or the Embassy to avoid any claims of violation of the attorney-client privilege."

Kevin shifted in his seat. He had lost round one, although Judge Davidson had tossed him a bone in the process. At least the prosecution wouldn't be seeing his memos to Draga—if they had kept all the materials separate as they claimed.

Kevin held his breath as he waited for the ruling on his contempt. Thirty minutes ago, he had been pretty confident. Now, he was not so sure.

"Second," Judge Davidson continued, "The Court is very troubled by the conduct of Mr. Anderson with respect to the protective order. However, out of an abundance of caution, the Court will reserve its ruling on the contempt issue until the conclusion of Mr. Zaric's trial. At that time, the Court will have a full record of counsel's performance from which to determine if this was an isolated incident or part of a pattern of misconduct."

The judge looked down at Kevin sternly.

"This is strike two, Mr. Anderson. You first showed bad judgment in taking on this case while you were seeking a job with the other side. Now, you delivered discovery materials to the Serbian secret police. I'm warning you. As they say in your country, 'One more strike and you're out.'"

Kevin was relieved not to be going to jail, but annoyed that Judge Davidson didn't dismiss outright the contempt. He was intending to hold it over Kevin's head as a threat during the remainder of the case.

"Third and finally," Judge Davidson continued, looking down at his book again, "all pretrial motions must be filed within thirty days. A hearing on those motions will be held in sixty days, on December 1st. Trial will begin on January 8th."

Judge Davidson quickly left the bench, leaving no doubt that his orders were final.

Kevin got up and walked back to Draga, who was being handcuffed for his departure to the prison. "You can release the room you saved for me," Kevin said. "And it looks like you're going to get your speedy trial."

"Now I just need to get the football scores from yesterday," Draga said.

"I could have gone to jail here and all you can think of is <u>football</u>?

The guards moved Draga toward the door.

"I'll be working my butt off for the next three months," Kevin called after him, "while you're studying the sports section."

When Kevin got home that night, Ellen had big news. "Dad, I have a loose tooth," she exclaimed as he walked in the door. "Look!" She showed him a tooth near the back of her mouth that moved from side to side.

"Great! Does the tooth fairy come in Holland?"

"We're going to find out. I hope the tooth comes out before I go to bed."

Kevin had already told Diane about the favorable ruling at the contempt hearing, but at dinner he gave her and Ellen more details about his day in court.

"Is that mean old guy going to be the judge at Draga's trial?" Ellen asked with one hand in her mouth wiggling her tooth.

"Fortunately, he'll only be one of three judges. For our pretrial motions and the trial, the whole trial chamber will be involved."

"Do you know who the other judges are?" Diane asked.

"The presiding judge is a woman, Juan Orozco of Chile. She was a Justice of the Chilean Supreme Court, and has been at the Tribunal for two years. I've heard that she's a nice person and a fair judge, but that Judge Davidson takes over in court. Sometimes he even rules on objections without consulting her."

"What about the other judge?" Ellen asked, carefully selecting a hard roll to try to dislodge the tooth.

"Judge Francisco Linares of the Philippines. He was President of the Philippine Senate before becoming a judge at the Tribunal. He's been a judge for less than a year, but from what I hear he's brought with him the strong law and order mentality prevalent in his country."

"Just the kind of judge you would have wanted in the states," Diane said.

"You're right," Kevin said wearily.

The phone interrupted their dinner.

"Will you get it, Ellen?" Diane asked. "It's probably for you anyway."

The Andersons routinely received two or three calls a night from Ellen's classmates with questions about their homework. Ellen had already established herself as one of the brainy kids in her class.

"I'm busy with my tooth, can you get it, Dad?" Ellen asked as she positioned the roll under her loose tooth in preparation for a big bite.

Kevin got up and answered the phone. "Ellen's Homework Service."

Ellen turned bright red. "That's the last time I let you answer the phone." She gave Kevin the evil eye as he handed her the phone. "Don't mind my dad," she said to her friend apologetically. "He's kinda weird."

Kevin and Diane continued their conversation while Ellen looked up something in her math book. "I did get some good news, today," Kevin said. "My investigator, Mihajlo Golic, came up with some information on Draga's kidnapping."

"The big guy we saw at Madurodam yesterday?"

"Yeah. He got copies of Belgrade police reports. The police believe the kidnappers were paid by people working with the U.N. Security Forces."

"What are you going to do?"

"Well, it's not exactly airtight proof, but it's enough to support a motion to dismiss the case based on an illegal arrest. We'll see what the prosecution comes back with."

The next morning, Kevin and Ellen left on their bicycles together. Ellen had wiggled her tooth out last night and was exclaiming over the shiny Euro coin the tooth fairy had left her. "Where do you think the tooth fairy gets the foreign money?" she asked Kevin.

"I don't know. Maybe there's a currency exchange booth at the fairy airport."

Ellen headed north to the American School, while Kevin went south to The Hague.

From his office in the Tribunal, Kevin called Nihudian.

"I can't find an investigator to work for Draga," Nihudian reported. "I think I talked to every investigator in Sarajevo."

"Damn, this defense lawyer job is tough. I used to have all kinds of investigators at my disposal. FBI, DEA, Secret Service. Now I can't even find anyone to help."

"I have an idea, Kevin. How about if I do the investigation, with the help of the students in my history classes? I'm not experienced in this kind of thing, but I would work hard and it would be a great learning opportunity for my students."

Kevin thought for a minute. He had no real alternative. "We could give it a try. If it seems like too much work or if it makes you uncomfortable, let me know."

"I would be honored to assist you, Kevin. I know you will be fair with the witnesses, so I have nothing to be ashamed of in helping you. And I owe you so much."

"You don't owe me anything. You already paid my fee, remember?"

Kevin felt better after talking to Nihudian. He wasn't a professional investigator, but he had been a policeman and was someone Kevin trusted. The latter counted for a lot these days.

After spending the rest of the week researching his other pretrial motions, Kevin headed over to the detention center for his regular Friday afternoon meeting with Draga. His client would have a fit if Kevin didn't show up in time to make their weekend football picks.

Kevin decided to pick up some pannekoeken for Draga and the guards. These were huge Dutch pancakes, the size of a Frisbee, which were made with fruit, cheese, meat, or just powdered sugar on top. The Dutch ate them for breakfast, lunch, or dinner.

"Have you ever had pannekoeken?" Kevin asked Draga when the two men met in the interview room.

"Pan-a-what-kin?"

Kevin opened the box and showed them to Draga.

"From the size of the portions, I like them already," Draga said.

As the two men dug in—cutting the large, thin pancakes with plastic knives—Draga pulled out the sports section and a piece of paper.

"You got lucky last weekend," he said. "You're ahead by 50 Euros. But not for long."

"If you want to give your money away, I'll take it. Let's see the lineup for this week."

Draga handed Kevin the paper and went back to work on his food.

"These are good," Draga said through a mouthful.

After Kevin had made his picks and endured Draga's predictions of doom, Kevin brought up the case. "I want to be clear with you what motions I'm filing on your behalf. I'm filing a motion to dismiss your case based upon an illegal arrest, as well as a motion for disclosure of intelligence agency files—the graymail motion. I want the Court to make the intelligence agencies reveal any information they have on you or the Black Dragons."

"What's the point of that?"

"Like I told you, sometimes there are secrets they don't want to reveal. Every once in a while they decide to drop a prosecution rather than have to reveal them."

"Dream on. You'd be better off spending your time studying the football teams."

"I seem to be doing pretty well so far. You're the one who needs to study."

$$* \qquad * \qquad * \qquad *$$

"All rise. *Veuillez vous lever.*"

The hearing on Kevin's motions gave him his first opportunity to see Judges Orozco and Linares. Alone at the defense counsel table, Kevin rose as the three judges entered Courtroom 1. On the opposite side of the courtroom, Charles Oswald and Bradford Stone stood confidently.

"Good morning, counsel," Judge Orozco said pleasantly. Her English was marked with a Spanish accent. "Mr. Anderson, do you wish to be heard on the motion to dismiss based upon the circumstances of your client's arrest?"

Kevin rose. "Yes, Your Honor."

Before he could speak, Judge Linares of the Philippines interrupted. "Counsel, I think we can save ourselves a lot of time here. Even if the arrest was illegal, you are not entitled to have the case dismissed. There is no precedent in support of the remedy of dismissal of the charges against the accused."

Kevin was about to offer a polite response when Judge Davidson broke in. "In any case, you don't have any proof that the arrest was illegal, counselor. These police reports you submitted are a bunch of hearsay. The prosecutor has submitted documents which categorically deny any U.N. involvement in your client's arrest."

"If you grant me a hearing, I will bring in the witnesses with firsthand information."

"We're not going to waste our time, counsel," Judge Davidson growled. "Your motion is denied. Court is adjourned."

The other judges looked surprised as Judge Davidson abruptly got up and began exiting the courtroom. Then Kevin realized that there had been no discussion about his graymail motion.

"Your Honors," he shouted, "there is one more motion to be heard today."

Judge Orozco had risen from her chair, and Judge Davidson was already on his way to the door.

"What motion is that, counsel?" Judge Orozco asked.

"My motion to require the prosecution to provide intelligence agency information." He did not want to refer to it as a "graymail" motion in open court.

Judge Orozco gave Kevin a puzzled look. She sat down and said, "I don't believe I've seen that motion."

"We don't know what counsel is talking about," Bradford Stone piped up.

Judge Davidson was still standing. "There are no other motions pending, counsel."

Kevin dug frantically through his papers. "Here it is, Your Honors. It was filed the same day as the motion challenging the arrest of Mr. Zaric."

Kevin offered the paper to the usher to be shown to the Court. "We have no record of any such motion being filed," the Deputy Registrar told the judges.

"We never received anything," Bradford Stone volunteered.

"What are you trying to do, counsel?" Judge Davidson asked gruffly.

"I have the stamped copy showing it was received by the Registrar, Your Honor. I filed it myself."

Judge Davidson was still standing. "There's nothing before the Court, counsel. Court is adjourned."

The judge turned to leave.

"May I file it again, Your Honors, since it has apparently been misplaced?"

Judge Davidson glared at Kevin; he had lost his patience.

"No," Judge Davidson shouted. "The time for filing motions has expired. Court is adjourned." He strode briskly off the bench, with the other judges following closely.

CHAPTER 12

▼

Four days later, Kevin was sitting at the dining room table having dinner with Diane and Ellen when suddenly there was a thunderous knock at the front door.

Ellen raced to the door. Before Kevin and Diane were even out of their seats, she had thrown open the door.

Two black figures yelled out in Dutch and threw something into the house.

"They came!" Ellen shrieked. "They came!"

Kevin saw confetti and small round brown cookies strewn along their hallway. A brown burlap sack had been left by the door.

Ellen picked up a cookie and popped it into her mouth. "Yum, pepernoten!"

It was December 5th, the day the Dutch celebrated the arrival of Sinterklaas, their version of Santa Claus. Instead of elves, his helpers were "Black Piets," descendants of the ancient Moors who were said to have met up with Sinterklaas in Spain and helped him distribute gifts to children who had been good. In reality, the "Piets" were neighbors, who had been given gifts by several parents to be delivered to their children.

Ellen scooped up some confetti and threw it in the air. "This is great!" she exclaimed. "I wasn't sure if Sinterklaas even came to American houses."

Kevin reached down, picked up one of the pepernoten, and took a bite. It tasted like a spicy graham cracker. "Hey, these are good."

Ellen spied the burlap sack by the door that had been left by the helpers. She looked inside and pulled out a large box. "Look, it has my name on it!" She tore at the wrapping paper, and then opened the box. "Ice skates!" She pulled out a pair of white leather ice skates. "The canals just have to freeze over this winter!"

The next morning, Kevin received a present of a different kind: a stack of witness interview reports from Nihudian. The reports were grim, and presented an unchanging pattern of brutality. The Black Dragons who first invaded a town acted with military professionalism and did not harass the civilians. They were men who were thought to be from Serbia and were unknown to the witnesses. Then, once in the camps, other men wearing Dragon uniforms—local Bosnian Serbs—appeared, and they routinely subjected the prisoners to beatings, rape and execution. The prisoners often knew these men. Kevin began to make a list of their names as he read the reports.

When he finished, Kevin called Nihudian and thanked him for his work.

"I don't feel successful," Nihudian replied. "I'm not sure I found anything helpful to you."

"It helps to know what to expect. What are these witnesses like? Believable?"

"You ought to come and see for yourself, Kevin. Most of them would talk to you. Maybe you can get a better idea what to ask them in court if you meet them in person. There are quite a few witnesses in Sarajevo. Why don't you come for a few days?"

"That's not a bad idea. My client won't tell me anything and if I don't come up with some cross-examination material, I'm going to look like an idiot at the trial."

A few days later, Kevin was on his way to Sarajevo. He anxiously looked out the window as the pilot announced over the intercom that they would soon be landing. He was looking forward to seeing Nihudian and meeting witnesses, but was unsure what to expect in Bosnia. Although the war had been over for five years, he knew that feelings still ran high among the Muslims, Croats, and Serbs.

Sarajevo had been awarded to the Muslims in the Peace Agreement, and Kevin wondered how safe he would be, although he had told Diane and Ellen there was nothing to worry about. But what if he was recognized from TV as Draga's lawyer?

The skyscrapers of the city came into view in the distance. Sarajevo looked like a big city in a bowl, with tall office and apartment buildings, and the pointed towers of Muslim mosques jutting into the air from a valley surrounded by large hills. When the plane got closer, Kevin saw that some of the buildings were just shells, with no glass in the windows and burned out interiors. One skyscraper was partially collapsed; a twisted rubble of steel and cement rising about five stories in a grotesque heap.

Kevin was reminded of a movie called "Welcome to Sarajevo" that he had seen back in the United States. It portrayed a bloody, dangerous place where people ran between buildings to avoid the constant snipers.

He was glad to see Nihudian's smiling face when he walked into the airport terminal after clearing Customs.

"Welcome to Sarajevo," Nihudian said warmly, extending his hand.

As he offered his own hand, Kevin shuddered.

Nihudian led Kevin to his car, an old red Volkswagen Golf. "I want you to meet my family. Then, we will start working. I have arranged meetings with six witnesses."

"Good work. Do you think we'll have any—security problems?"

"Well, we might if you are recognized. But most people here are too busy rebuilding to watch much TV. So, we'll just keep a low profile and you should be okay."

Kevin felt only slightly reassured.

Nihudian drove north from the airport, along the Miljacka River, which ran along the east side of downtown Sarajevo. Kevin saw the bright yellow and red tower of the Holiday Inn, where he would be staying. The hotel had been relentlessly shelled and sniped at during the war, but now, with a fresh paint job, it stood looking like any Holiday Inn in a major city.

As they drove, Kevin saw 19th century buildings that looked to be untouched by the war, such as an old post office, an opera building, and parts of Sarajevo University. The streets were filled with people hurrying about as in any American city.

"There's the old National Library," Nihudian said, pointing to a stately brown building with its windows blown out. "The Serbs shelled it during the war, and we lost many historical works. Then they claimed the Muslims did it themselves to look like victims." Nihudian shook his head sadly.

He pointed out Old Town Sarajevo, a mixture of stone mosques and small shops resembling a Turkish bazaar. "This is from the Ottoman Empire," Nihudian said. "It's what makes Sarajevo unique, and why the Muslims fought so hard to keep it."

Soon they parked in front of a large, gray apartment building. "This is home," Nihudian said. "My wife and daughters are anxious to meet you."

They walked up the stairs to the fourth floor. When they reached the apartment, Nihudian introduced Kevin to his wife and two young daughters, none of whom spoke English except, "Hello, Kevin," which they said in unison and had obviously practiced. The table was set with shiny silverware and fancy porcelain plates and cups. When they sat down for lunch, Nihudian interpreted as Kevin asked the girls how old they were, if they liked their school, and what they did for fun.

"We like to play with our dolls," the oldest said, "and ride our bikes."

Kevin thought of how little difference there seemed to be between these Bosnian girls and his own all-American daughter. Many Bosnian children had lost their fathers or both parents during the war. Fortunately, Nihudian's girls—bright, healthy and well-mannered—looked as if they had survived the violence with no outward signs of trauma.

After lunch, Nihudian and his family took Kevin for a walk around their neighborhood. They pointed out some buildings nearby that were riddled with holes from shells fired by the Serbs from a football stadium near the hills. Kevin watched as the girls played on the swings and climbed on monkey bars at a small neighborhood park.

"Your girls are wonderful," Kevin told Nihudian. "I'm glad you and your family can live here safely now."

"It is a shame that they cannot grow up like I did," Nihudian said, "side by side with Serbs and Croats. The war deeply divided this country and too many bad things happened for people to be able to forgive and forget so soon."

"What surprises me is that you can't tell who is a Serb, Croat, or Muslim by just looking at someone," Kevin said. "They're all Caucasians, and they look basically the same. I pictured Muslims as darker skinned people, like those from Iran or India. How did people know who was Serb, Croat, or Muslim during the war?"

"Their neighbors. The war turned neighbor against neighbor. When the Serbs invaded a town, they left the Serb houses standing and burned the Muslim houses, then looted them. You could see a street with some houses perfectly normal, and the ones on either side of them completely destroyed."

"Why did Serbs turn against their Muslim neighbors?"

"I think most did it out of fear. Fear that they would be treated as a Muslim if they did not go along. Fear that the Muslims would do the same thing to them if given a chance. That was the kind of propaganda Slobodan Milosevic put out all over Serbia."

Kevin looked at the children playing together in the park, and then up at the hillside where snipers had taken aim. It gave him a sudden shiver.

"You'll have four days to get to know Sarajevo," Nihudian said as if he could read Kevin's mind. "You'll learn to like it more." He looked at his watch. "We'd better get going to our first interview. It is with a judge, so we don't want to be late."

Kevin watched as Nihudian hugged his girls and kissed his wife goodbye. Then he led Kevin through his neighborhood until they came to an old shabby apartment building a few blocks away.

"A judge lives <u>here</u>?" Kevin asked.

"This judge is a refugee from another part of Bosnia. She was a judge in the northern municipality of Prijedor before the war. Many people fled to Sarajevo after the Serbs expelled them from their villages. When the war ended, the Dayton Peace Agreement divided Bosnia in two. The Serbs now govern the territory they took during the war, forty-nine percent of the country. They call it Republika Srpska. The Muslim and Croat Federation governs the remaining fifty-one percent of Bosnia. The Muslims are still afraid to go back to their homes in Serb territory."

As they climbed the stairs to the judge's apartment, it looked like this judge was living as a peasant. But the middle-aged woman who answered the door, with jet black hair streaked with grey, had a competent, intelligent air about her. She and Nihudian spoke in Bosnian for a minute, then she motioned to Kevin to come in.

She led them to a small table in the main room of what looked like a two-room flat. Kevin could see four other people sitting inside the other room, which looked to be a bedroom. "I know you are working for Draga," she said to Kevin as Nihudian translated. "I also know that you will be looking for some way to discredit me or use my testimony to help your client. But go ahead and ask your questions."

Kevin tried to break the ice. "I'm not trying to discredit you. That would serve no purpose. There are too many others like you who will testify. I just want to know some of the details of what you saw the Black Dragons do, and who in particular was doing it."

"Do you want to know the name of the man who raped me at Omarska?"

The judge looked Kevin directly in the eye without a hint of bitterness or shame.

"You were at the camp in Omarska? I thought only men were kept there."

"They kept a handful of women to work in the restaurant, prepare the food, clean the offices, that kind of thing."

"I do want to know the name of the man who raped you, if you don't mind."

"His name was Victor Vidic."

"Was he a member of the Black Dragons?"

"He claimed to be. He came to Omarska wearing a black beret and black uniform like the Dragons. He and his friends, who dressed alike, would beat prisoners during the day, then get drunk and rape the women at night."

Kevin didn't need to know the details of the rape, and for that he was grateful. He changed the subject, asking the woman about her life before she was arrested, about the ethnic cleansing of Prijedor by the Serbs, and her confinement at Omarska. By the end of the interview, Kevin's heart went out to her, and he felt terrible about how she and the others had suffered. He told her how sorry he was for what she had gone through.

Part of him was also sorry that he had come to interview her. It was much easier to cross-examine witnesses when they remained impersonal. He dreaded having to cross-examine this woman in court. What could he say? She was obviously telling the truth.

"I have just one more question," he said at the door when he and Nihudian were leaving. "As a judge, you have seen lawyers do their jobs for many years. Is there anything I should know to do my job?"

The woman hesitated. "There is one thing you might want to know," she said finally. "After the war started, many Bosnian Serbs were infatuated with Draga and his Black Dragons, but they couldn't be Dragons themselves. For one thing, they couldn't stay sober for a day. I heard they had their own black uniforms made up by a tailor in Sokolaz and wore them around pretending to be Black Dragons. I think your client was ruthless, but perhaps he is being blamed for more things than he is responsible for."

Kevin felt his heart beat faster. Ellen's preposterous Draga-impersonation defense had come alive. "Would you happen to know where in Sokolaz they got the uniforms?"

"It would have to be Stigic's Sewing Shop. Josef Stigic is the only tailor there."

"You must have been an excellent judge," Kevin said gratefully as they stood to leave. "Thank you for being so fair."

When he and Nihudian were back on the street, Kevin's spirits had soared.

"That's a great lead," he said to Nihudian. "Where is Sokolaz?"

"It's a town about 30 miles northwest of Sarajevo. But it's in Republika Srpska."

"I want to talk to that tailor."

"It's dangerous," Nihudian replied. "Sokolaz is the headquarters of the old Drina Corps of the Bosnian Serb Army. They're the ones who massacred 7,000 Muslims at Srebrenica. A Muslim and American would not be welcome in Sokolaz."

Kevin nodded, but he kept thinking how important conformation from the tailor could be as they walked back to Nihudian's car. "Where to next?"

"Our next witness is a damaging one. He saw Draga shoot his friend here in Sarajevo."

Kevin's heart sank. If what the witness said was correct, Kevin knew it meant that he was defending a murderer. Beyond that, he realized that his "Draga impersonation" defense wouldn't fly too well if someone saw Draga commit murder himself.

"But he lied about some things in his statement to the prosecutor," Nihudian said. "I just put some reports and photographs about him in the mail to you before you came. It will be interesting for you to talk to him. It might be difficult though. He was reluctant when I asked him to see you."

They drove to another section of Sarajevo, up a hill overlooking the city from the west. Kevin saw apartment buildings with gaping holes in them and some buildings that had not yet been repaired from the war. "This looks like a rough area," Kevin said.

"It was close to the front line of the fighting. The people who lived here almost never ventured out of their houses."

They got out of the car and walked up to a three-story building that had sniper holes in its walls. "Let me do the talking at first," Nihudian cautioned. "This guy doesn't like your client."

Nihudian knocked on the door of a first floor apartment. When the door was opened, a policeman appeared from inside. He spoke to Nihudian in Bosnian, then waved his arms.

Suddenly, four policemen came up from behind Kevin and Nihudian. They were yelling something Kevin did not understand. "What are they saying?" Kevin asked Nihudian as his arms were jerked behind his back.

Nihudian's face had gone pale. "They are saying that we are under arrest."

CHAPTER 13

▼

The policemen handcuffed Kevin and Nihudian and led them to a police car. Kevin felt beads of sweat forming on his forehead, though it was a brisk December afternoon. "What's happening?" he asked Nihudian.

The policeman pushed Kevin's head down as he placed him in the back seat of the car while another officer shoved Nihudian in from the other side. Kevin was breathing hard, and his thoughts flashed to the beatings and executions he had heard about in Bosnia. "Can you ask them why we've been arrested?"

Nihudian spoke in Bosnian to the police officer in the passenger seat.

"We'll be told that at the station," Nihudian reported.

Kevin blanched at the thought of going to a police station. He didn't trust police in third-world countries. He had seen one too many movies like "Midnight Express," a frightening story about an American in a Turkish prison.

They drove in silence down the hill into the center of Sarajevo. Kevin tried to sort out his thoughts. "Tell them I demand to see someone from the American Embassy."

"I don't think that's a good idea, Kevin. Let's wait until we get to the station."

They arrived at the back of the police station, and the policemen pulled Kevin and Nihudian out of the car. They led them through a hallway, which was crowded with families. The people all looked poor. Kevin guessed they were either families of people who had been arrested, or victims of crimes. He thought of his own family. He was glad he hadn't brought them on this trip, which Ellen had lobbied hard to make him do.

The officers left Nihudian and Kevin alone in a windowless room. The handcuffs were beginning to dig into Kevin's skin.

"What should we do?" he asked Nihudian.

"We have to find out what the problem is. We might be able to pay them a bribe."

Kevin would gladly have paid a bribe to have the handcuffs removed and to get out of there, but he didn't want bribery added to the charges. He thought the interview room was probably bugged, so he said nothing.

A few minutes later, a short, plain-clothed man in his forties with a thin black mustache entered. He said something in Bosnian and unlocked the handcuffs from Nihudian and Kevin. Kevin rubbed his sore wrists. He saw Nihudian reach into his pocket. Kevin thought he was getting money for a bribe, but Nihudian turned to him and said, "He wants to see our identification."

Nihudian took out his Bosnian driver's license and Kevin produced his American passport. Without saying anything, the man began copying the information onto a form that looked like a police report. Kevin wanted to demand an explanation, but thought it better to wait until the man was finished.

After writing down the information, the man spoke gruffly. Nihudian translated. "He wants to know what you are doing in Bosnia."

Kevin spoke directly to the policeman. "I am a lawyer for a person being prosecuted at the War Crimes Tribunal in The Hague. I'm here to interview witnesses who will be testifying at his trial. Nihudian is my interpreter." He tried to downplay Nihudian's role.

"Did you register with the Ministry of Justice before you began conducting an investigation in Bosnia?"

"No, was I supposed to?"

"Yes," the policeman replied through Nihudian. "It is required under our law."

"I'm sorry. I didn't know."

"We cannot have foreigners coming to Bosnia and bothering our citizens," the man said, shaking his head for emphasis. "This is a serious matter."

"I was authorized by the International Criminal Tribunal for the former Yugoslavia to come here. I did have official permission. And this man," Kevin said, gesturing to Nihudian, "he was just interpreting for me. He had no duty to register did he?"

"You still did not comply with our law," the man said sternly. "But you are correct about your interpreter. He is free to leave."

Kevin looked at Nihudian. "Go, before they change their mind."

"I can't leave you here," Nihudian replied. "You can't even speak to them."

"Let them get their own interpreter. You go and contact the American Embassy."

Nihudian reluctantly got up, and said something to the man. He walked out the door leaving Kevin and the policeman sitting across the small table from one another. Kevin wondered how they would communicate. He also felt an even greater fear now that he was alone.

"So you are the lawyer for the famous Mr. Draga?" the officer said in English.

Kevin was surprised to hear the man speak English. He quickly replayed the previous conversation with Nihudian in his mind, hoping he had not said anything inappropriate. "Yes, I was assigned by the Tribunal to represent him."

"He is responsible for the death of many in Bosnia," the officer said solemnly.

Kevin did not like the direction the conversation was taking. "That's what I am here to find out about."

"Is there any doubt?"

"Probably not to the people of Bosnia. But I wasn't here during the war, so I have to find out these things by talking to people who were."

The man shook his head. "You should have followed our laws."

"I didn't know about your law."

"You're a lawyer. You can tell that to the judge."

Kevin groaned inwardly. Was he going to have to stay in jail until he was taken to court? "What happens now?" Kevin nervously asked the man.

The man smiled for the first time. "You will be treated like any other person arrested in the Republic of Bosnia and Herzegovina. You will remain in jail until we complete our investigation. If we find that you have broken the law, you will go to court. If not, you will be freed, like your interpreter."

"How long will it take?"

"This is a very simple matter." The officer rose from his chair. "You have already admitted committing the crime. We should be able to wrap up our investigation in a few days." The man abruptly turned and walked out the door.

Kevin was alone in the interview room for the next two hours. He tried not to think about what the jail cells were like, or who else was in them. He tried the door, but it was locked. He prayed that Nihudian would get some help from the American Embassy. Otherwise, he would be stuck in a Bosnian jail for several days at least.

Finally, the plain-clothed officer reappeared.

Kevin dreaded having to leave the interview room for a cell.

"Mr. Anderson, you are free to go if you agree to depart Bosnia in the morning and not return in the future unless you have approval from our Ministry of Justice to conduct an investigation here. Do you understand?"

"I understand." Kevin suddenly felt light-headed.

"Do you agree?"

"I agree," Kevin replied quickly. He would figure out how to get the remaining witnesses interviewed later.

The man opened the door and indicated Kevin should follow him. At first, Kevin felt unsteady on his feet, but he walked quickly through the lobby. When the man pointed to the front door, Kevin practically broke into a sprint. When he burst out the door, he spied Nihudian standing next to his car in front of the building.

"Thank you, Nihudian," he said as they got into the car. "Damn, that was close."

"Let's go get a drink," Nihudian replied. He drove to a cafe nearby, as he explained how he had gotten the help of someone at the American Embassy, who had made some calls on Kevin's behalf.

"I owe you. I was going to have to sit in jail for days before I even saw a judge."

They reached the cafe and sat down, with sounds of American rock music blasting from the music system. "Want a beer?" Kevin asked Nihudian.

"We Muslims don't drink alcohol. But I'll have a large cappuccino."

"That sounds perfect."

Kevin sipped the cappuccino as he felt the tension leave his body. It was beginning to get dark outside. His mind returned to the judge and the tailor in Sokolaz who might have made uniforms for the men at Omarska. "Damn, I hate to leave without talking to that tailor," he told Nihudian. "His evidence might prove Draga's innocence."

Nihudian was silent.

"How long would it take for us to get to Sokolaz tonight?" Kevin asked.

"It's only about a 45 minute drive. But we'd be taking a big risk. It's in the heart of Serb territory."

"Yeah, but the Serbs will want to help Draga. He's their hero, right? I have the papers showing I'm his lawyer and you're his investigator."

Nihudian looked up from his coffee at Kevin. "I guess we can try it," he said. "No sane Muslim would go to Sokolaz at night, but we _are_ working for Draga."

Kevin felt emboldened by the adrenaline from the day's events, and desperately wanted to find something useful for Draga's defense. "Let's go for it. Then

I'll head back in the morning with something to show for my trip besides sore wrists."

The two men finished their drinks and returned to Nihudian's car. They drove north from Sarajevo, and soon passed a sign telling them that they were entering Republika Srpska.

"At least there's no border station," Kevin said.

Nihudian was quiet.

They headed up the hill towards the town of Pale, where the ski events for the 1984 Winter Olympics had been held and which had been the home of Radovan Karadzic, President of the Republika Srpska, during the war. Then they turned north just before Pale and continued climbing until they reached a plateau near Sokolaz.

"How are we going to find this tailor?" Kevin asked as they approached the town.

"He's probably well known. We can just go into a shop and ask."

They drove toward the center of town. "There's the headquarters of the Drina Corps," Nihudian said, pointing out two buildings set back from the road.

"Let's just go in there," Kevin said. "They'll probably send someone to bring the tailor to us if I explain to them how it will help Draga."

"I don't know," Nihudian replied.

They drove down the main street, but the shops appeared to be closed. Some were boarded up. "I guess we can ask at the Army headquarters," Nihudian said, and eased his car into a space in front of the old Sokolaz Hotel next to the Army building.

Kevin was feeling more confident as he got out of the car. Rather than worrying about the authorities, he would just go directly to them. This way, if there were any registration requirements or the like, he would simply be informed about them.

Nihudian walked tentatively behind Kevin as they entered the building.

A man in a green camouflage uniform greeted them in the lobby.

"Kevin Anderson," Kevin said, shaking the man's hand. "I'm the lawyer for Dragoljub Zaric in The Hague. I was hoping someone could help us get some information for our defense case."

Nihudian quickly translated as the soldier's puzzled expression disappeared. The soldier went into an office and returned a minute later. "Wait here," he said in Serbian.

Kevin felt confident that this was the best approach to take and that they would gain the cooperation of the Bosnian Serb Army. He heard footsteps from the stairs in front of him and saw a bald-headed man in an Army uniform walking briskly down the stairs flanked by two other soldiers a half step behind him.

The man walked up to Kevin and said something in Serbian. Nihudian translated. "He wants to see some identification."

Kevin took out his and Nihudian's appointment papers from the Tribunal. He handed them to the man. The man looked at them briefly and threw them on the ground. He yelled something at Nihudian.

"He can't read these papers in English," Nihudian said. "He wants to see our passports."

Kevin pulled out his American passport and Nihudian produced his Bosnian driver's license. The man looked at Nihudian's license. "A Turk?" the man asked scornfully. He said something in Serbian that Nihudian did not translate.

He looked at Kevin's passport, then barked a command to the two soldiers with him. One man grabbed Kevin's arm and the other Nihudian's and began leading them toward the front door.

"What's going on?" Kevin asked.

The man unleashed a tirade in Serbian. "He says he has no knowledge of this and we are to be put in a cell until he finds out what this is all about," Nihudian translated.

"Oh, for Christ sake. Tell him to get someone to read these papers to him."

Nihudian tried to speak to the man, but he and Kevin were hustled out the door. The soldiers led them next door to a small police station. They spoke to the police officer at the desk, who handed them a set of keys. The soldiers led Kevin and Nihudian behind some bars, down a hallway, and finally opened a steel door with one of the keys. One soldier told Nihudian to get inside and locked the door. At the next cell, the officer threw Kevin inside and slammed the door behind him.

Kevin found himself in a small stone cell with only a bench attached to one wall. But he did not feel as frightened as he had been at the police station in Sarajevo. He was, after all, working for one of the Serbs. Once the Army guy verified this, Kevin felt confident that they would help him, or at the worst send them on their way back to Sarajevo. Kevin wished he had thought fast enough to tell the officer that he could call Zoran Vacinovic at the Embassy in The Hague for verification.

Kevin walked over to the wall nearest to Nihudian's cell. "Nihudian," he called. "Can you hear me?"

"Yes," Nihudian replied. The sound was muffled, but audible.

"I'm really sorry about this. But I think it will get straightened out."

Nihudian was silent for a moment. "I hope so."

Kevin sat on the bench, suddenly feeling tired. What a day! They had been arrested by two separate governments. But if he could just get the information from the tailor, he could go home in the morning and it would all be worth it.

Kevin waited for about thirty minutes, making small talk with Nihudian through the wall from time to time. Then he heard voices in the corridor and the jingle of keys. He walked over to the door and could see some soldiers opening Nihudian's cell. Kevin stepped back, expecting his to be opened as well.

He heard sounds of the officers raised voices saying something in Serbian, then heard Nihudian cry out. Kevin felt a wave of panic as he heard a thumping noise and Nihudian shouting and moaning.

"Hey," Kevin yelled. "What's going on? Leave him alone! We work for Draga."

Kevin had a feeling of helplessness as the shouting and moaning continued. He banged on his door and yelled for the soldiers. They were probably coming for him next, he thought, and he began to get scared. Would he be able to survive their beating?

After what seemed like an eternity, there was an eerie silence from the next cell. Kevin looked out his window and saw some of the soldiers backing out of Nihudian's cell. Then, a single shot rang out like a firecracker exploding.

"Oh my God!" Kevin cried.

His heart was racing as he saw the soldiers come out of Nihudian's cell. They pointed in the direction of Kevin's cell, and spoke among themselves. Then, they turned around and headed in the other direction, leaving Nihudian's cell door open.

"Nihudian!" Kevin yelled racing to the wall separating their cells. He called Nihudian's name several times, and put his ear to the stone wall, but could hear no reply.

Kevin paced around his cell. His first instinct was to bang on his cell door, but he decided that calling the soldiers to his cell was not a good idea. His shirt was soaked with sweat as he paced around the cell, alternately looking out the window of the door and calling Nihudian's name.

Kevin heard nothing for the next five hours. He was exhausted with worry for Nihudian. Had the men taken Nihudian out of his cell without Kevin seeing it, or had they shot and killed him? Kevin prayed that Nihudian was alive.

Finally, Kevin's cell door was opened before Kevin even heard anyone approaching. A tall, handsome soldier with neatly combed dark hair appeared alone in the doorway. Kevin jumped up from his bench.

"Mr. Anderson," the officer said. "I am Major Nikolic, the Corps Communication officer. I speak English, so they called me down here to speak with you."

Kevin let out a breath and relaxed a bit. The man did not look like he was about to beat Kevin. "What's going on? What happened to my interpreter?" Kevin asked.

"You were very foolish to show up here without making arrangements. The Corps Commander is very upset."

"I'm sorry. I thought the Army would be able to help Draga. I was in a hurry because I have to return to The Hague in the morning. Where's my interpreter?"

Major Nikolic ignored the question. "I've translated your documents for the Commander. We've determined that you are Draga's lawyer, but we cannot help you. You will need to leave here immediately."

The major handed Kevin the documents from the Tribunal.

"Okay," Kevin said, taking the papers. "I'm very sorry."

Major Nikolic handed Kevin a set of keys. "Here are the keys to your car." He turned and walked out of the cell.

"But what about my interpreter?" Kevin asked as he followed the Major out of his cell. "Where is he?"

"I'm afraid there has been a misunderstanding," Major Nikolic replied as he walked down the corridor past Nihudian's cell.

Kevin followed, and then looked inside the cell.

Nihudian lay on the floor in a pool of blood.

Kevin ran into Nihudian's cell. He knelt down by Nihudian's head and looked at his face. It was chalky white and lifeless. "Nihudian!" He reached for his arm to check his pulse. There was no pulse.

Kevin's body shook as he put his head in his hands.

"You've <u>killed</u> him!"

"It was an unfortunate mistake," Major Nikolic said from the corridor. "I assure you that those involved will be severely punished."

Kevin looked numbly at the smooth-talking Major. He was too shocked to speak at that moment, and his brain was processing a flurry of thoughts at once.

"I can identify the men who did this," Kevin finally said. "I saw them."

"That won't be necessary. We'll be conducting a full investigation, and we will notify the family of the deceased immediately. I am sorry."

Kevin stood, and walked numbly out of the building.

Although he would not remember the drive, he somehow found his way to the Sarajevo airport and took the first flight out for The Netherlands.

CHAPTER 14

▼

At home, Diane insisted in desperation that Kevin quit the case.

After Nihudian's death, he felt as if he was in a constant daze. He had been the one who insisted on going to Sokolaz, despite Nihudian's reservations. Now, because of him, two little girls in Sarajevo had lost their father. While Kevin didn't have the will to resist Diane's stance, neither did he do anything to take himself off the case. He was stuck in limbo, as if he had become a numb caricature of whom he had once been.

Slowly, after a few days and some long jogs through the Wassenaar dunes, Kevin's instinct to fight began coming back. If he quit now, Nihudian's death would have been for nothing. Even if he lost, at least if he saw Draga's case through, he would vindicate the principle that even war criminals should receive a vigorous and effective defense. A Muslim man had died while trying to obtain favorable evidence for an accused at the Tribunal. The least he could do, Kevin decided, was to continue the pursuit of that evidence.

"I'm going to stay on as Draga's lawyer," he finally told Diane. He explained his reasoning as she recoiled with fear. "But I promise I'll never set foot in Bosnia again."

If she was relieved in the slightest, Diane didn't let on.

Kevin decided to try to get his hands on a list of the bona fide Black Dragons who were trained and enrolled under Draga's command. Under the Tribunal's rules of superior responsibility, if Kevin could prove that a crime was committed by someone impersonating a Black Dragon, Draga could not be held responsible for that crime. Kevin needed a roster of the Black Dragons to look for the name

Victor Vidic and other persons who had been identified as having committed war crimes.

He wrote Bradford Stone, but received a sharp reply that they had no such list.

Draga was sorry about Nihudian, but when Kevin asked him about the existence of such a list, his client was steadfast in not wanting to participate in his defense.

Kevin next asked Zoran Vacinovic, but Vacinovic said his government wouldn't serve up lists of its citizens that the prosecution might use to indict people for war crimes.

Kevin found the entire scenario unbelievably frustrating. In the U.S. Attorney's office, he could get his hands on a document by having an FBI agent serve a subpoena. As a defense lawyer, he was reduced to begging, and still he couldn't get what he needed.

That night, Kevin helped Ellen pack her suitcase for their long-planned Christmas visit to California. "Guess what?" he said casually. "What you said about people dressing up like the Black Dragons is coming true." He told her about what the former judge had said.

Ellen was proud. "You ought to listen to me more often, Daddy. I'll solve your cases for you."

"Well, solve this for me, Ms. Detective," said Kevin, sitting down on the edge of her bed. "How do I get a list of real Dragons to prove that the people who committed the war crimes are not on that list and therefore were not under Draga's command?"

"What are the choices?" Ellen always wanted her problems to be multiple choice.

"Number one, we get it from Draga. Number two, we get it from the Serbian government. Number three, we get it from the prosecution. But they've all said no."

"Elementary, my dear Daddy," Ellen said. "I choose number four."

"But there's no number four."

"Think outside the box, dude," Ellen said, giggling. "That's what you tell me."

"You're a big help, Sherlock. Here's your fee." Kevin reached over and tickled Ellen on her sides. She convulsed with laughter and scampered away.

Think outside the box. Good advice, Kevin mused.

It made him think of his old friend and former colleague, Bud Marcello, who had survived a long career in the bureaucratic FBI by doing just that—again and again.

*   *   *   *

Two days later, Kevin was lunching with Bud Marcello at Mac's in Santa Rosa.

"I still can't picture you as a defense lawyer, Kevin."

"It's not exactly what I had in mind either," Kevin admitted as he sipped a Diet Coke. "I never knew dealing with a client could be so difficult. I wish Draga would help with his defense. Some clients want to help too much, but this guy won't help one bit."

Bud was amused. "He wants to be a martyr. That's his choice. At least he can't complain about the outcome."

"I just can't play to lose. It's not my nature. Plus, I'm not convinced he did what he's charged with."

"Oh, an innocent client," Bud said, laughing. "You've turned into a real true believer, old buddy."

"That Tribunal is a prosecutor's dream. They hold all the cards. They almost put me in jail. Can you believe that? Then I filed a motion for intelligence agency files on my client and they pretended it never existed. Vanished, even though I had a file-stamped copy. It makes me think somebody is hiding something. I've been thinking that if I could get my hands on the CIA's records, they might have a list of men under Draga's command."

"That could break either way for your client, you know?"

"Yeah, well, right now I'm willing to take the chance."

Kevin had been edging up on something, but he let Bud take the lead.

"Hey, remember that lady and her husband who worked for the CIA and were convicted of selling information to the Russians? Andrew and Maria Jones."

"Sure do."

"You know, I handled a lot of the interviews with them."

Kevin <u>did</u> know. He had remembered somewhere over the Atlantic Ocean on the flight to San Francisco about Bud's involvement in the espionage case, wherein the Jones couple had eventually cooperated with the government in exchange for lighter sentences. Even in instances involving CIA officers, the FBI had jurisdiction to investigate criminal prosecutions of U.S. espionage laws.

"Maria is okay. She's Italian, you know?"

"A real <u>pisano</u>, huh?" Kevin grinned.

"She found herself in some stuff that was mostly Andrew's doing—that guy I did <u>not</u> like—and she went along for the ride. Anyway, she's doing her time at the federal joint in Pleasanton. Go see her and tell her ole Bud says howdy."

"It's worth a try," Kevin said, smiling inwardly, thinking: <u>How many retired FBI agents would consider a convicted CIA spy "okay."</u> Bud Marcello was one of a kind.

Bud took out his pen and wrote something in Italian on his napkin. "Show this to Maria." He handed Kevin the napkin. "In the meantime, I'll make some calls."

The next morning, Kevin drove to the women's prison and was led into a conference room near the warden's office. The prison resembled a college campus, except for the towering barbed wire fences that surrounded the facility. The inmates were allowed to roam freely within the fences, and after a few minutes, Maria Jones opened the door to the conference room and entered unescorted.

"Ms. Jones, I'm Kevin Anderson," Kevin said offering his hand.

Maria Jones shook Kevin's hand. "I was expecting you."

"That's good. A mutual friend asked me to show you this." He pulled out Bud's napkin.

Maria picked it up and read the note. She was a small, thin woman, who looked to be in her early forties. Her dark black hair was streaked with gray and pulled back in a bun. Her skin looked wrinkled and her eyes tired.

Kevin expected Maria to be cautious. She had received a twenty-year sentence, and Kevin figured that, like most inmates, she still clung to some hope of getting out earlier, either by cooperating further with the government or by filing post-conviction legal challenges. What he was asking her to do now did not fall into either category.

Maria smiled warmly. "Your friend has been good to my family since I have been in here. I'd like to pay him back by helping you if I can."

"I'd sure appreciate any help you can give me," Kevin replied, wondering what Bud had been up to with Maria's family, and if the Bureau had known about it. "It would be confidential. Obviously, you're not going to be a witness in my case. I'm trying to locate a list of men fighting in a paramilitary unit called the Black Dragons in the war in Bosnia. I represent the commander of that unit. They called him Draga."

Maria Jones' eyes widened. "You represent Draga?"

"Yes. So, you know about him?"

Maria ignored the question. "Has he told you what he did during the war?"

"Well, no. That's the problem. He isn't cooperating in his defense. He loves to talk about American football and eat pizza, but he hasn't told me a thing about his case."

Maria nodded understandingly. She was silent for a while.

"What do you know about Draga?" Kevin asked, practically holding his breath.

"I was in the unit that coordinated intelligence information on Yugoslavia. I know a lot about Dragoljub Zaric."

"Do you know where I could find a list of the Black Dragons under his command? There apparently were people in Bosnia going around committing war crimes pretending to be members of the Black Dragons. Those crimes are going to be hung around Draga's neck unless I can prove they were committed by people not under his command."

"So you really don't know." Maria put her hands together and brought them to her lips. She was obviously thinking of something, but Kevin couldn't seem to get it out of her.

"What don't I know?"

Maria looked down at the napkin in her hand. "This could get me in a lot of trouble, Mr. Anderson."

Kevin was perplexed. He decided to remain silent and see what Maria Jones would do.

She wrung her hands. "Your client was the most significant operative the CIA had in Yugoslavia," she said finally.

"What do you mean?"

"Draga worked for the CIA. He passed on the best intelligence information we had on the war and on President Milosevic."

Kevin couldn't believe what he was hearing. "How do you know that?"

"I read the reports of his handler, William Evans. That was my main job for three years at the CIA."

"I'm speechless," Kevin said after a long pause. "My client has never even hinted at such a thing."

"The Agency probably promised to take care of him when his trial is over. They did the same to my husband and me. Then they gave him life and me twenty years."

Kevin's brain was working overtime to digest this new revelation. Then, reality set in. "I'll never be able to prove it," he said dejectedly.

"Yes, you will," Maria said, looking Kevin directly in the eyes. "I kept copies of the reports."

A shiver ran through Kevin's body.

"My mother has them. She lives in Oakland." Maria wrote her mother's address on Bud's napkin, along with a short note. "She'll give you the papers. You might also want to talk to William Evans. He retired. I think he works for Hilton Hotels now, in security."

Kevin thanked Maria profusely. His mind was racing as he drove directly to Oakland to see Maria's mother. If what Maria told him was true—and he had no doubt that it was—how would this impact his defense of Draga? In passing vital information to the CIA, had Draga been working to prevent war crimes, not commit them? Could his first client as a defense lawyer really have been on the side of the good guys?

Kevin wondered why Draga hadn't told him of the CIA connection. Was he willing to sit silently in prison for the rest of his life? Or had the CIA promised Draga his freedom, as Maria, who knew about these things, had strongly suggested?

As he drove on the freeway, Kevin suddenly wondered if he was being followed. The prison authorities could have notified the CIA of his visit to Maria Jones. They could have even bugged the conference room at the prison.

Kevin got off at the next exit. He checked his rearview mirror; three other cars were also exiting. He waited at the red light at the bottom of the exit ramp. When the light turned green, he continued straight ahead and re-entered the freeway. He looked to see if any of the other cars were doing the same maneuver. They were not.

Although he was still not sure if he was being followed, Kevin was anxious to see Maria's mother as soon as possible. He wanted to get his hands on the reports before they disappeared like his graymail motion had vanished into thin air.

As he exited the freeway again and approached what he thought was the right street, Kevin decided to once again be cautious. He circled a few blocks, and then stopped to look at his map. He did not see anyone following him.

Maria said her parents had moved to Oakland from the East Coast after her imprisonment. Kevin could see they were living in a multi-ethnic, poor neighborhood of single-family homes. If the whites, blacks, and Hispanics ever started fighting each other in the United States like the Muslims, Serbs, and Croats had in Bosnia, this neighborhood would be ground zero.

Kevin passed the house. It was a white, wooden single-story house with a small lawn in front. There was an old Chevrolet Impala parked in the driveway. The house needed a paint job, but the lawn was immaculate and was landscaped with nicely kept bushes. Around the yard was a chain-link fence. In this neighborhood, by necessity, all the houses were well fortified with security bars on many windows and doors.

After circling the block and not seeing anyone following him, Kevin parked. He opened the chain-link gate and walked up a few steps to the front door. The screen door was closed, but the inside door was open.

"Hello," he called, "is anybody home?"

There was no answer. Kevin called again. There was still no answer. A feeling of dread crept over Kevin. People did not leave their front doors open in this neighborhood. Had someone been here before him? He rang the bell. No one came to the door. Kevin thought about calling 911 on his cell phone, but decided to walk around to the back of the house. He slowly backed down the steps and followed the driveway along side of the house. When he reached the back yard, he saw a woman tending to some plants.

She had apparently not heard his calls or the front doorbell.

"Excuse me," Kevin said from the edge of the yard.

The woman looked up. She was a stout woman with a wide, pleasant face. She looked to be in her seventies, and her brown hair was neatly in place. When she saw Kevin, she put down her pruning shears and walked over to him.

Kevin did not wait for her to speak. "I'm sorry to bother you. I'm Kevin Anderson, a lawyer from Santa Rosa. I've just come from visiting your daughter, Maria, and she asked me to come here and give you this." He pulled out the napkin and displayed it for the woman to see.

The woman looked surprised at the mention of her daughter. She took the napkin. "I need my glasses. Come on in." She led Kevin into the house through the back door.

Kevin found himself in a small kitchen with a wooden table placed against the back window overlooking the yard. "Sit down. Can I offer you a cup of coffee?"

"Oh, no thanks."

"How about some tea, or milk? I've got some soda, or even some wine."

"I'll take a soda, thank you."

Kevin looked around the kitchen. He saw the refrigerator, filled with photos held up by magnets. He had come to believe that you could tell a lot about a family by looking at what was posted on the refrigerator. From his seat at the table, Kevin saw pictures of a large Italian family, and several pictures of Maria in happier and younger days. He saw none of Maria's husband.

"I'm sorry, I don't know your name," Kevin said as Maria's mother came back to the table carrying a pair of eyeglasses and a glass of cola.

"Alice. Alice Mancini."

"It's nice to meet you. And thank you for welcoming me into your home."

"We don't get many visitors. All our family except Maria is back East."

Alice put on her glasses and read the napkin. On one side, she read Bud's note to Maria, and on the other, Maria's note to her. "This scares me. Maria has never asked me to get her papers before. I wish I could discuss this with my husband."

"Where is your husband?"

"He died two months ago."

"I'm sorry. I—didn't know."

Alice studied the napkin. "I will honor my daughter's wishes."

"Thank you so much."

Kevin waited at the kitchen table while Alice headed toward the front of the house. When she returned, she carried two shopping bags, which she put on the table.

Kevin reached inside one bag and pulled out a large mailing envelope. Inside the envelope was a four-inch stack of papers. Kevin started looking through them.

Inside the second bag, Kevin found the mother lode. There were about thirty reports from William Evans. Kevin flipped through the reports quickly. They were dated from 1992 through 1995, and contained information from Draga about upcoming military actions in which the Black Dragons would be participating. There were also reports from Draga of meetings he had with President Milosevic and others in the Yugoslavian government.

Reading this material gave Kevin goose bumps. He was holding dynamite in his hands. The information in these reports might not only clear Draga of war crimes, but could prove that President Milosevic was the one giving the orders to the Bosnian Serbs in the war in Bosnia. The U.S. government might also be badly damaged by these reports. They showed that it knew of the attacks on cities and towns in Bosnia before they happened, and had done nothing to prevent the thousands of deaths that followed.

Kevin could not contain his excitement. "This is the best Christmas present I've ever gotten. I'm going to take these and copy them right away. I'll have them back to you in an hour."

Kevin strode quickly from the house, the shopping bags tucked under his arms. He got in his car and drove to downtown Oakland, where he knew of a 24-hour copy center. It was rush hour, and Kevin found himself crawling along city streets. He looked in the rearview mirror. There were no signs that he was being followed. If someone had been following, Kevin suspected they would not have let these documents get into his hands in the first place.

At the copy center, Kevin made two sets of copies. He mailed one copy to himself in Holland just in case the other copy was somehow taken from him before he got there, or when he came through Customs. Kevin shook his head at the irony of his situation. Just a few months ago, as a federal prosecutor, he could show his credentials and be waved through Customs. Now, he was smuggling papers to avoid Customs agents.

When he left the copy center, Kevin saw a sports store featuring Oakland Raiders souvenirs. He decided to get a present for the #1 Raiders fan in The Hague. After this brief detour, Kevin returned the originals to Alice Mancini.

When Kevin arrived back in Santa Rosa, Diane and Ellen were not at the hotel. Kevin had hardly seen Ellen since they had arrived in California. She had so many sleepovers with her friends that she had not spent a single night at their hotel. Kevin sat down and studied the reports. He found one report that excited him. In 1992, Draga had furnished William Evans with a list of the Black Dragons. Unfortunately, the list had not been attached to any of the reports.

As he read over the reports, Kevin realized that he needed to find Evans. The man might be his star witness in The Hague. Kevin turned on his laptop computer and got on the Internet. After some searching, he found the Hilton Hotel Corporation website. He wondered whether he could locate an employee through the website. Hilton had thousands of employees. After searching the website, he came up with nothing.

A few minutes later, Diane and Ellen came into the room. "Hi, Daddy," Ellen said. When she saw the laptop, she asked, "Can I check my e-mail? My friends from Holland are probably wondering what I'm up to."

"Sure, I was finished anyway."

He watched as Ellen effortlessly accessed her e-mail, then squealed with delight as she read her messages from her friends. "Jennifer thinks she's getting a scooter for Christmas. And, Katie is going to Disney World."

Watching Ellen operate the computer with ease gave Kevin an idea. "Ellen, could you spend a minute being a detective again?"

"Sure, Dad."

"I need to try to find a William Evans who works for Hilton Hotels. I want to know what city he works in. How would I do that?"

"That's easy." Ellen turned back to the computer and typed in www.google.com. "This is a search engine. It searches all kinds of places on the Internet." She typed in the words "William Evans" and "Hilton".

Kevin stood, looking over Ellen's shoulders. Ellen scrolled down through several entries that appeared on the screen. Then she clicked on one of them. It was a newspaper article about the recent prosecution of a skimming operation at the casino of the Flamingo Hilton Hotel. The article said that Hilton's internal security staff, headed by William Evans, had uncovered the fraud.

"He's in Las Vegas, Dad," Ellen said matter-of-factly.

CHAPTER 15

▼

"Santa found me even in a hotel!" Ellen shouted.

She burst out of bed in their hotel room, flipped on the light, and looked at two wrapped Christmas presents at the foot of her bed. "Can I open them?"

Kevin looked at the clock radio on the night stand. It was 5:03 a.m. "Santa came early, it's still dark out. But go ahead and open them."

He and Diane struggled to clear their heads and open their eyes. They sat up in bed and watched Ellen attack the wrapping paper.

Her first present was a "Talk Girl" portable tape player. "This is great! Now, I can record messages in Holland and send them to my friends in Santa Rosa."

Ellen put the tape player aside and opened Santa's second present. The second gift was a "Password Diary." It was a journal for writing in, but to open it you had to say a password into the microphone on the side. It had voice recognition technology, so only the holder of the diary could get in, even if someone stole the password. Ellen was delighted. "I love it!" she squealed, hugging it to her chest.

Ellen tried out the diary right away.

Kevin was thankful that Santa had included batteries. He imagined himself driving around Santa Rosa at 5:30 a.m. on Christmas looking for a place that sold batteries. After Kevin, Diane, and Ellen opened their presents to each other, it was still early.

Kevin decided to jog up to Lake Ilsanjo in Annadel State Park. He started out fine, but found himself struggling once he got to the hills. He had been running in a flat country for the past six months, and he could definitely feel the difference. When he finally reached the lake at the top, Kevin's mind began working on how to approach William Evans in Las Vegas. He decided to get some advice from Bud Marcello.

Two days later, after getting Bud's input and assistance, Kevin flew to Las Vegas. When he arrived, he was met by two beefy escorts in a black Lincoln Town Car. A broad-shouldered, clean-cut young man, who looked like an NFL lineman, got out of the passenger's side. "You Kevin Anderson?"

"Yes."

"I'm Striker. Hop in." He held the door open.

Kevin got in the backseat. The driver turned around and said, "Nice to meet you, Mr. Anderson. I'm Jim Timmons from LST Security." He was about the same size as the passenger, which translated to huge and muscular.

Kevin knew from Bud that both escorts were former elite military and worked for CEOs and entertainers who paid top dollar for high-level security. Kevin did not have to pay for their services this morning—Bud had called it a "trade out." He hadn't asked what Bud would be trading back. He didn't want to know.

"Your man's at work this morning at the Las Vegas Hilton in the second floor security office," Timmons said as they headed down the Las Vegas Strip. "What do you want us to do?"

"I'd just like you guys to come in with me and wait in the reception area. I want Mr. Evans to see you, but I need to meet with him alone."

"Ten-four."

They drove to the front of the Hilton. The driver parked the car right in front of the hotel. Kevin saw him slip the bellman a bill. Greasing palms was the way business was done on the Strip.

As they took the escalator to the second floor, Kevin turned on the mini tape recorder he had brought in his jacket pocket, and spoke into it: "This is Kevin Anderson, today's date is December 27th, and I am in the Las Vegas Hilton Hotel to meet with William Evans, formerly of the CIA."

When they got to the suite of offices on the second floor of the Hilton, the three men approached the receptionist. "I'm Kevin Anderson. I'm here to see William Evans."

"Is he expecting you?"

"No, but something urgent came up and I need to see him as soon as possible."

The receptionist dialed a number on her telephone console. Kevin could hear her talking to Evans. She put the phone on her shoulder and looked at Kevin. "What is this regarding?"

"I'm afraid it's personal. It has to do with his previous employment."

The woman returned to the telephone and repeated what Kevin had said. Kevin hoped that he would not have to be more insistent. He was relieved when the receptionist hung up the phone and said, "Mr. Evans will be with you in a few moments."

Kevin stood between his two new friends as they waited for Evans to appear. In a few minutes, a short, tanned, gray-haired man came striding down the corridor from behind the receptionist. From a distance, Kevin quickly sized up William Evans; late 50's, former military, in shape, no-nonsense guy.

Evans looked at Kevin, dwarfed by his two companions.

"Mr. Evans, I'm Kevin Anderson. Thank you for seeing me without an appointment. I'm a lawyer from Santa Rosa, California, and I represent a friend of yours who is in trouble. Can I talk with you in private for a few minutes?"

Evans looked at the business card that Kevin handed him.

"Come into the conference room," Evans said, leading Kevin into a large room near the lobby.

Kevin's two escorts—who had given him a small radio-beam "panic button" to depress if he needed them immediately—remained by the receptionist.

Once inside the room, Kevin's eyes darted to a bank of closed-circuit televisions on one side of the room. The televisions monitored different locations on the casino floor.

Kevin and Evans sat down at a large table. "I represent a man you know as Draga. I was appointed to be his lawyer by the War Crimes Tribunal in The Hague."

Evans' face registered neither surprise nor recognition.

"He needs your help." Kevin paused and waited for Evans to speak.

The man's face was a mask. "I'm afraid I don't know what you're talking about." Evans denial came a bit too late, however, and was delivered without any hint of surprise.

Kevin wished he could have been videotaping their meeting.

"I don't have time to play cat and mouse. My client's trial starts the week after next. I want to show you some papers that I received."

Kevin took out copies of Evans' reports and placed them on the table.

Evans looked at the reports without saying a word. Beads of sweat began to form on his temple.

"Mr. Evans, my client risked his life for you and your agency. The least you can do is talk to me."

"Alright," Evans turned to Kevin. "I'll talk to you. Your client was the CIA's best asset in Yugoslavia. I know because I was his contact, as you can see. But you'll never get me to say that in court or anywhere else."

"Draga's going on trial for crimes that he is not responsible for. That's why I came to you. Can't something be done to help him?"

"He ran that risk from the beginning." Evans looked Kevin directly in the eyes. "I can't help him now."

"What about this?" Kevin pointed to the report that mentioned the list of Black Dragons. "Can you tell me where can I get a list of the members of the Black Dragons?"

Evans studied the report. "I don't know where you got these reports," he said, shaking his head, "but I'm sure as hell not going to help you get more."

Evans stood up. "I'm afraid that I've got another meeting. It was nice meeting you," he said, extending his hand mechanically. "Don't come back."

Kevin extended his hand, as well. In it was a subpoena.

"This is a subpoena for you to testify at Draga's trial, Mr. Evans. You have now officially been served. I had hoped that there was some other way you would help, but if not, this is what I have to do."

Evans' face reddened. "You're a dead man, Mr. Anderson."

Kevin's heartbeat quickened.

He followed Evans out the door into the lobby.

"Oh, Mr. Evans," Kevin took the tape recorder out of his pocket and held it up. "I'd be more careful about what I say in the future. Copies of your reports are already in the hands of someone I trust in the national news media. If anything happens to me, your picture will be on the cover of Time magazine."

Evans stormed toward his office as Kevin rejoined his two bodyguards. That last bit about the tape and the news media had been Bud's idea for keeping Kevin alive. The bodyguards were to get Kevin and his tape safely out of the hotel.

"Let's go, guys," said Kevin. "I think I hit a sensitive nerve."

The Lincoln pulled away from the Hilton with Kevin safely in the back seat, on his way to the airport. His heart was still beating rapidly from the excitement. He rewound the tape and played it.

To his relief, it had recorded perfectly, even the "you're-a-dead-man" part.

*   *   *   *

By the time he returned to Holland, Kevin was seeing his client in a new light. Whatever his combination of motives, Draga <u>had</u> been helping the good guys.

His first morning back, Kevin headed for the prison. When he got into the interview room, Draga looked happy to see him, then disappointed. "What, no food?"

"It's still breakfast time. The pizza places aren't open yet."

"I haven't had a good *pannekoeken* in months. You're letting me down."

Kevin pulled out the football results for the past three weeks. "I've got some more bad news for you. You owe me 40 more Euros. The Raiders lost two in a row."

Draga smiled. "The playoffs are coming."

Kevin shook his head. "Pretty soon you'll be saying 'Wait till next year!'"

"I've got this all figured out. You're doomed."

"I really need to talk to you about something important," Kevin said. He took out William Evans' reports and put them in front of Draga. "I want you to take a few minutes to look at these."

Draga looked down at the papers. He was silent. He began reading the first report, then flipped through the others. "What are these?" The bravado was gone from his voice.

"I think you know. These are reports of an American CIA agent named William Evans, who acknowledged to me that he was your handler."

Draga was silent—an admission to Kevin that the reports were true.

"I had a meeting with Evans when I was back in the United States. I'd like you to listen to our conversation.'"

Kevin took out the recorder, put the tape inside, and pushed the play button.

When the short tape finished, Kevin looked squarely into Draga's eyes. "I haven't asked you to trust me before, but I need you to trust me now. This information can make a huge difference at your trial. The war crimes law makes a commander liable for the actions of his men only where he did not try to prevent the crimes from occurring. You're not guilty of anything if you in fact tried to alert the CIA in advance. I don't know what your plan is, but if you think that the CIA is somehow quietly going to get you out of all this—after you're convicted—I think you are making a big mistake."

"The Tribunal is not going to let me go no matter what proof we have," Draga said finally. "All this will do is get me and my family killed."

Kevin took a deep breath. A crack in Draga's wall had emerged. "I'm not going to use this information without your approval. I promise you that. But if we don't use it at your trial, you'll probably spend the rest of your life in prison."

Draga looked pained. "They have taken care of me before. I have no choice but to trust them now."

"Do you have any promises from them in writing?"

"Of course not."

"What is their promise?"

Draga hesitated. "Someone from the CIA came here to see me shortly after I was arrested."

"Name?"

"Pete Barnes. He said after I'm found guilty, I'm to be transferred to the U.S. to serve my sentence. One day, they announce I've been killed in prison. They take me out of there and relocate me and my family somewhere else."

Kevin thought that over. "What if they don't keep their word? Or what if they can't put all that in motion? What then?"

"I have to trust them. I have no other choice."

"Yes, you do have a choice. You can help me win your acquittal."

Draga looked at Kevin as if seeing him for the first time.

"In my twenty years in federal law enforcement," Kevin went on, "I've never seen the CIA spring anyone from a prison in the United States."

Draga exhaled. "What do you suggest?"

"My first instinct is to run into court with this and tell everyone you're innocent."

"That'll get me killed for sure."

"What do you suggest?"

"Maybe we can use these reports, and this tape, as a bargaining chip to get me some kind of written guarantee that I will be cut loose."

"The CIA won't sign something like that. They know a copy will end up at the Washington Post. No, I think we should bring this out in court, maybe in a closed session. It would be a huge embarrassment to the U.S. government if it is revealed that they had advance knowledge of attacks in Bosnia and did nothing to prevent them."

"You're still really naive, Kevin. I don't trust these people at the Tribunal. They'll cover it up. I'd rather try to get something in writing from the CIA, and be found guilty."

"But you're <u>not</u> guilty. It's not right for you to be convicted for something you are not responsible for."

"What are our chances of winning the trial with the CIA information?"

"Truthfully, I don't know" Kevin replied. "The judges are expected to find you guilty. That's the norm in the Tribunal, and you're one of their biggest prizes. But if the truth came out, I'd like to think they would do the right thing."

"What are our chances of winning the trial without it?"

"Right now, close to zero. Those odds might improve if I can get my hands on the roster of Black Dragons."

Kevin and Draga's eyes locked. Kevin wondered if his ego was getting in the way. He wanted to win. "We need to really think this through," Kevin said. "I promise I won't use this without your permission. I don't want you worrying about that."

"I trust you, Kevin."

Kevin glowed when he heard Draga say those words. "How about helping me get the roster of the real Black Dragons for starters?"

Draga was silent for a minute. "Wait here." He waved to the camera, signaling for the guards. Kevin got up as well. When the guard came, Draga said, "I need to get some legal materials from my room for my lawyer."

Kevin was pleased. He hoped Draga wasn't going to get the sports section.

When Draga returned he handed Kevin a stack of papers. It was a computerized list, in alphabetical order, of the names and dates of birth of all of the Black Dragons.

"This is the same list I gave to Evans a long time ago."

Kevin looked through the list. He did not see Victor Vidic or any other names that he recognized as having committed war crimes.

"Thank you," Kevin said. "This means a lot."

Draga took a deep breath. "I guess we have crossed a bridge today."

Kevin nodded. "Yes. I've been hoping for this since the day we met."

Draga nodded. "Do I still get pepperoni pizza?"

"You bet. But there's no way I'm forgiving your gambling debts."

Draga's face broke into a grin. "What do we do next?"

"Well, I imagine that we'll be hearing from the CIA. Why don't I see if they'll put your deal in writing so you can make them honor it down the road, if that's what you want to go for."

"That's what I want to do. Getting the deal in writing would be very good."

"I don't like the idea of an innocent man being found guilty."

"Do you like the idea of an innocent man being found dead?"

"No."

Draga got up from his chair. "You've been pretty lucky at football, sport. Let's see how you play hardball."

CHAPTER 16

▼

That night, Kevin and Diane walked down the street to pick up Ellen at her friend's house. She was not exactly happy to see them. "Can't I play longer? Why do you always come on time? Don't you know what it means to be fashionably late?"

Kevin brushed off the cool welcome. "I'm glad you're having such a good time, but I haven't seen you all day."

"I haven't seen Katie for two weeks," Ellen protested as she came outside to walk home with Kevin and Diane.

Ellen soon forgot her complaint. "I'm going to listen to Harry Potter," she said as she walked between Kevin and Diane. "I've been dying to start the tapes since Christmas." She had gotten the four Harry Potter stories on tape for Christmas.

If the CIA decides to bug our house, Kevin thought, they're going to get an earful of Harry Potter.

It was dark when the Andersons turned onto their street and walked the last block to their house. Kevin heard a car come up from behind and was startled when it slowed to a stop along side him and his family. The car was a large dark colored Mercedes and appeared to be occupied by only the driver. Kevin squinted to make out the driver's face. Diane had stopped, grabbed Ellen by the hand, and pulled Ellen towards her.

"Mr. Anderson." Kevin recognized the man now. It was Zoran Vacinovic. "I was in the neighborhood. Do you have a few minutes?"

"Sure. Why don't you park your car and come in?"

Vacinovic pulled over to the curb while Kevin rejoined Diane and Ellen.

"It's the man from the Serbian Embassy. I need to talk to him."

"He's always 'just in the neighborhood,'" Diane noted skeptically.

Vacinovic patted Ellen on the head when they all walked into the Anderson's row house. "Please excuse the interruption on your time with your father."

"That's okay," she replied brightly. "I'm going to start listening to my Harry Potter tapes anyway."

Kevin led Vacinovic up to his office on the second floor, while Ellen and Diane stayed downstairs.

"That's quite a girl. You must be very proud of her."

"I am." Kevin closed the door. "What's on your mind?"

"I just wanted to talk to you before the trial started next week. As I have told you, it is very important to my country that a full record be made of the atrocities committed against the Serbs."

"But, Mr. Vacinovic," Kevin replied, "there is no way the court will allow me to introduce evidence of war crimes against Serbs to justify war crimes that they committed in return. The Tribunal has already specifically rejected this defense. An eye for an eye may have been the law on the battlefields of Bosnia, but it is not the law in the courtrooms of The Hague."

"They just want to trick you into playing by their rules. But in the court of public opinion, the atrocities committed against the Serbs over many years more than justify what was done. That is how Draga should be defended."

Kevin could see that Vacinovic was agitated. "My government views these trials at the Tribunal in a broader context. The West is trying to create a historical record that will condemn the Serbs for the rest of history. That record must be set straight through evidence of the wrongs done to the Serbian people."

"How can I do that when the Tribunal will refuse to hear that evidence?"

"Look," Vacinovic said, opening his briefcase, "some of the people in the Justice Ministry in Belgrade have drafted an opening statement for you to use." He handed Kevin some papers.

Kevin took the papers and began reading them. They were full of anti-Muslim and Croat rhetoric, with references to the Ottoman Empire and World War II. There was not a single mention of Draga. As he read the statement, Kevin tried to think of how he was going to handle this diplomatically. "I appreciate all the work that went into this."

Vacinovic smiled.

"But I can't use it."

The smile disappeared from Vacinovic's face. "Why not?"

"Because it's irrelevant at the Tribunal. I understand your government wanting to present their side of the story, but this is not a United Nations debate. It's a criminal trial. I'm defending a human being, whose freedom hangs in the balance. I have to try to win within the rules of the Tribunal. Otherwise, I'd be violating my duty to my client."

Vacinovic raised his hand to his head in exasperation. He stared at Kevin. "Mr. Anderson, I would think this over very carefully if I were you. A lot of people will be watching your opening statement and how you handle yourself in this case. I wouldn't want the wrong people in my country angry with you."

Kevin got up to end the conversation. "Well, you are a smart man, Mr. Vacinovic. You understand my problem. I will leave it to you to educate those in your government who don't. Good night."

He led Vacinovic downstairs. When they reached the door, Kevin opened it for Vacinovic.

"Say goodbye to your lovely daughter for me."

The next day, Kevin planned his cross-examination for the first few witnesses. The prosecution would begin its case with background testimony from academics and military personnel who had studied the war in Bosnia.

Kevin was interrupted by a long-distance call from Bud Marcello. "I have bad news. Maria Jones was put in solitary confinement."

"Damn," Kevin said. "I feel terrible."

"Just be careful, Kevin. You've got some people stirred up, I'm sure."

"I haven't heard from them yet."

"You will," Bud predicted.

Two more days passed. Kevin wondered if he would hear from the CIA, or if he would have to try and contact them. On the Friday before the trial started, he went out for his wet, early morning run on the streets of Wassenaar. He heard another runner behind him.

"<u>Goedemorgen</u>," Kevin said, giving his standard Dutch greeting to those he encountered in the morning.

"Good morning, Mr. Anderson," the man replied in English.

Looking at the man, Kevin kept his stride as he put his left hand inside his jacket pocket. Even on this main street in Wassenaar, they were alone in the dark at six o'clock in the morning. Kevin realized that he could be killed here quite easily. He hoped that the man just wanted to talk.

"Not too many of us early morning runners," Kevin observed.

The man was wearing a baseball cap and a striped jogging suit. "I'm Pete Barnes," he said. "Do you know who I work for?"

"Yes. You're the CIA officer who called on my client."

"You've got a great reputation in San Francisco. First class prosecutor, straight shooter."

"That's nice to hear."

"So you're not going to give us any trouble over those reports are you?"

"Not at all."

"We need them back, and the tape you made with Mr. Evans."

"What are you going to do for my client?"

"Exactly what I told him we'd do. Relocate him and his family after the trial."

"Do the prosecutors at the Tribunal know what Draga did for your agency?"

"I don't know. They wouldn't care anyway. He's their big trophy. They want to nail him."

"So how are you going to deliver on your promise to get Draga to serve his time in the U.S. and spring him from prison?"

"We have our ways. Don't sweat it."

Kevin kept running. He came to an intersection. "Mind if we make a left here? If we don't turn around, I'll be too tired to make it home."

Barnes was matching Kevin step for step. He was not laboring at all.

The men turned left and continued their conversation. They looked like two friends out for a morning jog.

"I'm a defense lawyer now," Kevin said. "It's my job to sweat this kind of stuff for my clients. If you put it in writing for Draga, you can have the materials. You can understand that without something in writing, your promise to him can't be enforced, or even proven."

"That's out of the question. We can't put anything like that in writing. You know that."

"We would only use it if you didn't keep your promise. Otherwise, I'm going to tell the judges all about Draga's role in my opening statement on Monday."

"The Serbs will consider your client a traitor if this comes out. He and his family will be killed. You wouldn't be that irresponsible."

"I thought it was your job to protect your informants. If you won't, my client is prepared to protect himself and his family. But I'm sure as hell not going to let him go down for a life sentence without fighting with everything I've got."

Barnes looked over at Kevin. Water dripped down from the bill of his cap. "I hate running in the rain," Barnes said.

"So do I, but in the Dutch winter, if you wait for a clear day, you wouldn't be running much."

"What's it going to take to get you not to use this stuff?"

"A promise to Draga in writing."

"What's your second choice?"

"I don't have a second choice. Give me a suggestion."

"We're really not in a position to do anything."

"Then, how do I know you'll be in a position to keep your oral promise to my client?"

"He'll have to trust us. We've always been square with him before. We've already sprung him from prison once—in Germany."

"I was a federal prosecutor for twenty years. I've never seen you guys spring anyone from a federal prison in the U.S."

"It's no problem."

"I'll tell you what. You get Maria Jones out of solitary confinement at Pleasanton before Monday, and I won't use the material in my opening statement. Then we'll talk again next week."

"I don't think we can do that."

"Then you sure as heck can't set up an escape for Draga."

Barnes was silent. They had just about reached Kevin's house.

"I've got to go," Kevin said. "The ball's in your court." He turned down the path to his house, opened his front door, and entered without looking back.

When he shut the door behind him, Kevin took off his wet Gore-Tex running jacket. He reached into the left pocket and turned off the tape recorder, then hit the rewind switch.

His tape collection was growing.

CHAPTER 17

▼

"All rise! *Veuillez vous lever.*"

The gallery for Courtroom 1 was packed for the start of Draga's trial. As he looked out to the other side of the glass, Kevin saw correspondents for the major television networks sitting in the press section. The public gallery was also packed.

"Prosecutor against Dragoljub Zaric, case number IT-96-30," the Deputy Registrar bellowed. "Counsel, your appearances, please."

"Charles Oswald and Bradford Stone for the Prosecution." Kevin looked over to the prosecution side of the courtroom. Their investigator, Allen Jacobson, and a paralegal flanked Oswald and Stone. Three more assistants sat in the row behind them.

Kevin stood up in his black robe. "Kevin Anderson for the accused." He sat alone at the defense table. Behind him, Draga was in his chair, wearing a bored expression and the Oakland Raiders jogging suit Kevin had brought back as his Christmas present.

"Good morning," Judge Orozco said pleasantly.

Judge Linares smiled and nodded to both sides. Judge Davidson stared straight ahead.

"Is the prosecution ready for trial?" asked Judge Orozco.

"Yes, Your Honor."

She turned to Kevin on her right. "And the defense?"

"We're ready, Your Honor."

"Very well," Judge Orozco looked pleased that there had been no last minute glitches. "Let's hear the opening statement for the prosecution."

Bradford Stone rose from his seat and took his place at the podium. "Your Honors," he began, "the evidence during this trial will show that the man seated at the far left of the courtroom, Dragoljub Zaric, known as Draga, is responsible for the murder of thousands of people, and the beating, torture, and rape of thousands more."

Stone pointed his bony finger at Draga. "The evidence will show that this man selected, trained, motivated, and commanded a group of vicious killers known as the Black Dragons, and that he and his men marched through Bosnia like a tornado, killing and destroying everything in their path."

Kevin noticed that the press in the gallery were furiously scribbling as Stone colorfully described the prosecution's case. But, strangely, Kevin felt relaxed. The trial was underway; he was at last on his turf.

Kevin had spoken with Bud Marcello yesterday. Maria Jones had indeed been released from solitary confinement. Kevin had also had a long talk with Draga last night. They had agreed that Kevin would make no mention of the CIA evidence, at least until the prosecution had rested its case. In the meantime, Kevin would work on getting the CIA's promise to Draga in writing.

Bradford Stone's opening statement lasted most of the first day. His assistants placed large color-coded maps and charts on the easel as Stone painstakingly detailed all of the locations in Bosnia where the Black Dragons had struck. Three scale models of the Omarska, Foca, and Keraterm prison camps sat on tables in the well of the courtroom, in front of the Deputy Registrar and usher. Stone pointed out the buildings in the camps where Black Dragons had called out prisoners for beatings, torture, and rape.

It was 3:45 when Stone finally sat down to the nods and polite accolades of the other members of the prosecution team.

Judge Orozco thanked Stone, and then turned to Kevin. "Mr. Anderson, in light of the hour, perhaps we should hear your opening statement tomorrow?"

Kevin rose. "Your Honors, the defense will not be making an opening statement at this time. Pursuant to Rule 84, we wish to reserve our opening statement until after the prosecution has rested its case and before we begin calling our witnesses."

Judge Orozco looked surprised. Judge Davidson appeared to be looking up Rule 84, as did the prosecutors. After a pause, Judge Orozco said "Very well. Court is adjourned until ten o'clock tomorrow morning. We'll begin then with the Prosecutor's first witness."

Kevin was back in his office for about twenty minutes when the phone rang. Zoran Vacinovic was livid. "You made no opening statement? What kind of defense is that?"

"We'll have our turn later."

"But you did not answer the prosecution's case when the world is watching. The Serbs will be vilified all over the world tonight as butchers. You could have refuted that, but by saying nothing you admitted it was true." The man was clearly upset.

"I didn't admit anything," Kevin replied defensively, somewhat shaken by the force of Vacinovic's anger.

"My government expects a vigorous defense for Mr. Zaric, not someone sitting on their hands. People in Serbia are very, very upset right now."

"I'm doing this the way I think is best. We've talked about this before. I cannot and will not defend Draga by claiming that the Serbs were the victims, because even victims have no legal right to commit war crimes." Kevin realized he was almost shouting. He tried to calm down. "I will defend Draga by arguing that he didn't commit any war crimes. That's how it has to be."

"We'll be watching," Vacinovic responded ominously, and hung up.

That night, after Ellen had done her homework and gone to bed, Kevin and Diane watched the coverage of the trial on the BBC and CNN. The media presented only the prosecutor's allegations against Draga. The BBC report included footage of a crowd of emaciated men with their ribs clearly visible, looking hopefully at the cameras through a barbed wire fence. These were the infamous concentration camp scenes filmed during the war.

"I can understand why Vacinovic doesn't like this kind of press coverage," Kevin said. "Those pictures still give me the creeps."

"Did Draga do that?"

"No. That's exactly the point of my defense. I'll let them paint all their gory scenes. Then I'll ask them to point out Draga in their picture, or men they can prove were under his command."

Before going to bed, Kevin put a new cassette into his tape player and stuck it in his jacket pocket. He expected to have company on his run the next morning. He had prepared a subpoena for Pete Barnes in the event that their negotiations broke down. He stuck that in his jacket pocket as well and went to bed.

The next morning was cold, but dry. Kevin headed south towards the center of Wassenaar on his usual running route. Barnes joined him at the same place as before.

"Morning."

"Morning, Kevin."

"Thanks for getting Maria moved."

Kevin casually put his left hand inside his jacket and switched on the tape.

"You're welcome. See, we can deliver."

"That's a good sign. And I delivered on my end as well."

"Yes, you did."

"Where do we go from here?"

"I still need the reports, and the Evans tape. Then, we're done."

"And I need something in writing to guarantee what you will do for my client."

"We absolutely cannot do that. This kind of thing does not get put in writing."

"So he just has to trust you?"

"That's right. It's non-negotiable."

"Well, you'll have to just trust us that we won't use the reports and tape. I'm not giving them back to you without having a way to enforce your agreement with Draga. That's non-negotiable."

The two men ran stride for stride in silence for a while. "Kevin, you're a highly regarded federal prosecutor with a great career. Don't make this hard on yourself and everybody else."

"I don't need this aggravation either, believe me. I've got a case to try. But I wouldn't be doing my job if I didn't insist that an agreement be in writing. Oral agreements spell malpractice for lawyers."

"You don't seem to understand. It ain't going to happen. Period."

"Then I guess I'll just hang onto the reports and tape."

Kevin turned onto his street. They were almost to his house.

"I didn't want to do this, Kevin, but you're so damn stubborn." He reached into his right pocket and took out an envelope. He stopped running.

Kevin stopped as well and turned back to look at the envelope.

Barnes pulled out some snapshots from the envelope. Kevin could see by the light of the streetlight that they were surveillance photos of Ellen at school.

Kevin went ballistic. "What're you doing? Picking on some eleven-year-old girl? This is how the United States government operates? That's pretty damn low. But as long as we're handing out presents, I've got one for you."

Kevin produced the subpoena from his jacket. "You've been served. See you in court."

Barnes looked up. His face was grim. "This isn't a game, counselor. We gave you a chance to do it the easy way. Don't blame us for what happens next."

*   *   *   *

Back at the house, Kevin mentioned none of his encounter with the CIA to Diane. He went directly to Ellen's room to check on her.

She looked so peaceful asleep, and was such a dynamo when she was awake. Kevin was still seething. The CIA wouldn't dare do anything to a little girl.

Kevin made some soft noises by scraping against a desk, moving a chair, and brushing by the strings of beads hanging from the ceiling in Ellen's room. He always woke Ellen up by making indirect noises instead of barging in and calling her name or turning on the light. Ellen had told him she liked being woken up gently and slowly.

Ellen sat up in her bed and yawned. She was wearing her Britney Spears night-gown, and her hair had been braided before she went to sleep to make it easier to comb in the morning.

"Good morning," Kevin said cheerily. "It's Tuesday, the 9th of January. And it's not raining in Holland today."

"I can't wait for it to snow so the canals will freeze over," Ellen stretched in her bed. "I can't wait to ice skate on them."

"That'll be fun, but not for me."

Ellen smiled. She and Diane were good ice skaters. Kevin couldn't skate at all. The few times he had tried at the ice arena in Santa Rosa he had staggered like a drunk, lurching for the walls on the side of the rink to hold himself up. He wouldn't even dare try skating on the canals, where there was nothing to hold on to.

"Let's get dressed. I've got a trial to go to, and you've got school."

Ellen sprung out of bed. "I'll race you," she said. "First one to get done with all their bathroom stuff and get dressed wins."

"That's not fair. I have to take a shower, and put on a suit."

"Tough luck, buddy." Ellen glided past Kevin into her bathroom.

Kevin turned and dashed down the stairs. His ploy had gotten her moving, but he wasn't about to concede defeat.

After Kevin had gotten out of the shower, but not yet dressed, Ellen yelled to him from downstairs. "You can take your time, slowpoke. I already won by a mile."

When Kevin finally finished and came downstairs for breakfast, Diane was making sure that Ellen had everything she needed for school in her backpack.

"What's going to happen at Draga's trial today?" Ellen asked.

"Not much. Just some expert witnesses giving the judges background information on the war."

"When can I come watch?"

"Maybe on a really exciting day."

"Do you promise?"

Kevin looked over at Diane. She was frowning.

"Well, I can't promise for sure. The Tribunal rules say you have to be sixteen to watch the trials. But I'll see what I can do to get a special exception made for you."

"I can be really quiet."

"I know that. You've been to more trials than most lawyers."

"You need to get going. It's 8 o'clock," Diane said to Ellen.

Ellen grabbed her backpack and headed out the back door.

"Since it's not raining, I think I'll bike today, too," Kevin said.

When he got to the Tribunal, Kevin found that he had thirty minutes to spare before court started. He went into to the holding area to visit Draga. He told Draga about the conversations he had with Pete Barnes and Zoran Vacinovic.

"I feel like we're walking a tightrope here. Your friends are unhappy because I am not fighting for you and the CIA is unhappy because I am fighting too hard."

"When everyone is unhappy, that usually means you're doing a good job," Draga said. "Let's just get the trial over with. I hate sitting here listening to that tight-ass Stone."

"I'm still trying to win your trial."

"That's what I like about you, Kevin. You're a dreamer. Just keep working on my deal with Pete and the boys. Let's see if we can move up the date of my proposed death."

The prosecution's first witness was a professor of Slavic Studies at Yale University. Kevin listened as prosecutor Charles Osgood led the witness through a lengthy description of his background and qualifications, including the books and articles that he had authored on the former Yugoslavia. Kevin leafed through the professor's thirty-page curriculum vitae as the man droned on about his numerous publications, and conferences at which he had presented papers.

Kevin looked at the judges. Judge Davidson, seated closest to him, was fidgeting with his pen. Judge Orozco, in the center, was alternately looking at the witness and down at some written materials she had in front of her. Judge Linares, seated furthest from Kevin, was staring blankly at the computer terminal in front of him, where the simultaneous transcript was being typed on the screen as the witness spoke.

By the time Oswald had completed his questions on the professor's qualifications, it was time for the morning break. Everyone in the courtroom rose, grateful for the opportunity to stretch and break up the monotony.

Kevin walked over to Draga. "This is torture," Draga complained. "I never did anything this cruel to any Muslim."

Kevin saw the guards on both sides of Draga unsuccessfully try to suppress a grin.

"Do I have to be here?" Draga asked.

"Yes, you do. If I have to be here, you have to be here." Kevin walked over to his briefcase and pulled out the sports section of USA Today. "Can I give this to him?" he asked one of the guards.

"Sure."

"Here's something for you to read. Maybe you can study for this week's NFC and AFC Conference Championships. You've got two weeks to go and I'm still ahead by 10 Euros."

Draga took the paper. "Bring me one of these every day. It will give me a reason to live. If I have to listen to this every day, I might kill myself."

Kevin shook his head. His client was turning out to be a real comedian, and Kevin's only friend at the Tribunal.

The professor's testimony lasted the entire day, and most of the next day. He had not made a single reference to Draga or the Black Dragons. An almost audible sigh of relief could be heard in the courtroom when Oswald finally announced, "Thank you, Professor. I have no further questions at this time."

All eyes turned to Kevin. He stood up and turned on his microphone. "Do you have any personal knowledge of any war crimes committed by my client, Dragoljub Zaric or by men under his command?" he asked.

"No, I don't."

"Thank you, Professor." Turning to Judge Orozco, Kevin said, "Thank you, Madam President. I have no further questions."

Kevin took his seat. He could tell that everyone in the courtroom was surprised. On the other side of the glass, he saw some of the press corps turning around and conferring with one another.

"Very well," Judge Orozco said after a moment. She turned to the prosecution. "Call your next witness."

The next witness, and the two that followed over the balance of the week, were also academics. They painstakingly traced the social, political, cultural, and military events prior to 1992 that led up to the war in Bosnia. Kevin asked each of the witnesses the same question and all acknowledged that they had no personal knowledge of any war crimes committed by Draga, or by men under his command.

By Friday afternoon, the visitors' gallery had all but emptied. "Trial by tedium," one of the reporters had called it. Kevin was grateful that the week had passed without any further contact from Pete Barnes or Zoran Vacinovic. For now, all was quiet.

It was only 3:30 when Kevin packed up his briefcase and headed for home. When he reached the Tribunal lobby, a reporter came up to him. "Mr. Anderson, do you have any comment on Toma Lanko's story?"

"I haven't seen it."

The reporter handed Kevin a paper. Kevin read the headline. "Draga's Lawyer Putting up No Defense."

"No, I don't have any comment," Kevin said, returning the paper to the man. His critics would just have to be patient. Revealing his defense would just tip off the prosecutors. He didn't trust Bradford Stone to play fair.

Diane was sitting in the living room when Kevin came in. "I'm home early. How are you doing?"

"Fine. I'm still waiting for Ellen to come home from school. She's usually home by now."

"Well, it's Friday. She's probably making some plans for the weekend with her friends."

They heard the siren of a police car in the distance. When the police car with flashing blue lights stopped in front of their house, both Kevin and Diane stood up. They saw a large woman get out of the police car and stride towards their front door.

Diane walked quickly to the door with Kevin right behind her. She opened the door before the officer could knock.

"What is it?" Diane asked worriedly.

Kevin held his breath.

"Kevin and Diane Anderson?" she asked with a Dutch accent. The woman's eyes showed concern.

"Yes?"

"I'm Detective Michelle Weber of the Wassenaar Police."

"What is it?"

"I'm afraid your daughter has been kidnapped."

CHAPTER 18

▼

Kevin felt a wave of panic engulf him.

Diane let out a single scream; a primal burst from some painful place deep inside. Then, she burst into tears. Kevin felt like doing the same, but he knew first he should listen to the police, ask rational questions, and otherwise keep his wits about him.

He leaned against the wall near his front door, the breath taken out of him. All he could see was the beautiful smooth face of the daughter he loved so much. And then, he realized that he, too, was crying. He heard Diane say something in a voice that didn't sound like hers. He took hold of her arm and together they led Detective Weber into the living room of their home that suddenly seemed very empty and quiet.

Kevin felt sick; a clammy, chilled feeling that made his stomach queasy. He was wracked with enormous guilt. Even without hearing the details, he knew it was all his fault. His work at the Tribunal had jeopardized his daughter's life. Why had he done it? He wished so desperately to turn back the clock and have another chance to keep her safe.

Detective Weber, a large motherly-type woman with curly brown hair, seemed to be waiting for the stunned parents to compose themselves. She looked like a Dutch Oprah Winfrey before Oprah's diet. "Take a deep breath," she suggested. "We need to talk."

"I'm sorry," Kevin moaned, one hand now covering his face. His fingers were wet with tears. He pulled out his handkerchief and dabbed his face. He summoned up all the will he could to be strong.

"Please, detective, tell us—what happened?" he finally got out.

The detective looked at Kevin, then Diane. She spoke slowly and deliberately. "Your daughter was riding her bike home from school with her friend, Jennifer Morris. From what Jennifer told us, a white van drove up and cut in front of them in the bike lane. Ellen and Jennifer came to a complete stop. When they did, the side door of the van slid open, and two men burst out. They grabbed Ellen, pulled her off her bike, and carried her into the van. It was over in seconds. The van sped off toward the highway."

Diane started sobbing again. Kevin put his arm around her shoulder. The information had focused him and given him a sense of purpose. He waited for more.

"We have officers all over the area looking for that van. We're doing everything we can to find your daughter."

Kevin immediately thought of the CIA and his last conversation with Pete Barnes. Barnes had warned him about something would happen next. Would the CIA really kidnap a little girl? Kevin's hopes rose a little. They might kidnap her as a message to him, but surely they wouldn't kill her. They could have their reports and tapes right now in a heartbeat. He didn't care.

"I'd like to put a tracing and recording device on your phone," Detective Weber continued. "If this is a kidnapping for ransom, the kidnappers will be calling here. Is that all right with you?"

Kevin nodded. "Please do everything you can," he pleaded. "We'll do anything to get our daughter back."

The detective walked over to the phone and attached a suction cup device to the handset. One cord was connected to a tape recorder, another to a headset. "If the phone rings, we'll be here to operate the equipment. Just listen carefully and watch our signals."

The talk of contact from the kidnappers made Kevin feel somewhat hopeful. He needed to tell the police everything he knew. "I might have some information that could help," he said.

In the time they had been talking, other uniformed police officers had arrived and entered the house. One of them, carrying a cellular telephone, came over and handed it to Detective Weber.

"Yes, I'm interviewing them," she said into the phone. "No, not yet."

She handed the phone back to the other officer.

"They found the van in Leiden. It was empty. They apparently had a switch car nearby."

"What does that mean?" Diane asked.

"It means we're probably dealing with professionals, not some child molester," the detective said. "Someone planned to kidnap your daughter and make sure they got away."

It made Kevin feel strangely better to think his daughter was in the hands of professional kidnappers. It also confirmed his suspicions about the CIA.

"I think the American CIA might be involved," he said.

Detective Weber gave Kevin a surprised look. Kevin realized he would sound like some conspiracy nut, but plowed ahead anyway. "I'm a lawyer for a man on trial at the War Crimes Tribunal in The Hague. I got my hands on some CIA reports that are very sensitive. Someone from the CIA has been trying to get them back. The last thing he said to me was something like he would not be responsible for what happened next."

Detective Weber pulled out her notebook and sat down opposite Kevin. "Now, tell me this again, slowly please."

Kevin started at the beginning, and this time telling the detective about the pictures of Ellen that Pete Barnes had shown him.

When Kevin was done, he felt relieved to have finally disclosed the secrets he'd been carrying around. At this point, with Ellen's life at stake, he wasn't going to play any games with anybody.

If Detective Weber was skeptical that the CIA would kidnap an eleven-year-old girl on the streets of Wassenaar, she didn't show it. The woman seemed very professional.

"Were you aware of this?" she asked Diane.

"Some of it." Looking sternly at Kevin, Diane added: "But I sure didn't know about the CIA threatening Ellen."

"I didn't want you to worry," he said lamely.

"You didn't warn me, either. Now look what's happened."

Kevin nodded numbly. He knew Diane was right. He was to blame for this.

Detective Weber brought Kevin back to the conversation. "About this Pete Barnes—do you have a way of contacting him?"

"No," Kevin answered. "I've only seen him two times. Both times he just showed up on my jogging route at 6 a.m."

Diane started sobbing softly. "Why haven't they called yet?"

"I don't know," the detective answered. "Each kidnapping is different. There's no way to predict when or if they will call."

Kevin got up and went to the bathroom. When he came out, he saw Ellen's scooter leaning against the wall near the front door. As he pictured her happily riding the scooter in front of the house, tears streamed down his face.

"Tell her about those Yugoslavians who kept coming to the house," Diane said to Kevin when he returned to the living room.

Kevin quickly composed himself. "It's probably nothing. I went to the Serbian Embassy for help on my client's case. A man named Zoran Vacinovic was supposedly helping me. He's come around here a few times to talk about the case."

"Who is this guy Vacinovic?" the detective asked.

"According to the prosecutor, he works for the Serbian secret police."

"This story gets stranger and stranger," the detective said.

Just then, the telephone rang.

Kevin jumped up off the couch.

Detective Weber raised her hand for Kevin to wait, then scurried over to the table where the phone sat. For a large woman, she was fast and agile. She pressed the "play" button and donned the headset.

"Pick up the phone," she told Kevin. "Keep them talking as long as you can."

Kevin was nervous, but anxious to pick up the phone before the caller hung up.

"Hello?"

"Kevin, this is Jennifer's mother. What's going on?"

The detective took off her headset and pressed the "stop" button on the recorder.

Kevin announced to the room: "It's Jennifer's mom." Returning to the phone receiver he said, "Can we call you back later?"

Kevin looked at the clock on the living room wall. It was 5:30. Ellen had been kidnapped an hour ago. It seemed like a week to Kevin. He would give anything to be able to hug his little girl again.

Through the living room window, Kevin saw that his neighbors had begun to gather on the sidewalk outside, near the police cars parked in front of Kevin's house.

"Do they know?" he asked.

"They don't know Ellen's been kidnapped," the detective said. "For now, the fewer who know the better. We don't want to spook the kidnappers."

Kevin liked his Dutch neighbors and knew they were concerned with all the police activity. Ellen had been a familiar sight in the neighborhood, racing around on her scooter or her bike. In Holland, much more than in America, neighbors looked out for one another.

Detective Weber went to confer with the other officers, while Diane used a cell phone to call Jennifer's mom.

The minutes passed painfully slow for Kevin as he sat in the living room. He stared at the telephone, willing it to ring. He didn't know what to say to Diane. It was all his fault—she knew it, and so did he.

Detective Weber came into the living room. "Mr. Anderson, we'd like your consent to search your house. It's standard procedure in these types of cases. There might be a scrap of paper or something that might help us find your daughter."

"Go right ahead," Kevin replied. He felt very comfortable with this detective. She showed him a consent form in Dutch and translated it to them in English. Kevin and then Diane signed and dated it.

Detective Weber put the form in her folder. Kevin heard other officers heading up the stairs. It occurred to him that twice in the last six months law enforcement officers had searched their home. Kevin didn't care; he'd do anything to get Ellen back.

The detective pulled out another form. "We'd like to take a taped statement from you," she said to Kevin. "This consent form advises you of your right to remain silent, to have an attorney, and informs you that anything you say can be used against you."

Kevin knew the Miranda warnings by heart. As he signed the form, a signal of caution crept into his brain. "Am I a suspect?" he asked.

Detective Weber paused. "Everyone is a suspect until we eliminate him or her. We don't want another Jon Benet Ramsey case here in The Netherlands."

He shuddered at the mention of the little girl found murdered in her home. Her parents had become suspects mostly because they had refused to speak to the police.

But Kevin wasn't concerned about himself. He wanted to do everything in his power to help Ellen. He signed the form.

Then, the phone rang.

Everyone froze again for an instant before quickly moving into position.

Detective Weber activated the tape player and gave Kevin the signal to pick up.

"Hello," Kevin said, his voice sounding hopeful.

"Mr. Anderson, this is Reuter's News Service. I'm sorry to bother you. I've a report that your daughter has been kidnapped."

Kevin's shoulders sagged. "Hold on one moment." He covered the mouthpiece and said to the others "Reuter's News Service." He saw Diane's face fall.

Kevin wanted to ask the officers what he should do. "Let me have your name and number and I'll call you right back."

"But can you confirm there's been a kidnapping?"

"I can't confirm anything. Give me your name and number."

The reporter complied and Kevin hung up. "Now what?"

"Get ready for a media circus," said Detective Weber, pulling the front curtains shut. "We'll need some more people out here, and some crowd barriers."

"Will this spook the kidnappers?"

"I don't know. It was inevitable, though. You'd better prepare yourself for a lot of publicity."

Kevin felt shaky. He didn't want to say anything that might hurt Ellen. "I'll just let your people talk to the press."

A few minutes later, Kevin began answering Detective Weber's questions on tape. During the interview, the phone rang three times with calls from reporters.

Kevin began to feel foolish as he played the tapes for Detective Weber of his conversations with William Evans and Pete Barnes. He was an idiot for playing games with the CIA. He should have left everything alone. Draga was a big boy. He'd known the risks of doing business with the CIA. Now, Kevin had put his own daughter in jeopardy.

"I got caught up fighting for my client. I never expected consequences like these."

"Have you received any other threats?" asked the detective.

"Not really. The Serbs are upset with me because they don't think I'm defending Draga aggressively enough. But I've received no direct threats from them."

"After hearing those tapes, I would say that lack of aggressiveness is not one of your problems," Detective Weber responded with a slight smile.

When the detective finished asking him questions, Kevin walked over to the front window. He peeked around the curtains. News crews were setting up their equipment, their lights illuminating the Andersons front door. It was 7:30, and there had been no word from the kidnappers.

"Where is my daughter?" he asked no one in particular as he looked past the camera crews into the dark night.

"Ellen, my sweet girl, where are you?"

CHAPTER 19

▼

There were no lights illuminating the old farmhouse where three adults and a young girl sat around a beat-up wooden kitchen table.

"You'll be staying here for awhile," one of the men said in English.

Ellen kept her eyes down, staring at the table. She was scared, and she wanted her mother and father.

"Don't try anything and no one will hurt you."

She had screamed when the men grabbed her from her bike and carried her into the van. She had tried punching, kicking, and biting, but she could not get away from the stronger men. They had told her that if she kept struggling they would have to tie her up. After that, she had sat quietly in the backseat of the van, between the two men.

The van had sped quickly onto the highway, and then gotten off the next exit. It soon came to a stop on a residential street. The men carried Ellen out of the white van and into a black van. She had sat in the back seat of this van for what seemed like an hour as the driver, a woman, took them through several small towns and finally to a rural area with farms, cows, and lots of grass.

Ellen had cried until she was drained. The kidnappers had spoken in Dutch among themselves, but it was beyond Ellen's simple understanding of the language. When the tears had stopped, Ellen had pulled herself in like a tortoise in a shell.

Now, sitting around the kitchen table as the two men smoked marijuana, Ellen finally got the courage to speak.

"Why are you doing this? What did I ever do to you?"

The woman looked at Ellen. "This is not about you. It's about your father."

"When do I get to go home?"

"That depends on him."

"Do I have to sleep here tonight?"

"Yes."

"Follow me. I'll show you your room."

She led Ellen to a bedroom at the end of the hall. It was a plain room with a single bed in the corner and a chest of drawers on the opposite wall. The walls were bare, and badly in need of a paint job.

Ellen shivered. The room was cold. "I don't have any clothes to wear to bed, or for tomorrow," she said, her voice a soft whisper.

The woman opened the top drawer of the dresser. There were clothes inside. Ellen took out a pair of pants and held them out. The size looked about right. She opened the other drawers and saw shirts, socks, underwear, and pajamas.

"There are a lot of clothes. Am I staying here for a long time?"

"I don't know."

Ellen looked around the bare room. She walked over to the window.

"The windows are locked," the woman said. "Your door will be locked as well. There are no other houses around. So don't get any ideas of leaving on your own. If you try anything, you'll be locked in the basement."

Ellen pictured a dark basement like the Chamber of Secrets in one of the Harry Potter books. She wasn't about to get in trouble with these people. If she did try to escape, she would have to be sure to succeed.

"It's time for you to go to bed. I'm going to lock the door now."

"Wait! Can I have my backpack so I can read a book?"

The woman retrieved the backpack. Before handing it to Ellen, she pulled out and inspected the contents. There were schoolbooks and notebooks, three pencil cases filled with gel pens, markers, and pencils, a bag of gym clothes, and a purse with lunch money. Satisfied, the woman left the items on the bed.

Ellen began placing the books on top of the dresser. "I'm going to need to do my homework in the morning."

"You'll be doing some farm chores, too."

"I don't know how to do farm chores."

"You'll learn."

The woman closed the door and Ellen heard the lock click. She sat down on the bed and cried softly. Her Daddy would find a way to rescue her, she told herself, as she got under the covers.

Emotionally exhausted, Ellen slept soundly that night.

*   *   *   *

Kevin and Diane didn't sleep at all.

At about 10 p.m., Detective Weber told Kevin that she would be leaving an officer inside the house to record any calls that might come in, and two officers outside to keep the press at bay. She and the rest of the police officers were going home.

Kevin felt a huge letdown when the police officers left. All of the activity in his home had sustained him. Now, there was nothing. He couldn't imagine going to sleep, not while Ellen was out there somewhere.

Diane, too, suffered a letdown. She sat on the couch, crying. "She's probably so scared. I feel so helpless."

"I know," Kevin said. "I feel like going out looking for her, or doing something. I hate just sitting around, waiting for someone to call."

No one did call.

The next morning, Detective Weber arrived at 11 a.m.

Kevin and Diane leaped up to greet her, anxious for any news.

"Have you made contact with the CIA?" Kevin asked.

"Our foreign ministry is working on that. We should hear this morning."

"Any other news?"

"No. Ellen's picture has been all over the television and in the newspapers. We've faxed flyers with her picture to every police department in Holland and all over Europe."

"Thank you," Kevin said. "I know you're doing everything you can."

"What about the kidnappers?" Diane asked. "Did you get any descriptions of them?"

"Unfortunately, Jennifer is the only one to have seen them, as far as we know. All she can really say is that they were two white males. Everything happened very quickly."

There was nothing more to say. Kevin paced around the house, waiting for more information. He went upstairs, took a shower, and changed into a new set of clothes.

*   *   *   *

At the farmhouse, even the loud call of a rooster had not awakened Ellen.

When she did wake up, the gray daylight of a cloudy Dutch morning illuminated the small room. Ellen sat up, ready to call out for her Daddy as she usually did when she woke up. Then she looked around and remembered where she was. She felt panic, then started to cry softly.

Soon, she got out of bed and walked over to the window. Outside, she saw a bright green field of grass, with cows grazing. She counted twenty-two black and white cows. She hoped she would not have to milk those big animals.

Ellen saw an old brown barn not far from the house. Between the barn and the house was a gravel area with some old rusty tractors and plows. Chickens and roosters were prancing about. She couldn't see any other houses from her window, just fields and trees off in the distance.

Ellen felt a shiver start from her bare feet on the wooden floor and work its way up her body. She quickly changed out of the pajamas and put on jeans and a long-sleeved shirt. The sizes fit perfectly. She wondered if there was another girl her age around, or if they had just stocked the house when they planned to kidnap her. She hoped there was another girl. If someone went to this much trouble, they were pretty serious about keeping her.

After she was dressed, Ellen realized that she had to go to the bathroom. She tried the door to her room. It was locked. She knocked on the door.

A few seconds later, the door opened.

"I need to go to the bathroom," Ellen told the woman.

The woman led her to the bathroom, next door to Ellen's room. Ellen went in and closed the door. She wondered if the bathroom window was also locked, but she was afraid to try it.

When she came out, the woman was waiting. "Come on, I'm going to show you around." She led Ellen around the house, pointing out the living and dining rooms, two other bedrooms, and the kitchen. Ellen saw the two men from last night sitting at the kitchen table. They didn't say anything to her.

"Sit down," the woman said, pointing to an empty chair at the kitchen table. She dished up a plate of eggs and some toast.

Ellen ate a few bites, but said nothing.

One of the men spoke in English. "These are the rules around here. You cannot go in the other bedrooms. There's no TV, and no phone. You cannot go outside the house unless one of us is with you. If someone else comes, we will have to lock you in your room until they leave. Any questions?"

Ellen stared at her plate and said nothing.

"And don't try to get away. There are no houses around here. If you try to escape, you won't make it, and we'll put you in the basement with the rats."

Ellen shuddered at the thought. She would be a good girl. "When can I go home?"

"We don't know yet."

"What do I do all day here?"

"There's always plenty to do on a farm. You can start by helping Anna with the dishes."

Anna. It was the first time that Ellen had heard any of their names. "What's your name?" she timidly asked the man who had spoken to her.

"You can call me Hans, and you can call him Jan."

"Are those your real names?"

Hans looked at Ellen with a frown. "What do you think?"

"No. In that case," Ellen declared, "you can call me Sarah. I've always wanted to be called Sarah."

"Okay, Sarah. Get going on those dishes."

CHAPTER 20

▼

The dishes at the Anderson house were going unwashed. Kevin and Diane stayed in the living room near the phone, waiting for some news of Ellen. Kevin paced, looking at the silent phone, then out the window. Diane read a book, trying to distract herself.

Shortly before noon there was a knock at the door. Kevin went to answer it. Detective Weber, who had been gone for a couple of hours, was back—this time accompanied by a tall, lanky man that a surprised Kevin recognized immediately.

It was Pete Barnes of the CIA.

"I believe you know Mr. Barnes," Detective Weber said.

Barnes offered his hand to Kevin.

Kevin shook it, waiting to hear the news.

"I'm sorry about your daughter," Barnes said. "Please know that we have absolutely nothing to do with this, I swear."

Kevin's first reaction was disbelief. Then his face sagged with disappointment. He had already worked things out in his mind. He would give the CIA what they wanted and they would give him what he wanted: his daughter. He felt shaky and sat down.

"I think we have to look at some other angle," Detective Weber said to Kevin and Diane. Diane, who had jumped up at the sound of the knock, sat down as well. She looked like she was having trouble comprehending the meaning of this information.

"How do you know whether to believe this?" Kevin asked Detective Weber, not looking at Barnes.

"The Dutch government made contacts with the United States government at the highest levels. They've given us their assurance that they had nothing to do with this."

Barnes looked at Kevin. "I'm sorry, I wish I could fix this, but I can't. It's not us."

Diane spoke to Detective Weber. "Are you satisfied that it's not the CIA?"

"Yes, I don't think they would lie to the Dutch Foreign Ministry."

"But intelligence agencies always deny things," Kevin interjected. "They've issued denials for the last fifty years of things they were proven to be responsible for."

"The people in our government do not think they would lie to us about this."

Kevin's mind was racing as he fought against accepting the information. He looked at Barnes. "It's a heck of a coincidence, then. I've learned not to believe in coincidences."

"Believe it," Barnes said firmly. "We had nothing to do with this. We'll help you find the people that did."

Diane seemed more prepared to accept this turn of events than Kevin. "If not them," she asked Detective Weber, "then who?"

"That's the question," the detective said. "Let's approach this from a different angle."

"I'm sorry," Kevin said to Detective Weber. "I'm having a lot of trouble just accepting someone's word that they're not involved. Especially an agency known for denying anything and everything."

"How can we prove we're not involved?" Barnes asked.

Kevin thought about that. "I don't know," he finally said. Turning to Detective Weber, he asked, "Didn't you say everyone was a suspect until they were eliminated?"

"They're eliminated," Detective Weber said firmly. "I have to rely on the judgment of the Foreign Ministry. We need to move forward, Mr. Anderson. Your daughter is out there somewhere."

Kevin thought of Ellen, and pictured her in some squalid house, chained to the walls—or worse. "I'm sorry. I guess I was clinging to the hope that there was some rational explanation for this and it could all be resolved."

"What about those people from the Serbian Embassy?" Diane asked. "Have you checked them out?"

"Not yet. It's a very sensitive thing to investigate someone from an Embassy. You remember that our Ambassador to Serbia and Montenegro was recalled when the U.N. people searched their Embassy here in The Hague."

Kevin remembered that all too well. The U.N. police had searched this very house that night. "Well, what can we do?"

Detective Weber pulled out her tape recorder and another interview form with Miranda-type warnings. After Kevin signed it, she turned on the recorder and asked Kevin to recount his contacts with the people from the Embassy from his first visit to his latest telephone conversation with Zoran Vacinovic.

"Mr. Anderson," Detective Weber said at the end of the questioning, "I have to ask this. You wouldn't do something like this as a stunt to get some advantage in your trial, would you?"

"Absolutely not. I would never put my wife or daughter through this."

"Will you give me our reports and those tapes?" Barnes asked.

"Yes, I will."

"Can you get them now?" Barnes obviously didn't want to take the chance of Kevin changing his mind.

Kevin got up from his chair. He began having second thoughts. The way Barnes had asked for them right after Detective Weber had challenged him had made Kevin reply quickly to clear his name. But what about his obligation to Draga? If he gave up the materials, he would have no way of proving that Draga had been helping the CIA and no way of helping Draga enforce his agreement.

As he went to retrieve the tapes and reports, Kevin hesitated. Why give the CIA the material if they could not help free Ellen? On the other hand, maybe the CIA had really kidnapped Ellen. If he gave them the reports, maybe they would release her, all the while denying that they had anything to do with her kidnapping.

Kevin's instincts told him to just give over all the tapes and reports. He needed to stop playing games. He would do everything he could to free Ellen. Draga's interests were just going to have to come second.

Kevin handed the reports and tapes to Barnes. "Please help my daughter."

Barnes reached for the materials, but Detective Weber quickly snatched them from Kevin's hand. "These may be needed as evidence in our kidnapping investigation," she said to Barnes. "We'll hold onto them for awhile."

Barnes looked surprised, but said nothing.

Kevin was surprised and delighted. Now, he had the best of all worlds. He had shown his good faith by freely giving up the materials, but they were in the hands of someone who would not deny their existence if they were needed for Draga's case.

"Do you have any other copies?" Barnes asked.

"No, they're all there."

"We'll probably need to give you a lie detector test on that."

"Fine."

After Barnes had left, Kevin said, "I don't know what to believe any more. I'm having a hard time with this."

"We're back to square one," Diane said, crushed. "Who would want to kidnap our daughter?"

"Mr. Anderson, I'd like to have you take a lie detector test this morning," Detective Weber said.

Kevin said nothing, wondering if he was now the prime suspect. "The quicker we erase any suspicions on you, the better."

"Of course," Kevin said. "I'm ready when you are."

"Let's go down to the Wassenaar Police Station and take care of that right now"

Kevin stood up and went to get his coat.

Detective Weber told Diane that she would have to answer the phone when it rang. Diane paled, then looked at Kevin. "Hurry back," she said.

Kevin knew she didn't want to be alone, and he felt terribly having to leave.

He kissed Diane goodbye, and went out the front door, followed by Detective Weber and another officer. A row of people with cameras lined the path between his house and the street. Lights went on and cameras flashed as Kevin stepped outside.

Reporters shouted questions in Dutch and English. Kevin didn't respond, and Detective Weber led him straight to a police car parked in front. They got into the car and drove the six blocks to the Wassenaar Police Station. A procession of journalists followed in their own cars. More pictures were taken of Kevin going into the station.

"Is he being charged?" one reporter shouted.

"Is he being arrested?" asked another

The cloud of suspicion that seemed to hover over Kevin made him nervous. He knew that polygraph tests were not considered reliable enough to be used as evidence in court, and were a subjective tool that depended greatly on the experience and skill of the examiner.

Kevin sat down in a windowless room and listened as the middle-aged polygraph examiner explained the procedure for the test. The examiner seemed exact and cautious, two traits that Kevin appreciated. He carefully explained that after a series of innocuous questions to establish Kevin's baseline readings, Kevin would be asked three relevant questions: Did he plan his daughter's disappearance? Did he know who had his daughter? Did he, or anyone on his behalf, retain copies of the CIA reports or tapes?

The examiner attached wires to Kevin's chest, arms, and fingers that would measure his breathing, pulse, and perspiration. The wires ran to a machine with a pen that moved up and down like a seismograph measuring an earthquake.

To fight his nervousness, Kevin kept silently repeating his mantra: "I have to help Ellen. I have to help Ellen…" He knew that if he remained a suspect, the police would divert valuable resources from the search for Ellen to an investigation of him. Things that should be done to try to find Ellen might not be done if they suspected Kevin.

The examination lasted an hour. By the end, a ream of paper had spilled onto the floor from the machine. When the examiner removed the wires from him, Kevin looked for some hint of how he had done. The examiner gave no clue. Kevin was exhausted, and anxious to get back home. He wondered if the kidnappers had called.

The examiner excused himself and took the papers with him as he left the room. Was it a bad sign that he had not told Kevin the results? Kevin was too tired to think it through. He felt like he was running on fumes.

After what seemed like another hour but was probably only fifteen minutes, the examiner returned to the room with Detective Weber. The examiner sat down across from Kevin and looked him directly in the eye. "You're telling the truth."

Kevin's eyes teared up; he couldn't help himself, the pent-up tension just poured out. In a few minutes, he went into the bathroom and washed his face. He looked like hell. His eyes were bloodshot. He felt unsteady; a touch dizzy. He knew he needed sleep.

When he got home, Kevin hugged Diane. "I passed their test," he said.

"What took you so long?" Diane had never doubted Kevin would pass.

Kevin took her hand. "I have to get some sleep. I can't think straight any more."

Diane had been drinking coffee. "I can't sleep while Ellen is out there. I'll wait by the phone, you go up to sleep."

Kevin trudged up to the second floor. He felt like he had just been hit by a truck. His head ached. His body was stiff. He took off his clothes, got under the covers, and closed his eyes. He was asleep in seconds.

When he awoke, it was 11 p.m. Diane was asleep beside him. Kevin felt rested, and anxious to hear any news. He got dressed, washed his face, and went downstairs. A young police officer was sitting in the living room near the phone, reading a book.

"Any news?"

"Nothing, sir, I'm sorry."

Kevin went back upstairs, not knowing what to do next. He had slept for about eight hours and knew that he could not go back to sleep. He looked at the stairs to Ellen's level, but he didn't think he could face going up to her room and seeing her things. He went into the bathroom, and took a shower.

After his shower, Kevin returned downstairs. He made sandwiches for himself and the officer. Now his body was all screwed up, he thought, sleeping during the day and being wide awake in the middle of the night. He and the officer sat at the dining room table, eating sandwiches and chips, and making small talk.

Kevin looked at the clock in the living room. It was 1:15 a.m. It was going to be a long night.

Then, the phone rang.

Kevin jumped to answer the phone.

The officer moved swiftly to the tape player, switched it on, and put on the headset. Kevin hovered over the phone, waiting for the signal to pick it up.

"Hello." He didn't think some reporter would call at this hour.

"We have your daughter," a man's voice said. The voice was deep, the words spoken slowly.

Kevin's brain was frozen for an instant.

"There is only one way you will see her again."

"How? I'll do anything. Just don't hurt my daughter."

"Your daughter will be killed unless Draga is released. You must win his case and you will have your daughter back. Otherwise, you will never see her again."

The phone line went dead.

CHAPTER 21

▼

When Ellen awoke on Sunday morning, she got out of bed hoping it would be her last day on the farm. She got dressed and knocked on her door.

Anna soon came and opened it.

"Do I get to go home today?" Ellen asked hopefully.

"Not today."

"I have to be back for school tomorrow."

"I don't think you're going to make it."

"Why? Does my dad have to pay some money to get me back?"

"I don't know. I'm just hired to take care of you while you're here."

"I want to go home."

Ellen ran into the bathroom and slammed the door.

When she came out of the bathroom, she ate her cereal in silence at the kitchen table. "I guess I'll do my homework," she told Anna when she finished eating. "Otherwise, I'll be way behind when I get back." She went into her room and returned with her backpack. Soon, her books and papers were spread out all over the kitchen table and Ellen was diligently working through her assignments.

"You know it's against the law to keep a kid out of school," Ellen complained.

"We don't want to break the law," Anna replied facetiously.

"Good. Tomorrow you can be the teacher and I will be the student and we'll have school right here."

"I don't know how to teach school."

"It's easy. You just teach me from the textbook, and then assign me a bunch of homework. I have all my books. I'll help you prepare a lesson plan if you want."

"We'll see. I'm not being paid a teacher's wage."

"Who's your boss?" Ellen asked. "Is it Hans or Jan?"

"That's none of your business, young lady."

"Does this have something to do with my dad's trial?" Ellen asked.

"You sure ask a lot of questions. Now, get back to your school work."

Ellen spent the next hour studying. Anna tried to read a book, but Ellen kept asking questions. "What's eight times twelve? How do you spell 'manufacture'?"

When she had finished, Ellen packed up her backpack and brought her books into the living room. "This will be our school." She took out a piece of paper and wrote, "Anna's schoolhouse." She taped it to the door.

"What are we going to do today?" Ellen asked.

"Today's Sunday. We rest."

"I don't want to rest, I'm bored. Can we bake bread? My mommy showed me how to do it."

"No, but we can feed the chickens. They need to eat every day. And the cows need to be milked."

Ellen made a face. "Can you do the squeezing part and I hold the bucket?"

Anna didn't respond. She and Ellen got their coats on and went out to the barn. Anna grabbed the feed bucket and carried it outside. The chickens and roosters scrambled over to meet them. Ellen reached into the bucket, and spread the feed around.

They were just finishing up when Ellen spotted a small brown and white dog sniffing around the barn. Ellen walked slowly toward the dog. When she was close enough, she knelt down and petted it. The dog licked her fingers.

"You're just a puppy. Where did you come from?" Ellen lifted the dog into her lap. "You don't have a collar." The brown and white puppy curled up inside Ellen's lap as Ellen stroked its back. "Where's your family? I'm missing my family too."

The puppy hopped out of Ellen's lap and played in the grass. When Ellen stood up, it got on its hind legs as if to imitate her, only to fall forward and try again. "Silly puppy, dogs can't stand on two legs." Ellen scooped up the dog and walked over to Anna. "Whose dog is this?"

"I don't know. I've never seen it before."

Ellen ran over with the puppy to Hans and Jan. "I found this puppy. Do you guys know who it belongs to?"

The men shrugged.

"Can I keep it? Please!"

There was no reply.

"Thank you so much," Ellen blurted out, "I've always wanted a dog. He's so cute. Wait 'til my mom and dad see this!"

Ellen put the puppy down gently on the ground. It started sniffing everything. "Come on," she said to her new friend, "we've got to make you a little home."

"Is it a boy or a girl?" she asked Anna.

"A girl."

"Great. I don't like boys. No offense."

Anna's face broke into a wan smile.

"Girls rule!" Ellen proclaimed, giving Anna the thumbs up sign.

"I've got to think of a name," Ellen said. She picked up the puppy and studied its face. "I've got it!" I'm going to name her Johanna. J for Jan, H-A-N for Hans, and A-N-N-A for Anna."

Ellen ran after the puppy. "Johanna, come here!"

✻   ✻   ✻   ✻

At the Anderson home, Kevin and Diane waited for news from the police. The call from the kidnappers had been brief, and Kevin knew the prospects for tracing it were poor. By late morning, Detective Weber arrived and told them that all they could determine was that the call had been made from a cellular phone somewhere in Holland.

They played and replayed the tape of the conversation. Kevin wished he had gotten the man to talk longer. The caller had a slight accent, but his English had been good. Given the fact that he had demanded Draga's release, Kevin was surprised that the caller did not have a Slavic accent. While he was still unwilling to completely rule out the CIA, Kevin knew that the goal of the kidnapers meant a wider field of suspects.

"I'd like to go visit my client," Kevin said. "If someone did kidnap Ellen on his behalf, maybe he might have some ideas about who."

"Does Draga know you have a daughter?"

"Yes."

The detective frowned. "Does he know she goes to the American School?"

"Yes."

"Maybe he had something to do with it."

"I really don't think Draga would have Ellen kidnapped. He'd probably kidnap Bradford Stone's child rather than mine. He would know that I'm the person at the Tribunal with the least ability to get him released."

"What do we do now?" Diane asked. "They may never call again."

"The call may not have been from the people who have Ellen," Detective Weber replied. "It could be some cruel hoax. The caller sounds Dutch or German. A high profile case like this brings out all sorts of crazies. It's strange to kidnap someone and then demand something that the victim has no control over."

"I want to go talk to Draga. I feel like he might be able to help."

"I'd like to have the conversation recorded," the detective said.

Kevin was silent for a minute. "I'm uncomfortable about that. We have an attorney-client privilege. And I feel strongly that he's not involved. He's too smart, and he wants to get his trial over with. How about if I just talk to him in private for now?"

"Well, that's your decision. If we have the conversation on tape, we can analyze it for small things that might tip us off if he is lying. But, I understand your concern."

Diane spoke up. "For God's sake, Kevin, we're dealing with Ellen's life. You have to do everything to help the police."

"I really don't think Draga is involved. I know him pretty well by now."

Diane stood up and walked away from the table.

Kevin took a deep breath. He didn't want to upset Diane. She was holding up amazingly well under the strain. Her daughter had been gone for two days now. But he didn't want to violate the law or Draga's trust either.

Kevin and Detective Weber were followed by a group of reporters when they left his house. When they arrived at the jail, he was led into the interview room.

Draga was already there, and he stood up as soon as he saw Kevin.

"I'm sorry about your daughter, Kevin. You look like hell."

"I feel worse than I look."

They shook hands.

"I'll do anything I can to help," Draga said. "Do you think this is about the trial? There's been all kinds of speculation on the news."

Kevin told Draga about the call that morning. Kevin watched Draga closely for signs he knew something about the kidnapping. "Do you have any idea who might be behind this?"

Draga thought for a minute. "I hate to say this, but there are all sorts of idiots in Serbia who might think up something like this. The thing that throws me off is that they think the caller might be Dutch or German."

"Are there any of your supporters that come to mind who might do this?"

"Lots of people. Just about any of the old Dragons on that list I gave you might have gotten some people together thinking this would help me. But they don't speak English, and they don't really know any Dutch or German people."

"The police think there's at least a possibility that the call might not have even been from the kidnappers. It might have been a copycat or hoax or something."

Draga nodded.

"I gave the CIA reports and tapes to the police detective. We can probably get them back if we decide to use them in your trial, but I had to turn them over. I thought the CIA kidnapped my daughter to get the reports back. Pete Barnes came to my house yesterday morning and denied it. I don't know whether to believe him or not."

"Let me know what I can do, Kevin."

Kevin shook Draga's hand before he left. "I really appreciate your attitude. It's funny, but you're the person I trust the most right now."

"I'm sick to think that your daughter has been kidnapped because of me."

Kevin left the visiting room and met up with Detective Weber. He told her what Draga had said.

"I'm positive he's not behind this," Kevin said.

When they left the detention center Kevin asked about Vacinovic. "Can I go talk to him?"

"We're still gathering intelligence information on him. Let's sit tight for a while. Everywhere you go, the reporters follow. If he is involved, I don't want to spook him."

When they returned to his house, Kevin told Diane about his conversation with Draga. She didn't ask if he had recorded it. Kevin suspected she already knew the answer.

"Judge Orozco's assistant called," Diane told him. "The Judge is offering to postpone the trial."

"No. I have to get Draga acquitted."

He took the phone number and called the Tribunal's legal officer. "I appreciate the Judge's consideration," Kevin said, "but please tell Judge Orozco that I don't want the trial delayed. I'm prepared to be in court tomorrow."

An hour later Kevin received another call from the legal officer. Court would begin as scheduled at 9:30 in the morning. Kevin was beginning to feel exhausted again.

Detective Weber left Diane and Kevin with one officer to monitor any calls, and two officers outside their front door.

"What are we going to do, Kevin?" Diane asked. "I feel so helpless."

"I'm going to try to win Draga's trial. That's all I can do."

"If that call was from the kidnappers, it sounds like they're prepared to hold her for a long time," Diane said.

Kevin agreed. "I hope they're treating her well." He did not express his next thought: <u>I hope she's alive</u>.

Kevin went to bed at eight o'clock that night. He tossed and turned, searching for the magic words he could say in court that would win Draga's acquittal and get his daughter back before something terrible happened to her.

CHAPTER 22

▼

Although he took his usual seat at the defense table in Courtroom 1, Kevin felt like a different person than he had been on Friday. It was as if he had an entirely new client: his daughter. This gave him a personal stake in the outcome that he had never experienced before as a prosecutor.

Everyone treated him differently as well. From the moment he came into the building trailed by news crews, people offered their sympathies and wished him luck.

Kevin looked up from the table when he heard a familiar voice. "Mr. Anderson, I'm so sorry about your daughter. I gave you the application to be defense counsel, and I can't help but feel this is all my fault."

Kevin saw a grief-stricken Mrs. Kelly.

"It's not your fault at all, Mrs. Kelly. You're the nicest person I know here."

Mrs. Kelly would not be consoled. She continued in her Irish accent. "If there's anything I can do, please let me know. And give my best to your wife. Poor dear, this must be frightful for her."

Kevin struggled to keep his emotions in check as he thanked the motherly Mrs. Kelly. He concentrated on keeping his professional demeanor in court. He had written an outline of what he wanted to say to the Court, and he reviewed it again.

"All rise. *Veuillez vous lever!*"

Kevin came to his feet as the judges filed into the courtroom.

Led by Judge Davidson, they all looked somber and grim. They sat down at their places as Draga was brought in from the door behind Kevin. Kevin was surprised to see that Draga was not wearing his jogging suit. Instead, he was dressed immaculately in a navy blue blazer, gray slacks, a white shirt and red tie.

Judge Orozco was the first to speak after the case had been called. "The Court wishes to express its sorrow to Mr. Anderson and his wife over the kidnapping of their daughter. We are all praying for her safe return."

Kevin nodded in thanks.

"We were prepared to postpone this trial, and not convene today. However, Mr. Anderson has requested that court proceed as scheduled this morning. We have honored that request. Mr. Anderson, do you wish to be heard?"

Kevin stood up and moved to the podium. "Thank you, Madam President," he said in a voice that sounded higher and shakier than he would have liked. "It is difficult for me to be here, knowing that my daughter is being held somewhere against her will."

He fought to choke back tears as he visualized Ellen. "Yesterday, we received a telephone call saying that she will be released only if Mr. Zaric is released. So I am here today to continue my efforts on behalf of Mr. Zaric. It is the only thing I can do to help bring my daughter back."

Bradford Stone rose from his chair. "Your Honors," Stone's voice had no trace of sympathy. "The prosecution would urge the court to replace Mr. Anderson as counsel for the accused, given the emotional state that he must be in. The situation has given him a personal stake in the case. I believe that it would impair a lawyer in the performance of his duties towards his client."

"I was thinking the same thing," Judge Davidson interjected. Turning to Kevin, he addressed him for the first time. "Mr. Anderson, I really don't think you should continue. You should be helping the police. You can't give Mr. Zaric's case your undivided attention under these circumstances."

Before Kevin could respond, Judge Orozco spoke. "I agree," she said, looking directly at Kevin. "As a mother, I can imagine the pain that you and your wife must be feeling. You're in no condition to participate in a trial."

Kevin was fighting a feeling of panic. He couldn't leave Draga's trial. It was his only hope of getting his daughter back. He took a deep breath and rose. "I want to continue," he said evenly, trying to keep the emotion out of his voice. "Perhaps it would be easier to sit home with my wife and wait for the phone to ring. But, my place is in this courtroom fighting for my daughter's freedom, as well as for my client's. It is true that I do now have a personal interest in the case, but that interest is the same as my client's."

Bradford Stone rose again. "After he is found guilty, the accused will most certainly claim on appeal that he received ineffective assistance of counsel. The

Court simply cannot allow Mr. Anderson to continue under these circumstances."

"Stop telling the Court what it can or cannot do," Judge Davidson spat. "What about the delay in the trial? A new lawyer would take months to prepare."

"Well, Your Honor, I have spoken to Mr. Krasnic this morning. He told me that he would be able to step in and assist the court within two weeks."

Kevin bristled. Krasnic couldn't prepare Draga's case in two months, let alone two weeks.

Judge Orozco looked at Kevin. "Mr. Anderson, I don't see how we can proceed in the absence of a waiver by your client, agreeing that your continued representation would not be a basis for overturning the verdict. And, I don't imagine your client wishes to waive anything."

All eyes in the courtroom moved to Draga, sitting behind Kevin, today looking like a natty businessman.

Kevin wished that Draga would do what it took for him to continue. He knew, however, that he couldn't ask his client to waive his rights over such a personal matter. But what would the kidnappers do to Ellen if Kevin were no longer on Draga's case? There would be no incentive to release her. She would probably be killed. Kevin closed his eyes and felt sick.

"Mr. Zaric," Judge Orozco said, "we are going to replace Mr. Anderson with Mr. Krasnic. Apparently he will be able to begin your trial in two weeks. Do you have any objection to that?"

Draga slowly rose from his chair. "Yes, I do," he said in a strong, firm voice. "I want Mr. Anderson as my lawyer. I want my trial to continue right now." He sat down.

Kevin was shocked and grateful. Draga had broken his courtroom silence for him. He looked at his client with deep appreciation.

Judge Orozco conferred with Judge Davidson. Then she turned back to the accused. "Do you agree, Mr. Zaric, that you will not be able later to challenge the result if you are found guilty on the ground that your lawyer was distracted, or had a conflict of interest, as a result of this situation?"

Draga once again rose. "I do agree," he said firmly. Then, looking at the visitor's gallery, he continued in a forceful voice. "I want those people who have kidnapped my lawyer's daughter to know that I do not want this. My lawyer is doing exactly what I want him to do. He is doing an excellent job. I am calling on those who are holding the girl to release her immediately."

Tears welled up in Kevin's eyes.

Judge Orozco was impressed as well. "Mr. Zaric. Thank you for that statement. It demonstrates character and compassion on your part. The Court is grateful to you for your actions here today. We hope that those misguided individuals who have taken Ellen Anderson will listen to what you have just said."

Turning to the prosecution, Judge Orozco said, "Call your next witness."

Stone stood. "Your Honors, with all due respect, we don't feel Mr. Zaric has adequately waived..."

"Call your witness," Judge Davidson boomed.

"Yes, Your Honor," Stone replied meekly. "The prosecution calls Witness A."

Kevin turned and looked back at Draga. Their eyes met. Kevin gave Draga the thumbs up sign. Draga winked back at him. Kevin pulled out his folder for Witness A.

The usher shut the curtain on the glass windows to the visitors' gallery. Whenever a witness whose identity was protected entered the courtroom, the curtain had to be shut. After the witness sat in the witness chair, which was shielded from public view, the curtains were reopened.

Kevin noticed for the first time that there was a full house today.

"Good morning, Witness A," Judge Orozco said.

"Good morning," the witness responded in the BCS language.

"Please read the oath from the card in front of you."

The witness read the oath, affirming that his testimony was the truth, the whole truth, and nothing but the truth.

"Witness A, the usher will now show you a piece of paper with a name on it. Please tell me if this is your true name."

The usher approached the witness with a piece of paper. "Da," said the witness, which meant "yes" in BCS.

Kevin had been given the witness' true name several months ago, but the public would not know the witness' identity. That was the Tribunal's way of protecting the rights of the accused to know and confront the witnesses against him, yet affording the witness some protection against retaliation.

"Mr. Stone," Judge Orozco said, "you may begin your direct examination."

Witness A's testimony was much like many of the stories in the reports Kevin had read. He had lived near the municipality of Prijedor in northern Bosnia, and had been stopped one day at gunpoint at a roadblock on his way to work. The Black Dragons manned the roadblock. He had been taken by bus to a school auditorium where he was held all day. He claimed to have seen Draga there, commanding the Black Dragons. At the end of the day, he was bussed to the Omarska Camp.

Once at Omarska, the witness and other Muslims were subjected to constant beatings and torture. Many of them were shot and killed. As the witness recounted these events, Kevin could not help feeling empathy for this man and all that he had endured. He was not a sophisticated man, and his testimony was devoid of any bitterness. He had lost his freedom, his home, and had been subjected to two months of horror at Omarska. Kevin had no doubt that everything the witness was testifying about was the truth.

Kevin's mind kept wandering to Ellen. Was she being held by the same animals who ran Omarska? He wouldn't even let himself think about that. He pictured Ellen sitting alone in a room somewhere, crying. Maybe the kidnappers would let her go after Draga's statement was publicized. Maybe the police would get some leads and find Ellen. As he looked over at the witness, Kevin realized that this man must have had similar thoughts about the fate of his own family during his days at the Omarska camp.

The witness described encountering a cruel man named Victor Vidic wearing a Black Dragon uniform. Vidic had come to Omarska, and had slit the throat of one man in the dining hall while the prisoners watched in horror. "This is what happens if you do not obey the Dragons," Vidic had said.

Kevin tried not to show any reaction. Draga could be convicted just on this testimony alone. Under the Tribunal's law of superior responsibility, a commander was liable for the crimes of his subordinates. It would be critical for Kevin to prove that Victor Vidic was not one of the Black Dragons.

Kevin thought of the CIA evidence. If he used it, he could prove that Draga warned the CIA about the ethnic cleansing scheduled for Prijedor before it ever began. Now that Ellen's life was at stake, Kevin could not afford to pull any punches. He would have to revisit the decision about the CIA evidence with Draga before the end of the trial.

The witness went on to describe how Vidic came to Omarska almost every day and called people out of the rooms. They would be taken to a white house on the property and be beaten or killed. The witness was ultimately taken to another camp and eventually exchanged for Serb prisoners held by the Muslim Army.

"Do you have any permanent injuries from these beatings?" Stone asked.

"Yes, I have constant pain in my spine, especially when it is damp weather. I get headaches every day. My vision in one eye is blurry. I limp with my left leg. And I have been treated for depression. Some days I do not get out of bed and lie there wishing Vidic had killed me. My life has been destroyed."

Bradford Stone paused. He took off his glasses and looked over at Kevin. "Your witness, counselor."

Kevin stood and moved slowly to the podium. He took a deep breath. Every eye in the courtroom was upon him. The sympathy for the witness hung in the air like a rain cloud waiting to expel its moisture.

"I am so sorry."

The man did not respond.

"You have a lot of courage to have survived all of this, and then to come here and talk about it again."

Still the man did not respond. Finally, the witness said, "Thank you."

"What happened to your family?"

"They were forced to leave Prijedor two days after I was taken. They left with the clothes on their back and whatever they could carry. They made it to Croatia and became refugees there, like many people from Prijedor."

"How many children do you have?"

"Three. Two girls and a boy."

"How old were they?"

"My oldest daughter was fifteen, my son was thirteen, and my youngest daughter was ten."

Kevin thought of Ellen. "I have an eleven year old daughter," he said for no reason in particular. "I'm in some pain now, too. But I can't imagine your pain."

"I am grateful that it was me and not them."

"I know. I'd change places with my daughter in a heartbeat."

Judge Orozco shifted in her chair. Kevin knew that these personal references were making her and everyone else uncomfortable. But he wanted to connect with the witness, and he felt himself making that connection. Witness A had let his back slide down in his chair a bit. It was time to move on.

"What was Draga doing when you saw him at the auditorium?"

"He was marching in front of a line of men in black uniforms. They were standing at attention. He appeared to be giving them orders."

"Did you see anyone at the auditorium mistreated?"

"No."

"Were you yourself mistreated there?"

"No."

"Did you see Victor Vidic at the auditorium?"

"No."

"Could you please describe the physical appearance of the people at the road-block and auditorium in the black uniforms?"

"They were young. They looked very strong and muscular."

"Did any of them have long hair?"

"No."

"Did any of them have facial hair?"

"No."

"Did you see any of them smoking?"

"No."

"Did you see any of them drinking?"

"No."

"Did any of them appear intoxicated?"

"No."

"Did they appear to be a group of well disciplined soldiers?"

"Yes."

Kevin paused, hoping to signal a contrast to the judges. "Did Victor Vidic have long hair?"

"Yes, he did."

"Did he have a mustache and beard?"

"Yes."

"Did you ever see him smoking a cigarette?

"Yes, he had a cigarette every time I saw him."

"Did you ever see him drinking?"

"Yes."

"Was he intoxicated at times?"

"Yes."

Kevin was pleased. He was making his points, while not having to attack the credibility of the witness. He tried to take it a little further.

"Victor Vidic wore the uniform of a Black Dragon, correct?"

"Yes."

"But you don't know if he was under Draga's command?"

"No, I don't."

"Did Vidic act like the men you saw Draga commanding?"

"No. The men at the roadblock and auditorium were professionals. Vidic was an animal."

Kevin took his seat, satisfied.

His defense of Draga—and Ellen—had begun.

CHAPTER 23

▼

Ellen looked at the clock in the living room, which she had now completely converted into a schoolroom. "It's 1:10. I'm hungry. Can I have lunch now?"

"You'll have to make it yourself," Anna replied.

They had spent the morning following Ellen's school schedule. After feeding the puppy, chickens and roosters, and milking the cows, Ellen had begun school precisely at 8:30. Since then she had covered Language Arts, Science, Social Studies, and Dutch.

"This is a hard day you have at school," Anna said.

"I know. Wait 'til you see the math. I'm in advanced math and we're doing pre-Algebra."

"You might be teaching me."

Ellen kneeled down and petted Johanna. Ellen picked up Johanna and the two of them played with a sock.

"I love this puppy so much. Can I take her with me when I go home?"

"If no one claims her."

"I'm not going home today, am I?"

"No."

"When will I go home?"

"I don't know. One day we will get a phone call and we'll be told what to do with you. That's all I know."

"I really miss my parents and my real school."

Ellen heard the sound of the front door opening. Johanna squirmed out of her arms and scurried over to investigate. She jumped on Hans' boots as he and Jan entered.

Ellen and Anna made sandwiches for everyone and they sat at the kitchen table.

"I have a job for you," Hans said when they were seated. "I want you to write a short letter to your parents. Tell them that you're okay. You can't tell them anything about where you are, what you're doing or about any of us. Just tell them that you're fine and that you miss them."

"Okay, I'll do that as part of my homework tonight."

Ellen was determined to give her parents a clue to help them find her. She didn't know where she was, just that she was on a farm. She thought all day about what she could write. Finally, she wrote a note and showed it to Hans. He did not spot her clue.

She hoped her parents would.

✳   ✳   ✳   ✳

When court adjourned after his cross-examination of Witness A, Kevin rushed to his office and called Diane. There had been no new developments at home. Next, Kevin headed down to the holding cell in the basement where Draga was kept when he was not in the courtroom.

Draga had loosened his tie and taken off his blazer. He looked like an executive at the end of a tough day at the office.

"I owe you, big time," Kevin said, shaking Draga's hand warmly.

"Maybe you'll forgive my football debts."

"What are your football debts?"

"Well, the Raiders lost the AFC Championship yesterday. Didn't you hear? I owe you 70 Euros. But the Super Bowl is in two weeks."

"I've been a little preoccupied," Kevin said, sitting down on the wooden bench bolted to the wall of the bare cell. "You sure know how to take advantage of a guy when he's distracted."

Draga laughed. "I learned that in the army. Act decisively when your opponent is at his weakest."

"Thank you for what you did today. You've done more to get my daughter back than anyone."

"Any word yet?"

"Nothing."

"You did good with that witness."

"Thanks. Only about ninety-nine more to go."

"Old Stone face over there didn't look too happy. I think you neutralized their best witness."

"Why did you round up civilians?" Kevin asked, wondering if Draga might break his rule and talk about the case now that he had seemingly broken his other rule and spoken up in court.

"Our orders were to detain all military-age Muslim males. It was up to the Bosnian Serbs to figure out who was a soldier and who was a civilian. We couldn't take a town and leave people there to attack us from behind."

That made sense to Kevin. "Will you help me win your case and get my daughter back?"

"I'll do anything I can to get your daughter back. But winning the case? I don't think that is possible, with or without my help."

"I can't believe they would hold my daughter for the whole trial. It's going to take at least a month. She's never been away from home for more than a week."

"Maybe they'll see that you're doing the best you can and let her go. I'll do what I can to pass the word in Serbia."

Kevin left the lockup and headed for home. The news crews were awaiting him outside the Tribunal guardhouse.

"Any news on your daughter?" one reporter shouted.

"Nothing."

"How do you expect to win Draga's trial? Nobody has ever been acquitted at the Tribunal."

"Draga's case is unique," Kevin replied. "I'm convinced that he's innocent."

Kevin realized that he sounded like a zealous defense lawyer. After twenty years as a prosecutor, he didn't know he had it in him.

When he arrived home, Diane was sitting on the couch in the living room. Kevin took off his coat and sat down next to her.

"This is so hard," she said to Kevin. "To sit here all day doing nothing while Ellen is being held somewhere." Tears streamed down her face.

Kevin hugged his wife tightly. "This is a nightmare."

"When is it going to end?" Diane sobbed.

"I don't know. I just don't know."

"Do you think she's alive?"

Kevin closed his eyes. "I think so. What would be gained by killing her? Then their game would be over and they would not have accomplished anything."

"What are they trying to accomplish?"

"Make the Court release Draga. Make me fight harder for him. Or maybe it is the CIA—trying to make it look like the Serbs. I don't know. It's insane."

"Will they hold her for the whole trial? I don't think I can take this much longer."

Kevin put his arm around Diane's shoulders. "Why don't you ask Detective Weber if there is something you can do to help, like going around with Ellen's picture or organizing volunteers?"

Diane pulled back. "I'm not good at that stuff. That's something you would do. I just want my daughter back." She burst into tears again.

Kevin felt Diane's resentment. He knew that she was unbelievably angry with him and blamed him for what had happened. There would be a time when that wound would have to be healed, or their marriage would not survive.

Although he was hungry and exhausted, Kevin sat with Diane on the couch for the next hour, talking out all of the possibilities.

"At least you have a purpose," Diane finally said. "You can go to court every day trying to win Draga's case. I haven't been out of the house since this happened."

Kevin knew that Diane was not really expecting a solution to their nightmare from him; she just wanted to talk, and express her feelings. But he couldn't help himself. "I've got an idea. Why don't you come to court with me and help on Draga's case?"

Diane frowned. "I haven't practiced law for more than eleven years."

"So what? You know a lot about Draga's case from listening to me. You don't have to handle any witnesses—just read the reports and give me some ideas. It'll look good to the kidnappers, like we are trying everything. It will get you out of the house, and we'll be together."

Diane was quiet. She looked down and squeezed her hands together.

Kevin knew she never liked the confrontation that took place in a courtroom.

"What would I wear?" she finally said, smiling.

"Let's go up to your closet and have a look."

They got up from the couch and went upstairs.

Kevin was pleased that Diane was considering helping at trial. The more he thought about this spur of the moment idea, the better he liked it. It would give Diane something to do, and it would help him as well.

"I would just be doing this for Ellen," Diane said, opening her closet door. "I never liked being in court."

"I know. But this is the best way we can help Ellen now. Let's go for it."

Diane stood looking in her closet, pulling hangers to the side and examining her garments critically.

"You'll be wearing a robe in court," Kevin said. "You just need a nice pair of shoes."

Diane frowned. Then she began going through her assembled shoes.

"I'm going to make myself something to eat," Kevin said after a few minutes. "Come join me when you're done."

When Diane came downstairs, she was still undecided.

"I don't really know what to do," she said. "I am such a mess—I can't decide what shoes to wear. How in the world am I going to be any help in court?"

"Why don't you sleep on it? You don't have to come tomorrow. Think about it for awhile."

Kevin ate his dinner alone while Diane went back to sitting on the couch. When he looked in on her, she was reading a novel. It was almost ten o'clock.

"I'm going to bed," Kevin said. "I can't stay awake any more."

"I'll be up in a while."

When Kevin's alarm went off the next morning, there was an empty space in the bed next to him. He got up to look for Diane. He went found her downstairs, sitting at the dining room table wearing a blue skirt, cream-colored blouse, and black pumps. She was reading one of Kevin's files from his briefcase.

"Does this mean what I think it means?"

"I'm doing this for Ellen," Diane replied wearily.

Kevin walked over to the table and gave her a kiss.

He remembered how they had once been a great team. Could they still do it?

When they drove to The Hague, Kevin filled Diane in on who would be testifying and who all the people were in the courtroom.

"What if the kidnappers call and I'm not home to answer the phone?" she asked.

"They'll call back at night. It'll probably be on the news that you are in the courtroom. I hope Ellen hears about this. She'll be so proud."

Diane shook her head. "I can't believe I'm doing this."

When they entered Courtroom 1, Diane looked out to the visitors' gallery. "This is weird," she said. "That glass between the courtroom and the audience makes me feel like I'm on the inside of a fish bowl."

Diane looked at Kevin warily. "Why do I let you talk me into these things? I didn't even want to come to Holland. Now you've got me in the courtroom helping defend a war criminal."

He smiled. "Must be my powers of persuasion."

"All rise! *Veuillez vous lever!*"

Kevin and Diane rose as the judges entered the room. "Prosecution versus Dragoljub Zaric, case number IT-96-30. Counsel, your appearances please," the Deputy Registrar announced when the judges had been seated.

"Bradford Stone and Charles Oswald for the prosecution."

Kevin spoke next. "Good morning, Your Honors. Kevin and Diane Anderson for the accused."

Judge Orozco's eyebrows shot up.

"I would like to introduce my wife, Diane, to the Court," Kevin continued. "She is also a lawyer, duly admitted to practice law in the United States. With the court's permission, she is here to help me defend Mr. Zaric, and to show those who hold our daughter that we are doing everything humanly possible on Mr. Zaric's behalf."

Judge Orozco smiled at Diane. "It's nice to meet you, Mrs. Anderson. I am sorry it is under these circumstances."

Diane gave a forced smile. Judge Orozco turned to the prosecution. "Is there any objection to Mrs. Anderson participating in the defense?"

Bradford Stone rose. "We've had no notice of this, Your Honor. But we continue to believe that it is inappropriate for Mr. Anderson to be representing Mr. Zaric given his emotional state and what has occurred this weekend. I hardly think that Mrs. Anderson's emotional condition can be any better."

Diane glared at Bradford Stone across the room.

"What a pompous ass," she whispered under her breath.

Judge Orozco turned to Judge Davidson and then Judge Linares and had short conversations with each of them. Then she turned to Draga. "Mr. Zaric, do you have any objection to Mrs. Anderson participating in your defense?"

Kevin turned to look at Draga, wishing he had a chance to talk to Draga about this first. Draga looked handsome in a light gray suit. His client had turned into a clothes horse. Kevin wondered where he was getting the nice threads.

Draga stood up. "I would welcome her help," he said gallantly.

Kevin smiled at Diane. The war criminal was turning into a prince.

"Very well then," Judge Orozco said with a smile. "Welcome to the Tribunal, Mrs. Anderson."

CHAPTER 24

▼

The prosecution's next witness was another Muslim from the Prijedor area who had been stopped at the roadblock, taken to the school auditorium, and then to Omarska. He had not seen Draga, but had seen and experienced firsthand the beatings by Victor Vidic at Omarska.

Kevin's cross-examination began as it had with Witness A. He elicited the facts about Vidic's unkempt personal appearance and smoking and drinking habits, as contrasted with the men in black uniforms the witness had seen at the roadblock and auditorium. Then he tried to extend his gains a little further.

"Victor Vidic is a brutal human being isn't he?"

"Yes, he is"

"Did he ever perform guard duty at the camp?"

"No."

"Did he ever do anything at Omarska other than show up and beat people or try to extort them?"

"Not that I am aware of."

"You knew him from before the war?"

"Yes."

"He was in trouble with the police for violent crimes before the war started, correct?"

"Yes, he was."

"He had been to jail?"

"I heard that he had."

"In fact, he was in jail when the Serbs took over Prijedor, wasn't he?"

"I'm not sure."

Kevin turned to the judges. "Your Honors, at this time I would like to introduce a document, to be designated as Defense Exhibit 1. It is a certified copy of the records of the Prijedor jail for the months of March through May, 1992."

Judge Orozco waited while the usher handed the document up to her and distributed copies for the other two judges and prosecutor. When she had reviewed the document, she turned to the prosecution. "Any objection?"

"Well, it's our document," Bradford Stone huffed. "He got it from us. We intend to offer this document into evidence ourselves."

"Very well," Judge Orozco said, ignoring Stone's complaint, "Defense Exhibit 1 shall be received into evidence."

"Thank you, Your Honor," Kevin replied. "I would ask the usher to display the document on the screen." The usher rose and placed the top piece of paper on a machine which projected the document on the computer screens in front of the trial participants and on the television screens in the visitors' gallery.

Turning back to the witness, Kevin asked. "Would you agree that this shows that Victor Vidic was in jail in Prijedor on the day of the roadblock and had been in jail for the two months before that?"

"Yes, that's what it looks like."

"You're not aware of any training that Vidic went through with the Black Dragons are you?"

"No, I'm not."

"He was about as untrained and undisciplined a man as you ever met, wasn't he?"

"Yes."

Kevin thought for an instant about stopping there. He had accomplished just about everything he had wanted in his cross-examination. Up to this point he had known the answers to the questions he had asked. From here on out, it would be a gamble.

"The prisoners talked among themselves about Victor Vidic, didn't they?"

"Yes."

"You had a lot of time on your hands."

"Yes."

"And Vidic was notorious at Omarska, especially after he slit that man's throat."

"Yes."

"Victor Vidic always wore the uniform of the Black Dragons, didn't he?"

"Yes."

"But it was well known among the prisoners that he wasn't really a Black Dragon, wasn't it?"

Kevin held his breath waiting for the answer. Because hearsay was allowed at the Tribunal, he knew the prosecution could not object to Kevin's question about what others had said out of court. He was guessing that the prisoners would have seen Vidic for what he was.

The witness appeared to be thinking about his answer. Then he spoke. Kevin waited for the translation. "There was a lot of talk that he was not really a Black Dragon."

Kevin took a shallow breath and plunged further. His trial lawyer instincts told him there was more gold in the mine. "Did anyone talk about where he had gotten the Black Dragon uniform?"

"Yes."

"Where had he gotten the uniform, from what you heard?"

"People said he had his Black Dragon uniform made by a sewing shop in Sokolaz."

"In your opinion was Vidic under the control or command of Dragoljub Zaric, known as Draga?"

"Your Honors," Bradford Stone was on his feet, interrupting. "We must object. There is no basis for this witness to give an opinion on that issue. He wasn't privy to the chain of command."

Judge Orozco looked at Kevin. "Mr. Anderson?"

"Madam President, this witness was in a position to make observations of Vidic's behavior and to evaluate information he received from others. Because of that, his opinion would be of some assistance to the Court."

"The objection is overruled. The witness may answer."

Kevin wondered whether the witness would back off now that the prosecution had signaled its displeasure with the way the testimony was going. Kevin had taken control; he just needed to maintain it for these last few questions. He repeated the question. He hoped the man was as honest as he seemed.

"I don't think Victor Vidic was under the command of Draga or anyone else. He just did what he pleased."

"He was not a real Black Dragon, was he?"

"No."

"Thank you. I have no further questions." Kevin returned to his seat. Bradford Stone stood up quickly to try to repair the damage. He asked several questions in which he tried to show that his own witness didn't really know what he had been talking about.

"You don't really know what the relationship was between Vidic and Draga, do you?"

"No."

"You don't know with whom Vidic shared the property he stole from the prisoners, do you?"

"No."

"And you don't know whether Vidic was acting on his own or on orders from Draga, do you?"

"No, I don't."

"Thank you, I have no further questions." Stone sat down, having neutralized his own witness. He looked annoyed.

"I have a question," Judge Orozco said. "What makes you think that Vidic was not under Draga's command?"

"He was a criminal before the war and he acted the same way during the war. He did not act like a soldier. And why would he have to pay someone to make him a uniform if he was a real Black Dragon?"

That question hung in the air as the witness was excused. While the man left the courtroom, Kevin whispered to Diane. "How are you doing?"

"Okay," she said. "You did great with that witness. I forgot how good you are."

"Thanks, honey. But wait until we get to the guy who saw Draga shoot someone."

"Mr. Stone," Judge Davidson said, "I have a question for you while we are waiting for the next witness. How many more witnesses will testify about crimes committed by this Victor Vidic?"

"About twenty, Your Honor."

"That's what I thought," Judge Davidson said. "Besides the fact that he wore the uniform, what evidence do you have that he was a member of the Black Dragons?"

"Well, um, it's part of a pattern," Stone stammered. "Other Black Dragons did the same things at other camps."

"Do you have any documents or records showing that Vidic was trained by the accused or his men?"

"No." A trace of annoyance crept into Stone's voice.

Judge Davidson continued his cross-examination of Stone. "Do you have any documents or records showing that Vidic was a member of the Black Dragons?"

"No."

"Just the uniform?"

"The uniform, and the pattern."

Turning to Kevin, Judge Davidson said. "Mr. Anderson, you don't seem to be disputing that Vidic committed these war crimes."

"That's correct, Your Honor. We do not dispute that."

"Your position is that he was not under the supervision or command of your client."

"That's correct."

Judge Davidson nodded. He turned back to Bradford Stone. "Mr. Stone, there is no point in wasting our time with twenty more witnesses about Victor Vidic. We'll listen to your evidence about the other camps and see if there is the pattern that you have alluded to. We'll listen to any evidence that links Vidic to the accused. But any more testimony about Vidic's individual crimes would be cumulative and a waste of our time."

"But, Your Honor," Stone pleaded, "these acts are in the indictment. We have to be allowed to prove them."

"You've already proven enough to convict the accused of murder, inhumane treatment, and torture, if you can prove that Vidic acted under the command of the accused. So let's get to the point and not waste our time."

Bradford Stone sputtered. "But—may I have a moment, Your Honor?" He turned to Charles Oswald. They huddled with their investigator, Allen Jacobson, and other members of the prosecution team. When they emerged, Charles Oswald addressed the court.

"Your Honors, if this is your ruling, we do not have any more witnesses for today. The remaining witnesses we had scheduled all deal with Vidic. We will have to recess until tomorrow."

Judge Orozco looked over at Judge Davidson, then at Judge Linares. After a few whispered words among them, she announced, "Very well, the court will be in recess until 9:30 tomorrow morning." The judges rose from their chairs and filed out of the courtroom.

Kevin turned to Diane. "Come on, I have someone I want you to meet." He walked back to where Draga was seated.

"This is my wife, Diane."

Diane stuck out her hand. "Nice to meet you."

Draga took her hand, lowered his head, and kissed it. "The pleasure is mine."

Kevin laughed. "Stop hustling my wife."

Diane looked taken aback.

Draga was smiling. "After two witnesses, you're two for two," he said to Kevin.

"They're going to regroup now."

"You can handle it," Draga said. Turning to Diane, he asked if there was any late word on Ellen.

Diane shook her head grimly.

"I am sorry. If I can do anything, let me know. I have children, too."

Diane managed to get out "thank you" as she looked down at the floor. The mention of Ellen had brought her back to the real world.

"I'll see you in the morning." Kevin said to Draga.

"I'll see if I can fit you in. I'm rather busy, you know."

Kevin laughed. "I'll get you a USA Today so you can read about your Raiders."

"For that, I will cancel my other engagements."

Kevin smiled and led Diane out of the courtroom as the guards took Draga out into the holding area through his special exit. "He's not so bad, is he?" Kevin asked as they walked down the hall in their matching black robes.

"I guess not. He seems to like you."

"There you go. The man has excellent judgment and taste."

As they drove home, Kevin and Diane talked about Zoran Vacinovic. "Somebody had to tell the kidnappers where you lived, that you had a daughter, and where she went to school," Diane said. "He certainly had that information."

"It's strange he hasn't called," Kevin said. "I'd like to go over to the embassy and talk to him. Maybe I can get a feel for whether he knows something. At the least, I can ask for his help."

"Don't do anything on your own, please."

When they arrived home, there were no more reporters in front of their row house. Kevin was glad to get some privacy back, but worried that their story was fading from the limelight. He didn't want people to forget about Ellen and stop looking for her.

When they entered their house, Diane checked their phone messages. There were none. Kevin checked their mail. There was a letter addressed to him. The return address said simply "Ellen."

Kevin yelled for Diane. "There's something here from Ellen."

Diane rushed over.

"Don't touch the envelope," Kevin said excitedly, "There might be fingerprints."

"Should we open it?" Diane asked.

"Hell, yes."

Diane got the letter opener while Kevin slipped a newspaper under the letter and carried the paper to their dining room table. Holding the envelope by the edges, he opened it. There were two pieces of paper inside. He unfolded the first. It read:

> **Start defending Draga and the Honor of Serbia or your daughter will die. She will only be free if Draga is freed.**

Kevin and Diane looked at the typewritten message on the first piece of paper from the envelope. It was unsigned, and appeared to be in a standard font from a personal computer. Kevin picked up the other paper by the edges. It was a note in a handwriting he immediately recognized.

> I am Fine. They Are treating me good. I hope they will Return me soon. I love you, Mommy and daddy.
>
> Ellen

Kevin looked at Diane. "At least she's alive," he said.

Tears had welled up in Diane's eyes. "What do these people want from us? You can't get Draga released. Why don't they realize that? Why don't they just let her go?"

"We're not dealing with rational people," Kevin replied. He studied the first note. "'Defend the Honor of Serbia.' That's what Vacinovic has been saying."

Kevin picked up the envelope by the edges to look at the postmark. It had been sent from Amsterdam. "At least she's close. They didn't take her to Serbia."

"Well, they wouldn't mail it from where she's at. And there's a million people in Amsterdam. How are they going to find her?" Diane lamented. "We'd better call Detective Weber right away." She walked over to the phone.

Kevin looked at the two notes again and the envelope which were lying on the newspaper on his dining room table. Maybe they would help the police find Ellen. Perhaps the printer on which the typed letter was produced, the postmark, or some fingerprints could provide a clue.

Diane hung up the phone. "She's on her way."

Kevin went upstairs to get out of his suit and into some comfortable clothes. Defend the Honor of Serbia, he thought. How am I supposed to do that?

When Detective Weber arrived, she read the notes. "Is this one your daughter's handwriting?"

"Yes," Diane replied. "I know how she makes the capital "E" in Ellen. It's her writing all right."

"We'll have these fingerprinted and analyzed. It's good news. Ellen's alive and the kidnappers may have given us some clues."

"This 'Honor of Serbia' business," Kevin said. "It's the same thing that Zoran Vacinovic was trying to get me to do. He argued with me when I told him the court doesn't allow the defense that the other side committed war crimes first. He said that the world was watching the trial and I needed to defend the honor of the Serbian people, not just Draga."

Detective Weber nodded her head. "We have been looking at Vacinovic. He's apparently highly placed in the Serbian secret police and well connected to the allies of former President Milosevic. He's assigned to The Hague to monitor the war crimes trials for the government."

"Do you think he's involved?" Diane asked.

"I don't know. We've been following him yesterday and today, but he's just gone to the embassy and worked."

"Can I go talk to him?" Kevin asked.

"Let's wait on that and give our surveillance a little longer."

"What should we do?" Diane asked. "What can we do?"

"You're doing everything you can. Going to court with your husband was a good gesture. It shows the kidnappers that you are willing to do everything to get your daughter back. Maybe that will give them more reason to think their demands will be met."

"Should we try to show that we are defending the honor of Serbia?" Kevin asked.

"Sure. The more they see you taking their demands seriously, the more likely we'll hear from them again."

Detective Weber took out some plastic bags and tweezers and began putting the letters and envelopes inside. "I'll send these to the Forensic Department. They'll look for fingerprints."

"I just want to look at Ellen's note one more time," Diane said. "It's the only part of her I have left."

Diane and Kevin looked at the note again.

"Not a word misspelled," Diane said.

"It's odd that she capitalized some words in the middle of a sentence, though," Kevin replied. "See, she's capitalized Fine, Are, Return and Mommy."

Kevin suddenly realized what Ellen had done. "I think she might be sending us a message. Those letters she's capitalized spell FARM. She's on a farm!"

Diane and Detective Weber looked at the note again.

"You're right," Diane said. "She likes those acrostic things. She wouldn't have capitalized those words for any other reason."

"That's quite a girl," Detective Weber said. "She slipped that past her captors."

"She almost slipped it past us," Kevin said. "Way to go Ellen!"

"What can you do if you know she's on a farm?" Diane asked the detective. "There are lots of farms in Holland, and we don't even know if she's still in the country."

"Well, we can concentrate on rural areas in Holland when distributing her picture. We can also interview feed-store owners and other businesses to see if anyone new has moved into a farm recently. I'm sure there are other things we'll think of."

As Kevin and Diane walked Detective Weber to the door, Kevin was feeling upbeat because Ellen was alive, and feeding them clues.

He wondered what it was like for her on the farm.

CHAPTER 25

▼

At that very moment, Ellen was eating dinner with Hans, Jan, and Anna.

"My mom doesn't make me eat green beans," Ellen said. "I don't like them."

"You should learn to like them," Anna replied.

Ellen grumbled and began picking at the beans. She ate a few green beans along with the pasta that Anna had cooked.

"Can I put in a few requests next time somebody goes shopping?" she asked.

"Like what?" Anna asked.

"Some Oreo cookies, fruit roll-ups, Pringle potato chips, that kind of stuff."

"Forget it!" Anna said. "You get fresh fruit, green vegetables, and granola."

Ellen groaned. "This is child abuse!"

Anna cleared the table while Ellen went out to the schoolroom.

"We're not getting any good treats," she said to Johanna as she bent down to play with the puppy. "I'll get you some good stuff when we get to my house."

Ellen wondered if her parents had received her letter. She hoped they had gotten her clue. Tomorrow, she would try to find out more about where they were so she could send another clue home.

If that didn't work, she'd have to look into a way to escape.

＊　　＊　　＊　　＊

The next morning, Diane and Kevin were in Courtroom 1 waiting for the judges to enter. They had decided to try to convince the court to allow evidence of the atrocities committed against the Serbs. At least they could show the kidnappers that they were trying to "defend the honor of Serbia." A stack of six law books sat on the desk next to Diane, who would write the brief.

The prosecution's next witness entered the courtroom a few minutes later. He had grown up in Sarajevo, the capital of Bosnia, and was working as a waiter in a restaurant there when the Serbs started shelling and shooting down from the hills with sniper fire.

According to the witness, he and his friend, Dimitri Bojanovic, had been driving near the airport one night after having a few drinks at a bar when two Black Dragons with rifles stopped them. The men ordered them out of the car and took them into a warehouse, where they were interrogated about the location of the Muslim positions and the kind of arms the Muslim Army had. Both men claimed they were only waiters and did not fight for the Muslim forces. The warehouse was some kind of command center for the Black Dragons. Dozens of men in black uniforms and black berets were coming and going from the warehouse.

After the initial questioning, the witness and Bojanovic were taken to another office. Draga was behind the desk. The witness recognized him from television. Draga was wearing the Black Dragon uniform. He stood up and towered over the men. "You have one last chance," he demanded. "Tell me the truth."

The witness said he and his friend, Bojanovic, steadfastly insisted that they had nothing to do with the Muslim Army. "We are just waiters. We work all the time, we don't have time to fight." Draga stared at them intently as they begged him to believe them. When they had finished, he sat back down. "Very well, you have had your chance. I will take you at your word. If we see you in a Muslim uniform, you are dead."

Draga told the two men they were free to leave. They scurried out of the warehouse and back into the witness' car. They couldn't believe that they had survived an encounter with the Black Dragons.

While they were driving home, according to the witness, Bojanovic wanted to tell a Muslim Army commander whom he knew about the location of the warehouse. He convinced the witness to drive up in the lower part of the hills so he could give the Muslims the location of the Black Dragons' command center. Bojanovic directed the witness to an area where the Muslim army apparently was hiding.

When the witness stopped the car, Bojanovic got out and began running towards the trench. Suddenly, a shot rang out. Bojanovic fell to the ground. The witness looked back towards where the shot came from. He had a clear view of Draga, just lowering his rifle. Draga and his men then stormed the trench where the Muslim Army was hiding.

The witness was yanked from the car and thrown to the ground. He stayed there for about an hour while the Dragons launched grenades into the Muslim position. He heard screams from inside the bunker as explosions ripped it apart. When all was quiet, the Dragons stormed into the trench. All the Muslim soldiers were apparently dead.

Draga came over to the witness after the fighting was over. He picked him up off the ground and dragged him to the body of Bojanovic. Bojanovic was clearly dead. "You two were very foolish," he said. "But thank you for the escort." He dropped the witness back to the ground on top of Bojanovic's body, and left. The witness was taken by other Black Dragons and later turned over to the Bosnian Serb Army. He was transported by bus to the prison camp at Foca, where he remained for a month before being exchanged for Serbian prisoners.

Bradford Stone looked at the judges, making sure they had understood every word of the witness' testimony. "Were you ever a member of the Muslim Army?" he asked.

"Never."

"Was Bojanovic?"

"Never. We were just waiters."

"Is there any doubt in your mind that it was Draga who fired the shot that killed your friend the waiter?" Stone asked in conclusion.

"There is no doubt. I saw it with my own eyes."

Stone turned to the judges, and removed his glasses. "I have no further questions of this witness."

Kevin was out of his chair, ready to start his cross-examination, but Judge Orozco called for the lunch recess. Kevin sat back down. He would have to wait.

Diane went back to the office while Kevin dropped in on Draga in the holding cell. "Got a minute?"

"Just one. I'm late for an appointment."

Kevin smiled. "Did you shoot that guy?"

Draga looked at Kevin. "Hell, yes, I shot that guy. He was going to tell the Muslim Army the location of our operations."

"What happened?"

"It was just like the witness testified. He's told it exactly the way it happened."

"Why did you let them go?"

"I figured they would lead us to the Muslim Army, and they did. We killed about 50 men in that bunker that night. Then the Bosnian Serb Army used it. It was a very strategic position."

Kevin was silent.

"Was that a war crime?" Draga asked.

"It depends on whether Bojanovic was an innocent civilian or a military person. This is what we call Monday morning quarterbacking. You make a decision in the midst of a war, then eight years later the lawyers are picking it apart under a microscope."

"Well, the witness told the truth. I'll just have to accept the consequences."

"He didn't tell the whole truth."

"What do you mean?"

"You'll see this afternoon."

"Well, speaking of quarterbacking," Draga said, brightening. "What is our wager on the Super Bowl? The Giants are seven-point favorites. Will you give me the Ravens and seven points?"

"Six points."

"You are a weasel. How much is the final wager? I need to make up my 70 Euro deficit."

"10 Euros."

"Oh, come on, for the Super Bowl. It won't even make the game interesting to watch."

"What do you want to wager?"

"A hundred Euros."

"That's chump change for you," Kevin said, laughing.

"I know, but I figure it's the most you can afford to lose."

"It's a deal. You can have the Ravens and six points for a hundred Euros."

Draga and Kevin shook hands on the deal. "One more thing," Draga pulled out a piece of paper with a large number of squares on it. "Do you want to buy a square in the prison football pool?"

"You are incorrigible! You're going to get three years for bookmaking on top of your war crime sentence."

Kevin went back into the courtroom. He double-checked his folder for the witness. The ammunition his friend Nihudian had gathered in Bosnia was there. A wave of sadness swept over him as he remembered the night Nihudian had died.

Kevin sat down and went over again how he would detonate Nihudian's ammunition that afternoon.

＊   ＊   ＊   ＊

"Good afternoon," Kevin began in a friendly voice.

"Good afternoon."

"Did I understand you to say that you were never in the Muslim Army?

"Yes"

"And neither was Bojanovic?"

"That's correct?"

"Were you ever in any military unit of any kind?"

"No."

"Was Bojanovic?"

"No."

"At the time of this incident with Draga you were both civilians?"

"Yes."

Kevin realized that he was repeating damaging information that Stone had already brought out, but he needed to close off all avenues of escape. He turned to the Court.

"Your Honors, with the assistance of the usher, I would like the witness to be shown what has been marked as defense exhibit 2."

The usher placed the document before the witness and distributed copies to the judges and prosecutor. "Sir, this is a certified copy of an application for widow's benefits filed by Bojanovic's wife. Do you see her name there?"

The witness studied the document. "Yes, I do."

"I'd like to offer defense exhibit 2 in evidence."

"Any objection, Mr. Stone?" Judge Orozco asked.

"Well, Your Honor, we've just received this document. We weren't aware of it before now."

"Very well. It will be admitted, subject to reconsideration if the prosecution lodges an objection."

"Thank you, Madame President," Kevin said. He turned to the witness. "Do you see where Bojanovic's widow stated that her husband had been on active duty with the Bosnian Muslim Army at the time of his death?"

The witness' eyes were fixed on the document. "Yes, I see that. But, I have not seen this paper before."

"I understand that. Do you know why Bojanovic's widow would state that he was in the Muslim Army?"

"Maybe she wanted to get some benefits from the government, I don't know."

"That would be dishonest, wouldn't it?"

The witness shifted in his chair. "I guess so."

"Do you see where she signed it under penalty of perjury?"

"Yes, I do."

"Are you suggesting that your friend's widow committed perjury to collect benefits from the government?"

"I don't know."

"But you do know that Bojanovic was a civilian at the time of his death?"

"Yes, he was."

"As were you?"

"Correct." The witness' eyes darted quickly over to the prosecution table, and then back to the document.

"Madam President, may the witness be shown defense exhibit 3?"

Judge Orozco nodded. The usher distributed the document and the copies.

"Do you recognize Exhibit 3?"

The man sunk lower in his chair, his eyes fixed on the document.

"I guess so."

"Why don't you tell the court what it is?"

"It's an application for compensation for the time I spent at the Foca camp."

"Is that your signature?"

"Yes."

"And you are applying for back wages from the Bosnian Muslim government for the time that you were imprisoned at Foca?"

"Yes."

"And do you see the part where you certified that you were on active military duty at the time of your capture?"

"Yes."

"You also signed this document under penalty of perjury, did you not?"

"Yes."

Kevin paused to let the answer sink in. He asked his next question slowly.

"So, which is the perjury, your statement in exhibit 3 that you were on active military duty, or your testimony in this courtroom that you were never in the military?"

The witness looked at Kevin, then at Bradford Stone. Then he looked at Judge Orozco. "Do I have to answer that question?" he asked her.

"You have a privilege to refuse to answer if the answer would incriminate you," Judge Orozco replied. "You can also consult with a lawyer if you wish, and we can appoint one for you if you can't afford one,"

Bradford Stone and Charles Oswald were huddling with their team. Kevin was sure they were not pleased at having their star witness given his Miranda warnings by the judge. Kevin looked over at the witness, waiting for an answer.

The witness paused, and looked over at the prosecutors. Finally, he said, "I lied on the form."

"So you committed perjury to your government?" Kevin asked, rubbing it in a bit.

"Yes." The man was still looking down.

"But everything you told this Court was the truth?"

"Right."

"You were never in any military?"

"Never."

"And neither was Bojanovic?"

"Right."

"You're sure about that?"

The witness hesitated slightly. He took a slow breath. "Yes," he said softly.

Bradford Stone came to his rescue. "Madam President, these questions have now been asked and answered three times. I object."

"Objection sustained. Move on, Mr. Anderson," Judge Orozco said.

Kevin was more than ready to do so—in fact, he couldn't wait.

"I would like the witness to be shown defense exhibit 4," he announced, pulling out one more folder. "May I approach the witness and show it to him myself. It's a photograph."

"Very well."

Kevin handed the usher copies to distribute as he approached the witness. He stood next to the witness and placed the photograph in front of him. "Do you recognize this photograph?" he asked.

The witness appeared to wince. He stared at the photograph of himself and Bojanovic with their arms around each other's shoulders, wearing Muslim Army uniforms with rifles in their outstretched arms. The judges looked at the photograph, then at the witness expectantly. The prosecution team huddled around the photograph, whispering furiously.

"Do you recognize this photograph?" Kevin asked again, looking down at the witness, just a few inches in front of him.

There was no answer.

"We got it from Bojanovic's wife. We know a lot more, as well. I think it's time you told the truth."

The witness did not move. He continued staring at the photograph.

Bradford Stone tried to break the awkward silence. "Your Honor, Mr. Anderson should be ordered to return to the podium. He's shown the witness the exhibit."

Without waiting for the Judge to respond, Kevin backed up, returning to his position, but keeping his eyes on the witness. Finally, the witness looked up at Kevin.

"Your friend's widow and children think he died for his people as a hero," Kevin said softly. "Are you being fair to his memory?"

Bradford Stone rose again. "Mr. Anderson keeps asking questions without giving the witness a chance to answer," he whined.

"Yes," Judge Orozco said. "Witness, do you recognize the photograph?"

"Yes."

"Go ahead, Mr. Anderson."

"I'd offer it into evidence, Madam President."

"Any objection, Mr. Stone?"

Stone was back consulting with Oswald and the others. He did not reply.

"Hearing no objection, defense exhibit 4 will be admitted," Judge Orozco said tersely. "Continue, Mr. Anderson."

"This is a photograph of you and Bojanovic, is it not?"

"It is."

"Were you and Bojanovic in the Muslim Army at the time of his death?"

The courtroom was still.

The witness looked from Kevin to the photograph, then he answered. "Yes."

Bradford Stone was once again on his feet. "Your Honors, I think the witness needs counsel at this point. Perhaps we should recess his testimony until he has an opportunity to consult with a lawyer."

Judge Davidson leaned forward on the bench. "We can do without your interruptions, Mr. Stone. Witness, you have just admitted to perjury before this Court on a most important point. You sat here all morning telling us you were civilians. Now, you are admitting that you were in fact in the military. We need to know the truth."

"We were in the military, Your Honor," the witness replied shakily.

"What were you doing near the airport that night?"

"Looking for the Dragons' headquarters."

"Did you tell this to Mr. Stone?"

Stone was on his feet. "Of course he didn't, Your Honor! We're as surprised as you are. We've been sandbagged by the defense. They gave us no notice of these documents or the photograph."

Judge Davidson ignored Stone. "Did you tell this to Mr. Stone?" he repeated.
"No."

"Where did you get the idea to claim you were civilians?" Judge Davidson
asked.

Kevin was now a spectator to the cross-examination.

"Before the investigators asked me questions, they explained to me that if
Bojanovic and I were civilians, they could convict Draga of a war crime. If we
were in the military, then it was just part of the war. I wanted Draga to pay for
killing my friend. So, I told them we were civilians. I didn't know that all this
would come out." He looked down again at the photograph.

"Mr. Anderson," Judge Davidson said. "I don't believe any further questions
from you are necessary."

"I agree, Your Honor." Kevin sat down.

"Mr. Stone," Judge Davidson said. The judge was clearly in control now.
"You don't have any more questions either."

Stone rose shakily to his feet. "No, Your Honor."

"The witness may be excused."

The usher quickly drew the blinds. The witness couldn't wait to get out of the
courtroom. When he had gone, Judge Orozco said, "I think we have heard
enough for today. We'll reconvene tomorrow at 9:30 a.m."

Bradford Stone leaped to his feet. "Madam President, I would ask that you
order Mr. Anderson to provide us with copies of all of his exhibits. He's being
quite unfair."

"No," Judge Davidson replied pointedly. "You know that the defense doesn't
have to disclose their impeachment in advance. You'd better warn your witnesses
to tell the truth."

Kevin couldn't help but smile. He looked down, trying hard to suppress it. He
looked over at Diane. She was looking at him with pride. He looked back at
Draga. He was reading the sports page. An admiring audience of one wasn't bad,
Kevin decided.

Silently, he thanked Nihudian for the legal ammunition he had provided.
Without it, Kevin knew he would have had great difficulty impeaching this very
critical witness, and no chance at all of winning Draga's acquittal—and Ellen's
release.

He just wished his dear friend had been here to see it.

CHAPTER 26

▼

At that moment, the trial of Draga was the furthest thing from the minds of the three kidnappers. They were doing chores in the barn when they suddenly heard the sound of a car coming down the road.

"Quick!" Hans yelled to Anna. "Hide the girl!"

Anna grabbed Ellen by the hand and led her to the back of the barn and one of the stalls for the cows. "Get down here," she ordered sternly.

Anna knelt down with Ellen; both were out of sight of anyone entering the barn.

Ellen, taken by surprise, started sobbing quietly. She hated being pushed around. Besides, the stall reeked of cow manure. Anna held her finger to her lips signaling Ellen to be quiet. Ellen obeyed.

Hans went out to meet the visitor.

Ellen could hear a car engine running. She looked through a small crack in the boards where she was huddled. She saw Hans talking to a man who was standing next to a pickup truck. The man handed Hans some papers, then got back in his truck.

Ellen considered trying to scream, but then she thought about the basement and the rats. Anyway, she wasn't sure the man could hear her over his engine. She watched him as he drove past the barn and back toward what she suspected was the main road. As the white truck passed she was able to make out the Dutch writing: "Province of Utrecht."

When the man had left, Hans returned to the barn and Anna stood up.

"It's clear now," Jan said.

Ellen stood up as well. "Who was it?"

"None of your business," Hans replied.

"I don't like it when you make me hide." Ellen stepped into the open doorway of the barn, wanting to breathe the fresh air and see the sky. "I want my mommy and daddy. I miss them."

No one replied.

Ellen sat down and played with Johanna. The puppy was licking her face and jumping all over her. "I'd like to write my parents another letter," she said. "Would you send it for me?"

"Maybe," Jan replied.

"I think I'll go do that now. It'll cheer me up."

"Okay," Anna said. She followed Ellen into the house.

Ellen went into the house, her head down. She sat at the table with a paper and pencil. "Province of Utrecht." How could she let her parents know?

When they had finished dinner that night, Ellen got out her letter and showed it to Jan. She had addressed an envelope as well. "Here's my letter. You can read it. I followed all the rules."

Jan looked at the letter.

"Will you send it? I'll give you the money for a stamp."

"We'll see," Jan replied.

"Here's eighty cents." Ellen took a small coin purse out of her backpack and counted out the coins. "We need to talk about an allowance. If I'm still here by Saturday, I think you should pay me an allowance."

"You're not serious," Hans said.

"I get eleven Euros a week at home. I do a lot more chores here than I do at home."

"Don't you have homework to do now?" Hans asked.

"You sound like my Dad. He doesn't even let me digest my food." She turned to Anna. "Men," she said, shaking her head as she got up from the table.

That night Jan re-read Ellen's letter, just to be certain. It looked harmless enough.

Without telling anyone, he mailed it the next day.

✳   ✳   ✳   ✳

The letter arrived on Saturday afternoon.

When Kevin pulled up in front of the house from a bicycle ride, Diane called to him from the door. "We got a letter from Ellen!"

Kevin dropped his bike and ran inside.

There was an envelope on the table, in Ellen's handwriting, but with no return address. The postmark was again from Amsterdam. This time there was no demand from the kidnappers, just a short letter from Ellen:

Dear Mom and Dad,

I miss you very much. Don't worry about me. I am being taken care of and am fine. I'm keeping up with my schoolwork, even my Dutch. I'm learning new words such as Ut, which means out, and recht, which means right. I hope that I will see you again soon, but don't worry.

Love,

Ellen

"Where's the clue?" Kevin immediately asked Diane.

"I was looking for that myself. Do you think there is something about out and right, like outright, or right out?"

Kevin read and re-read the letter. "I don't know, but she's trying to tell us something." He couldn't figure out what it was.

"Did you call Detective Weber?"

"Yes."

"At least Ellen is still okay. It's her handwriting all right."

"She seems to be okay, if you can believe the letter. But maybe they are making her write it."

An hour later Detective Weber arrived. She examined the letter. "This is strange. Why would the kidnappers just let her write home, with no demand or other communication?"

"I was wondering about that myself," Kevin said. "It seems like they're taking an unnecessary risk."

Detective Weber rubbed her chin as she studied the letter. "Up to now they've been very professional about everything. I don't see the purpose in sending this letter."

"I bet she's put a clue in this letter," Kevin said. "I just can't figure out what it is."

"I thought it might have something to do with the words 'out' and 'right,'" Diane said. "That's just kind of out-of-context. She picked those words for a reason."

"She spelled the word 'out' wrong," Detective Weber observed. "We spell it 'uit' in Dutch, not 'ut'. And she capitalized it. Wait a minute. When you put Ut and recht together, you get Utrecht. We have a province named Utrecht."

Kevin looked at the letter. "That's it! How big is the province of Utrecht?"

"Well, the good news is that it's the smallest province in Holland," the detective replied. "The bad news is that there are a lot of farms in the province."

"This narrows it down quite a bit, though, doesn't it?" Diane asked hopefully.

"It does," the detective said. "I'm going to get all our manpower over to Utrecht. And I'll get this letter fingerprinted. Your daughter is quite clever about feeding us information without her captors realizing it."

Diane and Kevin looked at each other proudly. Could this be the break they needed? They were afraid to get their hopes up too much, but both were ecstatic with the newest developments.

"I still think that Vacinovic is involved in this in some way," Diane said.

"Would you mind if I contacted him now?" Kevin asked Detective Weber. "If he's not involved, maybe the secret police have heard something in Serbia that might help your investigation."

"Go ahead. Our surveillance of him hasn't paid off. Just let me know in advance when you're going to meet with him."

Detective Weber packaged up Ellen's letter and took it with her to be processed.

"What do we do now?" Diane asked after the detective had left.

"What do you say we take a ride?" Kevin said mischievously.

"You mean to see for ourselves what the province of Utrecht looks like?"

Diane and Kevin got out their map of Holland. The city of Utrecht was located in the center of Holland, about a forty-five minute drive from Wassenaar. Upon arriving in Utrecht, Kevin and Diane visited the VVV, Holland's tourist agency, and got more detailed maps of the province.

Detective Weber was right, there was a lot of agricultural land in the province. They spent the afternoon driving around the small, country roads peeking down driveways leading to farm after farm.

"This is so frustrating," Diane said. "I can feel that Ellen is around here somewhere. But how do we figure out where?"

They became more discouraged as they drove on through the province. "We need more clues," Kevin said. "I hope we hear from Ellen again. She's gotten us this close."

When they returned that evening, there was a message from Detective Weber. The police laboratory had found some fingerprints on the letter and envelope.

Most were Ellen's, but they also developed some adult fingerprints as well. They were checking those prints in their databases.

"What a roller coaster," Diane said as she slumped on the couch.

Kevin sat down and took her hand. "We know she's alive. It's her handwriting on the letter, and it was postmarked yesterday. Thanks to Ellen, we've narrowed it down to the province, and we know she's on a farm. Now we have fingerprints, too."

"Oh Kevin, it's been eight days. Can you imagine what she's going through? She's never been away from home this long. Who knows the conditions she's being kept in."

Kevin tried to picture Ellen on a farm somewhere in the country they'd seen that day. He hoped she wasn't locked in some cold, drafty barn. The winter temperatures in Holland were hovering below freezing. He hoped she was not sitting somewhere, shivering in the cold.

The next day, Sunday, Diane and Kevin stayed home. Diane finished her brief. It was first-rate. She argued that although evidence of the atrocities against the Serb people were not a justification for war crimes, the evidence was relevant to explain the state of mind of the people who committed the acts.

"While the court may justifiably view the 'honor of Serbia' as irrelevant to the question of whether war crimes were committed," Diane had written, "it is legitimately relevant to the question of whether the crimes were carried out by the highly-trained group of dispassionate warriors commanded by the accused, or passionate and misguided men with whom the accused had no connection and over whom he exercised no control."

She ended her brief by attaching the note from the kidnappers as an exhibit, and making a personal plea. "The small amount of the court's time spent on this matter may make a lifetime of difference to our family. Please give us the latitude to present this evidence."

On Monday morning, the two of them went to court for another week of Draga's trial. They filed Diane's brief first thing in the morning, then spent the next five days listening to the testimony of Muslim witnesses who had been subjected to beatings, torture, and rape in the Serb-run camps in Bosnia. Kevin and Diane listened to tale after tale of horrible mistreatment and inhumane abuse.

Just as Bradford Stone had told the Court, a pattern emerged as the witnesses paraded before the Tribunal and told their stories. At each of the camps, Omarska, Foca, and Keraterm, men in Black Dragon uniforms had come to the facility and beaten, tortured, raped, extorted, and often murdered Muslim prisoners.

Kevin's cross-examinations were difficult. He had one goal during his questioning—to get the names of the men in black uniforms. He began compiling a list, which he had marked as defense exhibit 5. Whenever a witness identified an alleged Black Dragon, Kevin had them write his name on the list. His only hope was that at the end of all this testimony, none of the names on this list would match the list of real Black Dragons under Draga's command. So far, that part of his strategy had been successful.

The mood of the court, however, had swung against the defense, as the flood of heart-wrenching stories poured forth. Just before they concluded on Friday, Judge Davidson quizzed Bradford Stone. "We've heard the pattern that you have referred to, Mr. Stone. How much more evidence do you have?"

Stone was his arrogant self now that things were back on track. "We have just one more day of victims, Your Honor. Then we will present statements made by the accused to journalists, and speeches he made. We will then conclude with our chief investigator, Mr. Jacobson, as a summary witness. I expect we will finish our case on Tuesday or Wednesday of next week."

"We don't need to hear from any more victims," Judge Davidson said gruffly. "Finish your case on Monday." The judge turned to Kevin. "How long will your defense case be, Mr. Anderson?"

"I'm not sure, Your Honor. That depends in part on the Court's ruling on our motion to admit evidence of the atrocities committed against the Serbs."

Judge Orozco spoke next. "Yes, I believe Judge Linares is ready to provide the Court's ruling on that motion."

Everyone looked over at Judge Linares. He had been quiet for most of the trial, his expression unchanged as the witnesses had recounted the horrors of the Serb camps. "Mr. Anderson, I want to compliment you and Mrs. Anderson on your memorandum. It was outstanding. I also want to tell those who are still holding your daughter that you have done everything humanly possible to convince the Court to admit this evidence. However, it is the order of this court, as it has been in every case in which this issue has been raised before, that evidence of alleged atrocities against the perpetrators of war crimes is not admissible. It is simply not relevant. We will issue a written opinion in this matter in the near future."

Kevin looked at Diane and shrugged his shoulders. He was not surprised, and a bit relieved that he would not have to muck up his defense with evidence that was not going to be persuasive to the court. He just hoped that Ellen would not suffer for it. As Judge Linares had said, they had done all they could.

Judge Davidson looked at Kevin. "You have your ruling, Mr. Anderson. How long will your defense case be?"

Kevin looked back at Draga. There were still many things unresolved. Could they get the list of bona-fide Dragons into evidence through the chief investigator? Would they use the CIA evidence? Would Draga testify? Kevin looked back at Judge Davidson. "Can I give the Court an answer on Monday? My client and I have some decisions to make this weekend."

"Very well, but you need to be ready to start your evidence on Tuesday."

"Yes, Your Honor." The many unsettled questions about his defense made him very nervous.

"What are we going to do?" Diane asked when they were alone. "The trial is almost over."

"Win the trial for one thing. If the police don't find Ellen before the verdict, it's our only hope. I have an appointment to see Vacinovic this afternoon."

When Kevin arrived at the Embassy, Zoran Vacinovic greeted him at the door.

"Mr. Anderson," Vacinovic said, extending his hand, "I am so sorry about your daughter."

"Thank you." Kevin studied Vacinovic for any sign of insincerity. He really couldn't tell. He followed Vacinovic into the conference room.

"What can I do for you?" Vacinovic asked.

"I was wondering if you had any contacts within the Serbian intelligence agencies that might have some information about the people who kidnapped my daughter." Kevin looked at Vacinovic's eyes.

"Don't you think I've tried?" Vacinovic said, gesturing with his palms up for emphasis. He met Kevin's gaze. "When I heard about your daughter, I had the Ambassador call the head of our internal police agency. We have made weekly inquiries. There is no information in Serbia about who kidnapped your daughter."

"The note we got from the kidnappers seemed to be wanting us to defend the honor of Serbia. That's why I thought someone from your country might be involved."

"I don't know. Maybe it's the Muslims. They keep committing atrocities and blaming it on the Serbs. It's part of their strategy to get the United States to intervene on their side."

Kevin did not react.

"Believe me, Mr. Anderson, if there is anything I or my government can do to help get your daughter back, we will do it."

"Thank you. I brought you the brief we submitted to try to get the evidence of atrocities against the Serbs admitted before the Court. I think it's a good brief, but we lost that issue today. The judges won't permit it."

Vacinovic took the brief. "I hope the people who are holding your daughter are fairer than that court."

"Well, I'm still trying to win Draga's case. I'm fighting with every breath I have, for Draga and my daughter. But the trial will be over by the end of next week, so my time is running out."

Vacinovic stood up. "I'll let you know if I learn anything at all. And good luck in the trial, Mr. Anderson, although I suspect we both know the outcome."

Kevin left the Embassy, not knowing any more than he had when he came. He simply couldn't detect anything in Vacinovic's words or demeanor that indicated he was involved.

Despite Diane's instinctive misgivings, Vacinovic seemed clean to Kevin.

*   *   *   *

At the regional police headquarters in The Hague, less than a mile away, Detective Weber waited. She put her headset on as the wiretap in the Serbian Embassy signaled that someone had picked up the phone to make a call. The equipment showed that a call was being placed to Belgrade.

The interpreter translated Zoran Vacinovic's words for Detective Weber: "The court did not allow the evidence. The trial will be over in one more week. Then, you'll have to dispose of the package."

"I'll make the arrangements now," said the man at the other end of the phone. "The Dutch men and the woman will not be suitable for that job. I'll have to send someone from Belgrade."

"Do it yourself, Mihajlo. You know what the package looks like."

"Yes, a very sweet and lovely little package," replied Mihajlo Golic.

Vacinovic hung up the phone.

"Put out an all points bulletin for Mihajlo Golic," Detective Weber shouted to her assistant. "He's coming to Holland to kill Ellen Anderson."

CHAPTER 27

▼

"It's Friday night," Ellen said to Anna as she packed up her schoolbooks for the weekend. "Let's do something fun. I've worked hard all week."

"Yes, you have."

Ellen had forged ahead in math to solving algebra problems, as Anna frantically read the textbook to try to keep up. Finally, Hans had to be consulted. He apparently had better math skills than Anna. Now, every night after dinner, Hans was reluctantly correcting Ellen's math papers.

Science was an easier subject for everyone. Ellen was studying insects, and despite the cold weather, insects were in ample supply at the farm. Ellen had gone on an insect-gathering field trip—under Jan's escort to make sure she didn't wander away—and she had collected her specimens in several jars.

In language arts, Ellen had a real problem. She needed books to read, but there were none at the house and no English bookstores to go to. So, Ellen had taken to writing. She wrote daily in a journal describing her activities and her feelings.

Since Anna had liked history in school, she was an excellent social studies teacher, and this was Ellen's favorite class. Anna would tell Ellen stories about the different civilizations that she was studying in the textbook and then have Ellen draw pictures or write short stories about the culture. Ellen proudly hung up her pictures in the schoolroom, and kept all of her other homework neatly in binders, ready to turn in to her real school once she returned.

The subject in which Ellen learned the most was Dutch. Although Ellen's real Dutch teacher had only required Ellen to learn twenty vocabulary words a week, Anna had insisted that Ellen learn twenty a day. Since Anna, Hans, and Jan also spoke Dutch when talking among themselves, Ellen had picked up quite a bit of the language. She couldn't wait to show her Dutch teacher how much she learned. She was almost through the entire Dutch textbook, and the school year was only half finished.

Ellen had also worked hard this week trying to find another clue that she could pass on to her parents. She finally decided to use the license plate number from the black van that Jan and Hans drove. She still didn't know where she was, so she thought the license number was the best she could do. She had memorized it by repeating it over and over in her head. Ellen had written some more letters to her parents, but no one would agree to send them. She had to figure out another way.

"Please," Ellen begged at dinner. "Next week is the end of the quarter at my school. I need to go back there. They're going to flunk me if I don't turn in all this schoolwork. I can't have all F's on my report card for second quarter of sixth grade. I'm going to go to college, you know. Can I go home next week?"

No one answered her.

Ellen pulled herself up from the table and began washing the dishes. A few minutes later, she heard Hans' cellular phone ring. He carried it with him all the time, but this was the first time she had heard it ring. He walked into the bathroom and closed the door. When he came out, he went into the dining room and said to Ellen, "I think you'll be going home next week."

"Really? That's perfect! I can turn in my homework on time. I can't wait to see my mom and dad, and my friends. Oh, thank you, Hans."

She ran over and gave him a big hug.

When she went to bed that night, Ellen couldn't sleep because of the excitement of knowing that she would be going home soon.

Later in the night, Ellen got up to go to the bathroom. She looked at her clock. It was 3 a.m. They didn't lock her in her room anymore, so she walked to the bathroom quietly on her own. When she got there, she saw Hans' cell phone lying on the counter.

Ellen stared at the phone. Should she call her parents? She wanted to so badly. But what if someone heard her? She had only one more week, and she didn't want to spend it in the basement. What could she tell her parents? She didn't even know where she was.

The debate raged in Ellen's mind. She calculated the odds of getting caught. The bathroom was at the end of the hall near her bedroom and away from the other bedrooms where Anna, Hans, and Jan slept. Maybe she could say she had gotten really lonely if she got caught.

Ellen's instincts were to not break the rules. She was going home anyway, why risk it? She headed back to her bedroom. Just as she walked out of the bathroom, she had an idea. She took the cell phone, put it under her pajamas, and climbed back in bed.

She got under her covers and pulled them and her pillow over her head. She pushed the "on" button to the phone.

A small "beep" sounded. Ellen prayed that the blankets and pillow had muffled the sound. She dialed her home number and willed someone to answer.

*   *   *   *

Kevin was deep in sleep when he thought he heard the phone ringing. After a moment, he shook himself awake. It was still dark outside. He heard the ring again and raced to the phone in his office. He glanced at the clock. 3:16 a.m. It was either the kidnappers or some inconsiderate fool calling from the United States.

"Hello."

Kevin heard a soft whisper, "Daddy, it's me."

"Ellen! Where are you? Are you all right?"

"I'm fine, Dad. I gotta be quick. I'm on a farm in Utrecht. That's all I know. They say I'll be coming home in a week."

"Can you get away?"

"No, there are no houses around here. And someone is with me all the time."

"Are you being treated okay?"

"Yeah. I even have a puppy. Her name is Johanna."

"Ellen, who kidnapped you?"

"Two guys named Hans and Jan, and a lady named Anna. But that's not their real names. Dad, I gotta go. Write this down. 84 FG SJ. That's the license number of the van they drive. It's a black van."

Kevin scrambled to find some paper. "Give me that again."

"84 FG SJ"

Kevin repeated it.

"That's it," Ellen said. "I gotta go, Dad. I can't get caught using this cell phone."

"God, I wish you could tell me where you are!" Kevin exclaimed. His mind raced for questions to ask. He wanted to never let go of that phone until Ellen was safe.

"I really gotta go, Dad. They'll lock me in the basement if they catch me using a phone."

"Okay. We love you and miss you so much."

"Love you too. Tell Mommy I love her. Bye."

"Bye, Ellen, see you soon."

"Diane!" Kevin yelled, and ran into their bedroom, turning on the light. "Ellen just called!"

Diane sat upright in bed. Kevin repeated every word Ellen had said.

"Oh, God," Diane said. "I wish I could hear her voice. How did she sound?"

"Good. She wasn't crying or anything. She sounded like her usual self, but a little scared. She sounded sure she would be coming home next week. And she said to tell you that she loved you."

"Do you really think they'll let her go after the trial?"

"I hope so."

Diane immediately called Detective Weber's office with the news. The night dispatcher paged Detective Weber. A few minutes later the detective called. Kevin related what Ellen had said and the license number.

"We'll run this license plate right away," Detective Weber said. "We just got some other leads last night as well. I was going to call you this morning. We found some fingerprints on the envelope with Ellen's second letter. They come back to a Johan Oosten from Amsterdam. He's a Dutch male, about 25 years old, who has no criminal record. We contacted the Amsterdam police. Their files show that he's been a member of a socialist, left-wing student group, sympathetic to unpopular causes like the Serbs."

"Wow!" Kevin exclaimed. "That's a great lead."

"We had people looking for him last night in Amsterdam. He hasn't been seen since the day Ellen was kidnapped. He told his mother he would be gone for awhile on a job, but didn't say where he was going."

"Sounds promising."

"There's more," Detective Weber said. "We got a court order to wiretap Vacinovic's phone. After your meeting last night he called your old friend Mihajlo Golic in Serbia. They're behind this whole thing. They hired Oosten and some other Dutch radicals to do the kidnapping."

Diane had been right all along! She now stood by the phone with a quizzical expression on her face.

"I'd like to strangle that pot-bellied pig, Vacinovic" Kevin said between clenched teeth.

When he hung up the phone, Kevin told Diane everything. She overcame whatever temptation she had to get into I-told-you-so recriminations.

"I've had my hopes up so high before," she said, surprisingly calm. "I'm almost afraid to let them get up again."

"I know. The police work is out of our control. Let's go downstairs and work on Draga's trial. That's something we can do."

Diane made some coffee and Kevin got out his papers. It was just before 4 a.m.

"Here's the big question for the trial," Kevin said. "Do we go for broke and use the CIA evidence?"

"Why would you use it?"

"I think there are two ways to possibly win Draga's trial at this point. The best way would be to prove that Draga was working for the CIA and tipping them off to his military operations. With the CIA evidence, I can show that Draga more than discharged his duty as a commander to prevent war crimes. And it will put the damaging speeches and statements he made into a wholly different light."

"What's the other way?"

"The other possibility is to continue with our defense that the people who committed the war crimes weren't even under Draga's command, which is true. But William Evans from the CIA might be the only witness who could identify the list of bona fide Black Dragons that Draga gave me. As it stands right now, I've got a list of all the perpetrators of war crimes from the victim witnesses. That's defense exhibit 5. But I need the CIA evidence to show that these people were not on the list of people under Draga's command."

"Will Draga let you expose his CIA activities?"

"Well, it's actually my decision. As his lawyer, I have the right to make decisions on trial tactics. I did promise Draga that I would leave that decision to the end of the trial. It looks like that time has come."

The next day, Kevin brought <u>pannekoeken</u> with him to the prison. When he went into the interview room with their breakfast, Draga was his usual sports-obsessed self.

"One week to Super Bowl Sunday," Draga enthused. "The point spread is down to five points. I think I've got you."

"You haven't got anything. There's a saying in the United States: 'It ain't over till the fat lady sings.'"

Draga looked puzzled. "You mean, like in the opera? Well, just bring 30 Euros to court a week from Monday."

"We're not going to be in court a week from Monday. Your trial is going to be over this week."

That pronouncement seemed to have no impact whatsoever on Draga. "Well, you better come here and see me on Monday. In fact, use some of my winnings to buy us both a steak dinner and bring it with you."

"Is that all you think about—football and food?"

"Just about. Two of the three F's. The other one is not available to me."

Kevin got serious. "We need to talk about the trial."

Draga grimaced. "I like the way you're handling it. Just keep up the good work."

"Don't you care how it comes out?"

"I already know how it comes out, Kevin. We lose. I get a life sentence. I am transferred to the United States, and I get a new life in a year or so. We've had this conversation."

"I know, but now my daughter's life is wrapped up in this. It looks like Vacinovic and Golic are behind her kidnapping. That guy's not really your brother-in-law, is he?"

Draga's expression sobered. "No, he is not related to me at all—he is with the secret police. But, I don't like our odds, Kevin. We're playing against the house. Our chances of winning in this court are close to zero. I wouldn't bet on us."

"Not if I throw the Hail Mary pass on the last play and show them that you were playing for the home team all along."

Draga shifted uncomfortably in his seat. "Kevin, you've been straight with me all along. Let me ask you this. If we keep quiet and don't bring this CIA stuff up, do you think Pete Barnes and the boys will honor their promise to me?"

Kevin thought about that. He could say no and make it more palatable for Draga to let him use the CIA evidence in court, but he was not going to lie.

"I think they will," he finally replied. "They got Maria Jones out of solitary confinement. Plus, now a Dutch police officer has heard the tapes and seen the reports. I think the CIA will try to keep its word."

Draga looked like he was thinking; he said nothing for a while. "I think so, too, now that you got 'em on tape. That was the best thing a lawyer could have done for me. I'm so lucky I got you as my lawyer. No one else would have had the guts to do that."

Kevin held eye contact with his client.

"So, I don't have anything to gain by exposing that aspect of my life, and I have a lot to lose," Draga continued. "If we use it, my family will be in danger and the CIA won't honor the deal."

"But if you are acquitted, you won't need their deal."

"Kevin, you don't understand. If I burn my bridges with the CIA, even if I am acquitted, I lose. Remember that I have to go to Germany, then Belgium, and then Sweden to serve my time on my old cases. I'll serve more time in worse places than if I am convicted in this case."

"So the best result for you is if we lose," Kevin said slowly.

"That's what I've been trying to tell you from the beginning," Draga said. "I want to lose. Except, now, for one reason: your daughter."

"I guess this is what Bradford Stone meant when he claimed it presented a conflict of interest," said Kevin, beginning to feel thoroughly defeated.

"No. I know you, Kevin. You wanted to win my case from the very beginning. Your daughter's situation hasn't changed that." He stood up and stretched. "Will the CIA evidence make a real difference?"

"I think so," Kevin said. "Right now, we can't even use the list of Dragons you gave me without a witness who can identify it. By using the CIA evidence, not only can we prove that the men who committed war crimes weren't under your command, but we can show that you tried to prevent war crimes."

Draga started pacing around the room.

Kevin had never seen him this serious.

Suddenly, Draga stopped. "All right, I've made my decision. Screw Bradford Stone and the horse he rode in on. Let's use everything we've got and play to win."

"What about your family?"

"I'll have some people look after them. I brought this on my family for what I chose to do. You didn't bring anything on your daughter. You were just doing your job."

Kevin's eyes watered as he considered what Draga had just said. This alleged "war criminal" had more character than some of the prosecutors and judges at the Tribunal.

CHAPTER 28

▼

Kevin remained obsessed with his quandary over the CIA evidence. Would he be trading Draga's life for Ellen's? There was no guarantee that it would work. The kidnappers might kill her anyway or the Tribunal might still find Draga guilty. But he had to do everything in his power to save Ellen. Draga was right. She didn't deserve this.

On Sunday, Kevin made an appointment to see Detective Weber, who was working in a command post set up at the Utrecht Police Department.

"Any news?" he asked.

Detective Weber was wearing jeans and a plaid woolen shirt and looked as if she were ready to do some farm chores herself. She led Kevin into an interview room and closed the door.

"Golic is coming to The Netherlands," she said when they had sat down. "He's flying in from Belgrade on Tuesday morning. If we haven't found Ellen by then, we hope he'll lead us to her."

"That's great. Why do you think he's coming?

Detective Weber looked away for a moment. "I guess this is the end game for the kidnapping. When the trial's over, if you believe their demands, they will release Ellen if Draga is released."

"And if Draga is not released?"

"I don't know. They said to you on the phone that they would kill her."

Kevin felt sweat forming on his forehead. "What are you doing in the meantime?"

"We're looking for the van, Johan Oosten, the farm, the puppy, anything that will lead us to your daughter. The headmaster of the American School has been asking what they could do to help. Tomorrow they are closing the school for the day and bussing a few hundred high school students as well as parents and staff to Utrecht to knock on doors. We are providing them with pictures of Ellen and Oosten."

Kevin was moved how wonderful everyone had been since Ellen went missing.

He leaned forward, and lowered his voice. "On Tuesday, I have to start calling witnesses and producing evidence on Draga's behalf. I may need to use the CIA reports and tapes that I gave you the first day we met."

Detective Weber's expression gave Kevin no clue as to how she was receiving this request. He forged ahead. "If the judges know that Draga was working for the CIA during the war and giving them advance information about the military targets of his Black Dragons, I think it would significantly increase his chance of winning. And that would increase our chances of getting Ellen back if she's not found today or tomorrow."

"So you want me to give the materials back to you?"

"Well, I may want you to bring them to court on Tuesday morning. I haven't decided for sure yet. You see, it's not that simple. It may well be in Draga's best interests to lose the trial rather than use the CIA evidence."

Detective Weber gave Kevin a puzzled look.

He wondered if he was making sense. "If we don't reveal the CIA evidence, the CIA will probably keep their promise and Draga will be free in a year or two. But if we use it and, in the process, burn his bridges with the CIA, even if he wins he'll be taken to Germany, Belgium, and Sweden to serve his old sentences there. He'll end up serving more time than if he loses this case, and who knows what will happen to him and his family once his role with the CIA becomes known."

The detective nodded and her face softened. "That's a difficult problem for you then, isn't it?"

"It sure is. For Draga, it's better to lose the trial, but for Ellen I need to win."

"What does your client say?"

"He says to use the evidence and try to win. He said something like he made his choices and he and his family have to live with the consequences."

"That's unusual. Most criminals I know only look out for themselves."

"I'm not sure what I should do. But I want to know if you'll bring the evidence to court in the event I need to use it."

"Sure, I'll bring it to court. I'll need a subpoena to cover my behind with my superiors, but I'm not going to stand in the way of anything that might win your daughter's freedom."

"I brought a subpoena with me. I was hoping it would be okay with you."

Kevin took out the subpoena from his briefcase and handed it to Detective Weber.

She scanned it and put it down on the table. "That'll work."

"Do you think I should try and postpone the trial and buy more time for you?"

"You know, I think finding Ellen would be great, but having the kidnappers release her would be a whole lot better. Who knows what would happen if we find Ellen and have a confrontation with the kidnappers? She could be killed. Police officers could be killed. And the longer she stays with them, the greater the danger. So I would say to go ahead and finish the trial."

"Let me ask you—do you think I should use the CIA evidence?"

Detective Weber hesitated for an instant. "Yes, if it might make a difference between winning and losing the trial, I would. Your client is right. Ellen didn't do anything to deserve this. I think it's fair to use the evidence if it might save her life."

Kevin shook the detective's hand and walked from the station. The train and bus ride to his house were a blur as Kevin replayed his conversations with Draga and Detective Weber. He passed the American School and thought of the hundreds of people who would be lining up to be bussed to Utrecht tomorrow to help find Ellen. Everyone had been so unselfish. Would it be selfish of him if he sacrificed Draga for Ellen?

✳   ✳   ✳   ✳

When Kevin and Diane walked into Courtroom 1 the next morning, there was energy in the air as everyone anticipated the closing of the prosecution's case.

Bradford Stone strutted around the prosecution's side of the courtroom like an artist getting ready to put the finishing touches on his masterpiece.

Judge Orozco's legal officer came over and asked Kevin how many days he expected for the defense testimony, but Kevin was noncommittal.

"Check with me after the last witness."

At last, the usher commanded everyone to their feet and the three judges strode briskly to their places. They too seemed fresh and ready to move on to the next phase of the trial.

"Are you ready to call you next witness, Mr. Stone?" Judge Orozco asked after the preliminaries had been taken care of.

"Yes, Madame President. And I am pleased to inform the Court that we have consolidated matters so that this will be our final witness. We call Allen Jacobson."

A young, thin man with light brown hair came forward from the back of the courtroom. He read the oath and began answering questions on his background. Jacobson was from Israel, and had graduated from military college with honors. He had been an investigator with the Israeli Army for six years before being detailed to the United Nations to work as an investigator for the prosecution at the Tribunal. Three years ago he was assigned to the investigation of Draga, and had worked on the case ever since.

"How familiar are you with the activities of the accused and his Black Dragons?" Stone asked.

"Very familiar. During the course of our investigation, I have interviewed hundreds of witnesses and reviewed thousands of documents."

"Have you collected and organized these materials over the past three years?"

"Yes, I have."

"Can you show the court how you have done that?"

"Certainly." Jacobson appeared proud to show off the thoroughness of his work. He pushed a button and the terminals in the courtroom displayed what was on the screen of Jacobson's laptop computer. "I created a number of different directories for the evidence." He moved the mouse and double clicked on a file. The terminals showed an alphabetical list of directories with such headings as Foca, Omarska, and Prijedor.

"Can you show us an example of how you stored the data that was collected on the accused?"

"Yes, I can." Jacobson scrolled his mouse to the file labeled "Srebrenica" and double clicked. Another directory appeared with names of victims or incidents that had occurred in the city of Srebrenica. He chose the directory for "July 11, 1995" and double clicked. More directories appeared. He double clicked on one of them and a report of a witness to the murder of Muslim civilians on that day in Srebrenica appeared on the screen.

"Using these directories, have you been able to compile a complete picture of the activities of the accused and his Black Dragons during the entire war in Bosnia?"

"Yes, I have."

"Objection, Madame President," Kevin shouted as he rose to his feet. "He's referring to materials which may not have been disclosed to the defense."

Stone answered before even being called upon. "To the contrary, defense counsel is quite incorrect. All of the materials have been disclosed to the defense months ago."

Kevin was in no position to question this, since he did not know what was in the various directories on Jacobson's computer. He sat down.

"Objection overruled. Please continue, Mr. Stone."

Stone's face broke into his smug smile, his pursed lips showing only a bit of white teeth. "Thank you, Madame President." he bowed slightly. Turning to Jacobson, Stone continued. "Now, as part of your investigation, have you had occasion to collect and review public statements made by the accused during the war in Bosnia?"

"I have."

"Have you selected a number of those statements and made a composite videotape of them?"

"Yes, I have."

Turning to Judge Orozco, Stone asked for and received permission to play the videotapes. Kevin and Diane looked at their computer terminal as Draga's picture in full Black Dragon uniform appeared on the screen. For the next three hours, Stone played excerpts of interviews Draga had given to CBS' 60 Minutes, the BBC, CNN, and other media. He also played Serbian television news coverage of speeches Draga had given to civic groups, at military functions, and even in an address to the Serbian Parliament. The English translation streamed across the bottom of the screen like a stock market ticker.

Draga's message had been consistent. Using inflammatory rhetoric, he called for the creation of a greater Serbia through military action. He insisted that the Muslims must leave the Serb areas of Bosnia. He promised to kill anyone who resisted.

Stone finished his direct examination with a flourish. "Did your investigation reveal that the accused had in fact trained his men to kill?"

"Yes, he did."

"How many men were under his command in total during the war?"

"About 500."

"And how many people did they kill?"

"About 20,000."

"I have no further questions," Stone announced with a triumphant smile as he sat down.

"That stuff is awful," Diane said after the court adjourned for lunch. "These judges are ready to hang him. You'd better use that CIA evidence. It may be Ellen's only chance."

Kevin was silent.

"Are you going to put Draga on the stand?" she asked.

"No way. There's no way a judge would believe a word he said. If we use the CIA evidence, I've got to do it through William Evans' reports and the tapes I made."

Kevin decided to stay inside the courtroom during the lunch recess and prepare his cross-examination of Jacobson. He walked over to the witness box and saw that Jacobson's laptop was still there. He sat down in the witness chair. He was alone in the courtroom. He wondered if he would get in trouble if he looked at some of those files.

They claimed he already had the stuff anyway, so what difference did it make?

Kevin played around with the directories for a while, and then decided to look in the computer's recycle bin. He wondered what had recently been deleted from the computer. His heartbeat quickened when he saw the files. But before he could examine them, he heard a door open down at the prosecution's end of the courtroom and the voices of prosecutors Bradford Stone and Charles Oswald.

"What do you think you're doing?" Stone demanded when he saw Kevin sitting in the witness box.

The prosecutor rushed over.

Kevin quickly closed the screen for the recycle bin. "Nothing."

"You've got no business snooping in that computer. I'm going to report this to the Court." Straightening his tie, Stone sneered, "This may very well be your third strike that we've been so anxiously anticipating."

"I thought I heard Mr. Jacobson testify that everything in the database had been disclosed to the defense. If that's true, what's your problem?"

"I have a problem whenever I'm dealing with unethical defense counsel," Stone huffed. "You've proven yourself capable of just about any transgression."

Kevin got up and walked back to his defense table. "I'm sorry you feel that way."

"Where are your witness list and witness statements?" Stone demanded, following Kevin over to the defense side of the courtroom. "We're entitled to them now."

"You're entitled to them after you rest your case."

"Well, this is our last witness."

"Then you'll have the disclosure you're entitled to when he is done."

"How many weeks will your defense case take?" Stone persisted.

"I'll let you know when you rest your case."

"What a bloody ass!" said Stone, turning his back on Kevin and rejoining Oswald at the prosecution table.

Court reconvened a few minutes later.

"Mr. Jacobson," Judge Orozco said, "You're still under oath. Go ahead with your cross-examination, Mr. Anderson."

Kevin stood up and leaned on the podium. "That's a neat database you've created Mr. Jacobson," Kevin began.

"Thank you."

"Would you mind displaying your main directory on the screen for us?"

Without a word, Jacobson moved the mouse on his laptop and the main directory screen appeared.

"What order are the directories listed in?"

"They're in alphabetical order, sir, as you can see." A smug smile played on his lips.

"Could you just scroll down the list from A to Z so we can get an idea of the names of the directories?"

"Madam President," Bradford Stone interrupted. "This is a waste of the court's time. Mr. Anderson has had this material for many months. If he has a question about a particular document, he should get on with it."

"I take it that is an objection, Mr. Stone?" Judge Orozco inquired.

"Yes, I object to this line of questioning as irrelevant."

Jacobson, however, ever the efficient investigator, had started scrolling his directories while Stone voiced his objections. Kevin watched the screen intently, hoping to spot something specific that he could ask about.

"Objection sustained. Mr. Anderson, you'll have to be more specific."

"Yes, Madam President." One of the directories had caught Kevin's eye. "Mr. Jacobson, could you move to the A's?"

Jacobson complied. Stone looked ready to object again.

"I see a directory labeled 'Anderson'. What does that directory contain?"

"That contains pleadings that you have filed, correspondence you have sent us, and," Jacobson couldn't resist, "some of the court orders concerning your misconduct." A wide smile broke across his thin face. Kevin decided Jacobson had been spending too much time with Bradford Stone.

"Would you mind double clicking on that so we can see the sub-directories?"

"Certainly not, counselor."

Kevin studied the screen as a new group of directories were listed. He felt nervous as he frantically looked for something with which to continue his line of questioning. He feared another relevancy objection was seconds away. Then he saw something odd.

"I see a subdirectory called 'search'. Could you please double click on that so we may see what files are contained in that subdirectory?"

"Madam President," Stone bellowed. "This is absurd. Are we to sit here all afternoon looking aimlessly through the computer?"

Jacobson, however, had once again forged ahead and displayed the contents of the "search" sub-directory on the screens throughout the courtroom. When he saw that, Stone rose again. "I'm instructing the witness not to respond to Mr. Anderson's requests until the Court has ruled on my objection."

Jacobson quickly clicked back out of the "search" sub-directory.

Judge Orozco looked over at Kevin. "Mr. Anderson?"

Kevin looked up from the screen. "You asked me to be specific, Madam President. I am being specific. I have asked for a specific sub-directory and I am about to ask for a specific file."

"Very well. Objection overruled. You may continue."

Kevin breathed a sigh of relief. Once again he had spotted something in his frantic scanning of the file names. "Please reopen the 'search' subdirectory, and then open the file called 'memo1'."

Jacobson complied. A document appeared on the courtroom screens. It was a memo from Kevin to Draga, outlining their pretrial strategy. It had been seized during the search of Kevin's house when he had been suspected of delivering confidential material to Zoran Vacinovic.

"Where did this document come from?"

"Objection!" Stone shot to his feet. "This is irrelevant. It's a pure fishing expedition."

"Where are you going with this Mr. Anderson?" Judge Orozco asked, a touch of impatience in her voice.

"If you will let the witness answer this one question, I think you will see."

"All right. The objection is overruled, for now."

All eyes turned to Jacobson. "It came from the search of your residence, Mr. Anderson. You ought to know that."

"Have you reviewed the documents that came from that search as part of your thorough preparation of this case?"

"Of course. Mr. Stone and I have reviewed every document in this computer in preparation for trial."

"Thank you." Turning to the judges, Kevin continued. "Your Honors, when I challenged the search of my residence, the prosecution represented to this Court that it had erected a 'Chinese wall' and that none of the material seized from that search would be seen by any members of the prosecution team in this case. Judge Davidson ordered the material and all copies returned to me. Now we have found out that they violated your order."

Kevin looked at Judge Davidson. "Remember?"

Judge Davidson leaned forward. "There's nothing wrong with my memory, counsel." He shifted his glare towards the prosecutor. "What about this, Mr. Stone?"

Stone was whispering furiously to Charles Oswald. "Your Honors," Stone rose hesitatingly from his seat, "I don't recall exactly what Mr. Anderson is referring to. He's filed several pretrial motions, all of them without merit."

Stone looked disdainfully at Kevin, then at Judge Davidson.

"I remember it," Judge Davidson said, his voice rising in volume. "You represented that no one on the prosecution team would have access to the materials which were seized. I ordered you to return those materials. This document on the screen looks like it's covered by the attorney-client privilege. And now we hear that you and your investigator have retained it and reviewed it."

"Your Honor, perhaps there was a glitch in our office procedures. But we have not introduced any of these documents into evidence, so there is no harm to the accused. It's his counsel who has chosen to now display this document to the public."

Judge Davidson's face got red. "Mr. Stone, I'm sick and tired of hearing you shift the blame to defense counsel whenever you are called to account. This is a serious matter and you have apparently acted improperly."

Turning to Kevin, Judge Davidson was equally gruff. "On the other hand, Mr. Anderson, no materials from the search have been brought in to this trial except by you just now. So I don't see how your case is prejudiced by the misconduct of the prosecution. Go on to another line of questioning."

"But, Your Honor, the prosecutor's access to attorney-client privileged materials in their trial preparation is improper, even if they don't introduce the seized documents themselves. I move for dismissal of the charges against Mr. Zaric, and request an evidentiary hearing on the matter."

"Motion denied," Judge Davidson growled. He looked over at the prosecution table. "I'm not happy about this, Mr. Stone."

Stone tried to make light of the criticism. "Well, it's only strike one for us. Mr. Anderson's already got two strikes."

Judge Davidson ignored Stone and sat back in his chair, his face wrinkled in a frown.

Judge Orozco leaned forward "Do you have any further questions for this witness?"

Kevin clenched his teeth. These prosecutors could get away with anything in this court. They had just violated the attorney-client privilege as well as searching Kevin's home without probable cause. And they had gotten away with it. Judge Davidson has acted as if it was Kevin's fault for bringing it up.

"Yes, Madam President, I do." He turned to Jacobson, who did not look in the least bit chastised. "Let's go back to the main directory."

Jacobson complied.

Kevin was really fishing now, his mind frantically trying to recall his other pretrial motions that the prosecution had made factual representations about. Then he remembered the motion that claimed that Draga's kidnapping and arrest had been orchestrated by the U.N. forces.

"Mr. Jacobson, do you keep a time log or other record of the time you have spent on this investigation?"

"Of course. My bosses and Mr. Stone here always want to know what I have been doing with my time." He chuckled at his own attempt at humor.

"Could you please open the directory that contains those time records?"

"Certainly." Jacobson scrolled to the Time Slips program and opened the directory. Dates were listed for the past three years.

"Could you please open the file for July 21ˢᵗ?"

Stone was on his feet. "Objection, Madam President. This is completely irrelevant."

Judge Orozco shook her head. "Let's see where this is going for a little longer."

Jacobson opened the file. "What does it show you doing on that day?"

"I was in Bucharest, Romania, doing investigation."

"Did Mr. Stone know where you were and what you were doing?"

"Of course."

"What were you doing in Romania two days before Mr. Zaric's kidnapping and arrest?"

Jacobson did a double take. His eyes met Kevin's for an instant, and then darted to Stone. Kevin knew that Jacobson had now recognized the trap. If the U.N. had no knowledge of Draga's kidnapping until the kidnappers dumped him at the Romanian border, how could Jacobson explain his presence in Romania two days before the kidnapping?

Stone started to rise to object, then thought the better of it. He, too, realized the relevance of the question. He left it to Jacobson to wriggle his way out on his own.

"Mr. Jacobson?"

"Yes. I, um, I was in Romania doing liaison work with our U.N. forces."

Kevin let the vague explanation slide and got right to the heart of the matter. "Did you have any advance knowledge of Mr. Zaric's kidnapping and arrest?"

Jacobson was clearly uncomfortable. "Uh, what do you mean by advance?"

"Did you have any knowledge that Mr. Zaric would be kidnapped before it took place?"

"Madam President," Stone whined, rising to protect his witness. "Mr. Anderson is using his cross-examination to re-litigate pretrial motions which have already been decided. This is irrelevant to the issue of the guilt of the accused."

Judge Orozco was about to speak when Judge Davidson chimed in. "Mr. Stone, didn't the prosecution represent in connection with that motion that it had no advance knowledge or participation in the kidnapping of Mr. Zaric?"

"That's possible, Your Honor. I don't quite recall all the pretrial litigation. Mr. Anderson filed a number of frivolous motions."

Judge Davidson ignored the swipe at Kevin. "Mr. Jacobson, did you have advance knowledge of Mr. Zaric's kidnapping?"

Jacobson looked down. He slowly raised his head and looked at the judge. "Yes, Your Honor."

Judge Davidson turned to Kevin. "You may continue, Mr. Anderson."

"Did Mr. Stone have advance knowledge of Mr. Zaric's kidnapping and arrest?"

Jacobson shifted uncomfortably in his seat. Stone burst to his feet. "That is completely irrelevant and an unwarranted personal attack by counsel," he shouted, sounding indignant.

Judge Orozco was back in charge. "Objection overruled."

All eyes returned to the witness box. "Yes," Jacobson answered. "He knew."

"Did he help plan Mr. Zaric's apprehension?"

Kevin looked over at Bradford Stone. He was agitated, whispering to Charles Oswald. Jacobson looked over at them before answering to give them time to object.

Finally, it was Oswald who rose. "Madame President, we must respectfully object to this line of questioning as being privileged internal communications and going into matters of attorney work product." He sat down quickly.

Judge Orozco smiled. "You'll pardon us if we don't share your new-found concern for attorney work product. Mr. Jacobson, did Mr. Stone help plan the arrest of the accused?"

Jacobson shot one last look at the prosecution table. "Yes."

"Your Honors," Kevin said, "I again renew my motion to dismiss the case against Mr. Zaric and request a full evidentiary hearing on the legality of his arrest."

Judges Orozco and Davidson looked over at Judge Linares, who was reviewing a ream of papers in front of him. Judge Linares looked up.

"Mr. Stone, I have your response to the motion in front of me," Judge Linares said. "It appears that you clearly led the Court to believe that the United Nations had no advance knowledge of or participation in Mr. Zaric's kidnapping and arrest."

Stone rose, his arrogance gone for the moment. "I apologize if the court read our response in that fashion. I seem to recall that the main thrust of that response was that a person was not entitled to dismissal even if the arrest was illegal. In any event, we have not used any evidence seized in connection with the arrest and therefore the legality of the arrest is irrelevant."

Judge Linares did not respond immediately. He appeared to be studying the papers in front of him.

Judge Davidson broke in. "You are correct, Mr. Stone. The legality of the arrest is not relevant to the issues at this trial. Mr. Anderson, your motion is denied."

Kevin mustered every ounce of restraint to keep from slamming his fist in frustration.

Judge Davidson glared over at the prosecution table. "But that's strike two, Mr. Stone."

Kevin was furious. How could they keep getting away with this? He took a deep breath and tried to maintain a professional demeanor. He wanted to scream.

"Let's take a thirty minute recess," Judge Orozco said.

After the judges left, Kevin slumped in his chair next to Diane. "I can't believe this! These morons are ready to lock me up when I am accused of doing something wrong, and they won't do a thing to Stone who's been caught in two lies to the Court."

Diane patted his hand sympathetically. "You're doing the best you can."

"This is not a fair trial!"

A guard approached Kevin from the back of the room. "Your client would like a word with you."

Kevin got up and followed the guard to the interview room just outside the courtroom. When he got inside and the guard had shut the door, Draga sprang to his feet. He punched his right fist out, then his left, like he was shadow boxing. "One, two," he shouted. "You got him on the ropes. You're killing him. This is better than a heavyweight fight, Kevin. I love it!"

Kevin couldn't help but laugh, even though he was still angry. "My biggest fan, thank you. But I can't believe these rulings. These judges will tolerate all kinds of crap from the prosecution."

Draga started hopping around the room with his hands together in front of his stomach. "What are you doing?" Kevin asked.

"I'm hopping like a kangaroo. Should I do it in the courtroom and let them know what I think of this kangaroo court?"

"No, thank you. My, you are animated today. What did you have for breakfast?'

"I just love going to the prizefights, Kevin."

"Well, we may be landing a few punches, but the referees are the ones who'll declare the winner. And I don't like our referees."

"Any more news on your daughter?"

"Her whole school is out in Utrecht hunting for her right now. Hundreds of kids and grown ups."

"That's really something."

"And the police expect Golic to fly in tomorrow."

"Will they arrest him?"

"I don't think so. I think they'll follow him to Ellen."

"Listen, I need to make some arrangements for my family," Draga said. "Will the CIA stuff come up tomorrow?"

Kevin took a deep breath. "I'm not going to use it."

Draga's eyebrows arched in surprise. "Why not?"

"It's complicated, but in the end it comes down to integrity. I took on the responsibility of being your lawyer. And I have to act in your best interests."

"But what about your daughter?"

"All my life, I've believed that if I did the right thing, everything would work out. So, I've decided to do the right thing. I'm praying that it works out for Ellen."

Draga put his arm around Kevin. "You are the most courageous, honest person I've ever met." He squeezed Kevin's shoulders then pulled back. "I'll never tell another lawyer joke for as long as I live."

Kevin smiled.

Draga was grinning as well. "I like your attitude, Kevin. And I think you are right. If you do good, good will be done to you. I wish I had lived by that rule, I wouldn't be here right now."

"You gave me permission to use the CIA evidence despite the consequences to you and your family. I haven't seen that kind of character in anyone around here."

"Well, let's go kick some butt." Draga pumped his arms once again.

"I've got some good news for you, sports fan," Kevin said as he knocked on the door for the guards.

"What?"

"I think I might have strike three on Bradford Stone."

CHAPTER 29

▼

"Mr. Jacobson," Kevin began when court resumed. "I've had the usher place defense exhibit 5 in front of you. It's displayed on the screen as well. Do you see that document?"

"Yes."

"And from sitting in this courtroom during the entire trial, you know what this document is, don't you?"

"Yes, I do. It's the list of names of Black Dragons who our witnesses have identified as having committed war crimes."

"Is the list complete as far as you can tell?"

"Yes."

"Madam President, I offer defense exhibit 5 into evidence."

Judge Orozco looked over at the prosecution table. There was no effort to object to the seemingly harmless list. "Defense exhibit 5 will be received into evidence."

"Thank you, Madam President." Kevin turned to face Jacobson. "Now that we have a list of the people who committed the war crimes, I'd like to compare that to the list of members of the Black Dragons under Mr. Zaric's command. Do you have such a list?"

Jacobson hesitated for a moment, as if trying to recall. "No, I do not."

"Is such a list contained in your database?"

"No." Jacobson glanced over toward Bradford Stone.

"Could you please go to your laptop and return it to the main screen that you see when you first turn on your computer?"

Jacobson complied, a puzzled look on his face.

Kevin continued, "Now could you double click on the icon called 'recycle bin'?"

Jacobson didn't comply. His eyes wide, he looked at Stone, who leaped to his feet. "Madam President, I strongly object," said the prosecutor. "This is another fishing expedition. It is a waste of this court's time and wholly irrelevant."

Judge Orozco cut him off. "He's caught some fish already today, Mr. Stone. I think we'll let him continue for a while."

"Thank you, Madam President," Kevin said. "This won't take long."

Kevin instructed Jacobson to open the recycle bin.

Jacobson's face had gone pale. He did as directed.

"These are the files which have recently been deleted from the computer, correct?"

"Correct," Jacobson looked over at Stone again.

Kevin paused before asking his next question. He waited for Jacobson to look at him. "Mr. Jacobson, my next question is a career-breaker. I want you to think carefully before you answer it. Think of your livelihood, your family, your integrity."

Stone was on his feet. "This is totally improper. Counsel is badgering the witness."

"Ask your question, Mr. Anderson," Judge Orozco said, "without the drum roll."

Kevin smiled sheepishly.

The tension in the courtroom was palatable. Even Judge Linares was leaning forward waiting to hear the next question.

"Mr. Jacobson, did you delete the membership list of Black Dragons from your database?"

Jacobson was about to answer when Stone leaped to his feet. Finally realizing where this was going, he was desperate to stop it. "Madame President," he shouted, "this is outrageous! I caught Mr. Anderson breaking into our database during the noon recess. He was sitting in the witness box using Mr. Jacobson's laptop computer. He cannot be allowed to profit from this skullduggery."

Judge Orozco was silent, taken aback by the objection.

Judge Davidson, however, was impatient. "We're not going to waste any more time with this," he snapped.

Kevin, not sure what Judge Davidson meant, was determined to forge ahead. "Did you delete the membership list of Black Dragons from your database?" he repeated in a loud voice.

On the computer screen, a file labeled 'membership' could be seen among those in the recycle bin. Jacobson glanced at the screen, and then quietly said, "Yes."

"When?"

"On Saturday."

"Why?"

"I was instructed to do it."

Kevin couldn't wait to ask his next question. "By whom?"

Stone leaped to his feet. "Madame President!" His voice was booming with as much bluster as he could summon. "This is privileged information. It's entirely irrelevant to the case. I must instruct the witness not to answer."

Judge Davidson's face turned bright red. "And I instruct the witness to answer the question right now," he yelled. "Who told you to delete that file?"

Jacobson was now bent on saving himself. He didn't hesitate. "Mr. Stone."

All eyes turned to Bradford Stone. Even Charles Oswald was looking at him. Stone's face had turned crimson. He looked down at some notes.

All of a sudden there was a noise from behind Kevin. "Strike Three!" Draga yelled, standing up and waving his arm like an umpire calling a batter out. The guards moved forward quickly to restrain him. Draga sat down, a wide smile on his face. The guards couldn't help themselves. They broke out in laughter.

Judge Davidson ignored the outburst. His gaze was directly at Bradford Stone. The judge was livid. "Is that true, Mr. Stone?" he barked.

Stone rose slowly from his chair. "May I have a word with my co-counsel?"

Judge Davidson glared at Stone. "We'll be in recess for ten minutes," he announced. "I want a full explanation for this when we reconvene. That is an order."

The judges stood up and strode from the bench. Kevin saw Judge Davidson grab Judge Orozco's arm and say something to her as they left.

Oswald and Stone quickly left the courtroom as well.

Kevin noticed that there were no spectators today in the visitor's gallery. Pity, he thought. He hoped the news media was covering this session from the press room. He wanted the people holding Ellen to know the extent to which he was fighting for Draga.

"Was he hiding evidence?" Diane asked Kevin

"He sure was. I hope they don't let him out of this one."

"How did you find out?"

"I checked the recycle bin at lunch, just like he said. I saw the membership file."

Kevin couldn't wait for the ten minutes to be up. He turned around. Draga was laughing with the guards and repeating his umpire gesture. When his eyes met Kevin's, he shadowboxed three punches. At least the accused was enjoying his trial now.

The judges filed in exactly ten minutes after they had left. Their expressions were grim. Kevin noticed Charles Oswald sitting alone at the prosecution's table. Bradford Stone was nowhere to be seen.

Judge Orozco began by recognizing Oswald. "Madam President, You Honors, I would like to apologize to this Court for what has transpired this afternoon. We have suspended Mr. Stone, effective immediately. He will no longer be participating in this trial, and our office will conduct a full investigation into the matter."

Judge Orozco smiled grimly. "I think that is very appropriate, Mr. Oswald. Are you prepared to proceed with the trial?"

"Yes, Your Honor. And furthermore, I wish to advise the court that I had no knowledge of the deletion of these files until I heard about it in Court. Those files should have been turned over to Mr. Anderson months ago. I very much regret what has occurred here today."

Judge Orozco smiled again. She seemed satisfied that the problem that threatened to unravel the trial had apparently been solved.

Kevin, however, was not about to let it go so easily. "Madam President, I move to dismiss the case on the grounds of outrageous prosecutorial misconduct. Evidence has been hidden, misrepresentations and perjury have been committed in this very courtroom, and the attorney-client privilege has been shamefully violated. You must send a clear message that this cannot be tolerated in this Tribunal."

Judge Davidson interjected. "Mr. Stone has got that message loud and clear. You can now have the evidence that was withheld so that you're not disadvantaged by his misconduct. But we're going to decide this case on its merits. The Tribunal is here to seek the truth about what happened in the former Yugoslavia. Your motion is denied."

Kevin looked down and shook his head.

"Do you want more time to review the evidence?" Judge Orozco asked Kevin.

"No, I'd like to continue my cross examination."

"I'd like a recess so I could consult with counsel for the prosecution," Jacobson interjected from the witness box.

Judge Davidson glared at him. "That won't be necessary. We just had a recess. Proceed, Mr. Anderson."

"Mr. Jacobson, could you open the file containing the membership list?"

Kevin saw the mouse shake as Jacobson moved it to open the file. Beads of sweat could be seen on his forehead.

"What exactly is this?" Kevin asked when a list of names had been projected on the screens.

"It is a list of all persons who were members of the Black Dragons from the beginning of the war in Bosnia in 1992 through the end of the war in 1995."

"Where did you get it?"

Jacobson hesitated. He looked over at Oswald, who made no effort to object. "Do I have to answer that question?" he asked Judge Orozco.

"Yes, you do," Judge Davidson answered for her.

"We received it from the American Central Intelligence Agency."

"Are you convinced it is complete and accurate?" Kevin asked, avoiding further questions about the CIA.

"Yes, I am."

"I take it that you have checked the names of the people on defense exhibit 5 who have been identified in this court as having committed war crimes against this list of bona fide Black Dragons?"

"Yes," Jacobson's voice was barely above a whisper.

"Please tell the court the result." Kevin's voice dropped to match that of Jacobson.

Jacobson took a deep breath. "None of the people who committed war crimes were on the list of Black Dragons."

"So you have no evidence that the people who committed the war crimes were under Mr. Zaric's command?"

"That's correct."

"And that's why this file was deleted?"

Jacobson shifted in his seat. "I guess so," he said, never looking up.

Kevin could have stopped, but he had noticed one more thing. *This one's for you, Nihudian*, he thought.

Looking up at Jacobson, Kevin said, "Please open the file labeled 'Stigic.'"

Jacobson complied.

An invoice from Stigic Sewing Shop appeared on the screen.

"What is that?" Kevin asked, knowing it was the very piece of paper that Nihudian had died trying to help him retrieve.

"It's a copy of an invoice from Stigic's Sewing Shop in Sokolaz."

"What is the significance of this invoice?"

"Stigic made two dozen Black Dragon uniforms in 1992."

"For whom?"

"Victor Vidic," Jacobson was now sticking to the shortest possible answers.

"The same Victor Vidic who committed the brutal war crimes we have heard about in this court."

"Yes."

Kevin spoke clearly and with emphasis on each word. "He ordered these uniforms so he and his associates could impersonate the Black Dragons, correct?"

"Yes."

"I'd like to offer this invoice as defense exhibit 6."

"Defense exhibit 6 will be admitted," Judge Orozco said after seeing that Oswald was not objecting.

Kevin turned back to Jacobson. The man was not resisting any more. He just wanted to get his testimony over with. Kevin pressed on for the final thrust.

"You have no evidence that Mr. Zaric had any command or control over Victor Vidic or anyone else on defense exhibit 5, do you?"

"No." Jacobson conceded.

"You have no evidence that Mr. Zaric ever even met the people who committed the war crimes, let alone commanded them, do you?"

"No," Jacobson admitted.

"I have no further questions, Your Honor," Kevin said, taking his seat. He saw Jacobson's taut face relax.

"Any questions on redirect, Mr. Oswald?" Judge Orozco asked.

"No, Your Honor."

"Very well, the witness may be excused."

Jacobson got up from his seat and took his laptop with him to the prosecution table. He sat down at his usual place. No one looked at him and he looked at no one.

Judge Orozco looked to Oswald, who rose again. "The prosecution rests."

"Very well. I believe then that it is your turn, Mr. Anderson," Judge Orozco said lightly as the tension lifted from the courtroom. "It's almost four o'clock. Would you like to begin tomorrow?"

Kevin stood up. "The defense rests, Your Honors."

Judge Orozco's eyebrows shot up. "You mean you aren't calling any witnesses?"

"That's correct. They've just admitted everything I would prove. Mr. Zaric had no responsibility for the men who committed the war crimes."

"Very well, then," Judge Orozco said, collecting her thoughts. "We'll have closing arguments tomorrow morning at 9:30. Court is in recess."

Kevin turned and looked back at Draga. He walked over and Draga gave him a huge bear hug. "You destroyed them!"

Kevin smiled. "They're still the home team. I'll see you in the morning."

Kevin walked back over to the defense table to gather his papers. He sat down next to Diane. "Why didn't you use the CIA evidence?" she asked, her brown eyes boring in on him. "I thought you were going to do everything to save Ellen."

"I just couldn't, Diane. I had to act in the best interest of my client. It was the right thing to do. And besides, if these judges find Draga guilty after what they heard today, no evidence from the CIA or even God Himself is going to change their minds."

Diane got up shakily. "I hate you and your games." She ran from the courtroom. Kevin sat there in the courtroom, alone now, stunned. He had just finished the best cross-examination of his career. He had followed his instincts about the CIA evidence. But his instincts had, after all, caused him to lose Ellen.

Had he made the wrong decision? One that might cost his daughter's life?

✳   ✳   ✳   ✳

Ellen, in her room at the farm, heard the sound of a car drive up. She peeked through the curtains and saw Hans walk out of the barn and meet the car.

Ellen saw a brown-haired woman driving, and two young girls in the back. Ellen saw the woman showing Hans some papers. After a few minutes, the woman took back the papers and Hans stepped back from the car door. The woman started driving around towards the road. As she did, Ellen's eyes met the eyes of one of the girls. The girl looked familiar, like someone Ellen had seen at school. Ellen waved. As they pulled away, Ellen saw the girl excitedly bouncing in the car, tapping her mother's shoulder.

<u>I hope she recognized me</u>, Ellen thought.

When the car drove away, Hans rushed into the house. Ellen came out into the kitchen. Hans was talking heatedly in Dutch to Jan and Anna. From what Ellen could understand, the woman in the car was looking for Ellen, and had shown Hans pictures of Ellen and Jan.

Hans turned to Ellen. "We've got to leave here. Get you're stuff ready."

"What's happening?"

"Never mind. If you want to take anything, grab it right now. We're leaving."

Ellen thought of all the homework she had done. She ran around the house, gathering her homework binders and stuffing them into her backpack. She wondered if she should bring some clothes, but she had nothing else to carry them in. She put on her raincoat and stood by the door.

"Let's go," Hans said.

Ellen followed Hans and Jan out the door. Anna was behind her.

"Wait," Ellen yelled. She ran back into the house, and came out holding Johanna in her arms. "Am I going home now?"

No one answered her. Ellen thought they would get in the black van, but Hans led them through a field to a road behind the pasture that Ellen had never seen before. After walking rapidly down the road for a good five minutes, they came to a wooden shed the size of a garage. Hans unlocked the shed. Ellen saw an old blue van inside. "Get in the back with her," Hans told Jan. Anna got in the driver's side and Hans in the front passenger's side. Ellen squeezed Johanna as Anna turned the ignition.

"It's okay," Ellen bent over and whispered to Johanna.

"Wait. I forgot my wallet," Jan said suddenly. "I don't want it left in that house."

He ran out of the van, and back down the road. Anna pulled the van out of the garage and waited. Hans fidgeted around the van nervously. Suddenly, in the distance, they heard the sound of police sirens. The sounds were getting louder.

"We've got to get out of here," Hans shouted. "Let's see if we can get on the main road. If no one's near the farm, we'll go in and pick Jan up."

Anna drove the van slowly, with the lights out, away from the farm. When she reached a paved road, she turned the lights on. Hans gave her directions to get back to the main entrance to the farm. As they approached, they saw police cars parked near the road leading to the farm. They could see flashing lights down the road in the direction of the farmhouse.

"It's too late to get Jan," Hans said. "Just keep going by."

"Where to?" Anna asked

"Amsterdam. We're going to turn the girl over to the boss."

CHAPTER 30

▼

On the way home from the Tribunal, Kevin tried to talk to Diane, but she remained sullen and silent. He explained again why he had decided not to use the evidence of Draga's long-time cooperation with the CIA. Diane seemed unmoved.

Once home, Diane went up to their bedroom and shut the door. Kevin fixed some dinner for both of them, but Diane refused to come down to join him. Kevin sat in the dining room, eating by himself. It was 6:30, and he had a closing argument to give tomorrow. Why couldn't Diane have waited for one more day to vent her anger at him?

Kevin tried to work on his closing argument, but he knew that he would not be able to concentrate until he had resolved things with Diane. He went up to their bedroom. Diane was lying on the bed. She didn't move when he opened the door.

Kevin went over and sat on the edge of the bed.

"Can we talk?" he asked.

Diane did not respond. She was lying on her stomach, her face pressed against the pillow.

"Come on, we have to face this together. Right now, we both need to do everything we can to get Ellen back. Hate me when it's all over."

Diane rolled onto her side, turning her back to Kevin. "There's no point talking to you. You just go do whatever you please anyway, no matter what I say."

"That's not true. I do listen to you. I do respect your opinion."

Diane turned around and glared at Kevin. "You always think you're right, but Ellen and I have to pay for your mistakes. I'm tired of being a spectator while you play games with our lives."

Kevin took a deep breath. "Look, I'm convinced I did the right thing today. We have a real good chance of winning this trial. We showed today that the people they spent the last month prosecuting had nothing to do with Draga."

"Kevin, you are so damned blind. I've seen how those judges act. They're going to find some way to find your client guilty. And Ellen is still out there, her whole life riding on this stupid trial. I just hate it."

"Maybe the police will find Ellen. They had hundreds of volunteers out there looking for her today. They have a suspect, and a license number."

"We would have had a call by now if they found her. They've had almost a month to find her. This is so discouraging."

"Will you help me with my closing argument?"

"No," Diane shot back. "You don't listen to me anyway. Why don't you get your buddy Draga to help you? You obviously value his life more than your daughter's."

Kevin winced. "That hurt." He waited for an apology, but none was forthcoming. "I guess I'll get to work." He got up from the bed. "I'm going to prove you wrong about the verdict."

"I hope you do. For Ellen's sake."

Kevin trudged down to the dining room and began spreading out his notes. He remembered wistfully the evenings when it was Ellen who had her work spread out all over this same table. How he sorely missed her.

He was trying hard to focus on his closing argument when the phone rang at about 9 p.m. He let Diane answer it upstairs, trying to back off from being the boss of everything.

After about ten minutes, Diane came downstairs. "That was Detective Weber."

Kevin sprang from his seat at the table.

"They found the farmhouse where Ellen was being held, but they missed Ellen and the kidnappers by about five minutes."

Diane came over and sat down. She had been crying.

"A girl from the American School saw Ellen peeking out from behind some curtains," she went on. "The police arrested one of the kidnappers. The one whose fingerprints they have—Johan somebody."

Kevin had a million questions. "Where do they think Ellen is now?"

"They don't know. Johan told them that the other guy and the woman were driving a blue van. Detective Weber's got everybody in Holland looking for a blue van and the two kidnappers."

"How did they treat Ellen? What was the farmhouse like?" The questions gushed out of Kevin.

"I guess they treated her okay. A bunch of her drawings were pasted up around the house."

"What else did Detective Weber say?"

"The Johan guy said that they were hired by some people from Serbia to do this. He claims that his partner had made the contacts with the Serbs. He says he doesn't know who they are."

"Who's his partner?"

"I wrote down the name. It's Pieter van Dale. And the woman is Christina Trent. They're all connected with some Dutch left-wing political group."

"Do they have any other leads on finding Ellen now?"

Diane shrugged. "I don't know. She said that they expect that the guy, Golic, will contact the kidnappers after he flies in tomorrow morning. They'll be following Golic and they're hoping he'll lead them to Ellen."

"Damn! We almost had her back tonight."

Diane didn't reply.

"At least we know she's alive and has been treated reasonably well," he said.

"Maybe they'll harm her now that they're desperate and on the run." Diane said, starting to sob.

Kevin walked over to comfort her, but Diane got up from her chair and went upstairs. He went back to the dining room table. There was no way he could concentrate on his closing argument now.

He went up the stairs and into the bedroom.

Diane was back on the bed.

"I want to see the farmhouse," he said. "I want to see Ellen's drawings. Do you want to come with me?"

Diane looked up. "Yes. I was thinking the same thing."

Diane got dressed while Kevin called Detective Weber. She gave Kevin directions and said she would alert the officers at the farmhouse to let Kevin and Diane look around. She asked Kevin not to touch anything.

"Anything else new?"

"I think tomorrow will be critical," the detective said. "If we follow Golic, he should lead us to Ellen. We also have the number of van Dale's cell phone. I'm getting a court order to listen on that phone."

"Thank you so much for everything."

Kevin and Diane drove out to Utrecht in the darkness. Kevin tried to keep the topic on finding Ellen, although he couldn't resist saying that he was glad Detective Weber would be spending her time tomorrow looking for Ellen instead of testifying about the CIA evidence. Diane had softened a bit; she was at least speaking to Kevin. But the sub-freezing temperatures were not the only chill in the Anderson's car as they drove east toward what had been their daughter's home for almost a month.

When they went inside the farmhouse and saw Ellen's drawings, Kevin and Diane were both moved to tears. There was something about seeing these creations of their daughter that made her seem so much closer at that moment. They wandered around the house three times, each time seeing something new. When they had finally seen everything, they thanked the officers and drove off.

Diane slept most of the way home. It was almost 1:00 a.m. when they pulled up to their row house in Wassenaar.

Kevin was still too wired to sleep. He had a closing argument to give in a few hours in the most important case of his life. He went up to his office and began banging it out on his computer. When he was done, it was almost 5 a.m. There was no point in sleeping.

Kevin got on the Internet and checked the coverage of Draga's trial. He saw the Reuter's News Service headline first: "War Crimes Suspect Puts Up No Defense." He read the story, which had apparently been put on the wires from a story written by Toma Lanko for the Bosnia News Service. The story revealed that for the first time in the history of the War Crimes Tribunal, an accused had called no witnesses in his defense.

Kevin found Lanko's original story. Lanko made no mention of Bradford Stone or of Kevin's cross-examination of Chief Investigator Jacobson. Instead, he quoted unnamed sources in Serbia decrying the Tribunal's appointment of an American prosecutor to represent Draga. He also quoted the Registrar of the Tribunal as saying that it was the first time in the history of the Tribunal that no defense had been offered for an accused. He noted that thousands of dollars of public money had been disbursed to Draga's defense team for experts and investigators, and promised to look into how that money was spent.

Kevin groaned at the slanted and inaccurate coverage of the trial. This would just confirm the Serbs' suspicions of him. All he could do was pray that Ellen would be found today, or that the kidnappers would at least wait to hear the verdict.

Kevin went on his regular run at 6:00 a.m. He tried to put everything out of his mind except his closing argument. He went over the argument in his mind as he ran under the streetlights on another cold and wet morning. The more he thought about it, the more convinced he became that he was going to win Draga's trial.

Kevin didn't even notice the runner who came up from behind him until the man was running along side. When he looked over, Kevin saw Pete Barnes. "Thought I might find you here," Barnes said.

"Guess I'm predictable." Kevin said.

"You may be the least predictable guy I know," said Barnes, chuckling.

"I know this isn't a coincidence. What's up?"

"I just wanted to thank you, Kevin. Most lawyers would have used those reports and the tapes. They would have rationalized away their client's best interests in a thousand different ways to make it coincide with their own. But you stood tall, Kevin. I'll always have great respect for you for that."

"Thanks. I owe you an apology for accusing you of kidnapping my daughter."

"Hell, I would have thought the same thing if I were in your shoes."

"Well, I hope things turn out. They found the farmhouse where Ellen was kept last night."

"I know. Last night after I heard that you weren't going to name us in court, I mobilized our people. You wouldn't believe what is going on as we speak. We've got people at CIA Headquarters in Virginia listening to conversations and reading faxes from Serbia. We've got so much coverage this morning that we know when someone turns a light bulb on anywhere in that damn country. Your daughter will be found, I know it."

"I'm going to win this trial. One way or the other, I hope we get Ellen back soon."

"Give 'em hell today. We'll get Draga out of those charges in the other countries if you win."

"I was hoping you would."

When they reached Kevin's street, Barnes waved as Kevin turned left toward his house.

Kevin was pumped up as he ran up the stairs to his bedroom. He hadn't slept, but his adrenaline was racing and good news seemed to be right around the corner.

Diane was getting dressed when Kevin arrived. She was still subdued when Kevin greeted her and gave her a kiss. Kevin determined to ignore their problems for the rest of the day and do his part at helping win Ellen's release.

Kevin made small talk with Diane as they drove to the Tribunal. When they walked into the courtroom, he saw that a handful of people were in the visitors' gallery. Most of them appeared to be court and prosecution employees. It reminded him who was still the home team.

After the judges entered, Charles Oswald rose to give his closing argument. "Your Honors," Oswald began, "this is a case about murder, torture, and rape. It is not a case about prosecutorial misconduct. Please do not be distracted by the unfortunate events involving Mr. Stone. The bottom line is that despite too many regrettable incidents, this court has given the accused a fair trial, represented by able counsel."

All three judges listened intently as Oswald summarized the testimony of each victim who had testified. His paralegal flashed pictures of the victims on the courtroom screens as Oswald described their suffering. Oswald talked for an hour and a half, and did not once mention Draga.

Kevin shifted uncomfortably in his seat. Oswald was making a powerful argument, but what did it have to do with Draga? As if reading Kevin's mind, Oswald asked, "What is the responsibility of the accused for all of these atrocities?"

He then had his paralegal play a portion of the tape where Draga told Ed Bradley of "60 Minutes" that the Muslims should be forced to leave Bosnia and live in Turkey or some other country. "Bosnia is and always has been part of Greater Serbia," Draga was heard telling Bradley. "And if they won't leave on their own, we'll give them a choice. They can leave on a bus or in a box."

Kevin tried not to grimace.

Oswald played a few other excerpts, and then got to his punch line. "The evidence has shown that the accused fed the climate of fear and terror that led directly to these events in Bosnia. Just as a person who brews the poison cannot escape responsibility by claiming that someone else administered it, the accused cannot escape responsibility in this case for the horrible acts of inhumanity that he promised the world he would bring to Bosnia."

A feeling of nervousness swept over Kevin. Are the judges buying this crap? he wondered. They sure looked attentive while Oswald spoke. Oswald had done what prosecutors do when they have little hard evidence against the accused. He had focused on the victims and the heinous nature of the crimes, and glossed over who was responsible. Kevin had to make the judges see through that.

The court recessed for lunch before hearing Kevin's closing argument. Kevin remained in the courtroom. He smiled as he saw Allen Jacobson take his laptop with him as he left.

After going through his argument a final time, Kevin went down to the basement holding cell to talk to Draga. He told him the latest news about Ellen and the farmhouse.

"They're going to find her," Draga predicted. "You'll get a call any minute."

"I hope so," Kevin paced around the small room, more nervous than he wished to admit.

"Kevin, I want to thank you for everything you've done for me and my family. No matter what happens. You're the best damn lawyer I've ever seen. But more than that, you've been my friend. And I'll never forget that."

Kevin was touched. "You've been a great client and friend, too," he said, meaning every word. "I'm going to go out there this afternoon and win your case so you can reunite with your family. Then, I'm going to see my daughter again. Then, the Giants are going to squash the Ravens on Sunday. And then I'll call it a week."

The two men laughed.

Kevin returned to the courtroom to try to win his case—and Ellen's freedom.

*   *   *   *

A hundred miles away, an oversized, muscular man looked out the window of the train as it passed through the emerald green Dutch countryside.

Mihajlo Golic was on his way to Amsterdam. He had decided to travel by train, rather than fly into Schipol Airport. He didn't want to have to worry about getting his Beretta pistol through the metal detectors.

He had heard the news about Draga's trial. The American lawyer was a fraud after all. Imagine putting up no defense. It was an insult to the Serbian people. He took no joy in what he would do to the girl, but the lawyer had been warned. Now he would get what had been promised.

Golic walked into the bathroom and pulled out his cellular phone. He dialed the number for the man he knew as "Hans."

"Hello," Hans answered on the first ring.

"I'll be in Amsterdam in three hours time," Golic said in English. It was the only common language between them. "I'm on the train."

"We've had a problem," Hans said. He explained the events of the previous evening. "We're in a hotel in Amsterdam."

"I'd better pick up the girl this afternoon. It's getting too dangerous to hold her any longer."

"What about the trial?"

"The trial's a joke. The American didn't even put up a defense. The judges will be deciding the case by tomorrow. And there's no doubt what that decision will be."

"Call me when you get near Amsterdam. We'll arrange the transfer."

"I'll do that." Golic clicked off the phone and returned to his seat.

*   *   *   *

At the Wassenaar Police Station, Detective Weber also returned to her seat, after removing her headphones connected to the telephone monitoring device.

"Get everybody from the airport over to Amsterdam Central Station," she barked over her walkie-talkie. "He's not flying—he's on the train!"

The detective shifted her large frame and rechecked the 9 mm automatic revolver in her purse. She was a dead-eye shot, and today, she wouldn't hesitate to pull the trigger.

She looked at the picture of Mihajlo Golic taped to the wall in front of her.

"Be a good boy," she coaxed. "Come to Mama."

CHAPTER 31

▼

"What do you mean 'make the transfer'?" Ellen asked Hans when he had finished talking on his cell phone.

"We're going to take you to the man who will bring you back to your family."

Her eyes sparkled. "Then I'm going home today?"

"Possibly," said Hans, casting a glance at Anna.

Ellen walked over to Anna and gave her a hug. "I'm going to miss you guys."

Anna returned the hug. There were tears in her eyes.

Ellen went over to Hans and hugged him too. He awkwardly embraced the girl. Then he said to Anna, "We've got to talk."

The hotel room was cramped for three people and a dog. Ever since Ellen had woken up at 6 a.m., she had been bored. Hans and Anna seemed preoccupied. They were watching television, listening for any news about Jan. There was no mention of his arrest—only a story about Draga's trial. The announcer reported that no defense had been offered for Draga and said that a verdict in the trial was expected tomorrow.

Hans told Ellen that he needed to speak to Anna in private about something. "You know enough of our language now that we can't even talk Dutch in front of you," he said. "So I need you to go into the bathroom for a few minutes while we talk out here."

Ellen shrugged her shoulders. "It's okay. Come on, Johanna." She led the puppy into the bathroom and closed the door.

Ellen's eyes scanned the bathroom. She spotted a drinking glass sitting upside down next to the sink. She picked it up and held it to the wall. She could hear perfectly.

"I'm supposed to take her to the guy in about three hours," she heard Hans saying in Dutch. "I don't think he's going to let her go."

"What do you mean?"

"They're not even waiting until the trial's over. They're positive that Draga is going to be found guilty."

"What should we do?"

"It's really risky for us here in a hotel," Hans replied. "We can't stay here forever. I'll feel a lot better when we've gotten rid of her."

Ellen felt sad as she listened in the bathroom.

"I don't want anything to happen to her," Anna said.

"That's what I'm afraid of," Hans said. "When I took this job, I just thought we would be babysitting the girl until the trial was over. I didn't care what happened after that. But now that we've gotten to know her, well, things are different."

"Why don't you find out what their intentions are? Our deal was we hold her until the trial is over. They can wait for one more day."

"That's a good idea."

Ellen heard the bed creak and quickly put down her glass.

Soon, Hans called for her to come out.

Ellen and Johanna came out. "Hey, can we order room service?"

"Sure," Anna replied. "It's lunchtime anyway."

"I'm going out for awhile," Hans told Anna. "Make sure she's in the bathroom when the waiter comes to the door. And Johanna, too. We're not even supposed to have pets in this hotel."

Hans went out and closed the door behind him.

He hopped on the first bus and rode it for a few miles. He got off in a shopping district and found a public phone. He placed another call to Mihajlo Golic.

"This is Hans," he said when Golic answered. "I didn't want to use my cell phone any more. My partner may have given the number to the police by now."

"Does he know about me?"

"No. Let's meet in Leiden. Get off the train at Utrecht and take a local train to Leiden Central station. Go downstairs and I will meet you in front of the snack bar. Then we'll make the arrangements to transfer the girl. I had to get rid of my van because I think it's hot."

"Okay. I should be there in about two hours."

"I'll be there," Hans replied. "I'm throwing my cell phone away. I'll call you from a public phone if I don't see you at the station."

"All right," Golic said, and hung up the phone.

The big man was anxious to get it over with. He would take the girl out in the woods tonight after sundown. He checked his watch. It was 2:30.

*   *   *   *

The judges looked attentive as Kevin rose to the podium and began his closing argument. "It is true, as Mr. Oswald said, that this is a case about murder, torture, and rape. Unquestionably, all of those things took place during the war in Bosnia. But neither Mr. Zaric nor any of the men under his command committed any of these heinous war crimes. And for that reason, you must find him not guilty."

Kevin went on for the next fifteen minutes reviewing the war crimes described during the trial and the persons who committed them. Not one was a bona fide Black Dragon. He explained that Draga's public statements were a method of propaganda that was part of his military objectives of intimidation to encourage surrender rather than armed resistance. He argued that if the prosecution truly had a legitimate case against Draga, there would have been no reason for them to conceal evidence and suborn perjury during his trial.

"Yes, this is a case about murder, torture, and rape," Kevin continued. "But it is also a case about courage." He slowed his pace and looked directly at Judge Davidson. "The witnesses who have testified during this trial have shown extraordinary courage to survive the horrors of the war and then to relive them again in this courtroom. A little eleven-year-old girl, who had nothing to do with the war, my daughter Ellen, has courageously endured a month of confinement during this trial. And now, her life depends on <u>your</u> courage."

The judges—all three—were glued to his every word.

Kevin fought to keep his composure. "I know it will take tremendous courage on your part to render an unpopular verdict, but one that is compelled by the evidence. This Tribunal will be judged, ten, twenty, a hundred years from now, not by how it exacted revenge for the war in Bosnia, but by how it dispensed justice. When you write your verdict, you will be writing a page in history. History is replete with great men and women who had the courage to do what was not popular, but was right.

"And so I ask you—no, beseech you with every ounce of my waning strength—to do the right thing. There is not a shred of evidence that proves that Mr. Zaric, or anyone under his command or control, committed a single war crime. Dragoljub Zaric is not guilty. Please have the courage to say so by your verdict. Thank you."

Judge Orozco leaned forward towards her microphone. "Thank you, Counsel. The court will now deliberate in its chambers on the verdict. We will announce the verdict at 9:30 tomorrow morning."

Kevin rose warily as the judges left the bench, giving no sign of what their verdict would be. "That was a stirring argument," Diane said when Kevin had sat down. "You did your best. I know." She placed her hand over his.

Kevin looked back toward Draga, who was being led out of the courtroom. His client flashed a thumbs-up. Kevin remembered seeing Ellen do the same thing at his last trial in San Francisco.

Kevin walked back with Diane to their office. Kevin felt exhausted, as he did after every closing argument. It was not so much the strain of the argument, but the knowledge that the trial was over, that it was now out of his hands. The time spent waiting for a verdict was the most stressful moments of Kevin's life. By the time they had reached the office, the butterflies had already started fluttering in Kevin's stomach.

Diane called Detective Weber.

"Golic is coming by train," Diane reported to Kevin when she got off the phone. "They expect him to arrive at Amsterdam Central Station any minute."

"My God, we could have Ellen home before the verdict. I'd love to have her in court with me tomorrow."

Diane started to frown, but then changed her mind.

"Me, too," she said.

✳   ✳   ✳   ✳

Mihajlo Golic never made it to Central Station. As Hans had arranged from the public phone, Golic went to Leiden, where Hans was waiting for him at the snack bar.

"Where's the girl?" Golic asked.

"At the hotel."

"I have the money for your services, as agreed," Golic opened his jacket, showing Hans an envelope in his inside pocket. "One hundred thousand Euros. I will give it to you when you give me the girl."

Hans said nothing.

"I need a van, and some rope and tape," Golic continued.

"My partner has probably told the police about me by now. I think it would be better if you got those items yourself. Why don't you do that in the morning and you can pick up the girl tomorrow afternoon?"

"Very well," Golic replied.

It was getting late today. He needed time to rent a van and buy his supplies.

Hans gave Golic a business card for the hotel where they were staying. "No more phone calls," Hans said. "Just be in the lobby at noon. By then, the trial will be over, yes?"

"Perhaps."

"What are you going to do with the girl?"

Golic looked at Hans with steely eyes. "That's of no concern to you. You'll have your money."

Hans nodded uncomfortably. "Until tomorrow." He walked off into the crowd.

*   *   *   *

At six o'clock, Kevin couldn't stand the waiting. He called Detective Weber. "Has Golic arrived yet?" he asked.

"Something has gone wrong. We've checked every train arriving at Amsterdam Central Station. There's been no sign of Golic."

"What about the cell phone?"

"It hasn't been used since this morning. We found the blue van abandoned in Amsterdam, and we've been all over the area, but there's no sign of Ellen or the kidnappers."

"What are you doing now?"

"Still looking," the detective replied. "We're canvassing all the hotels around Amsterdam. We've got surveillance on Vacinovic and the embassy. Pete Barnes has got his people scanning all kinds of communications from Serbia. And we've contacted the families and friends of the two suspects who are holding your daughter."

Kevin related the conversation to Diane, trying to put a more positive spin on it.

"Let's go home," he said. "There's nothing more to do here, and I'm exhausted."

Diane drove while Kevin sprawled out in the passenger's seat. He couldn't sleep, but his body was drained of energy. If the police didn't find Ellen tonight, then it would come down to the verdict after all.

Kevin and Diane went through the motions of changing clothes and eating at home. They called Detective Weber every two hours. After the ten o'clock call, Kevin fell asleep on the couch in his clothes.

Kevin awoke at the sound of the telephone. He looked at the clock. It was 7:15 a.m. When he picked it up, he heard Diane already answering on the upstairs phone. It was Detective Weber.

"Barnes' people picked up a call from Golic to his wife in Serbia early this morning. He's in Amsterdam, said he had some business to take care of today and would be back in Belgrade tomorrow. We've got Golic's cell phone number now, and the CIA is monitoring it."

"Maybe he'll release her today," Kevin said.

"I hope so. What do you think your chances are in court?"

Kevin hesitated. "I think they're pretty good, but I'm not willing to gamble Ellen's life on it."

"Maybe we should try to get the judges to postpone the verdict," Diane suggested.

"I don't think they would," Kevin said, "or even that we should try. I feel okay about it and any delay might make the kidnappers suspicious. Plus, the press has been really bad. The Serbs might expect a guilty verdict and not wait for it. What do you think, Detective?"

"I've never heard of anyone being acquitted by the Tribunal," she admitted. "Do you really think you are going to win?

"I do. Their case was nothing more than smoke and mirrors. It fell apart."

"I'm thinking we should let things play out then," she said. "I feel that we're close to finding Ellen. But as I said before, it would be much safer if they released her voluntarily."

The detective wished the Andersons luck in court today and hung up.

Diane frowned when Kevin came upstairs. "I hope you're right, Kevin. Maybe you're so wrapped up in the trial that you're reading it wrong."

Kevin thought about that. He did get to believe his own arguments by the end of a trial—all trial lawyers did. But he usually could tell when he was going to win.

"I don't think so," he said thoughtfully. "After twenty years in this business, I think I have a pretty good sense of how a trial will come out."

"Not in this court," Diane muttered as she walked away.

Kevin went to his desk and picked up the lucky stone that Ellen had given him years ago. She had insisted he bring it to his verdicts. He clutched the stone, then put it in his pocket.

When Kevin walked into Courtroom 1 with Diane an hour later, he saw that the visitors' gallery was packed with reporters and various court personnel, including his old friend Mrs. Kelly, who waved unabashedly at him.

"All rise! *Veuillez vous lever!*"

CHAPTER 32

▼

"Mr. Zaric," Judge Davidson boomed. "The Trial Chamber finds you guilty as charged. You are hereby sentenced to imprisonment for the rest of your natural life."

Kevin felt his body sag from shock, then fear. He just managed to steady himself by leaning his hand on the table. Sweat popped out of his pores as he struggled to maintain his composure. He felt sick to his stomach. He had lost. Ellen was in extreme peril. How could this have happened?

Kevin couldn't bring himself to look at Draga or anyone else. He kept his eyes down on the table in front of him. He had failed. Somewhere far in the distance, Kevin heard Judge Davidson continuing to speak. "Mr. Zaric, you have the right to appeal this judgment. I am notifying you that you must file a notice of appeal within thirty days."

Kevin concentrated on trying to draw a breath. He was jolted out of his stupor by Draga's strong voice.

"I will not appeal your verdict," Draga said firmly. "It comes as no surprise to me. I committed no war crimes and you know it. But this court has nothing to do with the truth and even less to do with justice. I shall proudly serve my sentence as a prisoner of war."

Draga continued, as Judge Davidson sat uncharacteristically silent. "I want to say a final word to those who have kidnapped my lawyer's daughter. Release her at once. My lawyer did all he could in this kangaroo court. He is my friend. If you so much as harm a hair on her head, I will see that you are hunted down and shot like animals. That is all I have to say."

Draga sat down. His mention of Ellen had caused everyone to look at Kevin.

Tears welled in Kevin's eyes as he struggled to keep the dam of emotions inside him from bursting in the courtroom. He felt weak, on the verge of collapse.

Judge Davidson's gruff voice filled the courtroom. "Mr. Zaric, I find that you have knowingly and voluntarily waived your right to appeal this verdict. You shall be transported to begin serving your sentence forthwith. I am advised that the Registrar has determined that your country of confinement shall be the United States of America."

Judge Orozco then addressed Kevin. "Mr. Anderson, I want you to know I dissented from this verdict. I am praying for your daughter. Court is adjourned."

Kevin slowly rose to his feet as he held Diane's hand. She showed no outward reaction to the events. When the judges had filed out, the courtroom guards came up to Kevin one by one.

"You did a fine job, counselor."

"Tough luck, sir, you deserved to win."

"I'm ashamed of this place."

Kevin only nodded. Diane had already walked out the door toward the defense offices. He ran to catch up, and put his hand on her shoulder. When she turned around, he hugged her. They said nothing for several seconds as they clung to each other, desperately, in the corridor of the Tribunal.

"I'm so sorry," Kevin said, tears streaming down his face. "You were right all along—about everything."

Diane said nothing. She was not crying, and she did not make eye contact.

"Come on," she said, "I've seen enough of this place for a lifetime."

"Me, too," Kevin said haltingly.

They walked quickly down to the lobby and out the door before any reporters could see them. Still wearing their black robes, they got into their car in the underground parking garage.

"What do we do now?" Kevin asked.

"We pray for Detective Weber."

Kevin still felt weak and shaky. He knew that Diane had summoned her strength and resolve to fill the void, but all he could think of was that he had lost. He had failed Ellen, Diane, Draga, and himself.

"I let Ellen down," he moaned. "I pray to God they don't kill her."

Diane looked straight ahead, her face set with determination as she made her way through the traffic in The Hague. "They've kept her alive this long. There's no point in killing her. It won't accomplish anything."

"I want to believe that so much."

*   *   *   *

In a gray building in the center of Belgrade, a white-haired man turned off the television and summoned his aide. "Get Zoran Vacinovic on the line," he ordered in Serbian. When the call had gone through to his country's embassy in The Hague, he spoke firmly.

"Zoran," he said, "Call it off."

"Yes, Mr. President," Vacinovic replied. "Our man is here in The Netherlands. I will try and contact him at once. But may I ask why?"

"Draga knows too much," the President replied. "We don't want him singing like a bird. And he still has dangerous friends here. I think it is best if we accept his wishes in this matter."

"Yes. Well, everyone knows that his trial was a farce. Perhaps having the American lawyer and the fact that he did nothing was a good thing. It is just more evidence of the continuing atrocities committed against the Serbian people."

"That is what will be said on television and radio here," the President replied. "You do the same on your end."

The conversation ended. In another brick building, this one in Wassenaar, Detective Weber whooped as she put down the phone after an urgent call from the CIA's Pete Barnes.

"Yes!" she exclaimed, thrusting her fist in the air. "They've called it off."

*   *   *   *

Sitting in the van he had just rented, Mihajlo Golic loaded his Beretta. He filled the chamber, although he was certain only one bullet would be needed for the job. He took his cell phone and threw it in the glove box. He would leave it off. There would be no more calls.

He looked at the card of the hotel that Hans had given him, found the address on the map, and headed to pick up the girl.

*   *   *   *

After the call from his president, Zoran Vacinovic looked in his address book and found the number for Golic's cellular phone. He punched the numbers in right away.

There was no answer.

CHAPTER 33

▼

Ellen was again in the bathroom of the hotel room, her ear pressed to the drinking glass she held up to the wall. She could hear Hans and Anna talking.

"He'll be here in a few minutes," Anna said in Dutch. "What should we do?"

"We have to give her to him. We have no choice. If we don't, we won't get the money. A hundred thousand Euros. All our risk and our work this month would have been for nothing."

"Can we make it a condition that he not hurt her?"

"They don't care what we think."

There was silence in the room until Hans called to Ellen.

"You can come out now."

Ellen walked back in from the bathroom, Johanna at her heels.

"It's time to start packing up," Hans said.

Ellen's heart was pounding. "Can't you guys just drive me to my house? I'll show you how to get there once we get to Wassenaar?"

"Sorry," he said. "We have to follow our orders, too, just like you."

Ellen sighed, then reached into her backpack and pulled out two folded pieces of paper. "I made you each a card." She handed one to Hans and one to Anna. "It's something to remember me by."

Hans and Anna looked at the drawing on the front of their cards. Ellen had drawn the farm, with her, Hans, Jan, Anna and Johanna. "Thanks for being my family," it said on the inside.

When she saw it, Anna began to cry.

Ellen went to the chair and put her hand on Anna's shoulder. "Don't be sad."

Suddenly, Hans jumped up from the chair and reached into his wallet. "Sarah," he said, walking over to Ellen and Anna. "Here are 20 Euros. I want you to listen to me and listen good." He put the bill in her small hand and squatted down to her height.

"The man who is coming might try to hurt you. I want you to go right now. Walk over to that street," he said, opening the curtains and pointing, a sense of urgency in his voice. "Get on the first bus that comes and it will take you to Amsterdam Central Station. You need to get away from here."

Anna hugged Ellen. "Yes, Hans is right. You need to go, now!"

Anna looked up at Hans and squeezed his hand.

Ellen just stood there, feeling scared.

Anna raced around the room, grabbing Ellen's backpack and stuffing all of her books back in it.

"This is serious," Hans said to Ellen. "Go as fast as you can."

"Can I take Johanna?"

"No," Hans replied. "You'll be too noticeable. We'll take care of Johanna, just go." His voice was loud now.

Ellen wanted to protest, but she was too scared.

Anna put her backpack on her shoulders.

They escorted her into the hallway, and Hans opened the door to the parking lot.

"Good luck, Sarah," he said.

Ellen reached down and grabbed Johanna. "I love you, my sweet puppy," she said, tears streaming down her cheeks.

Anna took the puppy from her and gave Ellen a hug.

Ellen turned and walked away. Once in the parking lot, she started to run toward the bus stop.

*   *   *   *

It was precisely noon when Mihajlo Golic arrived at the hotel in the van.

The rope and tape were in the briefcase he carried, and he felt the comforting press of the Beretta lodged in the small of his back.

Hans was waiting for him in the lobby. "Follow me," Hans said.

Hans led Golic outside and gave him directions to the room. "The girl is in room 162. I don't want to be there when you take her. I'm leaving now."

"Who's with the girl?"

"She's watching TV with Anna. She will be no problem for you."

Golic nodded.

Hans gave him the key to the room.

"Now is the time for our payment," Hans said.

Golic reached into his pocket and gave Hans a thick envelope.

Hans did not look inside.

As Golic headed for the room, Hans walked in the other direction, away from the hotel. He turned down a residential street where Anna was waiting, holding Johanna. "Let's get out of here," he said.

Golic, carrying his briefcase with the rope and tape, approached the door to room 162. He heard the television. He knocked on the door. There was no answer. He knocked again, louder, but got no response. Finally, he reached into his pocket for the key and opened the door. He saw that no one was inside. He raced into the room, checking the bathroom. It was empty.

He had been tricked. Golic was furious.

He raced back to his van and withdrew the Beretta. He drove around the area, looking for Hans or the girl. The Dutch man would pay for this, he vowed. Meanwhile, he would set out for Wassenaar. Perhaps there was still time to find the girl.

*   *   *   *

Ellen boarded a train for Leiden where she could catch the bus to her house.

She had gotten to Amsterdam Central Station as Hans had instructed. She was scared and kept looking back, but no one appeared to be following her. She went to a phone to call her parents, but she didn't have her phone card and the phone didn't take coins. She decided she would just get home on her own. What a great surprise it would be to her parents when she walked in the door!

When the train arrived in Leiden, Ellen got off and walked outside to catch a bus.

She knew that the number 43 bus would take her to Wassenaar and to the bus stop a few blocks from her home. She waited a few minutes for the bus to arrive, and then got on. No one appeared to notice her. She sat looking out the window, knowing that in about ten minutes she would be safely back at her home with her Mom and Dad.

*   *   *   *

Detective Weber popped her third antacid pill of the day in her mouth. It had been a roller-coaster day.

First, there had been news of the verdict. Then, the President of Serbia himself had ordered that Ellen not be harmed. Finally, the frustrating knowledge that Golic was out there somewhere, probably with Ellen by now, and unreachable by phone. Vacinovic had been calling Golic's phone number for the last two hours with no response.

She thought about how Kevin and Diane must be feeling. The verdict must have been devastating. She decided to pay them a visit and wait it out with the parents, at least until she had some kind of additional information that she could act on.

*   *   *   *

The first to reach the Anderson home was Mihajlo Golic.

He drove by and looked in the window as he passed. There was no sign of the girl.

He parked his van a block away, behind some trees. He slowly walked back down the street, on the opposite side from the Andersons' row house, his Beretta tucked once again in the small of his back. He waited behind some bushes. He would be patient, but in the end, he would finish the job that he was ordered to do.

Golic knew he could not go back to Belgrade in failure.

*   *   *   *

Failure was the word that summed up Kevin's thoughts as he sat on the couch of his living room, staring blankly out his front window. How could he have done this to Ellen? to his family? How could he have been so naive to expect justice at the Tribunal?

<u>Take me</u>, he prayed to God. <u>Just let my daughter live.</u>

*   *   *   *

Ellen alighted from the bus, the weight of her backpack once again on her shoulders. It was just a few more blocks to walk on a cold, sunny day.

She pictured her mother, her father, and her room on the third level. It would be great to be home again. She only wished she could have brought Johanna with her.

*   *   *   *

Golic saw the young girl from about 50 yards away as she crossed the street.

Was it her? He walked forward in her direction, reaching for the Beretta as he strode. As she got closer to the row house, Golic was sure it was her.

He stood at the edge of the bushes now, concentrating on the small target now turning into the walk leading to the row house where the Andersons lived.

He raised his gun.

"Stop! Police!"

Golic was stunned. A large woman was on him, her gun thrust firmly in his ear.

Golic's weapon fell from his hand as Detective Weber pushed him roughly to the ground. Before he could react, his hands were pulled behind his back and handcuffed.

Ellen neither saw nor heard the commotion. She excitedly rang the bell by her front door.

Kevin lifted himself off the couch and padded over to answer the door.

"Daddy!" shouted Ellen as she leapt into his arms.

"Oh my God, it's you!" Kevin exclaimed, hugging her daughter, tears pouring from his eyes.

Diane screamed and ran over to them.

The three of them were hugging, laughing, and crying.

They were a family again.

*   *   *   *

News of Ellen's return spread through Holland like a North Sea gust. Kevin spent much of the afternoon and evening answering calls from reporters, friends, and Ellen's classmates. That night, Ellen proudly showed Kevin and Diane all the schoolwork she had done, and insisted that she wanted to go to school the next day to turn it in.

The morning after the greatest day of Kevin's life, he awoke to the sound of a dog barking. A few seconds later, he heard the sound of little footsteps racing down from the third floor. When he got out of bed, he heard Ellen scream: "Johanna!"

The puppy had been left at their doorstep, its leash tied to their front doorknob.

At about 8:00, just as Ellen was getting ready to leave for school, there was a knock at the door.

Kevin opened it.

The headmaster of The American School stood in the doorway; a crowd of people behind him. "We've come to welcome Ellen back to school."

Ellen came to the door. "This is awesome!"

The path from her door to the street, and then toward the school, was lined with children and adults. Some held signs that said, "Welcome back Ellen."

Ellen grabbed her backpack, stuffed with all the work she would show to her teachers. "Bye Mom, bye Dad," she called out as she went out the door.

Kevin and Diane watched as the headmaster led Ellen between the two rows of people, who were cheering and clapping. They saw Ellen accept high fives from her fellow students, and then disappear into the crowd.

"We're lined up all the way from your house to the school," Ellen's math teacher, Maureen Toohey, said to Kevin. "Every kid in the school is out here."

"And teachers, too," added Ellen's home room teacher, Kerrin Poiker.

Kevin looked at Diane. Tears were streaming down her cheeks. He put his arm around her as they watched the crowd following their daughter toward her school. When the throng had gone from sight, Kevin closed the door.

Diane held him tightly as they walked back and sat on the couch, saying nothing.

Johanna jumped up on their laps, licking the wet hands Diane had used to wipe away their tears of joy.

"I promise I'll never do anything like this again," Kevin said.

EIGHT MONTHS LATER...

To: KevAnd@aol.com (Kevin Anderson)
From: Raiderfan@carribean.net
Subject: None
Life is good. As you thought, they made good on their promise.
I will never forget you.
But you do owe me 30 Euros, plus interest, for the Super Bowl.
Interested in trying to get it back this season?

About the Author

Peter Robinson is a former Assistant United States Attorney and Trial Attorney for the U.S. Department of Justice. He is currently a criminal defense lawyer. Among his major trials are the prosecution of the Neo-Nazi group known as "The Order," and the defense of one of the "Montana Freemen."

In the summer of 2000, he moved with his family for a year to The Netherlands, where he assisted in the defense of a Bosnian Serb Army General at The Tribunal. He is currently defending the former Chief of Staff of the Yugoslavian Army at the Tribunal, and the former President of the Rwandan Parliament at the International Criminal Tribunal for Rwanda.

He lives in Santa Rosa, California, with his wife, Jeanne and their 14-year-old daughter, Jennifer.

0-595-30754-X